Dylan Lawson is a screenwriter whose credits include *Twin Peaks* and *The X-Files*. He lives with his wife and dog in Montana.

EVERY SECOND LOST

Elias Hawks's world changed forever when, as a teenager, he crashed his car and woke six weeks later to find he had lost the girl of his dreams — and very nearly his life. Eighteen years on, all Elias has left is his career as an accident investigator, and a ticking time bomb in his head from the traumatic brain injury he suffered. But then the girl reappears out of the blue to tell him that her daughter is missing, and Elias finds himself caught up in an increasingly deadly search for answers. With his health already hanging in the balance, Elias will have one last chance to make amends for the past — and one last chance to find the truth, even if this time it means paying for it with his life . . .

DYLAN LAWSON

◆

EVERY
SECOND
LOST

Complete and Unabridged

CHARNWOOD
Leicester

First published in Great Britain in 2013 by
Headline Publishing Group
London

First Charnwood Edition
published 2015
by arrangement with
Headline Publishing Group
London

A catalogue record for this book is available
from the British Library.

ISBN 978–1–4448–2528–2

Published by
F. A. Thorpe (Publishing)
Anstey, Leicestershire

Set by Words & Graphics Ltd.
Anstey, Leicestershire
Printed and bound in Great Britain by
T. J. International Ltd., Padstow, Cornwall

In memory of Elaine Koster

Acknowledgements

This work would not have been possible without the insight and wisdom of my agent Helen Heller and my editor Vicki Mellor.

Prologue

My name is Elias Hawks. I'm a student of accidents — no, I'm a result of one, more than one, actually.

The first one took place in the back of a 1979 VW bus — it was a high-speed head-on collision between my college student parents who had slipped away unnoticed from the beer-drinking taking place at a party to drive blindly into their future. Neither apparently had time to put on a seat belt or anything else that may have prevented my arrival.

That a second accident would later shape my life to an even greater degree could, I suppose, be called fate, if you believe in it, or bad luck, if you don't. I try to just stick to the facts rather than delve into metaphysics. And the simple fact of my life is that following the second accident some eighteen years after that first one, I now understand how and why they happen. That's my gift, if you can call it that. I see things others don't. I know how things can change in a blink of an eye, I see the details that lead up to the accident, and I know that no matter how much people want to relive that split second that altered their life, it ain't gonna happen. That's why I, more than anyone, should have known better, and why I should have turned away, but I didn't. But I'm getting ahead of myself.

She was the girl, the one who stays frozen in

1

time, in memory, never aging, always turning the same way, brushing her long black hair off her face and looking right into your eyes as if she knew every secret you had ever held close — including that you were in love with her from the very first moment you had ever seen her, and that you were scared to death of feeling something that intense.

The relationships that followed this first love have existed in muted shades of gray in comparison, or at least that's where they seemed to end up. Perhaps that's just what time does to memory, polishing feelings to the point that, in comparison, nothing ever shines quite so brightly. But still, that feeling must exist; it's why we keep trying to fall in love. To remember that terror we felt when we got within ten feet of *the one* and lost the ability to speak and reverted to some presimian state, convinced that if we tried to speak our heart would explode.

And then it happened.

Towards the end of my senior year in high school I found myself standing next to her in the cafeteria line. Tracy James had on an orange shirt, two buttons open at the neck and three silver bracelets engraved with African symbols wrapped round the deep-brown skin of her wrist. Her thin, strong body was that of a dancer, which brought a kind of grace to even the simplest of movements. As I picked up a plate of what passed for lasagna she turned and looked at me.

'I wouldn't eat that,' she said with a half-smile as if she held some secret understanding of its

2

origins. I promptly dropped it. The plate smashed on the floor at my feet, bits of hamburger and cheese filling the eyelets of my shoes. Smooth. Everybody in the cafeteria turned and looked at me in complete dreadful silence, and then the laughing started, one snicker and then another until it was all I could hear. I stood in terror for a moment, trying to find my way back to the planet, which had in an instant become unrecognizable, and then let loose before I even realized I had said it.

'Do you want to go to the dance?'

They were the first words I had ever spoken to Tracy, and they took four years and a slab of hamburger lasagna with American cheese to put into a sentence. Two words a year; Darwin's finches have nothing on me. The room fell silent again, I suppose waiting to see how what remained of me was going to be shot down in flames. She glanced briefly around the faces staring at us and then turned and her dark eyes fell on mine.

'Sure,' she said.

I thought it was the bravest thing I had ever seen anyone do in my short life, certainly the kindest. Or perhaps she just wanted to see if I danced better than I handled food.

I pulled up to her house on that Friday night four days later feeling like a guy who had just been accepted at Harvard with a D average. It wasn't the prom, but it could have been to me. As I opened the car door and stepped out she came walking out of her house and swooped around to the passenger side. I couldn't take my eyes off her. She seemed to move without even touching the ground. The tight black dress she wore fitted the curves of her body like a second skin. I was speechless . . . again. As she opened the door she spoke the last words I ever remember her saying.

'I'm glad you finally asked me.'

I promptly lost all feeling in my left hand. I thought I was having a heart attack until I realized I had a death grip on the door. I let go of the handle and the feeling began to return to my fingers as I ran cool comebacks through my head frantically looking for a response.

'Me . . . also,' I said, the words sounding like someone standing behind me had uttered them. She looked at me for a moment as if I had spoken in tongues, but there was no second-guessing in her eyes; nothing to suggest she was looking for an escape, then she smiled and got into the car.

It took another three blocks for me to get up the nerve to attempt speech again. As the streetlight turned green and I stepped on the gas I glanced at her. She was looking straight ahead; her long hair was tucked behind her ear, flowing down the line of her neck until it spilled over her shoulder. Her eyes seemed to catch the headlights of passing cars the way the facets of a diamond snatch light from darkness. I had never realized how beautiful an ear could be, how perfect.

'You . . . ' I began to say.

Out of the corner of my eye I saw the flash of chrome and headlight just before the impact. I heard Tracy cry out 'Don't stop!', then it was utterly silent. Glass showered the side of my face as the car began to spin and lift into the air. For a moment all motion seemed to slow, then Tracy's fingers took hold of my hand as the dark shape of the telephone pole came rushing towards us.

Then everything stopped, all movement, time, memory, the only sound was the snap of my skull cracking.

But that was a long time ago. Or it was until today.

1

Eighteen years later

One day at a time is now the rule; it has been since that night — one step, one breath, a heartbeat at a time. If I try to look beyond that it's easy to get lost. A twelve-step programme for recipients of TBIs, as the physical therapists call them, traumatic brain injuries to the rest of us. Brain injuries are like family, good or bad, you're never entirely free of them.

My parents divorced almost one year to the day of the wreck. They had made it through the worst of it, but the damage had been done and there were no more VW buses in their life to bring them back together. My father drifted away to another life, eventually remarrying and starting another family. We talk little and see each other even less. Ten years after the divorce my mother died one day while at the grocery store. An artery leading to her heart failed. There were no warnings, no headlights coming out of the darkness. One moment she was picking up a grapefruit, and then she was gone, and I was alone in this world.

'Any sensory anomalies?' the doctor asked.

I had been in a coma for six weeks before slowly re-entering this world.

'New or old?' I said.

'New.'

I see the neurologist every six months or so depending on things like sensory anomalies. I looked at the doctor for a moment and then at the walls of the examination room; the dull yellow paint appeared to soften to the point that if I reached out, my hand would pass right through it. There had been bleeding in the brain, blood vessels were damaged and weakened, something that I would learn through my mother's death that I was already predisposed to. The multiple skull fractures I suffered in the collision were like throwing gasoline on a fire. It remains the chief reason I'm sitting here, the fear that the structural integrity of one of those blood vessels will fail and send me back into oblivion. Not that there's a great deal they can do about it. It will or will not happen. These visits aren't about healing me; they're about anxiety management.

'Nothing out of the ordinary,' I answered.

'That's good,' the doctor said.

It can be easy to tire of doctors. Good ones, bad ones, indifferent ones, I've had them all.

'So you would say things are normal?' he asked.

My sense of what constituted normality hadn't been the same since that night. Sometimes I see things, or I believe I do. You're never entirely sure with brain injuries. Sometimes I confuse thoughts with reality. I can be thinking of food and the glass of water I'm holding will suddenly smell like clams in red sauce. A stop sign will turn green. I forget things that are said to me twenty seconds ago. I remember moments from childhood long forgotten. An aura will appear around a person's face shimmering like a prism. A child's laughter will sound like a scream. Sitting alone in a car I'll feel Tracy's hand take mine just before we impacted the telephone pole.

Some things I don't tell the doctor. I didn't tell him that on our last visit when he shook my hand I knew he was sick. I don't know how I knew it. It had never happened before and never happened again. I like to think of these little surprises as if they were gifts sent to me by a stranger. Don't question them, just accept it as a sign you're still alive, though for a while after that I did avoid shaking hands for fear that I might find out something I didn't want to know. Too much information is not always welcomed.

'How are the headaches?' the doctor asked.

'Hardly noticeable.'

'Blackouts, seizures?'

Things were looking up that way. It had been almost a year since my last blackout or seizure.

'None,' I answered.

'That's good.'

He shined a pen light across the cornea of my left eye. I thought I felt the point of light touch the back of my skull. The doctor stepped back and slipped the light away in his pocket. He had lost weight since he was diagnosed with lymphoma. His eyes had the look of a salesman who no longer believed in what he was pitching. He had been a robust man when I first met him. Holding a pen light now seemed a strain for him.

'How are the headaches really?' he asked.

'For someone with or without a titanium plate

in his head?' I asked.

'On a scale of one to ten?' he asked.

'Sometimes four, sometimes five,' I said.

It was a game we played during examinations. I would affix a number to a level of pain and a dying man would tell me that four or five was good. He took a deep breath; it seemed barely enough to keep a bird alive.

'Any issues that might be causing stress?'

I'm supposed to avoid situations, emotions that could increase my blood pressure. Love can be deadly, but when has that ever stopped anyone?

'I live a quiet monk-like existence at the moment.'

He looked at me with his sad eyes.

'Perhaps you shouldn't,' he said.

'Meaning I should find a girl and settle down.'

'Something like that,' he said.

'I've never quite found the right wording to tell someone I might be leaving the party early just when they fall in love.'

'They, or you?' he asked.

'Life is complicated.'

He smiled in the way that only a fellow traveler with his exit visa already stamped could.

'How's the job?' he asked.

I'm an accident investigator for insurance companies. I read the tea leaves of skid marks and twisted steel and snapped steering wheels. I can walk into a junkyard and see stories in crushed fenders and shattered windshields that most people would never imagine. I see truth in the way a door has been pushed in and a tire worn down by skidding across asphalt, a cracked steering wheel. And I'm really good with telephone poles. I know just how much force it takes to snap them. And I know when someone filing a claim's pain is real, or just a fiction to stuff pockets with cash. It would be foolish to deny the irony of it all. Some men are born to their careers. Others are broadsided into them.

'I'm looking into a Honda and Chevrolet Avalanche that met in the middle of an uncontrolled intersection. The results were predictable.'

The doctor took a tiny breath and made a note on my chart.

'I don't know how you do it, given your history,' he said.

'Given my history, what else would I do?' I answered. 'An accident is the one place I truly feel at home,' I said. 'Besides, last year there were fifty-eight thousand vehicle accidents in Los Angeles. Recession is not part of my vocabulary.'

He closed my chart and looked about the room as if the words he was searching for were floating about waiting for him to put them in order.

'Everything looks good, perhaps you should . . . live a little.'

'It's what may happen after I've lived a 'little' that concerns me.'

He took a tired breath; he used to fight with me more about these questions before he became ill.

'Maybe it's worth the risk,' he said.

10

I imagined reaching out for a grapefruit.

'If I'm about to have an aneurism, can you tell me when it's going to happen or fix it?' I asked.

He tried halfheartedly to smile.

'I'll seriously consider your advice,' I said.

He was used to losing this argument. But he still went through all the possibilities just as he always did. And in the end the grapefruit still won.

Finally he gave up for the last time.

'Hope isn't always a bad thing,' he said, though the words seemed hollow. 'If anything changes, you'll be seeing Doctor Keller next time.'

I would never see him again. I took his hand in mine and said goodbye.

★ ★ ★

The last rains of winter were behind us now. For a month, maybe two, Los Angeles would be as pleasant as a city of nine million people speaking a hundred and ten different languages, all bent on driving like a bat out of hell, can be. I sometimes think that seeing the world through car accidents perhaps shades one's view of human nature, but as a claims adjuster once said to me, I was made for the job.

From the doctor's office I drove over to a salvage yard on Lankershiem to take a look at a 2004 Honda Accord that had been broadsided by the Chevy Avalanche. It was a routine accident from the view of the claims adjuster.

Which to him meant that the driver of the

Chevy whom we did not insure was at fault, and therefore liable for damages to both vehicles and all medical costs incurred by the driver of the Honda as a result of the injuries sustained which included multiple lacerations, a broken hip and elbow, cracked ribs and a partially collapsed lung.

Routine. I have yet to meet a claims adjuster with an imagination equal to even a dull-witted golden retriever. Their world is a simple one; to make sure the other guy pays.

Enter me, not because I tell them what they want to hear, but because when I tell them that the angle of impact was exactly ten degrees from center, which places the vehicle in the intersection a full five seconds before the other vehicle entered, you can take that information to the bank, which a whole lot of lawyers have done.

I parked next to the salvage yard offices and walked through the stacks of crushed vehicles waiting their turn to be shipped off and melted down into Slinkys and guardrails. The Honda sat inside a fenced enclosure where they kept vehicles still involved in investigations.

It was a silver four-door before the Avalanche took it out like a baby pine tree. The left front tire was flat and draped over the rim. From the back of the front fender to the middle of the rear door the side of the car had been crushed inward approximately twenty inches.

I stepped up to the open window and looked inside. The airbag hung limply, the driver's seat had been knocked loose from its anchor and twisted from front to back where the door pressed against it. Given the distance the door had been crushed inward and the weight difference of the two vehicles, the Avalanche would have been traveling close to forty miles an hour, fifteen over the speed limit.

I took a breath and felt tightness in my chest. The driver would have turned his head just in time to see the Chevy grill before it hit him. When it struck he was thrown violently to his right and then struck an instant later by the inflating airbag. A sense of weightlessness would have taken hold of him as the car flew across the intersection and then, like an astronaut hurtling to earth as gravity returned, the car came to an abrupt halt. There would not have been a sound for a moment or an understanding of what had happened until the pain from his first breath as his lung began to collapse brought everything into searing focus.

I reached out and placed my hand on the crushed door and then stepped back.

'Routine,' I whispered.

I made some measurements, took some photographs and then drove back around Elysian Park and headed towards downtown and my building next to Little Tokyo. It's not a neighborhood in the conventional LA sense, if the word conventional can be applied to Los Angeles. When I had first moved there, the warehouses had been filled with artists, head-banging musicians, drug addicts, architects, the odd movie star and just plain lost souls who never quite found their way into a normal career path, but it was a place where having a titanium plate in your head allowed me to fit more naturally in than a street with lawns and backyard barbecues. Gentrification has made its move now and more than a few buildings are filling up with young hip professionals, but so far my building has withstood the assault.

As I pulled up outside the building, I noticed the car parked on the other side of the street. I notice cars. I can usually guess what kind of person is stepping out of one before they open the door. A 2009 Volkswagen Jetta. A good safe vehicle with side airbags, scored well in government crash tests. It was too new to be owned by anyone in the building, by which I meant it was too normal. I decided it belonged to someone coming to visit their daughter or son, or to buy a painting to hang in their living room.

I wasn't even close.

As I walked to the entrance of the building the door of the Jetta opened and a woman stepped out. She hesitated for a moment and then started walking across the street directly towards me. She wore a waist-length black leather jacket with the collar turned up and black jeans and boots. Dark glasses covered her eyes. There was a slight hesitation in the movement of her right leg. Not a limp, more like an ill-placed comma. Her body was thin, like a dancer. Her once long black hair was now in short dreadlocks. She stopped a few feet away from me and reached up and removed her sunglasses. Her skin was just as dark and rich as

I remembered. Her eyes still filled with the same mystery I had lost myself in once before. My heart skipped a beat, and my knees buckled.

'You,' I said, picking up right where I had left off eighteen years before.

2

She looked at me for a brief moment then glanced nervously around, her eyes finally landing on my shoes, I assumed to see if there was any lasagna present.

'You haven't changed,' she said, apparently still impressed with my conversational skills. 'I wasn't sure you would remember me.'

Her dreads curled around her ear, which was just as perfect as it had been that day. I thought the part of me that had existed before the accident and the broken wiring in my head was long gone. I was certain that I had forever lost that eighteen-year-old who could still feel wonder and go all to pieces because of the way a hand brushed a strand of hair off a forehead. But all evidence at the moment, including my racing heart, suggested that I had been misinformed by doctors who had told me that some things in my life were never going to be quite the same because of the injuries I had sustained.

'You haven't changed either,' I said, barely managing to get enough air in my lungs to speak.

Tracy half smiled and dismissively shook her head.

'If only that were true,' she said, her voice tinged with longing or maybe just time.

'Well, that makes two of us,' I answered.

Her eyes nervously looked me over in a way that people did years ago when seeing me for the first time after the accident. A quick glance to see if the screws that held my head together were visible.

'I've often wondered how you were doing,' she said.

Apparently not enough to have sent a card, but I did nearly get her killed on a first date that lasted a grand total of four blocks, so it wasn't as if she owed me anything. Still, after all the surgeries and the pain and recovery, she could have called. Why didn't she? And why appear now?

'Someone from school told me you were down here. I was hoping we could talk,' she said.

I had lost touch with everyone from school. Comas will do that. The world and the people you wake back up to aren't quite the same. Or, more precisely, their world is often unchanged, it's yours that is unrecognizable. I suppose it's possible someone from that time knows where I live, but I suspected it was just a convenient answer that avoided the real reason she was here.

'Would you like to come in?' I asked and she nodded.

I stepped over to the door, opened it for her.

'I'm on the third floor.'

She stepped past me into the lobby. I wasn't sure, but the subtle scent that lingered as she slipped by me seemed to be the same one I remembered from the night of the accident, though I don't think it was perfume. It was just her.

We walked silently up the three flights. The length of time it took to reach my loft was nearly identical to the time it took to drive four blocks into oblivion years earlier. As I slipped my key into the door and pushed it open I took a quick glance to my left to make sure there wasn't a flash of chrome and headlights barreling in on us.

Upstairs my neighbor, a thirty-five-year-old guitarist, was wailing away on a polka version of a Hendrix song.

'Interesting building.'

'That's Buzz,' I said. 'He works at home a lot.'

I opened the door and Tracy stepped in and looked around.

'I like this,' she said.

Buzz in one of his more contemplative moods described my loft as a postmodern car wreck. Instead of art on the walls, I collected front-end grills of cars, classic ones, bent and twisted from some long-ago collision. Makers that no longer exist are a preference. I've got a Nash Statesman, a 1951 Studebaker Champion, a 1960 Austin Healy Sprite, and a 1954 Packard convertible. I find them comforting in their own way — relics of past lives, slightly damaged fellow survivors. The rest of the loft could be anywhere or anyone's, the furniture, mostly second-hand, I found in garage sales and vintage shops.

Tracy glanced at one of the grills but clearly didn't find the same kind of solace that I did in their company. I showed her over to my small kitchen table, but instead of sitting she stepped over to the counter by the window and leaned back against it, her hands holding tightly on to it.

I offered her a drink but she said she was fine.

'I should have apologized to you a long time ago,' I said. 'It wasn't much of a date.'

She shook her head.

'I would imagine that's hard to do when you're in a coma,' she said.

'I tried to contact you several months after I got out of the hospital, but your parents said you had left for school.'

She nodded and looked out the window at the skyline of downtown. My eyes drifted down to the graceful line of her hands. There was no wedding band on her finger.

'What do you remember about that night?' she asked.

I shook my head.

'I remember picking you up at your house, and I remember the telephone pole.'

'Nothing else?' she asked.

I looked at her for a moment. I was wrong about her being unchanged. There was something else in her eyes that wasn't present on that long-ago night. Doubt, perhaps, but who reaches thirty without that.

'I remember the way car lights reflected off your eyes,' I said without thinking. Apparently I had made some conversational advances in the last decade or so. 'And I remember you took hold of my hand just before we hit the pole.'

'And that's all?'

'Yes.'

She turned to me. Even full of doubt or whatever else they carried, her eyes still made me weak at the knees.

'It was the best and worst night of my life,' I

said. She crossed her arms over her chest, smiled ever so briefly, and then looked away.

'I came once to the hospital, but you were unconscious, a machine was helping you breathe, I couldn't handle it.'

'I sometimes have dreams that I'm suffocating, not very often, thankfully.'

'I went to college shortly after that and didn't come back until a few years ago. I think partly it was that I was angry with you for a very long time.'

It was probably unrealistic to have assumed she had come to see me after all this time to declare a long unfulfilled love.

'That seems understandable,' I said. 'Given the way the date turned out.'

She shook her head.

'I had wanted to be a dancer.'

'I remember,' I said.

'It was impossible after that night.'

It took me a second to make the leap behind her words.

'You were injured?' I said. 'No one told me that, or if they did it was lost in my broken head.'

'It would have been nothing to anyone else,' Tracy said. 'Torn-up knee . . . end of career.'

The slight pause in her step that I had noticed as she crossed the street.

'I'm sorry, I should have known.'

'I think you had your own problems,' she said.

'A few.'

She looked at me, a slightly puzzled look on her face, her eyes full of a question.

'So you don't remember?'

'What?' I asked.

She took a deep breath as if to steady her nerves.

'Dancing,' she said.

I didn't think I had heard her correctly.

'Dancing?' I asked.

She nodded.

'You really don't remember, do you?'

'Are you saying we made it to the dance?' I asked.

Tracy tried to smile, but it seemed uneasy.

'Yeah . . . you were really nervous, but you danced really well.'

'I did?'

'Yes.'

I stared into the blank empty room that is my memory and, as usual, there was nothing there.

'You sure it was me you were dancing with?'

Her eyes found mine and she nodded.

'All night; we surprised a lot of people at school.'

'I would have liked to have remembered that,' I said.

'No one ever told you?' she asked.

I shook my head.

'After the coma and months of rehab, it didn't really matter, my old life was gone; it took everything I had to find my way in the new one. I lost touch with everyone, moved on.'

'It's a good memory,' Tracy said.

'Me dancing, a good memory?'

She smiled again, this time it appeared easier.

'Yeah.'

'The accident happened after the dance?' I asked.

She nodded.

'The truth is I should have thanked you a long time ago.'

'For ruining your life?'

She shook her head.

'No,' she said softly, 'for saving it.'

'I don't understand,' I said.

'When we hit the pole, my leg was pinned between the seat and the dash.'

She took a breath then walked over, sat down at the table and clasped her hands tightly together in front of her.

'I was screaming,' she said and her eyes found mine for a brief moment, and then, like a wire that had been reconnected inside my busted skull, the telephone pole came flying out of the darkness and I heard the sickening sound of the crush of metal and the shattering of glass. I took a deep breath trying to steady myself, but my heart began to pound against my chest as the sounds of the crash bounced around in my head.

' ''Oh God',' I said softly. 'You were screaming 'Oh God'.'

She nodded.

'I don't remember anything else,' I said.

Memory is funny. Like luck, it comes and goes, you can't hold on to it, but you feel it, it's there, just as if you could.

'You freed me just before the car caught on fire.'

She reached out across the table and took hold of my right hand.

'You saved my life.'

I shook my head.

'That's not possible,' I said. 'I've read the police report. It didn't say anything about this. All it stated was that a male victim lay on the pavement unconscious, either having been thrown or having crawled from the car.'

She withdrew her hand and tucked it under her arm.

'It didn't say anything because I never told anyone,' Tracy said. 'You freed my leg and then pulled me to the pavement . . . ' She paused and clenched the muscles in her jaw. 'Blood began to come out of your nose and then your ear and you collapsed.' She paused and took a moment to catch her breath. 'I thought you were dead.'

'Almost.'

'And I thanked you for being a hero by being angry, I'm not very proud of that.'

I had questioned hundreds of accident victims, some innocent of any wrong, some as guilty as hell. It's not difficult to understand who's telling the truth and who's lying through their teeth. Tracy wasn't lying, though I still didn't believe this was why she was here, but truth and believing are two different things. My truth, the one I had been living with for over a decade, was that shit happens that's out of your control, some good, a lot of it bad. There was nothing in the fine print about being a hero.

'I should have told you this a long time ago. You saved me from the wreck . . . and probably a very bad career as a dancer.'

'It would have been nice to have known

23

something good had come out of that night.'

'I'm sorry.'

'I guess you had your reasons,' I said.

Tracy started to say something, but stopped.

My hand was trembling; little bursts of light were going off inside my head, the kind that signal a coming event or sensory anomaly after too much stress. I stood up from the table and walked over to the sink, turning on the faucet and splashing my face with cold water.

I wanted to say something, but my head began to spin as I struggled to catch a breath. It wouldn't have changed my reality to know this, but it would have felt good. And feeling good about something is not to be underestimated. I took a breath and then another, then I felt her hand on my shoulder.

'Are you all right?'

I glanced down at my feet and saw the melted cheese slide off the toes of my tennis shoes like a calving glacier. I managed to calm my breathing.

'This happens from time to time when I . . . one of the benefits of brain injuries, my head doesn't process things well sometimes.'

Her hand moved gently across my shoulder.

'I didn't come here to upset you.'

I shook my head.

'I'll be fine.'

Her hand lingered on my shoulder for a moment.

'I had no idea what you've lived with, I'm so sorry,' she said softly and then her hand slipped away, though I could still feel it there.

'I would have liked to have seen you dance

. . . on stage,' I said, and then turned around. She had walked back to the table and was sitting down, staring at her hands.

'Does this happen to you often?'

'From time to time. Comes and goes.'

'I'm sorry.'

I watched her for a moment, the way I once had across a classroom, but it wasn't the same. There was no turning the clock back that far in time. Did she have more surprises? Something told me she did.

'Don't be, the way I see and feel the world is mine, not anyone else's idea of what the world should be. It's a fair trade.'

Tracy's lips were silently moving as she played out a conversation in her head.

'Why did you come here?' I asked.

'Could I have that drink now?' she asked. 'Water is fine.'

I filled a glass from the sink and brought it to her. As she picked it up, her hand was shaking and she took the glass in both hands as she drank, quickly emptying it.

'You didn't come here to tell me we had danced, did you?'

She looked into the glass and shook her head.

'My name is Sexton now. I have a daughter,' she said.

Buzz began riffing on 'Beer Barrel Polka'.

'What's her name?'

'Charlotte.'

'How old is she?'

'She just turned seventeen.'

She tightened her hands into fists.

'I heard you're an investigator,' she said. 'I'm hoping you can help me.'

I sat down at the table across from her as I began to play out the words to Buzz's riffs in my head. *Roll out the barrel* . . .

'Was she in a car accident?'

She looked at me for a moment with a puzzled expression and then shook her head.

'No, why would you think that?'

'That's what I do, I investigate accidents.'

It took her a moment to process my words then a look of disappointment crossed her face.

'Oh,' she whispered and then shook her head. 'I've made a mistake, I shouldn't have come here, I thought you were a different kind of investigator. I have no right to ask anything of you.'

She started to rise from the table.

We've got the blues on the run . . .

'Has something happened?' I asked.

Tracy stood up but once on her feet she didn't start for the door. She looked around the loft for a moment as if not sure what to do and then turned back to me and nodded. Her eyes were moist, but there was more than pain in the tears, there was fear, and panic just behind that.

There it was, the reason she had walked back into my life. It wasn't guilt or any sense that she had wronged me. And it wasn't because she missed my food-handling skills, but that wasn't necessarily a negative thing.

'I don't know where else to go, I thought you could help.'

The voice in my head I hear when I interview

accident victims or sit in doctor's offices began sounding off. *Don't look at her hair, or her perfect ear or the way her wrist is slightly bent. The past is dead* . . .

'Maybe I can,' I said, as she slowly reached up and tucked a dread behind her ear.

Buzz let go with another riff. *The gang's all here.*

'Why don't you sit back down and tell me what's happened.'

She placed her hands out on the table in front of her and stretched out her fingers.

'Twelve days ago my daughter and I went to the mall. She wanted to check out a store and pick out something on her own so I went to another one. It's something we do, each go to a different place then meet for lunch and show each other what we've found. I waited at the restaurant for half an hour then went looking for her at the stores I thought she might have gone to. When I didn't find her I went back to the restaurant. She never came. No one remembers seeing her. There hasn't been a call, nothing . . . one moment she was in my life and then the next she was gone.'

'I'm sorry.'

She started to say something, but lost the words.

'What do the police say?'

'They consider her a runaway.'

'And you think they're wrong.'

Tracy nodded.

'I know they are. Charlotte would not have run away, that's not her.'

'What about her father?'

'We're divorced.'

'Could she be with him?'

'No.'

'You're certain.'

'He died two weeks ago in an accident.'

My heart skipped a beat.

'What kind of an accident?'

'Car. I don't know much about it except that he was driving alone. Just one of those things.'

She looked at me hesitantly.

'I guess we know about those, don't we.'

I nodded.

'Did Charlotte have any trouble in school — drugs or boyfriend?' I asked.

'The police asked the same questions.'

'What did you tell them?'

'No.'

'And they didn't believe you.'

She shook her head.

'They said it's not unusual for a parent to be unaware of their child's secret life. They say that when she gets hungry or tired of whatever she's running from, she'll either come home, or . . . '

Tracy let the rest of the sentence fall away, unwilling to say the words. She took her lower lip between her teeth, then reached out and touched my hand.

'My baby's out there, and I can't help her.'

I took her fingers in mine.

'I shouldn't have bothered you with this, I'm sorry.'

My heart began to increase in speed.

'It's all right. Why don't you tell me what

28

you've done so far?'

'She's listed on the National Crime Information Center missing children's website, I put appeals on her Facebook page, and I hired a private investigator.'

'When?'

'Eight days ago.'

She slid her hand back across the table and held both hands tightly across her chest.

'His name's Lester. He came highly recommended.'

'Has he found anything?'

'I don't know, I haven't heard anything. I went to his office, but he wasn't there. He hasn't returned my calls, nothing, he seems to have vanished.'

The titanium plate in my head felt as if it had touched a live wire and Buzz began to play again.

We'll have a barrel of fun . . .

'You saved me once,' Tracy said.

An aura of faint shimmering colors began to creep into the edges of my vision.

'I'm not a hero,' I said.

'You were for me.'

Was that really true? Or was it what she needed to tell me in order for me to help her?

'I figure out who did what and who is telling the truth when a Mercedes and Toyota smack into each other, I don't do this kind of investigation. I don't know anything about teenagers except that they have a lot more car accidents than adults.'

She reached out across the table and took my

hand in her long perfect fingers. Tears began to fill her eyes. My heart began to pound.

'I have nowhere else to turn, no one to turn to,' Tracy said, her voice on the edge of breaking.

I looked down at her fingers wrapping around mine. Had we really danced?

'I'm not who . . . '

I looked up to see the light reflecting in her eyes like diamonds, and then my head began to spin, then the room and my heart began to pound with panic. I tightened my fingers around hers trying to hold on to consciousness.

'You . . . ' I said, and then all movement, all sounds, all light, stopped as I hit the floor.

3

I looked into her eyes and she didn't look away. It was like slipping into a dark pool of water with no bottom.

'Just follow me, just move with my moves,' she said softly.

She placed her hand on mine and slowly moved it up my arm until she rested it on my shoulder and then she twisted her hips just enough to brush against mine, then her fingers reached out gently and touched my neck.

Her lips started to move in a whisper. Then I felt the faint sense of movement, like the ground shifting in a 3.5. There were voices, calling from another room, unrecognizable, speaking in clipped, single words. A hand touched my neck; others took hold of my arms and legs . . . lift . . . I was moving, faces passed by, staring in shock, a wheel squeaked, a door opened, then closed. I smelled the night air, the sweet hint of pollution . . . then everything sped up until it was all a blur and then only the voices and the sounds were there.

I've got . . . can you . . . lift him on three . . . nothing . . . a siren begins to spin through my head like a flame, an engine speeds, traffic, the voices begin to blend together . . . lights come and go, faces like flash cards appear and then vanish . . . the air rushes past, a door opens, more movement, faster and faster then it stops

. . . a blue glove . . . nothing . . . once more . . . the light in my eyes is like the sun . . . clear . . . again . . . hands hold my head . . . again . . . and then hands over my mouth . . . I can't breathe . . . I taste the plastic, like old gum filling your mouth, one piece then another and another until it slides down my throat and I begin to suffocate.

'Elias.'

I open my eyes and gasp for a breath.

'Dude . . . you all right?'

The air slips into my mouth like cool water. There's no tube down my throat.

'Elias?' said Buzz.

He was leaning over, staring down at me. What looked like an aura surrounded his face, but it was just his bright red hair. I tried to get up but Buzz's hand held me down.

'Slowly,' he said. 'Let me look at your eyes.'

He moved his finger back and forth in front of my face like an annoying insect on a hot summer night.

'You passed out.'

My breathing and heart were racing. Buzz took hold of my wrist checking my pulse.

'Try and slow everything down,' he said.

Panic began to take hold.

'It's over, you're all right. Look at me.'

Things began to slow.

'One breath at a time.'

The panic slipped back into its hiding place.

'This hasn't happened for a while, has it?' he asked.

I shook my head. I took another breath. I could still feel the breathing tube like a piece of bread caught in my throat.

'We should get you to a doctor, you could have a bleeder.'

Was he right? Was this the moment I had been waiting for? It didn't feel like it was, but what does that moment feel like? No instructions come with it. I took another breath, slower this time, didn't smell any grapefruit.

'No, no doctors,' I said. No respirators, no comas, no dreams.

'You sure?'

I nodded.

'Your pulse is slowing, that's good.'

Buzz had thick black glasses, hair down to his shoulders and the scent of dope hung about him. Someone once described him as what happened when Rod Stewart had sex with a Muppet. The T-shirt he was wearing read *Coltrane died for our Sins. Kenny G lives because of them.* He spent eighteen months in Iraq as a medic before coming home, plugging in his guitar and lighting up one joint after another. When he wasn't reinventing polka he played the occasional studio music for TV shows, and did a few things I probably wasn't aware of that may or may not be legal.

'You had a visitor,' he said.

I bolted upright and looked around the loft.

'She's gone.'

I looked over to the door.

'Don't rush this,' Buzz warned.

'We were dancing,' I said.

'You were dancing . . . really?' he said skeptically.

I shook my head.

'Not here, a long time ago.'

My head still felt a little uneven. Like the way you feel after being in a boat all day when you step back onto land.

'You saw her?' I asked.

'She came and knocked on my door when you passed out. I came down and checked. I told her this happens to you sometimes.'

'Did she say anything?'

Buzz shook his head.

'No, she just held your hand for a few minutes, then left. Who is she?'

'A memory.'

'A beautiful one.'

'Yeah, always has been.'

Buzz leaned in.

'You want to get up?'

My head was still adrift. I turned and looked out the window. The light outside was failing.

'What time is it?' I asked.

'Almost six, you were out a little over an hour.'

I reached up and Buzz pulled me to my feet. I wasn't quite ready to stand so I took a seat at the kitchen table. I quickly looked around to see if Tracy had left anything behind, a note, a phone number. There was no evidence that she had been here, except that I could still feel her fingers wrapped around mine.

'You all right, Elias?'

Was I? I reached up and ran my hand over the side of my head where the plate lay.

'Better,' I said.

'So who is she?' Buzz asked.

'The girl of my dreams,' I said.

Buzz stared at me for a moment.

'As in THE girl?'

'That's her.'

Buzz shook his head.

'Not possible, I've done a thorough study and they do not exist, it's a myth.'

'A little mythology never hurt anyone,' I said.

'Tell that to the Greeks.'

I looked down at my hand which she had held; the feeling of her fingers had slipped away.

'Wait, are you saying she's the one from the accident?' Buzz said.

'Yeah, that's what I'm saying. She asked me to help her,' I said.

'Help?'

'Yes, it's when you render assistance to someone in need.'

Buzz shook his head and smiled.

'Not always. I could tell you stories.'

'Don't.'

I pushed myself up from the table, walked over to the window and looked down at the street where her Jetta had been parked. Buzz came over and stood next to me. He looked down at the street where I was staring and then at me.

'So, after all this time, without so much as a note or some wilting flowers at the hospital, she shows up and asks you for help.'

I looked out to the north towards the lights of China Town which were beginning to glow.

'That's what she did.'

'Tell me you said no,' he said.

'I'm not sure what I said, I passed out.'

35

Buzz shivered as though a glass of cold water had been poured down his back. He shook his head and then stared out into the city.

'She should have at least slept with you out of simple courtesy before asking for help.'

'She said her daughter's disappeared,' I said.

'What about the father of the kid?'

'Dead.'

'And the police?'

'They think she's a runaway.'

Buzz shook his head.

'Elias, no one, particularly someone that beautiful, just appears out of the past and asks for help. The world just doesn't work that way. It's like saying I was in Iraq to fight for democracy.'

Out over the hills of Elysian Park a police helicopter began circling with its spotlight burning a hole in the fading light.

'Let her hire someone.'

'She did. He's found nothing.'

'Rabbits vanish, not people. If the girl ran away, it's for a reason. Now is your chance to just walk away.'

'She told me we danced that night,' I said.

'The night of the accident?'

'Yes.'

'I thought you never made it to the dance.'

'So did I.'

'And you believed her.'

'Why would she lie?'

'You really need me to answer that?'

I shook my head.

'So what do you do?' Buzz asked.

'I still help her.'

Buzz pounded the table with his fist like he was hitting a buzzer in a game show.

'Wrong answer! The correct answer is why in a city of ten million people, did she come to you?' he said.

'She told me that I saved her life at the accident.'

Buzz's jaw nearly fell off its hinges.

'This is turning into a hell of a date,' he said.

'Too bad I don't remember any of it.'

'And convenient for her.'

'And if it's true?'

'That you danced the night away and saved her life all in one night?'

I nodded. Buzz took a deep breath and stared out the window.

'You want some advice?'

'From a man playing 'Beer Barrel Polka'?'

'No one can give you back the things you lose,' Buzz said. 'Trust me, I'm an expert on the subject. Go find a nice head-on collision to investigate.'

'That would be the sensible thing to do.'

'You've seen this girl twice in eighteen years, the results have not been good either time. You don't know anything about her, her daughter or how they got to this . . . It's a private world you're thinking of stepping into, and you have no idea what's in there. Maybe your head was telling you something.'

'How many sensible people do you know with titanium plates in their head?' I said.

'I know a guy who is good at finding things out about people.'

'You mean bad things.'

'Anyone can find out good things, it's the things people don't want others to know that they keep hidden. I'll talk to him, see if he can fill in a few of the blanks about your dream girl before — '

'Before what?'

'Before you get back in a car with her.'

He waited for me to protest, but instead I nodded.

'And get your ass to a doctor.'

Buzz turned and closed the door behind him as he walked out. I stepped back over to the window and looked down to where Tracy had parked. Buzz, in his weird way, was probably right. She picked me for a reason I didn't understand completely yet. But she still picked me, and that was the part Buzz didn't grasp. Perhaps you can't get back the things you lose, but maybe you can find something else to fill that hole inside.

From upstairs the soft sound of Buzz playing 'Taps' on the guitar drifted down. I took one last look at the empty spot on the pavement where I had seen her step out of the car then turned and looked back into the loft.

'Sensible,' I said to myself.

I walked over to the door and instead of locking it, I pulled it open and stepped into the hallway.

4

How do you find someone who is missing when it's you who is lost? I didn't think about where I was driving, though I knew where I was heading. I couldn't have gone anywhere else, even if I had tried. I had looked into that empty space that holds the secrets of my life and tried to peel back the darkness to let a sliver of light in. I had lived since the night of the accident with known history that was at least settled, if not complete. It gave a kind of order to everything that had followed.

With one sentence, Tracy had changed that.

We danced all night.

Did we? Did I really save her life? Was part of the incompleteness inside of me a reflection of her dark eyes as I held her in my awkward arms?

I stopped the car across the street from the high school and stepped out. I had never returned here after the accident. They had given me my diploma while I was unconscious, and once I had woken and stepped back into the world, the recent past was a stranger to me. The places, the people, I no longer knew this world — or, more correctly, I had been thrust into a new world that made this one irrelevant, so I stayed away from it.

Lights were on in the building. People were walking in the front door. The sign out front was lit up . . . 'Parents' Night, everyone welcome.'

I crossed the street, joined the line of people stepping through the doors. Inside the lobby dozens of parents milled about having as many conversations. The look on their faces wasn't unfamiliar to me. I'd seen them at accident sites and post-accident interviews of parents whose teen had wrecked the family mini-van — a combination of fear and confusion, false bravado and complete cluelessness. But the conversations that were flying through the lobby like parenting missiles were new.

'She told me I was too obsessed with success . . . I've tried everything . . . he's a stranger . . . I found out she was a lesbian at the kitchen table . . . nothing but straight A's and then he tells me he's found God . . . I thought it was drugs . . . she said it was lack of a reliable global future . . . he told me that he was gender neutral . . . I thought I knew her . . . I'm afraid to ask . . . she doesn't want what we have . . . he won't talk to his father and I don't know how to . . . three-hundred-dollar cell phone bill . . . he said he wanted to be a carpenter and I just broke down . . . they accused him of cheating on his SAT . . . she told us she no longer respected our marriage . . . '

A hand touched my shoulder and I spun around. A woman in her early fifties with short-cropped gray hair, wearing a whistle around her neck and a nametag that read Mrs Hansen, was standing there.

'Are you here for the personal growth or the academic achievement meeting?'

I hesitated. I already understood that I knew

40

nothing about teenagers, now I could add parents to that list. It was as if I had just been dropped off on a deserted island only to find it inhabited by a group of desperate survivors from some terrible disaster.

'Growth, I think.'

She smiled.

'First time? Don't worry, you're amongst friends.'

She pointed me down the hallway where the crowd was slowly moving. I followed the parents until I reached the first hallway and walked away as fast as I could, the parents' conversations echoing against the walls until I turned down another hallway and parent night slipped away.

The names on classrooms and the signs posted on walls were unfamiliar, but I knew these halls just the same, as if a portion of time had frozen inside the building. I knew the smell, the sound footsteps make on the tiles, the way voices travel. I didn't think I knew where I was going, but when I turned down another hallway and stopped at a set of double doors with rectangular wire-reinforced windows, I knew where I had been going all along.

I reached out, pushed open the doors, and stepped inside. A single light at the other end illuminated the gym. I walked across the wood floor until I reached the middle of the court. Had Tracy told me what she thought I wanted to hear? Had I imagined the words, or did these walls still hold them?

Just follow me . . .

I closed my eyes and tried to press against the

door that shuttered my memory, but there were no ghosts spinning around the dance floor, no words being whispered from the top row of the gym's seats.

Perhaps Buzz was right.

A sound came out of the darkness — a jangling of bracelets on a wrist as they settled around my shoulder. I thought I heard a whisper: *Move when I move.*

'You're in the wrong place.'

I spun round to see a figure standing at the doors to the building.

'Are you looking for the meetings?'

He took a few steps into the gym, a set of keys making the noise on a ring on his belt.

'Parents' Night is in the other side of the building.'

'Sorry.'

I started walking towards him and the doors. He was a heavy-set man, his hair combed over his thinning scalp.

'I tell them to put up more signs, but they don't listen to me.'

He stepped back to the doors and pushed them open as I approached. He had on a blue shirt that had a name tag on it: Frank. He looked to be nearing sixty. If he had been at the school when I attended, I didn't remember him.

'Go down to the far end and take a left,' he said.

As I stepped past him his eyes looked me up and down.

'You're not really here for Parents' Night, are you?' he said.

I stopped.

'Excuse me?'

'You came in here for someth'n' else.'

'How did you know that?'

He shook his head.

'I see it a lot, guys come in here to relive the big shot they made that won the game, or the shot they missed that lost it. Happens all the time.'

He looked at me and suppressed a laugh.

'So did you make it, or did you miss it?'

'I don't remember.'

He looked at me for a moment, trying to decide if he should call security or not. Apparently he made a decision because he smiled.

'Then consider yourself lucky. There ain't nothing here but an old wood floor. The shot never changes.'

I glanced back in the gym.

'Perhaps.'

His eyes held me for a moment, then he turned and walked away through the doors to the gym, his keys jingling on his belt.

★ ★ ★

It was a short drive from the school; in ten minutes I pulled to the side of the road and stopped several car lengths from the intersection. I had never once returned to the site of my accident. Half a dozen times over the years I had come to within several blocks of it only to turn away. The riot of sensations inside as I came close was just too raw — like pulling a piece of tape off an open wound. So I avoided it, and

43

whenever I had questions about what happened that night, I just opened the accident report, read over my history, which I had come to accept, and put it back in the filing cabinet where it was out of sight.

I closed my eyes and took a breath.

Look at me . . . Tracy whispered softly, then her voice trailed off and there was nothing else, not her hand reaching out to take mine just before the collision, no headlights, nothing, not even the telephone pole racing towards us.

If I remembered the accident report correctly, Tracy and I had been driving from the south, which was to my left, heading north. The car that had struck us had come from the east. I stared into the empty intersection and my heart began to beat heavily against my chest. Why hadn't I questioned it before? If, as I remembered, we were driving from Tracy's home towards the dance, we would have entered the intersection from the right side, not the left. But if what Tracy had told me was true, and we had made it to the dance and were heading home, we would have entered the intersection from the direction I was pointed now, not from the left.

If the report was right, neither of those things had happened, so what did and why?

The headlights of a vehicle appeared in my mirrors, the car paused several hundred feet behind me for ten or perhaps fifteen seconds, then moved down the street and slowed as it passed me. It was a dark Ford Taurus. The windows were tinted, though I could see the ember of a cigarette glowing inside. It stopped at

44

the intersection and didn't move.

One minute she was in my life, and the next she wasn't.

The passenger window lowered, a hand reached out and dropped the cigarette onto the pavement. I don't know why, but I opened my door and stepped out. The Taurus still didn't move. I took a step then another and then the window of the Ford rolled back up and the car took a left and drove off.

I walked over to the corner of the intersection where the '86 Volvo of my mother's had come to a rest after we were struck. There was no telephone pole standing there any longer. A four-inch gouge had been taken out of the concrete of the gutter, but that could have been from anything — urban decay, LA slowly crumbling . . .

I kneeled down to touch it and the headlights came rushing out of the darkness and then Tracy's voice: *Don't stop.*

I turned in the direction the car had struck us. The street was empty except for a cat that ran across the road and disappeared into the shadows of a house.

'Don't stop,' I whispered.

Had I? Had I ignored Tracy's warning? Did my foot hit the brake, was that why it happened?

I turned and looked south in the direction we had been driving according to the report. The red taillights of the Taurus faded into the distance and then disappeared. Whatever else was down that road wasn't visible in the darkness, or my memory.

I walked back to the car and slid in behind the wheel, but didn't turn the ignition on. My head throbbed with a headache, my muscles felt as if I had run a marathon. Doctors had always advised me to remain quiet for twenty-four hours after a blackout; if I ignored their advice I might end up in the vegetable patch.

'What's happening to me?' I whispered.

If I had thought that I would find answers etched in the concrete or the wood floor of the gym I wasn't even close. Two words had come back, a warning not to stop. Had I ignored it? Was that why we crashed, or did we crash because I had listened to her? If I had found out anything it was just more questions.

It was nearing midnight now. I was too tired to drive, and with my head the way it was, oncoming headlights hitting my eyes could feel like a struck match touching my optic nerve. I reclined my seat and lay back to get some rest before trying to drive home. In little more than a breath or two I drifted off to sleep.

The dreams came in waves, one after another, each pushing further and deeper into that empty room that fills so much of my past. There were hands lifting me, sirens, lights, voices of strangers, the sound of breathing, but not a person's breath, it was mechanical, a relentless in and out, in and out, never resting, never altering its rhythm, just endlessly pushing air.

Don't stop.

I bolted up in my seat at the sound of her words in my ear. My hands were gripping the wheel as if bracing for impact. The headache had eased with rest. I took a deep breath and released the wheel then looked to my left, the intersection was empty. Dawn was just breaking.

The streets were just beginning to come alive with traffic as I drove home. The first deliveries of food were arriving at Chinatown restaurants. The scent of roasting duck and garlic drifted out from kitchens already well into their day. A street sweeper moved through downtown with its large brush taking away the previous day's trash. Prospective jurors were filing into the courthouse building. Stockbrokers in BMWs were just arriving at the large trading firms to begin the day's moneymaking.

I stopped in Little Tokyo and had breakfast at a Mexican café next to a noodle shop and tried to make sense of what had already happened over a plate of eggs and beans and salsa.

I lingered for over an hour drinking coffee, watching the street life out the window. Trucks of art headed for the museum. Japanese business-men in thousand-dollar suits, telephones held tight against their ears. Homeless drifting up from the railroad tracks to begin a new day of pan handling, squad cars moving out from Parker Center to begin their shift.

Don't stop became no clearer, and the beans got cold.

I parked in our lot on the side of the building and as I made my way to the entrance I paused long enough to check out the make of every vehicle within sight. Not a VW Jetta anywhere, no perfect ears or jangling bracelets, not a slab of lasagna in sight.

Let it go, I thought. If Tracy had told me the truth and I had saved her life at the accident, then according to Buzz I was ahead of the game and should walk away.

I walked slowly up to the third floor then down the hallway to my loft. Buzz was playing music, but softly now; he had moved on from the previous day's polkas to a soft ballad. Across the hallway I could smell fresh paint being mixed in another neighbor's loft. Slightly burned coffee drifted from another. All was as it should be. After a shower I would call the office and find a nice parking-lot fender bender to investigate and I would leave the past where it belonged, securely encased in titanium.

I started to slip the key into the door.

Who was I kidding? How could I walk away? This was my chance, and if I didn't take it I would never step out of the glare of the oncoming headlights that had held me in their grip for eighteen years.

But if Buzz was right, the blackout was a warning; if I ignored it, I risked losing everything . . . the word hung in the air like a breath on a cold night. I pushed the door open just enough to look in at my collection of mangled front ends and twisted grills . . . everything.

Don't stop . . . there was a flash of chrome . . . don't . . . brakes squealed . . . her fingers touched mine . . . Did you make the shot or miss it? Don't.

I slipped the key back out and closed the door as I left.

5

Tracy's address was listed on the missing children's website. As the crow flies her house was perhaps ten miles from the loft, but as it was becoming apparent, nothing, not cars, and most certainly not lives, ever moves in a straight line in Los Angeles.

The home was on Emelita in North Hollywood a few blocks west of the 170 freeway. The street was a nice tidy row of bungalows with lawns and magnolia trees — a postcard of suburban America in all its glory. I parked across the street and sat there without making a move to get out of the car. There was no Jetta parked out front, or in the driveway.

A small picket fence painted bright yellow surrounded the yard. The windows that I could see had curtains drawn; the others were behind a thick bunch of bird-of-paradise plants. The house itself was painted in the bright purple you see in Mexican folk art, the front door in aqua green. On the front yard there was a sign that read: Heal the Bay.

In the moments I had imagined her life over the last eighteen years, this would fit nicely — a house full of life, happy, normal. The gap between imagination and reality was widening by the second. What had happened to her in that time? How many blank pages were there yet to be filled? How do you go from dreams of the Bolshoi to a suburban street and a missing daughter? Had the accident done all that? It couldn't be that simple.

When I looked more closely at the house it became apparent that the reality behind the postcard front was that all was not well. Newspapers and takeout menus were scattered across the front porch. The plants in the yard were dying of thirst. The curtains weren't drawn to keep the light out; they looked more like bandages on open wounds.

The voice in my head began whispering again and again.

Why you, why did she come to you?

Did I really think she would just waltz back into my life because she believed I could save her? How do you even go about it? I glanced into the rear-view mirror.

Walk away.

I started to reach for the gearshift, then stopped, then started to reach again and stopped again. Then I saw the white Jetta come around the corner and down the block. She pulled into the driveway without looking in my direction and parked next to the house and got out.

Don't get out, don't, no, no, no.

I was already out the door and walking across the street.

Fool!

What else is new?

As I passed a withered agave plant slumping towards the dried grass of the lawn, Tracy reached the front door, slipped the key in and started to open it, then turned and watched me approach.

She wore a T-shirt under a loose open sweater and jeans. I reached the steps to the landing and stopped. Beyond getting out of the car I hadn't actually worked out what I was going to say or even do, but here I was.

'Are you all right?' she asked. 'I was worried, your neighbor said he would take care of you.'

I nodded.

'For me, I'm pretty good.'

She took a step and closed the door behind her.

'I shouldn't have bothered you, I'm sorry,' Tracy said.

'It's no bother.'

I noticed her hand was tightly clutching the doorknob as she talked.

'No, you should really forget I came. It would be better that way.'

I took a half-step towards her up the steps and I noticed her hand tightened on the door.

'For whom would it be better?'

'You,' she said. 'It wasn't right for me to ask you, I didn't understand. You should just forget it,' she said, trying too hard to sell the words.

'I'm tired of forgetting when there are things I would like to remember.'

I took another step, her fingers tightened even more around the handle.

'Memories are overrated,' she said softly.

The muscles of her chin trembled.

'Are they?' I asked.

Tracy took a deep breath and looked past me into the street.

'Yes,' she said. I think she believed that.

'I went back to the school last night, walked into the gym,' I said.

She pressed herself back against the door almost as if my words had pushed her. She looked at me for a moment and then shook her head.

'Why would you do that?' she asked.

'I wanted to remember what it was like to dance with you.'

Nervously she tried to swallow, then looked away.

'Did you?'

'A little, not much.'

She shook her head.

'It was just a dance. I'm sorry; I didn't realize you had . . . ' She glanced at my head.

'Problems,' I said.

She took a breath and looked away.

'You could have gone to anyone for help. Why me?' I asked.

'I told you last night.'

'Because I saved you once.'

She nodded, then glanced at me.

'I used to think of the way you were that night, your blond hair, hazel eyes . . . If you had known how attractive you were, no girl would have had a chance. When I saw you I thought you were the same, but you aren't the same, are you?'

'No, I'm not.'

Tracy looked at me sadly. 'Neither of us are,'

she whispered, her eyes full of more than just the passage of time.

Tracy sat down against the front door and looked out towards the street.

'The night of the accident,' I asked, 'just as we entered the intersection, you said to me 'Don't stop' . . . you were trying to warn me about the car.'

Tracy shook her head.

'I don't remember.'

'I didn't listen, I tried to stop. It was my fault, wasn't it?'

Again she shook her head.

'Doesn't matter, you don't owe me anything.'

I sat down next to her.

'Does to me.'

She shook her head again, started to say something, then paused and said something else.

'Don't blame yourself.'

'I have one gift, if you can call it that. I see details that others look right past, like it was a picture, with the sounds, smells, everything. I don't know if I would be any good at this, but I would like to help.'

Tracy's hands tightened into fists. She took a shaky breath.

'You don't know anything about me,' she said, barely above a whisper.

The baggage carried in those words appeared to press down on her shoulders to the point where I thought she might collapse.

'I don't have any room for anything or anyone in my life who can't help me, do you understand?' she said and turned to me, her eyes moist with tears. 'If I lose Charlotte, I'm lost.'

'What happened to you after the accident?' I asked.

I'm not sure how long the silence lasted. Tracy just stared at the street as if it were a stream flowing past, watching the currents twist and turn, waiting for the waters to reveal the secrets they held under the surface. Were they mine she was looking for, her daughter's, her own?

If she saw something there, nothing in her eyes gave it away and when finally she did speak, the voice and the words seemed only half to belong to the woman sitting next to me. Perhaps the rest belonged to the girl I'd once danced with, or maybe it belonged to some other time and place that she kept locked away from all eyes, even her own, or maybe what I saw wasn't hers at all.

She had left for college not long after the accident.

'My parents thought the discipline, the study, would be good, and help me to move on, so I began classes that summer.'

She shook her head in wonder.

'They were so clueless.'

For almost an hour she told me about what happens when the shattered dreams of an eighteen-year-old collide with reality.

'I lost myself,' she said. 'I don't remember much of it, I was drunk, or high most of the time. I thought I could push it all away, but the more I partied the worse it got. I thought I was being punished, so I just kept partying to punish myself more.'

She stopped for a moment and stared again at

54

that stream as if something had broken the surface.

'Then I crashed again,' Tracy said. 'I got pregnant.'

Her eyes found mine for a brief moment then looked away.

'That was the first time Charlotte saved my life,' she said. 'My parents had wanted me to lose the baby, they didn't understand that if I did that . . .'

The words slipped away for a moment.

'I was eighteen, so I made my own decision and a child brought a child into the world.'

The memories appeared to overwhelm her for a moment and I realized what she had been seeing in the stream passing us by. She was watching herself, twisting and turning, struggling to stay above a current she had no control over.

'That dream didn't work out exactly as planned either,' Tracy said just above a whisper.

When she had finished talking, Tracy looked back out at the street. There was no stream reflected in her eyes any longer, just the cold reality of her life. Had she told me everything? I doubted it — after all, no one tells anyone everything. She was right, I didn't know her, but it didn't matter to me. A door in my past that had been locked now had a crack in it, and I wanted to step all the way through.

Tracy leaned her head on my shoulder, took a deep breath.

'What do we do now?' she whispered.

I know Buzz would have told me to get up and walk away, but I couldn't. Yesterday and for as long as I could remember I was alone; now, perhaps, I wasn't. And if the blackout I suffered meant that a clock in my head was beginning to count down the minutes left, I didn't want to waste a single one of them. Even if it was possible that I was chasing little more than shadows of a life and a girl that was lost years ago.

'I need to know everything that happened on the day she disappeared,' I said, looking down the street with its perfect suburban houses. 'Every detail, no matter how small — a gesture, a single word, a car that drove a little too slowly past. I need to know who her friends are and who isn't a friend. Who she talks to on-line, what she likes, everything that happened in the days before she vanished, and everything that has happened since. And I'll need to know the things you don't want to tell me.'

'What things?'

'The secrets inside this house.'

There was surprise or perhaps fear in Tracy's eyes.

'Secrets?'

I nodded.

'We all have them.'

Her eyes briefly found mine, as if she was searching for what secrets of hers I had already found. Then she looked away and nodded.

'All right.'

6

Walking through the house to her daughter's room at the far back corner, I felt like an intruder. Buzz was right; this was a private world I was stepping into. The fact that I wasn't certain whether I was here for her or me gave more weight to the feeling that I was a trespasser peering through an open window.

We stopped at the door, which had a photograph of Charlotte staring into the camera waving a finger. Below the picture were the words: Don't even think about it. Below that was written: A room of one's own.

Until this moment everything that had happened so far had the quality of a story told in the third person — a work of fiction about the past that resembles reality but has the distance of time. The eyes staring out from the photograph changed that in a heartbeat.

Charlotte no longer was just a name or a tiny thumbnail on a website. She was real, with the perfection of youth in her face. I could see in her eyes a reflection of the girl I had danced with, the lines of her face were a little rounder than Tracy's, the skin a little lighter, the lips not quite as full.

'The policeman who came after she disappeared thought this meant she was an angry, rebellious teenager.'

'Cops don't read much Virginia Woolf,' I said.

Tracy looked at me and almost smiled.

'Maybe it's because I was a dancer, I never could sit still long enough to read much. When Charlotte was younger she always seemed to have her head in a book, now it's the computer or the phone.'

She paused for a moment, looked over to me.

'I remember you were always reading in school,' she said.

'I had to learn to read all over again after the accident,' I said. 'Actually, it was a way to watch you without anyone noticing.'

She smiled.

'I noticed.'

The smile slipped away as she turned back to the bedroom door. Tracy took hold of the door handle, hesitating just long enough before opening it to suggest she still felt as if she were betraying her daughter's wishes by stepping inside, then she opened it and we walked in.

About the time that I was hoping to occupy teenage girls' bedrooms I had traded it all in on a room in intensive care, but I guess you could move this room to the Smithsonian as a representative of the category and no one would bat an eye. There were posters on the wall: a rock band, one for saving the planet, an anime-like drawing of a dragon, a bed with stuffed animals, a desk with a computer on it, snapshots taped on the wall behind the computer. Everything was exactly as it should be, it was perfect, and it was this perfection that made me uneasy; nothing is perfect, particularly lives.

I stepped over to the desktop; there was a

small collection of silver and braided-fiber bracelets, some of them looked like the same ones I remembered Tracy wearing on the night of the dance. The photographs on the desk were mostly of Charlotte alone, one had her mother standing with her next to a giant redwood tree; two others appeared to be with girlfriends, not one with any boys. On the bed were a small brown bear, a skunk, and a snake with purple spots and a green furry tongue.

I could feel her presence in the room. I could see her slipping a bracelet on her wrist and sleeping in a bed, her hand on a purple snake with spots.

'She reminds me of you,' I said.

Tracy shook her head.

'She's smarter than me.'

I slowly looked around the room. Where do I begin, how *do* you begin? There were no skid marks, no bent steel or shattered glass. What hubris made me believe I could do this? My heart began to pound against my chest.

'I don't — ' I started to say.

'What?' Tracy asked, her eyes locking on me with a fierce intensity that seemed unwilling to accept any hesitation.

Think, look around the room, find a place to enter the intersection.

'What?' she repeated.

I looked back to Charlotte's desk, the photographs, the bracelets. I remember how they softly jangled as Tracy's hands moved.

'Tell me something about her, something only you would know,' I said.

Tracy looked about the room as if searching for a memory.

'When she was small, she was afraid to fall asleep, she wasn't afraid of the dark, just falling asleep. So I would get in bed with her and she would tell me a story.'

'What kind of stories?'

'Sometimes they would be adventures she would take with her stuffed animals, I remember one in which she went to the moon with her bear. Other times it would be an adventure with me . . . ' Tracy started to say something else, then stopped.

'What?' I asked.

She took a slow, deliberate breath.

'What is it?' I asked again.

'That was a long time ago.'

I looked over to the drawing of the dragon, it wasn't a romantic version of a child's rendering; there was a raw, violent quality, not the stuff of fairy tales, not one that ended happily.

'What about now?' I asked.

Tracy took a deep breath. 'I'd like to show you something,' she said, then walked over to the computer and I followed.

She opened a file and the screen filled with a video. It was a play from school. Charlotte stood in the middle of the stage in a lacy white dress, looking out over the audience as she delivered her lines. She spoke in a faint southern accent that had a hint of the San Fernando Valley in it. There was a sweet quality to the voice that only youth can produce — a kind of perfection that hasn't been touched by time. I wasn't even hearing the words, just listening to the sound. I couldn't take my eyes off her. When she smiled, dimples appeared on her cheeks.

'That's my baby,' Tracy whispered, then it became too much and she turned it off and stepped back to the bed and sat down.

I walked over and joined her. I sat in silence for several moments replaying Charlotte's voice over in my head. I had never heard her speak, but it wasn't a stranger's voice. It seemed part Tracy, part the dream I had lived with for so long.

'What did the policeman look at when he came in?' I asked finally.

Tracy shook her head.

'Nothing, I think he had made up his mind what had happened before he even stepped into the room. She's a black teenager. In the eyes of an LAPD cop that makes her little more than a criminal in training.'

'He said nothing?'

'He told me to look at her computer or her phone for any messages that seemed out of place, asked if she kept a diary and to look at it if she did, and if I found something, to call him.'

'Does she keep a diary?'

Tracy shook her head.

'It's all about Facebook and her phone.'

'And you found nothing on either.'

'Nothing on Facebook, her phone is with her. I've called it hundreds of times. Left message after message . . . ' The words slipped away from her. 'The service provider is supposed to alert me or the police if there's any activity on it.'

'And there's been none.'

'No.'

'Are you good with computers?' I asked.

Tracy shrugged her shoulders.

'About average.'

'And Charlotte?'

'It's their language, isn't it?'

'You didn't find anything on it?'

'No.'

I glanced at the snapshots on the wall.

'You've talked to her friends.'

'Yes, none of them have heard anything or know anything.'

'Did you believe them?'

'That's what the private detective I hired asked me.'

'How did you answer it?'

'They're teenagers, what's truth to them isn't necessarily the same thing it is to a parent.'

Once more I looked around the room. No imperfections, nothing out of place, it resembled a stage set more than a room where a life was being lived, particularly a life that quoted Virginia Woolf on the door. A seventeen-year-old girl without a single secret, was that possible?

Uneasiness settled into the pit of my stomach. I imagined that if I closed my eyes I would feel the room begin to slide across the pavement towards some terrible collision.

'You've gone through the room, all her clothes, every drawer?'

'Everything,' Tracy said.

'May I look at her computer?' I asked and she nodded.

I stepped over to the desk, opened the computer and looked at the files.

'I've been through every file, every application,' Tracy said. 'There's nothing there.'

I opened her Facebook page and stared at her profile picture. Her hands were held up in front of her face, illuminated by a flash the way a celebrity would try to block the taking of a picture by paparazzi. Behind her hands you could see enough of her face to know that she was laughing.

There were eleven hundred and sixty-two friends listed.

'How many of these do you think she actually knows?' I asked.

Tracy shook her head.

'I don't think knowing someone means the same thing for kids now as it did for us.'

'How many of the names do you recognize?'

'Fifteen. I counted them. I posted on her page asking all of her friends for help.'

I scrolled down the page. There were perhaps three-dozen postings from friends asking for Charlotte to contact them and to come home. There were no replies from Charlotte.

'Forty responses out of eleven hundred and sixty-two friends.'

Tracy nodded.

'What about her locker at school?'

She shook her head.

'Nothing that didn't belong.'

I looked over her profile information. There seemed nothing there that shouldn't be. She listed the music she liked, movies, books, politics, healing the oceans and saving tigers. Nowhere on her computer was there a hint that she had opened a page, or replied to a friend, that had taken her into a place she didn't belong.

I stepped back from the computer and looked at Tracy.

'What mall was it?'

'Sherman Oaks Galleria.'

'Was there surveillance video?'

Tracy nodded.

'She was seen by two different cameras at two different times. Once she was with me, and ten minutes later by herself.'

'No camera picked her up leaving the mall or in the parking lot?'

'No.'

'Did she ever go into the store where she was going to shop?'

'She never made it there.'

Tracy walked me through the day Charlotte vanished, step by step from when they woke in the morning to when they went to the mall just before lunchtime. She replayed the drive, the conversation, the things she remembered seeing and where they had parked in the lot. Aside from a white car she couldn't identify honking the horn at them to move after the light had turned green, nothing stood out that seemed any different from any other Saturday.

I sat down on the desk chair and looked around the room. It was like I had walked into an accident site, but there was nothing to indicate that something had gone terribly wrong. I wanted to say to Tracy that people just don't vanish, but I knew that wasn't true either. Bad things, terrible things do just happen; we had some experience with that. But no one, especially a teen, is perfect. Tracy was hiding something, the question was why.

'You told me last night that Charlotte hadn't had any boyfriends, is that true?'

Tracy clenched her fists.

'You're not telling me everything, are you?' I said.

She hesitated then shook her head.

'Why?'

'I wanted you to . . . not get the wrong impression.'

'How many?'

'Two that I know of.'

'Sex?'

'Hooking up is a form of recreation to most kids, doesn't mean much. When I found out about the first one I got furious with her. We had a fight and I said some things that I shouldn't have. After that I think the next hook-up was in anger at me. I think she was showing me that she wasn't going to make the same mistake that I did.'

'Did you talk to the boys she saw about her disappearance?' I asked.

'I tried, they said they knew nothing. If it wasn't true, I couldn't prove it.'

Tracy looked at me uneasily and then looked away.

'I didn't want to become one of those parents who become consumed with everything their kids do. I know parents who have hired computer experts to watch their on-line activity; others who track their every movement with GPS. I wasn't going to do that to Charlotte. Even with our issues, we still trusted each other, love each other.'

'But?' I asked, sensing there was more to it.

She took a deep breath.

'Perhaps I was wrong,' she whispered.

Tracy got up and walked over to the chest of drawers and opened one.

'I found these after she was gone. They're not new, they've been worn.'

Tracy pulled out a leather thong and bra.

'You don't wear these things because they're comfortable, you wear them for . . . others,' Tracy said.

'Who might she have worn them for?' I asked.

'I don't know,' she answered.

I looked over to Tracy. The sum knowledge of my understanding of her was that for a very brief moment a long time ago, I thought she was perfect. Who she had become or even was then was as much a mystery to me as Charlotte's disappearance. Perhaps it wasn't her daughter who had opened the wrong door and invited disaster into their lives. Perhaps it was her, or something her ex-husband had done before he died. What pain had they inflicted on each other? Did the trail of wreckage from the divorce lead all the way to Charlotte's last steps in the mall?

'If I'm going to be of any help, I need to know everything. Do you understand?'

She turned and fixed her eyes on me.

I wouldn't eat that if I were you.

She started to answer, then hesitated.

'You're asking if there is something in my life that may have caused this?'

I nodded. 'The things you don't want to tell me.'

She looked down at the floor and shook her head.

'All you really know about me is that I was eighteen once, and you had a crush on me.' She looked back at me and smiled. 'You probably didn't even know that I had one on you, did you?'

'That was beyond even my capacity to dream,' I said.

Her eyes seemed to look past me, searching for a memory that she could cling to that was as real as the present, then she looked away, still not having answered the question about her past.

'I've made a lot of mistakes,' Tracy said. 'Some poor choices.'

'Everyone does.'

She shook her head.

'Not everyone. Have you?'

'I drove down the wrong street once.'

She looked around the room then placed the underwear back in the drawer.

'I'd like to go talk in the other room,' she said as if her daughter was still here and she didn't want to confess her sins in her presence.

We walked down the hallway past the family photos arranged on the walls. I recognized Yosemite, San Simeon, Central Park, Dodger Stadium, a birthday party, a graduation picture. On first glance they looked like any other

67

family's collection of memories, but by the time I had reached the end of the hallway the same feelings I found in Charlotte's room pervaded the memories behind the glass. Each picture was perfect, but somewhere in that perfection hid an uneasiness that I couldn't point to. It was as if in each picture another person stood just outside of the frame of the photograph, unseen, but there, holding a key to a secret of what the photograph really showed.

I followed Tracy into the kitchen and took a seat at the table as she poured two cups of coffee and then sat down across from me and stared out the window.

'For a while after Charlotte was born everything was perfect. I was in love, I had a beautiful daughter, and I didn't care any more that I wasn't a dancer. It didn't last.'

'What happened?'

She started to speak, then stopped, looked down into the dark liquid of her coffee cup and whispered something to herself and shook her head.

'I've never told anyone this,' she said, her uncertain eyes catching mine for just an instant, then looking away. 'Ever.'

She sat in silence for a moment, waiting for the words to slip away from where she kept them securely hidden.

'My husband was two men. The one I married who swept me off my feet and the one I met on one of those spring days when the sky is so blue it seems painted.'

She paused as if to catch her breath, but there

was more than that, almost, fear.

'Charlotte was three. We were having a barbecue. I dropped his burger on the ground, I started to laugh and as I reached for it I heard him coming at me ... ' She paused and a shudder went through her.

'He picked up a lawn chair.'

I felt her shudder go right through me as I heard the sound of the chair swinging through the air.

'I turned to him.' Her hands began to tremble. 'I didn't recognize his face.'

The leg of the chair made a sharp crack as it hit the side of her face.

'It happened so fast.'

His fist closed around her shirt just below the neck as he slammed her to the ground.

'I remember the sky because I was staring at it as he held me down on the grass with his hands around my neck. I was screaming at him, or trying to.'

She exhaled heavily and took hold of her shaking hand with the other one.

'It was nearly a year before it happened again. The second discussion, as he liked to call them, happened in the living room.'

The images and sounds came at me like a power point on high speed. Hands, a mouth open in a scream, the sound of Tracy hitting the floor, fabric ripping as he dragged her across the floor.

'At first he just liked to choke me, but as time passed he got bored with that so he came up with more interesting forms of discussion. I thought he would change, that I could fix things. It's amazing how comfortable you can get with fear, even while it's eating you apart.'

Tracy fell into silence. Her breathing, having sped up, began to slow like an engine that had run too fast.

'Being a victim isn't your fault.'

She nodded and held on to the coffee cup with both hands.

'Remaining one was,' she whispered.

'I doubt it's that simple,' I said.

'Simple? No, it was never simple.'

She took a heavy breath and closed her eyes. I didn't want to ask the next question, but it was there waiting in her eyes.

'Did he abuse Charlotte?' I asked.

She drew her legs up onto the chair and wrapped her arms tightly around them.

'He said he didn't, his rage was directed at me, not her.'

'What did she say?'

She shook her head.

'She said he never touched her,' Tracy said, barely able to get the words out.

'Did she know about what he was doing to you?'

'He was always very clever about hiding what he did to me so that she wouldn't see it. There are a lot of ways to hurt someone without leaving bruises behind. But eventually, towards the end of it, he was getting more and more violent and not even he could cover up what he was doing. I stopped coming up with excuses about why my arm or neck hurt.'

'What was her reaction when she found out?'

'She loved her father. When she found out, it was confusing for her, she didn't want to believe it at first.' She sank back into the chair as if just talking about it took a physical toll the way his blows must have.

'What is the old saying . . . what doesn't kill us, makes us stronger.'

Tracy looked out the window. 'It's not true.' She took hold of the coffee cup and raised it slowly to her mouth, her hands gently trembling. She took a bird-like sip and then set it back down on the table.

'I used to think about you after he would do something. I would be lying in bed at night staring into the darkness and I would think about you pulling me out of the burning car, and I would tell myself that what was happening to me was punishment for having not been there for you when you were in the hospital.'

'That's not the way life works.'

She shook her head. 'At three in the morning, that's exactly how it works.'

'You said he died in an accident,' I prompted.

'Just less than a month ago.'

'Do you think there's any way Charlotte's disappearance could be connected to his death?'

'I don't see how. It wasn't for several weeks after the accident that . . . she was gone.'

'What were her feelings about him?'

'After the divorce we never talked about him.'

'Never?'

She shook her head.

'Abuse doesn't slide into conversations easily.'

'What was her reaction to his dying?' I asked.

Tracy sat with that for a moment and then shook her head. 'I think she acted the way she thought I wanted her to.'

'Which was?'

'Relief that a nightmare was finally over for good. If she felt anything more than that she never let me know.'

Tracy seemed to struggle with the next breath, like trying to breathe through a heavy cloth. Her hand not closed around the coffee cup began to tremble again.

'It wasn't the life I ever imagined,' she said softly, her brown eyes looking at me sadly. 'I guess you know about that.'

'A little.'

'Can we talk about something else?' she said almost as if she hadn't fully escaped from her husband's fury.

'When was the last time you heard from the investigator, Lester?'

'There was a message from him when I got home from your place yesterday. He asked me if I knew the names Sophie or Anna. He said he wasn't sure if it meant anything but he would check it out. I'd never heard them before. Apparently there was some connection with the names on a number of Charlotte's Facebook friends' pages.'

'But not on hers?'

'No, I checked.'

'Did you call him back?'

'Yes, but I just got his service,' Tracy said.

She sank back in her chair with exhaustion. I

had little doubt that at the rate she was going, at some point there would be nothing left and whatever was inside her that made Tracy who she was, would simply vanish like her daughter.

'Do you have a picture of her I can use?' I asked.

She nodded.

'What are you going to do?'

'I'll start from the beginning, the day she vanished,' I said. 'Retrace everything you did that day. Talk to everyone who might have seen something but didn't realize it or had just been asked the wrong question so they didn't think about it.'

Tracy looked at me for a moment.

'Like looking at skid marks at an accident.'

I nodded.

'Something like that.'

'What about your job?'

'They owe me some vacation.'

A tear fell down her cheek and she wiped it away.

'Are you good at what you do, Elias?' Tracy asked, her voice breaking with desperation.

I thought I felt one of the screws in my head slowly tighten.

'I was made for it,' I said.

7

Where is the line between memory and reality? How do you know when the shadows of yesterday give way to the sunlight of the present if the violent touch of a hand around your throat feels more real than the caress of the present? How do you find your way back?

As much as her memory allowed we did everything exactly as she had done the day Charlotte vanished. We left the house and followed the route they had taken to the mall. As we turned west on Burbank, Tracy's eyes appeared to focus in a way they hadn't before, but she wasn't seeing anything outside the car, or at least outside the car on this day.

'Tell me what you're thinking,' I said.

Tracy started to shake her head and confusion seemed to slip back into her gaze.

'You were remembering the drive with Charlotte?' I asked.

She looked out the window.

'What did you talk about?'

Tracy shook her head.

'It was just chat. I don't — '

'What was she wearing?'

She took a breath to slow things down.

'Jeans, a yellow shirt and a green Abercrombie hoody.'

'And you talked.'

Her eyes settled on a street sign as we drove past.

'Not yet. She had been fiddling with her iPod until we made this turn,' she said.

I followed her directions and turned south.

'Charlotte looked over to me and smiled, but it was different.'

'How?'

'There was something else there in her eyes for just an instant,' Tracy said.

'What was it?'

'I don't know.'

We passed a palm tree that had fallen over onto the pavement and was being cut up by several Mexican gardeners with chainsaws and machetes.

'Did you talk then?'

She nodded.

'Tell me.'

Tracy took a breath and closed her eyes for a moment, trying to find her way back, then opened them and began to replay the conversation.

'*Maybe we should do something else,*' Charlotte said.

'*Like what?*'

'*Something that means . . . something.*'

'*What would you like to do?*'

'*I don't know, I'm just thinking.*'

'*This is fun, nothing wrong with that, right?*'

She turned and looked out the window. '*Right.*'

In the distance the mall came into view.

'Then what?' I asked.

'She asked me a question. It caught me by surprise.'

Tracy said something softly to herself as if she were trying to coax her daughter's words back to the present.

'*If you could do things over again, what would you do differently?*' *Charlotte asked.*

'How did you answer?'

Tracy looked straight ahead.

'I didn't. I made a joke about breakfast. Stupid,' she whispered and shook her head. 'Why would I have answered her like that?' she said, as if, had the words been chosen differently, none of what followed would have happened.

'You were just talking, you didn't know what was going to happen next,' I said.

'It would have been better to have said anything other than what I did say,' she said in frustration.

'We probably wouldn't say half the things we do if we knew what was coming, but we don't get to do that.'

'Not once had she asked me something like that. But she did on that day, of all days, and less than an hour later she was . . . ' Tracy turned to me. 'Why did she ask that question?'

'I don't know.'

'She knew something was going to happen,' Tracy said, her voice filling with the edge of fear.

'It's possible, it's also possible that it was just a question.'

Tracy looked out the passenger window at the traffic moving by.

'You don't really believe that, do you?' she said.

'Probably not, but believing something is possible isn't the same as it being true.'

We turned at Riverside into the mall and found a parking space near where they had stopped on the day of the disappearance. Neither of us made a move to get out of the car, and neither of us said a word for several moments as her daughter's words seemed to hang in the air about us like dust.

'Regret,' Tracy said softly. 'She was asking about regret.'

'Yours?' I said.

Tracy shook her head.

'Have you ever asked someone a question that was actually about yourself and not them?' she said.

'I wouldn't use the things that have gone on inside my head as a benchmark of human behavior.'

'What if she had done something that had got out of control?'

'The underwear?'

'Maybe.'

'Then there will be evidence of it, and we can follow it.'

Tracy's eyes held on to my words as if they were a rope that was tied around Charlotte's waist that she could take hold of and pull her back from the darkness. As I looked at the shopping mall I couldn't escape the feeling that I was stepping into an intersection where two cars had violently collided.

'What happened next?' I asked.

Tracy got out of the car and we followed the same path into the stores that they had taken before.

'Did you talk when you were walking in?'

'No, she put her iPod back on.'

I do my best to avoid malls, and not just because statistically more accidents happen in a large parking lot than anywhere else. The amount of visual and audio stimulus to a brain with as many damaged wires as mine can be overwhelming at times.

We followed a short corridor lined with pictures of long-ago orange groves in the San Fernando Valley that I suppose were meant to put the kind of consumer free-for-all that took place within its walls into a historical perspective, though the connection of citrus groves to Bloomingdales and Foot Locker seemed a bit of a stretch.

Inside the mall the orange trees had been replaced by large palm trees, which soared up towards the second level of stores.

'We walked to the center, there's a fountain,' Tracy said.

We passed Abercrombie, Ann Taylor, Apple, The Body Shop and Cebu, Disney, Gap, Gap Body, Gap Kids, Guess, Crew, and then stopped next to the fountain outside a store named Utopia. Music and the sound of the voices of shoppers blended together into a strange rhythmic murmur that didn't come from any one place, but was just everywhere, like voices in a dream, speaking in your head.

'We were to meet in the food court upstairs in one hour,' Tracy said.

'And she said nothing else on the way here?'

'No, not on the way.'

Tracy looked around at the stores, her eyes falling on a Victoria's Secret sign. She took a short, clipped breath and whispered . . . 'Secrets.'

'Tracy,' I said.

Her eyes remained on the sign as if perhaps it held some sort of answer.

'Then what happened?'

'Charlotte started to walk away then looked around and said something.'

'What?'

' 'No following me — promise?' '

Tracy stared in the direction Charlotte had walked, her eyes landing on any girl who appeared to be Charlotte's age.

'I promised and turned in the other direction, just like she told me to.'

'Where did you go?'

'I just walked and looked at things. Got a coffee and sat on a bench for twenty minutes and watched the people pass by.'

'And in an hour you went to the food court?'

'A little before.'

'And you have no idea which, if any, stores she went to?'

Tracy shook her head.

'I circulated a picture to every store in the mall, no one remembers seeing her.'

I looked in the direction where Charlotte had walked away.

'Where was the camera that picked her up?'

'Right down there,' she said, motioning in the direction in which I was looking.

At that end of the mall was a department store.

'Bloomingdales,' I said, looking at the store at the far end.

'She wouldn't have gone there, she didn't buy from the big stores, only local ones, it was a political thing for her.'

We walked in that direction until I saw the surveillance camera perched above one of the elevators to the second floor.

'Was that the camera?' I asked.

'I think so.'

We walked over and stood directly under it and looked in the direction in which the camera was pointed. A girl in her late teens walked by us, listening to an iPod and talking on a cell phone.

'Was that about where Charlotte was walking?' I said.

Tracy watched the young girl for a moment.

'I guess so.'

'Don't guess, be sure.'

'Yes, that's it.'

'Did she turn or walk straight?'

'Straight.'

'No pauses?'

'No.'

'How many paces was she in view of the camera for?'

'Does that matter?'

'What I've learned in accident investigation is that everything matters, no matter how insignificant or unconnected. It's all part of the final picture.'

80

Tracy's eyes moved across the floor where her daughter had walked, counting out the steps she had taken.

'Seven or eight.'

'You're sure?'

She nodded. The set of stairs leading to the second floor was perhaps four or five paces beyond where the camera was positioned.

'She didn't go upstairs,' I said.

'I don't think so.' She shook her head. 'How does that matter?'

'It's one step.'

'To where?' Tracy asked.

I took Tracy by the arm and guided her in the direction Charlotte had walked.

'How was she walking?' I asked.

'What do you mean?'

'Was she walking slow, fast, normal?'

Recognition flashed in Tracy's eyes.

'I always thought she walked as if her feet barely touched the ground. There was her world, and then there was the world where the rest of us lived in.'

The words touched me in a way I wasn't expecting. Piece by tiny piece Charlotte was coming alive to me.

'That's how you walked when we were young,' I said.

She shook her head.

'I don't remember that.'

Tracy looked at me and reached out and touched my arm, then looked back to where Charlotte had gone.

'Was that how Charlotte was walking?' I asked.

She thought for an instant and then shook her head.

'No,' she said in amazement as if she had just seen a piece of a puzzle that suddenly fit.

'How?'

'She wasn't in her world . . . she was walking faster.'

When we reached the point where Charlotte would have walked out of view of the camera, I stopped.

'What happened next?' I asked.

She struggled with an answer and shook her head.

'Was she looking down at her iPod, around at stores, did she seem focused on something?' I asked.

'Focused?'

'You said she wasn't in her world?'

'No, she was looking up.'

'Straight ahead towards Bloomingdales?'

Tracy stared ahead at the entrance to the store another hundred paces on and shook her head.

'I'd forgotten,' she said in surprise. 'She glanced back over her shoulder.'

'Was it a casual glance or like she was looking for something?' I asked.

Tracy thought a moment then nodded.

'It wasn't casual. She was looking for something.'

'Could you see her face in the camera?'

She nodded.

'It looked like she was . . . nervous,' Tracy said.

'Then what?'

'She looked ahead again, but her head was turned a little.'

'Which way?'

'To the left.'

I looked down the line of shops.

'Hard left or just a little?'

'Just a little.'

My eyes stopped along the wall between two stores. There was a drinking fountain and next to that a doorway recessed in the wall. I stared at it for a moment then looked back at the camera and then back at the door.

'And then she was out of view?' I said and Tracy nodded.

I looked over to the door and started walking towards it, Tracy following a step behind. There was nothing written on the door to give away what was behind it. Tracy stepped up behind me, staring at it, taking in every inch of it as if looking for some trace that this was where her daughter had gone.

I began to reach for the handle when it turned. I stepped back as the door swung open and a young Hispanic man wearing a green janitor's uniform that looked one size too big for his thin frame stepped out and started to close the door behind him.

'Where does this go?' I asked him.

He looked up, surprised by my question. He looked at us both for a moment and shook his head.

'No public,' he said through a heavy accent.

'*De dónde va esto?*' I asked.

He looked at me suspiciously for a moment.

'Maintenance,' he said.

'We need to see inside.'

He shook his head.

'No public — ' he repeated.

I slipped my wallet out and flashed my ID from the insurance company just long enough for him to get the impression that it actually meant something. Then I reached into my pocket and took out the picture of Charlotte which Tracy had given me.

'Have you ever seen her?'

He barely glanced at the picture and quickly shook his head.

'No.'

'Please look closely, she's my daughter,' Tracy said.

The janitor looked at the picture again and shook his head.

'No, I didn't see her.'

'Is this door always locked?' I asked.

He nodded.

'No one ever leaves it unlocked?'

He glanced nervously around and shrugged. I took that as a yes.

'Open the door,' I said.

The janitor stepped over to the door, took a key from his belt and opened it. A dimly lit hallway led another thirty feet to a set of double doors. I heard a whisper in my head.

Charlotte was running now, her breathing faster with each step as she glanced back over her shoulder to make certain no one else came through the door.

I took Tracy's arm and quickly walked to the

set of doors and pushed them open.

Faster, she kept going faster.

The smell of stale food and garbage filled the air. A series of trash dumpsters lined one wall. On the far wall was a vertical loading-dock door. Next to that was a small entrance and exit door.

I crossed the floor of the loading dock to the exit door and pulled it open. Bright sunlight flowed in. The traffic of Riverside Drive streamed by outside. I stepped back in and looked around the dock. On the wall opposite the door was a metal bracket and a cable.

'No camera,' I said.

The janitor shook his head and shrugged.

'How long has it been out?'

'I don't know.'

Tracy was standing in the open door, staring out into the bright sunlight. I walked over to her. Her eyes were watching the traffic streaming by, but I doubted they were actually seeing any of it.

'She was here, wasn't she?'

I nodded.

'It makes sense. There's no image of her leaving the building because there's no camera.'

'Was someone chasing her? Was that why she looked back over her shoulder before coming out this way?'

I watched the cars pass by one after another for a moment, searching for how to say what I was thinking.

'She was rushing, but I don't think anyone was chasing her.'

Tracy looked over to me and shook her head.

'I don't understand.'

'If someone is following you in a public place, the last thing you're going to do is run down an empty hallway. All she would have had to do was scream for help if she was frightened.'

'Then what was she looking at?'

'I think she looked back to make sure you weren't watching her.'

The words seemed to snatch the breath from Tracy. She turned away and looked about the empty loading dock and then back out into the sunlight struggling to draw a breath.

'Me?'

'Yes.'

'You're saying my daughter did this? She just walked away?'

'I think so.'

Tracy crossed her arms on her chest and clenched her hands into fists. 'You figured all this out, just like that?' Tracy asked, her words filled with frustration.

'I figured out which door she went through, that's all.'

'I thought you were here to help me,' she said, shaking her head, trying to keep her fear and anger in check.

'I am.'

'And you think the police are right. You think she ran away . . . from me.'

'I didn't say that.'

Tracy shook her head, her eyes desperate to understand.

'I think she chose to step through this door. I don't know why or where she was going.'

Her fists began to relax their grip and she looked out into the sunlight. Her body began to tremble, but it wasn't from cold. She looked at me for a moment then turned away and sighed.

'I think a part of me kept hoping that because no one could tell me how or where she vanished, it was somehow less real, that it was all a mistake and that one day I would walk into her bedroom and there she would be, reading or listening to music.'

Her eyes moved about the loading dock and the dumpsters with their smell of day-old food and diesel exhaust from the garbage trucks.

'Now I know it's real,' Tracy whispered with a terrible finality. 'This is where I lost her.'

Tracy then stepped out into the sunlight and looked up and down the street as if searching for the next line or mark on a map pointing in the direction her daughter had gone from here.

8

Were there more secrets sheltered inside Tracy's battered heart? Was that what Charlotte was fleeing, or was it her own secrets she feared would follow her? There were no maps to follow, no more cameras, no fleeting images of Charlotte turning and looking over her shoulder before walking away, nothing at all to point in the direction she had gone, and even less understanding of why. All we really knew was what door she had stepped through to walk away from her life.

From the mall we drove across the Valley. Tracy spoke in fragments as she recognized a store or restaurant where they had gone shopping or eaten a meal.

What do you think about this . . . maybe just the two of us . . . do you remember what I ate here before, it was spicy . . . what if . . . could we . . . I was thinking . . .

The more intensely she tried to recapture the moment, the further it seemed to slip from her until her words sounded like those written on a postcard from someone you had not seen in years, and in that distance, I could hear the sound of her heart breaking a little more each time until finally she let go of words altogether and just watched her memories pass in silence.

A few of Charlotte's friends agreed to meet at a small Thai café not far from their school. To the south the Hollywood hills rose up, the Valley stretched out in every other direction. The smog that had filled the sky earlier in the day had been blown towards the coast by a warm breeze slipping over the mountains from the desert.

We arrived early and parked across the street. Tracy started to open the door and I reached over and touched her arm.

'I'll need to talk to them alone.'

She started to shake her head and a flash of fear appeared in Tracy's eyes.

'Why?'

'Part of my job in accident investigation is to know when people are lying to me,' I said.

Tracy looked at me uneasily. Was she afraid of what I might discover, or what I wouldn't?

Classes had let out for the day and groups of students of various ages were beginning to walk past the car carrying backpacks and bags while working phones and iPods. Tracy's eyes moved from student to student as if she was looking for some clue they might have held to Charlotte's disappearance.

'Look at them,' she said softly.

A girl started laughing into her phone. A boy held his hands above his head as if surrendering as a girl pushed him away.

'Look at them,' Tracy said again. 'Strangers . . . we think we know them, but we don't . . . we can't, not everything. It's like trying to balance a needle.'

She looked over to me. 'You think they'll be freer to talk without her mother there?'

A girl screamed and then jumped onto the

back of the boy she was walking with.

'Perhaps,' I said.

The students moved on, more groups began to pass; more dramas began to play out in glances and gestures. Tracy looked over to the café and nodded.

'No, you're right. I'll wait here.'

★   ★   ★

I ordered a cup of tea and took a seat at a window table and waited. The air in the restaurant smelled of lemon and garlic and, for a very brief instant, juicy fruit gum which the cashier was chewing. Or at least that's what my head was telling me; it was though it could have been pork and chilies and I wouldn't know the difference.

The first to arrive was a thin girl with jet-black hair, a pale complexion and a small silver nose stud. She stood nervously outside, glancing around, waiting for the others. From the description Tracy had given me I recognized her as April, one of Charlotte's closest friends. One by one the others arrived, Lola, Hunter and Morgan. They quickly entered into an intense conversation with lots of head shaking and nodding as they also fiddled with their iPods and made and received at least two phone calls each all without seeming to miss a beat of the conversation taking place.

They knew something, or at least believed they did. They appeared to be at ease with themselves

90

in a way that I don't remember being at that age. They were all dressed in jeans and loose-fitting shirts and T-shirts. The boy Hunter looked a little like a young Eddie Vedder, something he clearly cultivated. The illusion that I would more easily enter into their world and get information because I wasn't a parent quickly slipped away when I realized I was no more at home with them than I was with the adults at Parents' Night. They're a tribe, and they're going to make damn sure that they don't give away the family secrets to anyone who might use them against one of them.

When some sort of a consensus was reached, they stepped into the restaurant and immediately located the alien sitting at the table by the window. They glanced at each other, seeming to pass along some silent message, then walked over.

'Mr Hawks?' said the one boy.

I stood up.

'You're Hunter,' I said.

He nodded and introduced the girls.

'We don't know what we can tell you that we haven't told anyone else,' he added, a bit too rehearsed.

The girls all nodded except for April, whose eyes remained firmly planted on me.

'We all want the same thing, right?' I said.

'Sure,' said Lola.

'Absolutely,' added Morgan.

April didn't say a thing. The waiter stepped up and they all ordered Thai iced tea.

'Have any of you been in contact with

Charlotte — Facebook, or phone, tweets, anything?'

They all shook their heads.

'We already told everyone this,' Morgan said, then looked down at her phone and checked a text.

They were all distracted, and only appeared half interested. If any one of them were worried about their friend they didn't show it, except perhaps April, but that might have been because she wasn't as good an actor as the others.

'She was running from something at the mall,' I said.

That got their attention.

'How do you know that? No one said anything about that before,' Lola asked.

'It's what I do,' I said. 'I look at things and people and see what others don't.'

'You're like psychic?' Morgan asked, I think seriously.

'No.'

She looked disappointed.

'But you're not a cop,' Hunter asked.

I shook my head.

'What are you?' asked April, speaking for the first time. There was an edge in her voice that wasn't present in the others'.

'I might be the best friend Charlotte has,' I said.

April glanced at the others then looked back at me.

'You don't even know her,' she said.

'True.'

'Are you being paid to find her?' she asked suspiciously.

I shook my head.

'Why are you doing it, then?'

'I'm a friend of her mother's, she asked me to help.'

'What kind of friend?' she asked, clearly loading the question to the gills.

They all glanced at each other and Morgan snickered.

'What does that mean?' I asked.

'Maybe you should ask her,' Morgan said.

'Ask her what?'

April shot Morgan a look.

'Not for me to say, talk to your friend,' said Morgan.

I clearly wasn't trusted enough for inside information.

'I will,' I said.

'What was Charlotte running from?' April asked, getting back to the point.

'I was hoping one of you might have some ideas,' I said. 'A reason, a person, a name, something she did, something she didn't do . . . anything?'

They all shook their heads without hesitation.

'What makes you think she did something?' April said.

'Happy people don't disappear,' I said.

'You know a lot about happiness?' April asked.

I shook my head.

'I know about disappearing.'

'How do you know she isn't gone because she wants to be?' said Lola.

Lola had too much make-up on and was dressed more expensively than the others or, at least, she was dressed to get the maximum amount of attention without appearing to be seeking it. Her question appeared to elicit an angry reaction in April's eyes.

'Wish we could help,' Morgan quickly interjected.

Hunter shrugged. 'What can we say? One day she was here, the next she wasn't.'

'She's not a bunny in a magician's hat,' I said.

'I was just saying — '

'She could be in trouble,' I said.

I looked them over again for any more reaction or chinks in the armor but none appeared. I pushed back from the table and stood up. I was wasting my time.

'Sorry,' Lola said and smiled in a practiced sort of way that I remembered pretty girls doing in high school when they were brushing me off.

I started to leave, then stopped.

'Do any of you know Sophie or Anna?' I asked.

A waiter dropped a handful of silverware and April jumped. The other three looked at each other and shook their heads.

'I don't think so,' Hunter said.

The girls nodded in agreement a beat too quickly.

'They're friends of yours on Facebook,' I said. 'All of yours.'

Morgan forced a laugh.

'What's so funny?'

'What world are you from? I have, like, sixteen

94

hundred friends,' she said.

'Eighteen hundred,' added Lola.

'Same,' said Hunter. 'It's about community, it's not personal.'

I looked over to April.

'How about you?' I asked.

She looked at me for a moment then out the window.

'Can't help you,' she said.

'Too bad.'

'If there was something we could do, we would do it,' April said.

From the look in April's eyes it seemed to be the first honest thing any one of them had said.

'Lucky Charlotte,' I answered.

I left the four of them in the restaurant and walked out to my car. Were they all lying? At the very least they weren't telling me everything, but that isn't always the same as lying, just ask Tracy.

I slipped into the passenger seat as Tracy's eyes locked on me.

'What did they tell you?' she asked before the door was closed.

I turned. What was it the kids knew about her? What other surprises was she still holding on to?

'Do they know anything?' she asked.

Did they? And was it about Charlotte, or was it about Tracy? Or were the two of them part of the same abyss?

I shook my head.

'Whatever it is they know, they didn't tell me,' I said.

Tracy shook her head.

'Welcome to my world.'

'One of them suggested I ask you.'

Tracy took a slow breath as if letting the meaning of the question become clearer as she took it deeply into her lungs.

'Me, ask me what?'

'They didn't say,' I said.

If she knew the meaning of the question, her eyes gave nothing away.

'I'm going to find out,' she said angrily and started to reach for the handle of the car door.

'Wait,' I said as the door to the café opened and they stepped out.

The kids said a few more words to each other, perhaps it was heated, then again perhaps it was just natural teen drama.

'If they know something we can't let them walk away.'

'We won't,' I said.

'Then what?' Tracy said in frustration.

The conversation ended and Hunter, Lola and Morgan went in one direction and April in the other.

'We follow her,' I said.

Half a block down April stopped and got into a yellow Honda Civic and headed south down Colfax towards the Hollywood Hills. I spun the car around and began to follow, Morgan's question lingering in my head.

What world are you from?

Good question.

9

We followed April south, the houses getting a little bigger the closer we came to Ventura Boulevard. A few blocks short of Ventura she turned west onto a street lined with tall magnolia trees, their branches holding great white blossoms that hung over the road blocking out the late afternoon sun.

April pulled to a stop in front of a two-story post-modern-looking house that was all straight lines, industrial-looking metal and concrete colored a pale shade of rose. The lawn had been replaced by gravel, cactus and ice plants. A white Mercedes station wagon was parked in the driveway.

I stopped in front of another house and turned the engine off as April jumped out of her Honda and ran up to the front and rang the bell.

'Does this place mean anything to you?' I asked.

'No,' Tracy said.

The door opened a moment later and a woman with short-cropped dyed red hair stepped out. She wore expensive-looking jeans and a loose black sweater. She was perhaps forty and had the look of what someone once called a recovering actor, which, in LA, took in a large segment of the population.

'I've never seen her before,' Tracy said.

The woman gave April a hug and they quickly

entered into what appeared to be an intense conversation that seemed to surprise the woman, then they disappeared inside.

'Tell me about April,' I asked.

'What do you want to know?'

'Can you think of a reason she would want to hide something about Charlotte?'

Tracy nearly smiled as if I had inadvertently said something funny that I didn't get.

'What did I say?' I asked.

Tracy shook her head.

'I'm a parent of a teen, I can think of a hundred reasons she would conceal something like that . . . it's the natural order of things.'

'Has she been in trouble?'

'She had some alcohol issues about a year ago, but she got through it . . . as far as I know.'

'How close is she to Charlotte?'

Tracy thought about that for moment.

'They were very close . . . I think recently they may have drifted apart a little, I'm not sure, and I don't know why.'

The front door of the house opened and April and the woman stepped back outside. April was carrying a brown grocery bag filled with something under her arm. She turned back to the woman, said something, reached out and touched her hand, then started for her car.

As she walked away the woman remained in the doorway watching, occasionally reaching up and wiping her eyes.

'She's crying,' Tracy said.

'You sure you don't know her?' I asked.

Tracy nodded as April got into her Honda and

drove on. As we started to follow, the woman in the door glanced in our direction as we passed. There were circles under her eyes as if crying was a daily occurrence. Even for a recovering actress, she looked far too thin.

'What was it April said to you that makes you think this means something?' Tracy asked.

'It wasn't what she said, it was what she wasn't saying.'

Tracy took a deep breath full of nervous energy.

'A brown paper bag . . . I don't have time to waste, Elias, not a second. Tell me you're not wasting it.'

Was I? How many secrets could you fit into a grocery bag? I looked at Tracy for a moment and started to lie, to tell her I knew exactly what I was doing, that what was inside that bag held all the answers, but stopped myself.

'You don't know, do you?'

I started to say I didn't.

'No, don't,' Tracy said. 'It would be better if I believed in something.'

* * *

For an hour we followed April on the 101 freeway heading north across the Valley in the crawl of rush-hour traffic. Studio City, Sherman Oaks, Encino, Tarzana, they passed like endless pieces of memory momentarily remembered, then just as quickly lost as another one replaced it, none holding any more meaning or uniqueness than the previous one.

How could you not get lost here? A city built on dreams captured in grains of silver and projected in the dark. A land with no water of its own, sold to millions as a paradise where not even the ground you walk on is guaranteed to be there tomorrow. It was made for disappearing in.

At Topanga Canyon, April left the freeway and headed west towards the ocean. Tracy said little, preferring to keep her eyes focused on the yellow Honda ahead, as if to lose track of it would risk her daughter slipping away all over again.

As we topped the Santa Monica Mountains and began winding our way down to the coast, the sun began to slip into the vanishing point where the darkening sky disappeared into the water. In twenty minutes we were driving along the coast road into Malibu. We passed through the village and then turned off the coast road and down a long tree-lined drive towards the ocean.

As the sound of surf became audible April pulled into a parking lot in front of a sprawling redwood structure that looked half nature preserve and half doctor's office and walked inside with the paper bag.

Tracy pulled to a stop in the back of the lot and stared at the entrance. A small sign next to the doors read: Clear Life Clinic. Tracy looked at it in silence for a moment, a conversation seeming to take place in her eyes, then she shook her head.

'I should have known,' she said.

'What?'

'The paper bag.'

'You know this place?'

She kept her eyes on the entrance and shook her head.

'Never been here.'

Tracy looked away towards the tall trees, which were swaying in the breeze like kelp moving with the swell.

'It's a rehab clinic, they're all alike,' she said, her voice charged with emotion. 'They prefer to have things brought to patients in bags, harder to smuggle in things.'

I started to ask but she stopped me before I could.

'No, it couldn't be Charlotte, a minor can't be admitted without the consent of a parent or guardian. She's not here. April must be visiting someone else.'

Tracy glanced at me, an uneasiness filling her eyes.

'This won't help us,' she said.

She started to reach for the keys to start the car.

'How did you know about the bag?' I asked.

Tracy pulled her hand from the keys and sat in silence for a moment, the muscles in her jaw stiffening with tension.

'You can't guess?'

I shook my head. Tracy seemed to turn her eyes inward towards a place difficult to visit.

'I did a lot of self-medicating when . . . at different times.'

She looked over to me as if expecting the glare of judgment. I knew the look. It's the quick glance over my head to see what part of it has the screws stuck inside.

Was that what Morgan was referring to when she suggested I ask Tracy? Was it drugs or alcohol? Or were there still more pieces of the puzzle in the eyes of the girl I had once danced with, more mysteries to be uncovered?

'Sure,' I said.

She started to say more but let the rest of it go and looked over at the clinic doors the way you might look at a former lover with a mix of longing and relief.

'For a while it dulled the feel of his punches,' Tracy said softly, 'then it just dulled me.' She looked back at the trees as if seeking shelter in their movement. 'I lost my way,' she said.

I shook my head.

'You were pushed.'

Tracy clenched her fists as if the fight she waged inside was ongoing.

'Are you sure you want to keep — ?'

'Yes,' I said.

A tear slipped down her cheek and she wiped it away.

'I should be home in case . . . ' She was working hard to sell the words. 'Charlotte might call.'

I nodded.

'I'll talk to April when she comes out, then we'll go,' I said.

She took a breath and composed herself.

'You still think there's a connection to what was said to you at the café?'

If I understood anything it was that people, like cars, don't crash without a reason. April hadn't come here by chance after avoiding my questions. Why was what remained unanswered?

I looked at Tracy; were there still more mysteries in those eyes, did they hold the key to my own secrets? Was that what I was ultimately searching for? The answer to what I had or hadn't done in that intersection?

Don't stop.

The ocean breeze picked up the scent of the eucalyptus trees surrounding us. Tracy's eyes found mine and she started to say something then stopped herself, looked up at the gathering darkness of the sky and took in the bittersweet scent of the trees as if it were a shirt of a lover that still held his presence.

'Things should have been different,' she said softly.

What if, could be, should have, if only . . . I knew those words by heart.

'Talk to her,' Tracy said.

I got out of the car and walked across the parking lot, and as I reached April's Honda, another vehicle came around the corner into the lot and its headlights hit me. I felt Tracy's hand in mine, the scent of the trees seemed to swirl about me like a dust storm, I started to feel lightheaded, her voice was there again.

Faster . . . don't . . . don't . . .

I raised my hand to block the light. I felt the motion of the car as we were thrown towards the telephone pole.

'I can't fucking believe this!' came from behind.

The headlight was turned off and I turned.

April was standing a dozen paces from me.

'You fucking followed me!' she said angrily.

The motion in my head towards the telephone pole began to slow. I sat back on the hood of the Honda to steady myself.

'What the fuck is wrong with you!'

I shook my head.

'That's a long story.'

The motion stopped and I took a breath, the scent of eucalyptus vanished as though a switch had been turned off, for an instant the faint hint of colors shimmered in the dark sky then they, too, vanished and all that was left was the movement of the trees in the wind.

'I told you at the café — '

I was fully back in the moment.

'You didn't tell me anything,' I said, cutting her off.

April gritted her teeth and shook her head.

'You had better be gone when I come back out,' she said and started to turn back towards the clinic.

'Why won't you help your friend?'

April spun around on the words.

'Help? What the fuck do you know about help!'

A door opened and April looked over and saw Tracy get out of her car.

'Fucking great. Why don't you ask her how much help she's been?'

'Who did you come to visit?'

She shook her head.

'None of your business.'

'Was it Sophie?'

'No.'

'Anna?'

The wheels began to turn in April's eyes.

'Who was the woman at the house that gave you the bag?' I asked.

April looked over towards Tracy and shook her head.

'I'm not talking to her.'

'Why?'

'Are you totally clueless? What do you think Charlotte was running from?'

Anger filled her eyes as she looked at Tracy.

'It's her fault. She was supposed to be her mother, not a junkie.'

I looked over to Tracy as April's words seemed to go through her like arrows. Her shoulders sank and she turned away and reached out to hold on to the car for support.

'Nothing is that simple, April,' I said.

'No shit, you read that in a book.'

'Will you talk to me?' I asked.

April spent a moment trying to figure a way out of it, but either she didn't see one, or she decided to talk for her own reasons, perhaps even to do the right thing.

'Not here, and not around her,' she said.

I walked back over to Tracy. She was trembling when I reached her. I started to say something but she shook her head.

'I'm all right . . . just go.'

She started to get into the car, but I reached out and grabbed her hand. Her fingers closed around mine and she turned back to me, put her arms around me and whispered, 'I'm sorry,' then pulled away and got into the car and drove off.

10

April drove us back along the coast towards Santa Monica without saying a word for miles, fiddling with the radio, cigarettes, the mirror, phone, anything to keep words at bay.

I didn't push it; at some point whatever she was keeping bottled up inside was going to come flying out at terminal velocity. As we approached Sunset and she tossed the third half-smoked cigarette out the window, the silence finally became more uncomfortable than talking.

'So,' she said as she fumbled for another smoke in her bag. 'Why are you doing this?'

'Tracy asked for help.'

She laughed dismissively.

'She's good at that.'

'We haven't seen each other since high school.'

She shook her head in disbelief.

'So you're like the first boyfriend come back to rescue everyone. Can you do all that?'

She looked at me for a moment, perhaps it was because so much of my own youth had been taken away, but what I saw in April's eyes didn't reflect any part of what little I remembered about being seventeen. I felt like a character who belonged in an old silent newsreel.

'It is Anna in that clinic, isn't it?' I asked.

She hesitated then reluctantly nodded.

'What was it you had to come all the way out here to tell her?'

'She won't see her parents, I bring her things every week.'

She put another cigarette into her mouth but didn't light it.

'But that's not why you came tonight.'

She took a drag on the unlit cigarette and shook her head.

'So why?'

'You,' she said. 'I figured you would eventually find her.'

'Is she hiding something about Charlotte?'

'Everybody's hiding something.'

'Does she know where Charlotte is?'

'No,' she said far too quickly, but she wasn't lying, at least about that.

'Then why warn her about me?'

She started to answer, then stopped then started again.

'Because she's a mess, and I don't want her to be hurt any more than she already is.'

'I'm not trying to hurt anyone.'

She lit the cigarette and shook her head.

'That's what everyone says at first . . . why doesn't it ever work out that way?'

'Because we weren't made unbreakable,' I said.

She glanced at me; her eyes holding more experience than should be accumulated in seventeen years.

'You don't know anything about Charlotte except what her mother told you, do you?'

I shook my head.

'Charlotte spent most of her life taking care of her mother because she was too high to do the things a mother should be doing.'

'I know some of it.'

'Maybe she's better off where she is,' April said.

'Charlotte's father beat and abused her mother,' I said.

The surprise in April's eyes was all the answer she needed to give.

'It began when Charlotte was just four,' I said.

April started to shake her head.

'Charlotte would have told me that.'

'Everybody is hiding something, right?'

April glanced uneasily at me, her concrete view of the world having developed cracks.

'She would have told me that,' she said, shaking her head in denial.

'Like she told you why she ran?' I said.

She pulled the car over and stopped, jumped out and walked a few paces away and stared out at the ocean. I gave her a moment then joined her. She took another drag on the cigarette, working hard to put things back in order.

'Why didn't she tell me these things?' April asked in confusion.

'I don't know. Maybe she was scared, or frightened, maybe something else.'

She sunk down onto the sand and stared out at the white foam of the waves rolling up the beach.

'She should have told me,' April said softly to herself.

'Will Anna talk to me?' I asked.

She took another drag on the cig.

'Maybe, I don't know.'

'Did Charlotte and Anna share secrets?'

April tossed the cigarette into the sand.

'It's possible,' she said.

'Did you share any of them?'

Her entire body seemed to stiffen as she tried to contain a bad memory.

'I got away from that,' April said.

'From what?'

She shook her head.

'Is that why you and Charlotte had drifted apart?' I asked.

Surprise registered in her eyes.

'What did you get away from, April?'

She bit down on her lower lip as she tried to decide whether to trust me. Reluctantly, she appeared to come to a decision and got up.

* * *

We drove towards Hollywood on Sunset, past the long sloping lawns of Brentwood and the gated compounds of Bel Air mansions. I didn't ask any questions, didn't try to coax any more information from her. April watched the passing landscape with a kind of dismissive glare that wasn't to be found on any of the tour of the stars' homes bus rides.

Occasionally she would whisper something to herself. 'Look at this . . . what's wrong with these people . . . this is so sick . . . '

Was it because I had missed those years in my own life that it felt impossible that she could seem so old and so young at once? Her world wasn't mine, at best I could guess at her experiences, but she was the perfect reflection of the city she grew up in. Wired 24/7, fast, pretty, youthful skin and eyes that sang with clarity and were as fragile as glass. But like the walled mansions we were passing, April's exterior didn't feel entirely real.

Her presence was equal parts performance, panic and pragmatism. We're all sold on a dream version of LA. The rich holing up behind their gates, the immigrant slipping across the border, the family struggling to meet the mortgage, the pool man with a screenplay in his back pocket, the single-parent nurse, the kid shooting hoops in South Central, the salesman, the actor, the waiter, the limo driver, the suburban kid who takes the first drink or hit of ecstasy believing that it will all be different for them because in a city where reality is sold and bought like a product on a store shelf next to Gap jeans and Prada glasses, how could anything ever possibly go wrong?

What's wrong with these people is that we are these people.

We drove through Beverly Hills then into West Hollywood and the strip of restaurants and clubs and hip hotels. The early shift was beginning on the nightly crawl from club to club and the first of the cruisers were prowling the boulevard in their Bmers, Camaros and Mustangs.

As the traffic began to back up, April began to recite local history as she understood it, or because it gave a kind of order to a world that seemed to resist it.

She wasn't talking to me. I don't think she

looked at me once. I was as much a part of that landscape as the movie billboards and the lines outside the clubs.

'John Belushi OD'd there . . . River Phoenix here . . . Liberace died of Aids in there . . . Janis Joplin OD'd, the actor Sal Mineo got stabbed . . . Art Linkletter's daughter jumped out a window, Jan Berry of Jan and Dean crashed, William Frawley of *I Love Lucy* dropped dead and was dragged into the hotel lobby.'

We passed through the heart of old Hollywood and then the Cinerama dome and all the new construction that had begun with the real estate boom. Crossing over the 101 freeway, April looked at the hillside below the bridge the way a tourist might look at the Chateau Marmont. Then she glanced at me and said the first words that didn't seem to belong to her.

'A girl named Kelly died under here, I think she was from Ohio or some place like that.'

We drove a few more blocks and then April turned off Sunset and down a dark street to a dead end where all the dreams finally ran out of road. An abandoned warehouse filled the end of the block. In the glow of the headlights I could see that it was surrounded by a chain-link fence with a graffiti-scrawled For Sale sign.

'What is this?' I asked.

'It's not the Valley,' she said as if a continent separated us from where she lived rather than just the Hollywood Hills.

April's eyes moved across the building for a moment then she turned out the lights and the engine. Beyond the building I could hear the white noise of the traffic from the 101.

'Kids hang out here sometimes,' she said.

'Kids?'

'There were some Trance Raves here, but the cops got on to it and busted them; now it's just a place to hang and sleep. Cops don't have time to bother with it unless something bad happens . . . then it's too late.'

'Runaways,' I said.

She shook her head as if I had misspoken.

'Most of them prefer to think of themselves as future stars . . . like it's the natural evolution of getting high.'

'Is that what Charlotte wanted?'

April shook her head.

'No. Anna wanted to be a star. She has the looks — so does Charlotte, but she's smarter than that.'

A light flashed in one of the broken-out windows of the building followed by the orange glow of a cigarette in the darkness before it backed away and vanished.

'You came here with Charlotte?'

'We hit a few raves. After the cops broke up the parties I used to come back with Anna and just hang out and get high. I spent a few nights here; at first we thought it was cool. Like we were free for the first time.'

'What bad things happened here?' I asked.

Her breathing became quicker.

'It changed.'

'How?'

'At first it was just pot and occasionally E, then a form of meth called Strawberry Quik

112

began to show up. Everyone said it was different and wasn't dangerous. Like pop rocks. It wasn't true — just look at Anna.'

'Did Charlotte get involved with it?'

April shook her head.

'Not then. I don't know about recently.'

'Could she have come here with Anna?'

She hesitated.

'I knew Anna from a different school. Charlotte only knew her from Facebook.' She tightened her fists in frustration.

'Are you sure of that?'

She shook her head.

'Things had been changing, something was going on with her.'

'And you don't know why?'

'No.'

'What about Sophie? Would she know?'

'Like I told you before, I don't know Sophie.'

'You also told me you didn't know Anna.'

'Anna's a friend, I didn't know you.'

Was that the truth? If it wasn't, it was probably a form of truth as she saw it anyway.

'Have you looked for Charlotte here?' I asked.

'A few times, it was useless.'

I started to open the car door.

'Don't,' April said. 'It wouldn't be safe for you.'

'Why?'

She glanced at me and tried not to smile.

'You look like a tourist.'

'I'm not a tourist.'

She shook her head.

'It's what we used to call someone with money

113

from the suburbs who was looking for sex or drugs. They usually get robbed.'

I closed the door.

'How many other places are there like this?'

'A lot.'

'Could she be with someone?' I asked.

'You mean a guy?'

I nodded.

'No one I know, unless they're lying.'

'Are they?'

She didn't hesitate.

'I don't know that many people who only tell the truth, do you?'

'Why did you show me this?' I asked.

''Cause it's the right thing to do,' she said. 'That's what you're doing, right?'

Her eyes landed on me, daring me to answer. Was that what I was doing, the right thing? When Tracy first stepped out of the car, doing the right thing wasn't even on the map, and even if it was, was I doing it for her or for me?

April glanced at her watch and started the car. I suspected there was more she had to tell, perhaps a lot, but I had already pushed her far enough for the moment. We fell thankfully into silence as she drove me back downtown and stopped outside my loft. I started to thank her but she blew it off.

'You'll have to get permission to talk to Anna from her mother. I'll talk to her.'

I thanked her anyway and started to get out.

'I like that you didn't try to lie to me,' she said.

'About what?'

'That you're in love with Charlotte's mother.'

I glanced at my feet to make sure that they weren't covered in lasagna.

'We're just — '

'I just want Charlotte safe, I don't care about the rest.'

I got out of the car as quickly as I could before she dissected me any further and started for the building.

'He was her stepfather, not her father,' April said.

I turned, not sure I had heard her correctly.

'Her real father was some other guy in college who wouldn't marry her mother.'

'Does Charlotte know?' I asked.

April nodded.

'She figured it out.'

She looked at me for a moment.

'I guess Mrs Sexton didn't tell you, did she?' she said and then drove away.

11

I stood outside long after April had driven away. Did it matter that Tracy hadn't told me the truth about Charlotte's father? Was not telling me the same as a lie? I imagined there were reasons she left out that bit of personal history from her story but what about the others? Perhaps it didn't matter, except that for a brief moment I had allowed myself to feel a part of something, of someone, and then just as quickly I was an outsider again.

A couple of times as I walked up to the loft I took out my phone to confront her or threaten to walk away if she didn't tell me the entire truth, and each time before I dialed I'd hear Tracy's voice calling out her warning . . . *Don't stop, don't* . . . and then I would put it back into my pocket unused.

Upstairs Buzz was still playing the soft ballad. Across the hall I could smell coffee being brewed in another neighbor's loft, in another, oil paint being mixed. All was as it should be, except for me; she had reached out and pulled me by the hand from my solitary world, and I didn't want to go back to it. Even April saw that. I was in love with her, but which Tracy was I in love with, which story, which secret?

I reached my loft and as I started to slip the key into the door it opened a few inches. Had I forgotten to lock it? I didn't think so. I inched forward and looked through the opening in the doorway — there were no lights on, the faint glow of downtown was spilling through the windows.

I pulled the key out and ran my finger over the lock and the jam. There was no damage. Nothing had been forced open. I held my breath for a moment and listened for movement — the only sound was the soft chords of Buzz's guitar. I stared into the darkness trying not to imagine what hid behind the door, then reached inside and ran my hand along the wall until I found the switch and turned the light on.

Nothing grabbed my hand, nothing moved. I pushed the door open and stared into the loft. Nothing appeared out of order and I stepped inside. Perhaps I had left the door unlocked. I began to walk through the room taking a quick inventory of everything present. Nothing was missing, but it wasn't what someone had taken that I was sensing: it was what they had left behind. The air held the memory, like a whisper just loud enough to hear but not understand. The faint scent of cigarette that had clung to their clothes from a previous smoke had remained after they had left.

I started to double-check everything again when I noticed one of the drawers in my filing cabinet next to the desk was open a crack. The drawer was marked HISTORY. Inside was filled with files I had gathered on Tracy's and my accident and then all the medical papers from years of treatment. My entire life, or what had become my life, was contained in those papers.

I pulled the drawer open. The files were neatly arranged, categorized and divided giving order to all the events from the moment I turned to see the headlights coming at us, to my last doctor visit. It was what I had instead of memory.

I ran my fingers over the top of the files until they landed on one that felt as if it hadn't been placed completely back into the drawer. I couldn't remember the last time I had looked at it. Perhaps I hadn't replaced it properly back in the drawer. I carefully lifted it out. It was the accident file. I began to flip through the pages to see if anything was missing and stopped on a photograph of my parents' mangled and burned car. I hadn't looked at it in years. It was of the passenger side of the car — the side I had rescued Tracy from, if that were true. The dash was collapsed just where she said it had pinned her leg. I took it out and stared at it for a moment looking over all the details that I might now see, knowing what Tracy had said, but no burst of memory let loose. It was like looking at an old newsreel with no more relation to me than the *Hindenburg* going up in flames.

I started to replace it in the file then stopped and raised it to my face — it was here too, the scent of cigarettes. Or was it? Maybe it was the crossed wires in my head, maybe it was car exhaust drifting in through the window or dust or soot or any of the thousands of other particles floating around in LA's air. That's what it was, why the hell would anyone be interested? It's nothing, right?

I started to shove the file back into the drawer

and heard the creak of a floorboard behind me, then another. I slipped the file into place then slammed the drawer shut and spun around.

'Dude, where you been?'

It was Buzz. My heart eased back into my chest and I took a breath.

'You been with her, haven't you?' he asked.

Defining 'with' at the moment seemed a bit of a stretch.

'I'm helping her,' I said.

Buzz shrugged. 'Fools rush in.'

'You hear anything down here today?' I asked.

'Hear what?'

'Anything.'

'I've been recording all day. Headphones. Why?'

Perhaps it was nothing. Let it go, it was the wires in my head, that was all.

'No reason,' I said.

Buzz looked at me for a moment as if he were about to say something then he turned and walked a few steps towards the door before he stopped and looked back.

'You been smoking?'

Boom!

The building seemed to rock with a 3.5. I glanced back at the file drawer then around the rest of the loft.

Boom boom. The edges of my vision began to soften. My heart rate began to race. I took a breath; the air was filled with a sharp odor, like a Turkish cigarette. I turned as I heard the creak of a floorboard across the room from behind the closet door. I took a step towards the door, then

119

another. The edges of my vision began to darken. The floor creaked again, then the handle of the closet door began to turn and I stopped.

'Run.'

I reached out towards the handle.

'Don't.'

My fingers touched the handle. The door flew open and a bright light came rushing towards me.

'Elias.'

I walked across the room over to the closet door, hesitated for a moment then reached out for the handle and pulled the door open. The faint scent of cigarettes was here too, but there was nothing else. What the hell was happening?

'You all right?' Buzz asked.

I pushed the closet door closed and then turned.

'I'm the picture of health,' I said.

12

I would sleep for a few hours, then would wake and check the lock on the door and the chair I had wedged under the handle, then fall gradually back to sleep until a distant car horn or siren broke the night's silence and I would repeat the process all over until dawn thankfully put an end to it.

April did what she said she would. Anna's mother agreed to meet us the following morning. Tracy picked me up just after ten. Several times as we drove back to the Valley she started to ask me about what I had learned from my talk with April, and each time she backed away from pressing me for details, either afraid of the answers or of her reaction to them.

In truth, what I had learned about Charlotte had less to do with where she might have gone than where she had been and, as yet, there were no breadcrumbs left on the pavement for us to follow.

I didn't tell her about the files in my loft, not because I didn't believe it had happened, though if I tried hard I could almost convince myself it hadn't — almost. I didn't tell her for the same reason that I didn't ask about Charlotte's real father.

I had walked into a world filled with secrets; having one or two of my own that Tracy didn't know felt like a kind of insurance — though, from what remained, a bit fuzzy. Perhaps to keep myself from getting too close to her.

Anna's mother greeted us at the door before we had even rung the bell. Up close she was prettier than from a distance. She was dressed as if she were on an audition for the role of the mother of a troubled teen on *Law and Order*. Not too expensive, stylish without appearing to have taken any time to think about it.

What the clothes couldn't hide were the signs of stress in her face, the darkening under the eyes, the lines on her forehead, the muscles of her jaw which seemed in a permanent state of clench. From looking at the thinness of her frame I doubted she was getting enough to eat — even for an actress.

We did the introductions. Her name was Bre Sorenson.

She walked us through the house, which seemed to have fallen out of a page of *Architectural Digest*, and guided us into an open, sunny kitchen that was all stainless steel and soft pale yellows and whites and hanging copper pots.

'I have to apologize, my husband can't be here,' she said, then poured us coffee and took a seat at the table.

She wrapped her hands around her coffee cup like it was a handhold on a cliff face. She took several sips as she appeared to try to work something out in her head, then finally spoke.

'I understand you would like to talk to Anna?' she asked.

'Yes,' Tracy said.

'So would I,' she answered matter-of-factly without any sense of self-pity clinging to the words. 'Your daughter is the one who is missing?' she asked and Tracy said yes and filled in the time line of Charlotte's disappearance.

Mrs Sorenson listened as if she already knew each word, each detail, each heartbreak before Tracy spoke them. When Tracy was finished, Mrs Sorenson sat in silence for nearly a minute.

'Did they know each other?' she asked finally.

'On Facebook, perhaps more,' I answered.

'When she first learned to drive she didn't know the way to school because when I drove her she was always staring at the phone from the moment she got in the car.'

Her eyes seemed to be searching for a detail — the x on the map where things had first gone wrong in her daughter's life.

'We used to give her a little wine cut with water at dinner like they do in France. She wanted to be an actress. She had an agent. Everything was planned.'

She paused for a moment, then her words began to flow in a stream that gained momentum as she spoke.

'We gave her too much freedom, or not enough, we talked about everything, we wanted her to set goals, we pushed, she never was denied anything, the clothes, phones, she never needed anything from us that wasn't given, it was all part of the plan, she knew what she wanted, she was accepted at a good school, she had dreams and we were helping her get it. No matter how much we wanted everything for her there just wasn't enough time, we were all so busy working that we missed the warning signs that should have told us that she was losing control of what was real and what was not. We didn't see it at first or we didn't take it seriously and when she did try to reach out to us, we didn't listen and she said we were selfish and self-obsessed and when we tried to help we did everything you are supposed to, listened to all the experts, took her to the best people and it was all wrong and she just drifted away from us, from everything.' She took a breath. 'How are you supposed to know, how?'

We talked for an hour longer but the details that came added little to what she had already said. If there was a direct connection between Charlotte and Anna's life she was unaware of it, which, in the end, meant little, but she agreed to let us see her, if only in the hope that her daughter might reach out through us to her.

'She's making progress every day, small steps . . . we're certain of it,' she said, trying to sell herself as much as us on the words.

Perhaps all we really needed to know was there in Anna's mother's eyes. A confusion as disconnected from her own life as her daughter was from hers. And the more treatment theory she quoted, the more twelve-step protocols she outlined, the further she appeared to drift from any understanding of why her daughter's life had slipped away in the time it took to glance the other way.

13

Walking through the large wooden doors of the Clear Life Clinic was a bit like stepping into a fairyland of peace and harmony. Furnishings by The Four Seasons. Catering by Wolfgang Puck.

The staff were all dressed in khaki pants and polo shirts in tasteful pastel colors. Even by Malibu standards they all seemed unnaturally fit and attractive.

The ground rules the clinic personnel laid out for our meeting with Anna were simple. No sound recording, no video. Never use the word disease. Questions regarding her treatment protocols are not allowed. Do not discuss her family, her drug abuse and addiction unless she brings it up. Do not discuss others who may be enrolled at the clinic or ask questions about specific personnel employed by Clear Life Clinic either past or present. Staff may choose to monitor. At any point staff may terminate the meeting if it is deemed for the patient's benefit. At any point . . . if found . . . if necessary, etc., etc.

At a thousand dollars a day the lawyers were very thorough.

We were led outside to several benches sitting on a broad expanse of lawn that stretched to the edge of the bluff overlooking the beach. The gray line of the marine layer had drifted far offshore. In the bright sunshine the water appeared so blue that one wondered if it was included in the price of admission.

We waited a few minutes and a male staff member came slowly walking out across the lawn with Anna. She wore sweats and a tight-fitting fleece hoody which she hadn't pulled up.

I watched Tracy's eyes as they approached, taking in the way she walked, moved her hands, tilted her head as if she were reading from the parent code of teen body language that tells when your child is doing well in school, in love, lying, depressed or snorting crack. Or perhaps it was just the shared knowledge of addiction that guided her gaze.

The staff person introduced us by our first names.

'I'll be right over there if you need me,' he said, motioning to another bench thirty yards away.

Anna smiled and gave him a hug.

'Thanks, Reese, I'll be fine.'

Reese's eyes lingered on her for a beat longer, then nodded and walked away. Anna watched him all the way to the bench then finally turned to us. Her eyes were a light gray, her short hair dyed jet black, her skin as white as the foam of the waves breaking on the shore below us. She wore a bracelet on her wrist that identified her as a patient. In each ear lobe there were multiple piercings but she wore no jewelry.

She looked us each over with the eye of a gambler deciding on a bet. Then she smiled with the practiced ease of a beauty queen.

'If we stand here a minute before we sit, it will

126

give Reese the impression we're having normal small talk and he won't bother us,' she said, and then looked out at the ocean crashing below us. 'Isn't it fucking beautiful?' There was a manic edge to her voice.

She glanced back at Reese.

'OK, we can sit now.'

We sat down across from each other. A battle appeared to be raging inside Anna to be still as she crossed and uncrossed her legs and constantly fiddled with a zipper on her hoodie or rearranged her hair.

'You're here because of April.'

'Yes.'

'But I've never met you, right?'

Again I answered yes.

'You're not friends of my mother or father, I'd remember, but you have that look.'

'What look?' I asked.

'Parents.'

'Just me,' Tracy said.

She looked at Tracy for a moment, then at me.

'You don't look like a policemen, so what's that make you?'

'A friend.'

She turned back to Tracy and smiled.

'What?' Tracy asked.

'I was wondering how long you've been clean?' Anna asked.

How did she know, what did she see that I had missed? Tracy looked at me, almost embarrassed.

'A while,' she answered.

'Thirty-two days for me . . . it sucks.'

She glanced over towards Reese and smiled

sweetly then looked back at us. 'What the fuck do you want?'

'We're looking for my daughter Charlotte,' Tracy said.

Almost out of reflex Anna started to shake her head, then stopped.

'April's friend?'

'Yes.'

'Don't know her.'

'You're friends on Facebook.'

'Am I?' Anna smiled. 'One big happy global family,' she said sarcastically.

'You never went to the warehouse off Hollywood Boulevard with her?' I asked.

'The party house?' she said and shook her head. 'Like I said, I don't know her, never seen her. Unless I was high and don't remember.'

'How about Sophie?' I asked.

If it was possible, I seemed to have surprised her, the name appeared to send a jolt of energy through her entire body. 'What about her?'

'You know her?' I asked.

She smiled at some kept secret perhaps. 'Yeah.'

'Would she know anything about Charlotte?'

Anna shrugged. 'Maybe, maybe not. I think she may have mentioned her name — pretty sure.'

'How do we find her?'

She looked at me suspiciously.

'You sure you're not a cop?'

I shook my head. 'I'm afraid of guns,' I said.

She looked us both over for a moment then appeared to come to a decision about us.

'You're looking for a threesome, aren't you?'

'What?' asked Tracy in surprise.

'Sophie's really good.'

'We're looking for my daughter,' Tracy said.

'Sure,' she said as if not hearing a word, her energy growing more intense with each word.

'Would you know how to get in touch with Sophie?'

She shook her head.

'You don't really think I'm here because of drugs, do you? That's just what my mother tells people.'

'Why are you here, Anna?' Tracy asked.

Anna crossed her arms across her chest, glanced at Reese and leaned towards us.

'I'm here because they don't want me to be a star.'

'A star?' I asked.

'They saw my video, that's why, it's not the drugs, I can quit drugs any time. I just do that to relax. I feel better when I'm high. She — my mother — is afraid I'll be more successful than her, she never got a series. One pilot, that's all she ever did and it didn't even air.'

'Who told you you're going to be a star?' I asked.

'The director, the other actor.'

'Were you in a movie?' Tracy asked.

'It's just a way to get an agent.'

My stomach began to turn uneasily. Again Anna glanced at Reese then pulled her legs up onto the bench as if it was the only way to stop them from taking flight.

'I'm a great fuck, just ask them, I have a great body, they'll tell you, men, women, both. I'm a natural and from there I can go on to do anything, TV, movies, I'll be a celebrity.'

'You were in a porn video?' I asked.

She smiled with a kind of confused pride. 'I've heard Marilyn did one.'

'What're their names?' I asked her.

She hesitated.

'Why do you want to know?'

'Would they know Sophie? We might like to talk to them,' I said.

The wheels turned for a moment in Anna's eyes as she searched through the haze of memory.

'They took my phone away, I don't have any numbers. One said his name was Art, maybe, I don't remember the other one — Jack, maybe; he really liked fucking. He said I have the best ass of any girl ever.'

'Would Sophie know their names?'

She shrugged her shoulders then, as she looked at us, a switch seemed to be thrown inside of her. Her energy appeared ready to ignite and she took another quick glance at Reese then turned back to us and whispered.

'Who are you people really?' she asked.

I started to answer but she cut me off.

'If you get me some meth, I'll suck your cock, I'll fuck both of you if you want, you can do anything you want to me . . . you could get me out of here. Can you do that? Can you . . . please let me — '

Reese stepped up behind her and placed his hand on her shoulder.

She brushed it away and jumped to her feet

130

and began shaking her head.

'You're all fucking assholes!'

She glared at us both for a moment then looked over her shoulder at Reese.

'What are you looking at, wonder boy?'

Just as quickly as her rage had appeared, she seemed to surrender back into her gilded cage and laughed in a manic, strange way at us.

'You don't know what you're missing,' she said and turned and began to walk away with her keeper right behind her.

Tracy reached out and took my hand.

'Get me out of here,' she whispered.

14

Every day we wake, we build on those first rays of sunlight coming through the window by understanding that a day much like it had come before this one and one had come before that and so on.

But when I woke from the coma that didn't exist, it was as if I had read halfway through a book and had begun to flip back through the pages and found them all blank.

In time, by taking small steps, by embracing the pieces of me that had made it back to the world damaged, and not trying to find what I had lost, I had found a way, if not to fill those blank pages, at least to know I had a place in whatever was to be found in the pages ahead.

If I picked up a rose and it smelled like car exhaust or if a hamburger tasted like fish, I embraced them as if it was a secret world which only I was privy to. Instead of my anomalies becoming disabilities, I turned them into cherished friends who showed me a world that felt richer and fuller than everyone else's.

That was how I found my way back — until now.

What the hell was this? Not even in the endless dream state of the coma had my nightmares ever once come close to the dark world Anna inhabited. How did she get there? At least I knew where mine began and why. Was there any such point of origin in Anna's life? A moment in the video of her in the school play where you could say, 'Right here, this is where it began.'

One look at her mother's bewildered eyes and you knew no such moment existed.

There was no proof that any of what had happened to Anna was connected to Charlotte except that I could feel the pull of that nightmare dragging me in, perhaps just the way it had Charlotte, and none of my skills as the detached outsider seemed able to stop the slide.

★   ★   ★

We started to drive away from the clinic, then Tracy abruptly pulled to a stop, jumped out and stepped around to the back of the car and vomited. She was sitting on the ground leaning against the bumper when I walked around the back of the car. I kneeled down and gently wiped away some saliva from the corner of her mouth.

'I'm trying not to imagine the things I'm thinking, but I'm not doing a very good job,' she said.

'We don't know if there is any connection in any way to Charlotte,' I said.

'I didn't think there could be anything worse for a parent than what I had been going through,' she said.

Tracy looked at me and then glanced back down the road towards the clinic. I wouldn't have thought it was possible that her eyes could be filled with more doubt and fear than they already were, but I was wrong.

'Please tell me you have a plan,' Tracy said softly.

A plan? If there had been one it had slipped through my fingers. I scrambled to find something to say.

'If there's a connection between Anna and Sophie to Charlotte, maybe the investigator found it; we need to talk to him.'

'And if he hasn't?' she asked.

I had no real answer.

'We find the next door she stepped through after leaving the mall.'

'The mall,' Tracy whispered, trying to reorient herself.

★ ★ ★

We got his service when we called him so we drove to the investigator's offices at Ivar and Hollywood Boulevard. They were across the street from the spot April had pointed out as the place where Fred Mertz on *The Honeymooners* had dropped dead from a heart attack outside the old Knickerbocker Hotel.

A private investigator that specializes in missing children could find worse places for an office. Even though the film business long ago left Hollywood for glass corporate towers in Century City and the Valley, it still drew runaways like moths to a flame, thinking it was a place of dreams. From the tour April had given me I imagined Lester Investigations must do a thriving business.

134

'The office is on the third floor,' Tracy said as we reached the building.

A group of Japanese tourists were kneeling next to Fay Wray's star on the pavement having their picture taken with a man in a Gorilla suit. We walked up to the third floor and stepped out into a bright hallway that had been freshly painted. We passed a few empty office suites that were in the process of renovation. The other offices on the floor appeared to be affiliated with show business, a talent agent's office, location scouts and a catering service.

'It's at the far end,' Tracy said. 'The windows look out towards the Hollywood sign.'

I imagined that was intentional, in order to give parents from Omaha looking for their children a sense that Sam Spade himself would be coming to the rescue but I kept that to myself.

'How much did you pay him?' I asked.

'Five hundred-dollar retainer, then eighty dollars an hour after that is exceeded.'

Lester Investigations took up the last two corner offices on the floor. The name was stenciled on the smoked-glass door along with the words *Trust is our Business*. From inside the sound of a vacuum cleaner drifted out.

I opened the door and stepped into a small reception area. There was no one waiting. There were half a dozen chairs, a table with magazines, an old poster on the wall with the young faces of Judy Garland and Mickey Rooney. In the center of the floor sat a janitor's cart. The sound of the vacuum cleaner was coming from the other side of the walled-off reception. The faint odor of burning rubber or oil was present in the air. No one appeared to be sitting at the desk of the reception area behind the sliding-glass window.

I walked over to the sliding-glass window waiting for someone to step up but nothing moved behind it.

'Was there a receptionist when you were here before?' I asked.

Tracy nodded. 'Yes.'

I knocked on the glass and got no response.

'They must be having the office cleaned,' Tracy said. 'He told me that often he would not be in the office if he was following leads.'

I knocked again on the window then slid it open. Papers were laid neatly out on the receptionist's desk. The computer screen was dark. The chair was pushed back. Beyond the receptionist's office a hallway led towards the other offices. The vacuum sat unattended at the head of the hallway, little puffs of dust coming out of the bag.

'So where's the janitor?' I said.

We stepped through the door into the receptionist's area and I walked over and turned the vacuum off. I noticed what sounded like the hum of a printer coming from down the hallway.

'Is anyone there?' I called. There was no response.

'Maybe the janitor took a break,' Tracy said.

'Maybe,' I said, a sense of uneasiness growing in my gut.

'Is something wrong?' Tracy asked.

I turned and glanced at the vacuum. For a

moment it looked strangely like a telephone pole.

'Why would anything be wrong?' I asked, trying not to reveal my growing apprehension.

She shook her head as if she already knew something was happening.

'I don't know.'

Was Buzz right? Was there more Tracy hadn't told me, and of the things she had, how much of it was true? Did it really matter? Who wouldn't shade the truth to save their child?

'Which office did you meet in?' I asked.

'Back right.'

'Hello?' I called out again.

There was only the faint hum of the printer coming from down the hallway. Tracy stepped up behind me and placed her hand on my shoulder.

'Maybe we should come back later,' she said, my unease having spread to her.

Out of the corner of my eye I noticed something on the floor under the receptionist's desk — a broken coffee cup.

'I'll just take a look,' I said.

'I don't like this,' Tracy said.

I tried to smile, but it wasn't very convincing.

'I'm sure it's nothing.'

I crossed the receptionist's office over to the hallway. There were two doors on either side. The doors on the left were both closed; the two on the right were open. The sound of the copier or printer seemed to be coming from the back right office where Tracy had met with Lester.

'Mr Lester?' I said.

There was no response. I stepped over to the

first door on the left and opened it. It was a rest room and empty. I started to turn when I noticed something and looked back at the sink. There were a few inches of standing water in it, dark water. I took a step in, then reached out and flipped on the light. In the light, the dark water turned bright red with blood.

I backed quickly into the hallway and started to turn towards the first open door on the right. A hand reached out from behind and touched my arm. I spun round, raising my arm. Tracy jumped back, her startled eyes staring at my clenched fist. I looked at her for a moment and lowered my hand and unclenched my fist.

'What is it?' she asked nervously.

I shook my head.

'There's blood in the sink. It's probably nothing, the janitor must have cut himself, that's probably why he's not here.'

'Cut himself vacuuming?'

Her words settled uneasily over us.

'Don't touch anything,' I said.

'I don't understand.'

'It would just be better if you didn't,' I answered and stepped over to the open door of the first office and looked inside. It was untouched; nothing seemed out of place, there was no sign of anything being wrong.

'Let's leave,' Tracy said.

'The last office is the one you met Lester in?' I asked.

'Yes,' she said.

I turned and stepped over to the open door to Lester's office. The office had been ransacked

— no, that wasn't quite right, something else had happened. There was no order to the wreckage in front of me, this wasn't the result of someone looking for something. This wasn't a fender bender in a parking lot. This was the equivalent of a rollover at seventy — uncontrolled and violent. A lamp lay shattered, furniture overturned. There was a shoe lying in the middle of the floor — a black loafer.

I took a step inside and stopped. There was a computer on the desk. Behind the desk on a shelf, a printer hummed with a paper jam. Blood spots had sprayed across the wall to the left. On the floor behind the desk, the legs of the owner of the shoe were visible, his sock half pulled off his shoeless foot from crawling across the floor.

I quickly stepped around to the other side of the desk to see if he was alive. The man whom I assumed was Lester was lying on his face, his arms at his side. The desk chair lay overturned next to him. His face lay in a pool of blood that had soaked into the carpet and begun to dry. The pink of an open gash was just visible through his short dark blood-matted hair.

I tried to take a breath but my lungs refused to cooperate. I had seen countless accident-scene photographs involving fatalities. I had even been called to a few accidents where the victims were still covered by yellow tarps. Death in car accidents had become part of the natural process of millions of people living in close proximity. It may be tragic, but not unexpected. This wasn't the same. I looked down at the body stretched out at my feet and the little voice in my head began screaming. *Run, right now, and don't look back.*

I couldn't, and the longer I looked the more the events that had ended with this became clear. The fight had begun in the center of the room. Furniture was knocked over, a body had been thrown against the wall breaking a picture frame, and then he had been hit in the back of the head, which had knocked him to the floor. Drops of blood that I hadn't noticed before traced his path as he tried to crawl behind the desk seeking shelter or maybe a weapon in the desk.

The attacker tried to stop him and pulled off the shoe, but Lester kept crawling until he slipped behind the desk and was attacked again. Perhaps he had been hit once more and that stopped his movement, but it wasn't how it ended. On the side of his neck there were purple bruises that appeared to be shaped like fingers; he had been choked. Blood had been wiped off the keyboard. The computer had been used after the fight. It was why there was blood in the sink; the attacker had had the presence of mind to wash their hands.

My heart began to race. I closed my eyes and took several deep breaths, trying to regain control before my head followed my heart and a full-blown neurological event followed.

Get out, run.

The acrid odor of the blood began to smell like eucalyptus. I started to feel lightheaded; the edges of my vision began to shimmer. I was slipping.

Run, faster, run, don't stop.

'Oh my God,' came from behind me.

I turned. Tracy was standing in the doorway, staring in disbelief. Her hands reached up to cover her mouth. The sight of her put a halt to the slide.

'Don't come in here,' I said.

'No . . . ' The rest of the words left her as she gasped for breath. 'Is he — ?'

'Yes, he's dead,' I said. The finality of the words seemed to settle my heart rate and my head began to follow.

Tracy's hand started to tremble and she looked over her shoulder as if she was about to bolt.

'I don't understand.'

'Someone killed him.'

'Killed?'

'Yes.'

She shook her head, unable to make sense of what I had just said.

'No, no, no, this can't be right,' she said, her voice teetering on the edge of panic. 'Why would he be dead?'

I glanced back at the body, trying not to imagine that this had anything to do with Tracy or Charlotte.

'I don't know.'

Tracy turned and started to run and I went after her.

Run, don't stop, faster, faster.

I reached her as she stepped into the outer office and grabbed her arm. She tried to pull away.

'No, no!'

I put my arms around her.

'It's all right.'

She shook her head. 'We have to get out of here!'

'I have to look at something.'

She started to protest but stopped.

'You think this has something to do with . . . '

She shook her head.

'I want to make sure it doesn't,' I said.

Tracy looked back towards the office, hesitated for a moment then nodded. I let go of her and walked back to Lester's office and stepped around the desk. When I looked down at the body my heart began to race again.

Slow it down, think, what do you see, this is what you do.

The computer on the desk had been moved to the side to make it easier to look at after Lester's body had fallen to the floor. My heart began to slow again. I tried to take a deep breath.

Keep looking.

Tracy stepped back into the doorway, holding on to it as tightly as she could.

'We have to go,' she said, her voice quivering.

This is what you do, what do you see?

My breathing relaxed.

'We have to go now!' Tracy said with a blank stare.

'Not yet,' I said.

Her eyes looked down at the body.

'Don't,' I said. 'Don't look at him, look at me.'

Her eyes locked on to me and she struggled for a breath.

'I want to look at this before the police,' I said.

'He's dead! What's there to look at!'

I picked up a pencil off the desk and hit the space bar on the keyboard. The computer lit up. A printer application was on the screen; a second warning window had opened. *Job stopped, printer not responding.*

I stepped over to the printer and pulled out the piece of jammed paper then slipped in a new one. The printer started to hum and I looked back at the screen of the computer as another window opened. With each word I read my heart rate doubled. *Job resumed printing Sexton file.*

I reread it again and then another time to be sure that I was seeing the words correctly. The printer loaded the paper and it began to slide through.

'What is it?' Tracy asked.

A single sheet worked through the printer and then it stopped. I picked it up and flipped it over. It was blank, not a drop of ink on it.

'It says it was printing your file,' I said.

Tracy stared at me and shook her head, the panic returning to her eyes.

'My . . . I don't . . . why would my file be . . . '

I stepped back to the computer. *Sexton file job complete.*

'You're saying whoever did this was printing my file?'

'Yes.'

Panic began to take hold of her.

'Why?' Tracy said.

I clicked on the second window on the screen and it opened. *Sexton folder.* I opened it. Inside were two files and another folder. The first file was named Sexton. The second one was titled Derek Sexton. I opened the first which was the last job printed. There was nothing in it; the file had been emptied.

'Who's Derek Sexton?' I said, looking at the second file.

Tracy stared at me for a moment as if trying to understand the question.

'What?' she said, barely able to speak.

'There's a file with his name on it. Who is it?' I repeated.

She shook her head.

'Who's Derek Sexton?' I said.

Tracy took a hesitant breath, her eyes continuing to look about for a way to get out of the room.

'That was my husband.'

I opened it. Its contents had also been deleted. I clicked on the untitled folder and it opened. It contained a single file. If it was possible for things to get more uncertain, they just had.

'There's another file,' I said. 'Sophie.'

'Jesus,' Tracy whispered.

I clicked on it and it came up just as the others had — fucking empty. I looked down at the body, the stillness of death robbing it of definition and giving it the appearance of an oversize rag doll, an unreality that was only betrayed by the presence of so much blood. I stepped back away from the desk and walked across the room to Tracy. Her eyes were dull with the shock of what she had seen, or perhaps just incapable of processing anything else that took her another step away from the

144

life she had known.

'What's happening, Elias?' Tracy whispered.

The thing you remember about being in a coma, if you can even describe it as memory, is the feeling of losing one's place. Time loses meaning, there's no up, down, direction doesn't exist, light, darkness, not even the sounds one hears appear to come from a specific direction, even the beating of your own heart seems unconnected to anything understandable.

Until this moment I wouldn't have thought that feeling was possible to replicate, but I was wrong.

'Is there anything you might have forgotten to tell me, anything, the smallest detail?' I asked, hoping to find something to steady the ground I was standing on.

Tracy's eyes stayed on the body for a moment and she shook her head.

'No.'

The ground seemed to shift uneasily under my feet. When you've interviewed as many accident victims as I have you learn to hear the truth in their words as clearly as you can hear the echo of untruth from those that are shading it. Tracy had just lied.

15

It was easy to imagine running out the door and not stopping, the words 'Don't stop' echoing in my head, fueling every step. But I didn't — we didn't. Charlotte was in the other direction, somewhere just beyond where Lester had been beaten to death.

The first squad car arrived within a few minutes, then a second and a third and fourth. A patrol sergeant questioned us, then a detective. Thirty minutes after that I was sitting in an interrogation room across a table from two detectives in the Hollywood division.

The woman detective had short-cropped blond hair that she dyed and wore square black-rimmed glasses which were trying very hard to be hip. I guessed she was in her mid-thirties and doing her best to appear to still be twenty something. Her thin features gave her the appearance of a pissed-off bird. The second officer introduced himself as Detective Rodriguez. He was older than the lieutenant by a few years, wore a bright red tie and had a lazy left eye. He had the build and presence of a former marine.

'Lieutenant Delgado will be sitting in while we talk,' Rodriguez said, then asked me to once again explain what we found when we walked in the office.

He listened without comment, occasionally

taking notes. The lieutenant didn't take any. When I was finished Rodriguez began.

'What is your relationship with Ms Sexton?' he asked.

It wasn't the first question I was expecting them to ask.

'My relationship?'

'Are you involved with her?' he asked.

'I'm a friend.'

'Friend?' he said sarcastically.

'We knew each other in high school.'

Rodriguez smiled like a man reading a secret diary. 'She was your girlfriend?' he asked.

'No, just friends,' I said.

'You never asked her out?' Rodriquez asked.

I don't know why I didn't answer the question, but it seemed like a good idea given that they hadn't asked me a single question about the dead body in a murder investigation.

'What does this have to do with anything?' I asked.

'Just curious,' Rodriguez said, obviously getting pleasure out of the game of interrogation.

Delgado glanced at the responding officer's report from Lester's office.

'So, you're helping her to look for her daughter,' she asked, then returned to just observing.

'Yes.'

'And that's why you had gone to see Lester?' Rodriguez asked.

'Yes, she had hired him.'

'Any particular reason you went today?'

'He called Tracy about a name,' I said.

'What name?' he asked.

'Sophie.'

'Why didn't you just call him?'

'We did, he didn't answer.'

'No shit.'

Delgado held the report out towards Rodriguez and pointed something out. He looked at it and then smiled in a dismissive self-satisfied way.

'Says here you're an accident investigator for an insurance company,' Rodriguez asked.

'Yes.'

Rodriguez smirked.

'You think her daughter's disappearance is an accident?' he asked.

'No, I don't,' I answered.

'You know the difference when something is an accident and when it isn't,' he said.

I nodded. Rodriguez reached into his jacket pocket and removed a small photograph and placed it in front of me. It was a picture of a wrecked car, lying on a slope upside down; its roof collapsed, the doors and fenders heavily damaged. It was a BMW, perhaps five or six years old from what I could tell.

'Does this look like an accident to you?' he asked.

I glanced at the license plate number, and then at the marks along the side and the pattern of denting on the back end.

'What would you say happened here?' he asked.

'What does this have to do with Lester?' I said.

Rodriguez smiled.

'Humor us.'

I picked up the picture and looked more closely at the damage to the car.

'From the amount of deformation on the front and back end I would say the car cartwheeled one or two times, then slid on its side for a period, then hit a rock or a stump where the door is dented which flipped it over into a tumble of two or three rotations before coming to a rest on the roof. For that amount of damage to happen it probably would have had to travel somewhere between a hundred and twenty-five to two hundred feet down a slope of at least forty-five degrees.'

The two detectives stared at me for a moment, then quickly glanced at each other. I assumed that meant that I had accurately described what had happened.

'You describe it like you were there,' Rodriguez said.

'I'm good at my job.'

'Was it an accident?' he asked, loading the question full to the brim.

'As opposed to what?'

'Something else,' Rodriguez said.

'You asked me what happened, not why, I don't have enough information to tell you that,' I said, trying to contain my growing unease.

'What was your relationship with Tracy's husband?' he asked.

There it was, the reason for all of this. The car in the picture was the one he died in, and somewhere on that slope where he crashed a line led directly to what Lester had found in searching for Charlotte. No doubt Delgado and Rodriguez suspected that somewhere it also connected to me.

'I never met him.'

'I thought you said you were friends, and you never met her husband?' Rodriguez asked.

'Until a few days ago I hadn't seen Tracy since high school.'

'Some friend,' Rodriguez said.

'We lost touch.'

'Because she got married,' he asked.

'Because of an accident,' I said, realizing it was probably a poor choice of words as they were coming out of my mouth.

Rodriguez looked at me and smiled.

'Let me guess, a car accident.'

'Yes.'

'You were together?' he asked.

I felt like I had a shovel in my hand and I was digging a deeper hole with every word I said.

'Yes.'

'On a date?' she asked.

'A dance.'

'That's sweet,' Rodriguez said.

'I was injured, we didn't see each other after that.'

'And out of the blue after all these years she comes to you for help,' Delgado asked.

'Yes.'

'Must have been some dance,' Rodriguez said.

'I don't remember,' I said.

'She must have,' said Delgado.

'Do you have any idea why all of Lester's files on Ms Sexton are missing?' Rodriguez said.

'I would say that whoever killed him deleted them,' I said.

'No shit. You deduce that all on your own?' he said arrogantly.

The voice in my head was begging me to shut the hell up. The rest of me was getting frightened.

'I would say that since they are missing and he's dead it was more of a conclusion resulting from physical evidence based on fact rather than inference,' I said.

'You infer anything else?' Rodriguez said.

'The bruising on the left side of his neck where he was choked was more intense than the hemorrhaging on the right side of his neck, indicating a left hand that is dominant and stronger.'

They looked at me in silence for a moment.

'It can be dangerous to play detective, Hawks,' Delgado said.

'I'm just trying to find a lost girl,' I said.

'Where were you last night around ten o'clock?' Rodriguez asked.

Telling them that I had driven right past the office last night with April was probably the wrong thing to say.

'Was that the time of death?' I asked.

'Just answer the fucking question,' he responded.

'Resting. I had a neurological event.'

'Is that something like a rave?' Rodriguez said.

'It's a kind of seizure resulting from a brain injury. I have a titanium plate in my head.'

'I have plates in my kitchen. Did you kill Lester?' he asked.

151

My heart pounded against my chest. Had I heard him right?

'Did you get in an argument with him and things get out of hand?'

My head began to spin.

'Was there something he discovered that you wanted to get rid of?'

The walls seemed to move.

The questions came at me as if he had tipped over a box full of them. Some I heard, some I didn't, others seemed to strike me in the chest like a fist — did you . . . when was that . . . are you sure . . . what time . . . did he . . . was that why . . . do you really believe . . .

The floor fell out from under me and I was running through the dark. Tracy's voice was there. *Faster, faster, come on, run faster, don't — '*

The fall stopped.

'Hawks?'

I opened my eyes. The ceiling glowed a bright yellow. Delgado and Rodriguez were staring down at me.

'You there?' Delgado said.

'This one of your raves?' Rodriguez said.

My head slowed down, my heart was still going.

'You want to get up?'

She took my arm and helped me back to the chair. Delgado glanced over to Rodriguez and gave a nod towards the door. He didn't seem to like the idea, but he reluctantly stepped over to the door.

'What do you know about Ms Sexton and her

152

husband?' Delgado asked.

I had to run the question through my head to make certain I had heard it right.

'Her ex-husband,' I said.

'Who said they were divorced?' she asked.

I started to answer then stopped myself. Delgado smiled, pleased that she had surprised me.

'She tell you that?' Delgado said.

'Sure your name isn't pigeon, not Hawks?' Rodriguez said, smirking as he stepped out.

'They were separated, but not divorced,' Delgado said.

There could have been a dozen good reasons for Tracy to have lied about that to me, but at the moment, I couldn't think of one.

'You really didn't know?' she asked.

'Does it really matter?' I said.

'I don't know. I'm not the one she lied to.'

'He was abusive, I don't really need to know more than that,' I said.

'He was more than abusive.'

'How much more?' I asked.

'On several occasions he nearly killed her,' she replied, her eyes almost appearing to care.

'You don't think his death was an accident?' I asked.

'According to the coroner he died as a result of injuries suffered in a single vehicle accident, cause undetermined. If it wasn't an accident it would have taken someone with extensive expertise to make it look like one.'

I could feel her stick the bull's-eye on my chest.

'You mean someone like me,' I said.

She shrugged.

'Well, it's Sheriff's Department jurisdiction not ours, and they seem convinced it was just an accident,' she said. 'Either way I don't care, I'm not a homicide cop, I'm in vice and narcotics. Rodriguez, on the other hand, cares a lot. If you had something to do with Lester's death he will burn you at the stake.'

Had I heard her right, vice?

'Why are you here?' I asked.

'I have a curious nature,' she said, avoiding the question. She took out another picture and put it in front of me. From the quality I guessed it was either from a driver's license or a mug-shot. It was a man in his thirties, long brown hair, the edges of a web tattoo on the side of his neck just visible. His eyes had a wild, penetrating quality.

'Have you ever seen him before?' she asked.

'No.'

'Sure?'

I nodded.

'Who is he?' I asked.

'A friend of Sexton, a real piece of work.'

'Am I free to go?'

'You all right?'

I nodded and she gestured towards the door.

'Of course.'

I got up and walked over to the door. As I reached for the handle Delgado stepped over.

'How much do you know about her daughter?' she asked.

'All I need to,' I said.

'And you're sure you don't know Sophie.'

154

'No.'

'If you find her, I would like to talk to her,' she said.

'I'll keep that in mind.'

I started to reach for the door.

'Do you trust Ms Sexton, Elias?'

'You know a reason I shouldn't?'

Her eyes narrowed, but she said nothing.

'I hope you know what the hell you just stepped into.'

Delgado reached out and opened the door.

16

The fact that I had been wrong about which was the first lie Tracy had told me didn't really surprise me. But a man had been beaten to death and a cop was pointing his finger directly at me. I hadn't done anything wrong, but it was of little solace, perhaps made it feel even more threatening. The clock was ticking on Tracy's secrets.

She was waiting in the lobby of the station when I stepped out with Lieutenant Delgado walking a few steps behind me. I noted the flash of surprise in Tracy's eyes when she saw Delgado, then she quickly turned and walked out of the building. She was at the car waiting when I caught up with her. What the hell was I doing?

Don't get in the car. Just walk away.

'What did she ask you?' Tracy said, her voice full of tension.

I glanced back at the building. Delgado was standing in the doorway watching.

'You've met Delgado before?'

She nodded, but offered nothing else.

'What did she ask you?' she repeated.

I wasn't in the mood for a free exchange of information. I needed something back from her and just looking into her eyes wasn't going to be enough.

'Why don't you tell me,' I asked.

She started to shake her head.

'They wanted to know if I had killed Lester,' I said.

The muscles in Tracy's jaw tensed and she glared at the building.

'Imagine my surprise.'

She turned and got into the car and I walked around and climbed in.

'You need to tell me a few things,' I said.

She took a few breaths, trying to calm herself.

'What?' she said tersely.

'The truth,' I said.

She started to shake her head in protest or perhaps in confusion at the meaning of the word.

'If you want my help, this is the time to tell me everything,' I said.

She resisted, then grudgingly nodded.

'Why was Sexton's name in Lester's file?' I said.

Tracy looked back at Delgado. 'Not here.'

I slipped the key in and turned over the engine. We drove north away from the station crossing Sunset and Hollywood Boulevard, heading up towards the hills.

When I was driven away from the hospital after waking from the coma, the world I had watched pass by through the windows of the car was an unfamiliar one. Not because I didn't know it, I recognized the streets, I knew the neighborhoods, I'd eaten in this restaurant, been to that movie theater dozens of times. What I didn't understand was how I fitted into it any longer. The person I had awoken to wasn't the same one who had gone to a dance. I was a stranger in my own body, spying on a life that had belonged to someone else. So each day as I healed I would try to find ways to make this new life reconcile with the old one until one day when, completely unnoticed, my damaged head with its faulty wiring became me.

And now it had all happened again, seemingly in reverse, and the world I thought I had found my place in had changed again, but this time instead of headlights racing out of the darkness, the instrument of change was secrets, and one or maybe more than one of them had taken a man's life, perhaps two.

We stopped on an empty corner of Mulholland with a view stretching from the towers of downtown all the way to the coast. A warm breeze was blowing out towards the ocean where a thin brown ribbon of pollution hung over the slate-colored water. Tracy got out of the car without a word and walked over to the edge of the hill and sat down. I stepped over next to her but didn't sit.

'I've tried not to imagine where she might be because if I do, I see her everywhere,' Tracy said longingly. 'I even see her in other young girls. I could be looking at her right now, she could be in one of those cars, or sitting at a window in a building looking at me and I'm helpless to do anything.'

'Tell me about Delgado,' I said.

Tracy took a deep breath and nodded.

'She interviewed me once in the hospital after Derek had beaten me. She offered me a deal to help put him away. When I said no, she accused

158

me of wasting her time.'

'Put him away for what?'

'Drugs.'

'Using or selling?'

'Both.'

'About a week after his accident she came to my house and asked me some questions about it.'

'Delgado wanted to know if you had killed him?'

She nodded. 'I said no.' Tracy glanced at me as if to gauge my belief. 'She tell you that?' she asked.

I nodded.

'She also said he nearly beat you to death several times,' I said.

Tracy reached behind her right ear and pulled back her hair. I noticed her hand was trembling. A thin raised scar and suture lines of about four inches ran up and disappeared into the hairline.

'I know a little something about head injuries,' Tracy said, then stared down at the traffic moving along Sunset. 'That was the last time,' she said. 'He used my head to open a door with.' She bit her lip and shook her head at some private thought. 'Aren't you going to ask me?' she said.

Had she killed him? She turned and her brown eyes fell on mine the same way they had all those years before, but there were things inside them now that no seventeen-year-old eyes ever held.

'No, I don't think so,' I said.

Tracy took a breath, then turned and looked into the distance.

'I dreamed about it, I prayed for it from

159

whoever might be listening,' she said wistfully, 'but I didn't kill him. When I heard he was dead, I thought it was finally an answer to my prayers. I was wrong about that.'

'Who was Charlotte's real father?' I asked.

The flash of surprise in her eyes lasted for just a moment, but it was enough to know what April had told me was true.

'Who told you that?' she said, not yet ready to give it up.

'Charlotte told April.'

My answer took the wind out of her and she whispered her daughter's name with a heartbroken wince.

'You hadn't told her?' I asked. 'You didn't think Charlotte knew?'

She shook her head and worked her way through what she was going to say.

'He was just a guy I met before Derek. A one-night stand. I don't remember his name.'

'That's why you didn't tell her?'

She nodded.

'How do you tell your daughter that her mother was the party slut? I was ashamed.'

'Why didn't you tell me you were still married?' I asked.

'He was dead, I didn't think it mattered. I wanted you to like me.'

'Do you know what the truth is?' I asked.

She clenched her fists and shook her head as her eyes moistened with tears.

'Charlotte knew about the abuse, didn't she?'

Tracy closed her eyes and lowered her head. 'Only at the end. You try to hide things because you're afraid the shame will be worse than whatever he does to you.' Her eyes drifted back to the line of cars moving along Sunset, past the rows of billboards of the latest blockbuster films.

'Why is the life you imagine never the one you live?' she said, the sad tone of regret filling her words.

'I don't know.'

A flash of sunlight reflected off a windshield down below. The lines around Tracy's eyes tensed and she looked back at me.

'The only question the police asked me was where I was last night. Why did they talk to you for so long?'

I looked at her, trying not to lose myself in the details of her face that seemed unchanged since that day she came to my rescue in the cafeteria line. Did I trust her? Or was it the idea of her that I had lived with for so long that I wanted to believe in?

'They talked to me for so long because I'm an accident investigator,' I said.

It took a moment but the meaning of the question seemed to register in her eyes as if a cold hand just touched the back of her neck.

'Oh, my God, what have I done to you?'

'Was there anything between Charlotte and Derek that could be a connection between what's happened?'

'You mean more secrets.'

'Yes.'

Tracy started to shake her head to say no, then stopped herself.

'I don't know.'

17

There was no separating us now. And it was too late to listen to that voice in my head telling me to run. Either by chance or by design we were right back in my parents' car, sliding towards another collision.

A vice cop had drawn a line from Tracy to her dead husband. Somewhere that line crossed paths with Anna, and probably Sophie, and from there perhaps it led straight to Charlotte. But how?

Anna would be no help. She was already too lost in a nightmare version of the Hollywood dream. It was nearing six o'clock when we met April at a coffee shop not far from the mall where Charlotte had disappeared. It wasn't that I believed she had lied to me in our previous meeting, but if we had any chance of finding Sophie it would be with her help.

April showed up twenty minutes late, listening to her iPod and texting someone as she walked through the door of the shop and took a seat at our table. She wore a collection of bracelets that covered the spectrum of colors and causes on her wrist. Her clothes had a kind of chosen casualness that must have taken half the morning to put together.

She didn't protest Tracy's presence this time. More than once as she ordered her coffee I saw her stealing glances at Tracy as if she were trying to find evidence of the abuse, and perhaps even trying to find her way to forgiveness, or at least understanding.

'I thought we were done,' she finally said.

'Did you know about Anna and the porn?' I asked.

The question appeared to cause her pain. She reached up and pulled out the earpiece of the iPod.

'Not when it was happening, but I should have.'

'How?'

'She was a friend, I just should have.'

'It's the people we're close to who sometimes are the biggest mystery,' I said. 'You didn't do anything wrong.'

'Feels like I did,' she said sadly.

'Anna can't help us.'

'No kidding.'

'That leaves you,' I said.

'You think I wouldn't tell you if I knew where Charlotte was?' she said defensively.

'That's not what I'm asking,' I said.

'We need to find Sophie,' Tracy asked.

'I told you everything I knew, I told the detective you hired everything I knew — '

'You talked to Lester?' I asked.

April nodded.

'When?' I asked.

'Last night after I dropped you off, he called.'

'He was murdered last night.'

April reacted as if she didn't understand.

'He was beaten and strangled to death,' I said, hoping to add clarity.

April's face flushed though she did her best to appear unfazed by it.

'Murdered?' she asked nervously.

'It's important that you tell me exactly what you told him,' I said.

'Nothing. I told him I didn't know her.'

She looked over to Tracy.

'I'm sorry, Mrs Sexton. I don't know anything else.'

Tracy reached out and took hold of April's hand and squeezed it. 'I know you don't, that's OK, April,' Tracy said.

'No it's not,' I said.

Tracy looked at me in surprise. 'What are you doing?' she said.

'You haven't told us everything, April.'

April grabbed her bag and started to stand up.

'Whoever killed the detective probably killed Charlotte's stepfather,' I said.

Her grip on the world was quickly slipping away. I knew the look well. She stared at me for a long moment, unsure of whether to flee or stay.

'I don't understand, I thought he died in an accident,' she said, her voice raising an octave with fear.

'It's possible that it wasn't one,' I said. 'Now tell me the things you haven't said about Sophie.'

'I did — '

'We think she may know where Charlotte is,' I said.

She shook her head.

'Charlotte didn't know her,' April said.

'How do you know that?' I asked.

164

'She would have told me.'

'Like Anna telling you about the porn.'

For the first time in her young life April had run out of things to say.

'Whoever killed the detective last night is looking for Sophie as we speak,' I said. 'And after they find her, they will begin looking for Charlotte.'

'Why?' she said softly.

'Something about porn and drugs, I don't know.'

April looked down at her hands and took a deep breath.

'She made me promise,' she said softly.

'Sophie?' Tracy asked.

'No, like I said, I've never met Sophie.'

'You promised Charlotte,' I said.

She nodded.

'What was it?'

'Charlotte told me one day a few months ago about this amazing girl she'd met. She said she was unlike anyone she had ever known.'

'What did that mean?'

'Charlotte said that Sophie did and said things that she had never heard or seen anyone do. She called it a fearless life.'

'Is she in your school?' I asked.

April shook her head.

'No, I would have figured that out. She met her somewhere else,' she said.

'You don't know where.'

'Might have been a club, I'm not sure,' April answered.

'A club?' Tracy asked.

She nodded.

'Charlotte didn't go to clubs,' Tracy said, then immediately realized how foolish the words had sounded. 'You didn't always do homework when you got together on weekends.'

April shook her head.

'You and Charlotte are best friends, why didn't you meet her?' I asked.

Disappointment registered in her eyes.

'I wanted to. All Charlotte said was that Sophie had a lot of secrets and that some of them were dangerous, so she was careful about whom she would meet.'

'What did dangerous mean, was it drugs?' I asked.

She shook her head.

'I don't think so. Charlotte doesn't like to be around drugs.'

'What was it, then?' I asked.

She looked nervously over to Tracy.

'I would just be guessing,' she said.

Tracy filled in the blanks for herself.

'Are you saying my daughter was having a relationship with Sophie?' Tracy asked.

A flash of hurt or perhaps jealousy registered in April's eyes. 'I'm not sure.'

'I think you are,' I said.

Tracy held on to the arms of the chair as if the ground was moving under her feet. 'Are you saying Charlotte's a lesbian?' she asked.

April shook her head. 'Charlotte said things that made me think it was possible they were more than just friends, but she also said that Sophie had a boyfriend.'

166

'Do you know the boyfriend's name?' I asked.

She thought for a moment.

'I think it was Tyler.'

'Do you know anything about him?'

'He was hot. That's about it.'

That seemed to be the truth.

'What did Charlotte say?' I asked.

She glanced again uneasily at Tracy.

'Are you sure you want me to go on?' April said.

Tracy nodded.

'Tell us,' she said.

'Some of it was ideas, kind of out there, some were sexual things.'

'Sexual?' Tracy said.

'Yeah.'

'What does that mean?' Tracy asked.

Tracy's surprise seemed to astonish April.

'What do you think, she said the three of them were intense.'

'The three of them?' Tracy said in disbelief.

'I don't think Charlotte would want me to say anything else about that, it's kind of personal.'

'The three of them were having sex?' Tracy asked.

April nodded.

'What kind of ideas did she talk about?' I asked.

'I think she was getting radicalized. You don't have to look around very hard to know the world is pretty fucked up.'

'She never talked to me about any of this,' Tracy said.

'Yeah, I know,' April said.

'You know . . . Why wouldn't Charlotte tell me?' Tracy said.

'Common ground, I guess,' April said coolly.

'What are you talking about?'

April hesitated to continue.

'Go on, tell me,' Tracy said.

'Charlotte thinks of you as a victim. She didn't want to be like that. I think that's why she became so active on the net, she could create her own reality there.'

The words seem to strike Tracy with the force of a blow and her face flushed. She closed her eyes and sat back in the chair as if waiting for her world to right itself.

'Did you meet Sophie on Facebook through Charlotte?' I asked.

'I got a friend request one day from her, I assumed through Charlotte.'

'And you've talked on-line?'

She nodded.

'What can you tell us about her?'

She glanced at Tracy, aware of the damage her words had already done.

'Tell us,' I said.

Tracy reluctantly nodded.

'She seemed cool and she scared me a little,' April said.

'How?' I asked.

'I don't know how to put it exactly. I guess she sounds like she's willing to do or say anything.'

'Have you communicated with Sophie since Charlotte disappeared?' I asked.

'Couple times right after it happened, but nothing for more than a week.'

'Did you ask her if she knew where Charlotte was?'

'Yeah. She didn't exactly answer, but I think she knows something,' April said.

'Why?'

'She said Charlotte was a warrior and that everything would be fine.'

'A warrior?' Tracy said in disbelief. 'Fine? It's not fine.'

April took a casual breath.

'I'm just telling you what she said.'

'Have you continued to try to talk to her?'

April nodded.

'I've posted on her wall and sent her messages, but she hasn't responded.'

'Is there any information on her Facebook page that would help us find her?'

'There's nothing personal, she just posts statements, keeps them up for a few days then removes them.'

'What about a picture?'

'Not like you're thinking.'

'Can you show me?'

April picked up her phone and connected to Sophie's page and held it out to us. On the screen was a face, hidden in silhouette, a few faint lines of a face but nothing more. I looked over the rest of her page. April was right, there was nothing there that would guide you to her. A single statement in bold letters was all there was.

Do you know who you are? Fighting for every second is the only way to beat the lies.

Tracy looked at me and shook her head, barely clinging to what was left of her battered reality.

'Have you seen Tyler's page?' I asked.

'No,' April said. 'He wasn't listed as a friend on either of theirs.'

'Would you post a message to her for me?' Tracy asked.

April looked at me.

'I'm not sure that's a good idea,' she answered.

'I need you to do this, April,' Tracy demanded.

I looked over to Tracy.

'April might be right about that,' I said.

'What are you talking about?' she asked in surprise.

'If a message from you shows up, Sophie will know that April has sent it.'

April nodded. 'I promised Charlotte.'

'You can break that promise,' Tracy said.

'If April breaks that confidence and Sophie does know where Charlotte is, we could lose that connection,' I said.

'I can't do nothing,' Tracy said, her voice rising in a mixture of fear and frustration.

'We won't,' I said.

Tracy stared at me for a moment then started to say something but lost the words. She shook her head and stood up looking around the room for a moment as if she were lost and searching for an escape.

'I'll be outside,' she said and quickly walked out.

I reached out and picked up April's phone and looked at Sophie's page.

'May I try something?' I said.

April hesitated.

'You can alter it if you want,' I said.

She nodded in agreement.

'You said you think Charlotte met Sophie at a club?'

'I'm not positive, but I think so.'

'Which club?'

'We go to the Echo a lot.'

I hadn't been inside, but I had heard of it. It was a head-banging indie rock club on Sunset in Echo Park. I typed out a few words on Sophie's page and then held it out for April to read before I posted it.

I've found something you need to see, can't post, meet me at the Echo.

'Do you think that will work?' I asked.

April looked it over for a moment and then shrugged.

'What have I found?' she asked.

'If she responds, just say an answer to a secret that you can only tell her in person, then get her to meet you at the Echo.'

April thought about it for a moment then nodded and posted the question on Sophie's page.

'It's done.'

'Did Charlotte ever talk about her stepfather?' I asked.

'She used to.'

'What does that mean?'

'They used to be close, but that changed.'

'When?'

'I'm not sure, some time in the last six months, she wouldn't talk about it.'

'Was it the abuse?'

April shook her head.

'I don't know specifics, I just know she was afraid of him towards the end.'

I wrote my name and number down on a card and slid it across the table to her.

'If Sophie responds, call me,' I said and then started to get up to leave as April looked at the card.

'You're him,' April said.

'Him?'

She nodded.

'Charlotte said there was this guy in her mom's past that she had been in love with but had lost.'

The word love hung in the air and my heart skipped a beat. Whatever I had imagined for all those years the one part that had always remained firmly planted in the realm of dreams and distinct from any reality of what had gone on between us was that Tracy had actually been in love with me.

'I don't think that's accurate. We knew each other in high school,' I said.

'She said everything that hadn't worked out in her mom's life could be traced back to one moment when everything changed and she lost him.'

I felt like I had just fallen over a cliff.

'Did Charlotte tell you anything else?' I asked.

She nodded.

'She said that her mom told her that he had died.'

'I guess it can't be me, then,' I said.

'Charlotte didn't believe her, she used to make up stories about what had happened between them and why he disappeared. In one she said he had run away because of a broken heart to France and had become a painter, in another he had been disfigured in an accident and had become a monk in India and lives on the top of a mountain. She even made up one where he came back and rescued her after she had been kidnapped by pirates.' She smiled. 'We were pretty young when she made up those stories. I've never been to France or India.' April shook her head. She appeared for a moment much older than she was. 'You're trying to rescue her,' she said.

'I'll let you know if I find any pirates,' I said and started to leave.

'She also said his name was a bird's name.'

I turned.

'If you hear from Sophie, let me know,' I said.

'You are him, aren't you?' April asked. 'She said she found your picture in a yearbook once.'

Was it really possible that Tracy had been in love with me all these years?

'Do I really look like the kind of person that people make up stories about?' I said.

April shook her head.

'I don't know, what do people in stories look like?' she asked, then picked up her bag and walked out.

18

Tracy was sitting in the car motionless, her gaze fixed on some point ahead that I suspected only she could see because it probably only existed in memory. In her hand she held a small photograph of Charlotte from her wallet.

I slipped in behind the wheel but made no move to start the car.

'We sent a message to Sophie. If she responds, April will let us know.'

Tracy closed her eyes and took a deep breath.

'Can you tell me something?' she asked.

'I'll try,' I said.

She looked down at the photograph, her eyes seeming to search for the physical evidence of what April had just told us.

'I love my daughter more than I ever imagined you could feel anything. She is in every heartbeat, every breath I take. Any meaning that might ever come from my life is because of her.' Tracy looked up from the picture. 'I don't understand this. How is it possible that I knew so little about her? How can it be that Charlotte was two people, one of whom is a complete stranger?' A tear slipped out of the corner of her eye and down her cheek. 'What was it you said? Sometimes it's the people closest to us who are the biggest mystery.' She wiped away the tear. 'What did I do? Why is this happening?'

'I don't know,' I said.

Tracy turned to me.

'Am I being punished?'

I shook my head. 'I don't think it works that way.'

'Even if I get her back, how will it ever go back to the way it was?'

'Nothing ever goes back to the way it was.'

She turned to me, her eyes holding on to mine for a moment, then she looked away into the distance.

'It's almost as if my daughter disappeared into the Internet like it was a living, breathing thing that snatched her away to another life. What do we do?'

'We sent Sophie a message, April will call us if she contacts her.'

'So we just wait?'

'No.'

'Then what?' she said, grasping for straws.

'We go someplace I don't think you're going to like.'

Tracy turned and looked at me.

'Where?'

I had let it go until then, but I couldn't any longer, perhaps it had been a small lie, but I still needed to know why.

'Your husband.'

'What about him?'

'Why did you tell me you were divorced?'

She exhaled heavily, closed her eyes for a moment and shook her head.

'Why?' I asked again.

'Does it really matter?'

'You tell me.'

She shook her head.

'It doesn't.'

'You didn't think I would help you if you were still married.'

She turned to me. 'I'm not used to believing in people.' The air rushed out of Tracy's lungs and she struggled to take another breath, then she tightened her hands into fists and stared at them in her lap. 'I would say anything to anyone if it would help me find Charlotte.'

Did I really know if I could trust her? What did I believe?

'Even me?' I asked.

She looked up from her hands and glanced at me, her eyes avoiding mine. 'No, that's different. I wanted you to believe I was someone worth caring about,' she said softly.

'You might have tried the truth.'

She looked back at her hands and shook her head.

'When you live a lie for as long as I did, you begin to think that's how everything works.' She fell silent for a moment, then looked up. 'What now?' she said.

'Have you been to either your husband's gallery or his apartment since he died?'

She shook her head. 'No.'

'Has anyone been in them?'

'The police,' Tracy said.

'Delgado?'

'I don't think so, just the Sheriff's Department.'

'Do you have access to them?'

She thought for a moment.

'They gave me an envelope with his effects

176

from the accident. I haven't looked at it but I think his keys are in there.' Tracy looked at me uneasily. 'You want to look inside them?' she asked.

'Are you OK with that?'

The pace of her breathing increased.

'Sure,' she said in a less-than-convincing tone. 'He can't hurt me ever again, right?' she said, not entirely believing it.

I turned over the engine.

'No, he can't,' I said.

19

We drove to Tracy's house and she retrieved the envelope from a desk drawer where she had kept it since the police had given it to her. She carried it out to the kitchen and set it on the table. The simple act of touching it seemed to cause her pain.

She took several steps away and crossed her arms over her chest, staring at the large manila envelope with the name Sexton written on it like it was an intruder in her home.

'I'd rather not open it,' Tracy said nervously.

I stepped over to the table, undid the metal clasp on the envelope and poured the contents out onto the table. The sum total of what her husband had carried with him the day he died amounted to a wallet, a little less than a dollar in loose change, two key rings, one in the shape of a silver dollar that had four keys on it, the other with a small bottle opener that held two keys.

'This doesn't seem right,' I said.

'What do you mean?' she asked.

'Did the police say anything about keeping any of his things?'

'Not to me. Why?'

'There's something missing.'

Tracy stared at the items for a moment.

'How do you know that?'

'The one thing everyone carries isn't here.'

178

Tracy looked down at the contents of the envelope.

'His phone.'

'Was he the kind of person who might have forgotten it?'

She shook her head.

'Never.'

'Could have been lost in the accident, thrown out a window as it tumbled down the canyon or just missed inside the wreck.'

'Does that happen a lot?'

'No, not a lot, but it happens.'

'Where else could it be?'

Before I could reply Tracy answered herself. 'Oh, that,' she said.

'Yeah, that.'

'The person who killed him has it,' Tracy said.

I nodded and then reached down and pulled the two key rings aside.

'Do you recognize either of these?' I asked.

She nodded.

'The silver dollar ring is for the gallery, the other must be the apartment.'

Her eyes stayed focused on the keys and she took a tentative step closer to the table.

'What is it?' I asked.

'I don't remember there being four keys on it, there were three before.'

'You're certain?'

'No, but I think so.'

'What about the other key ring?'

'I've never seen them before. I never went to his apartment.'

Her eyes shifted to the wallet, moving over the

worn brown leather as if, hidden inside its folds and creases, his violence still lurked.

'Are you OK?' I asked.

She hesitated and then nodded. I picked the wallet up and opened it. From his driver's license picture Derek Sexton stared out from death. There was a smile on his face, but what came out of his eyes appeared entirely different. The joy present in the smile had been replaced by a kind of fury barely able to contain his menace. Even if I had not known the history of their relationship, the violence in his eyes was startling. That this man was the one Tracy had chosen to share a life with was beyond my ability to imagine.

Opposite the driver's license was a clear plastic holder that appeared to hold credit cards. I flipped through it until I reached that last holder that held a photograph in it. It was a picture of Tracy, but it wasn't the one I knew. Her left eye and cheek were swollen from being beaten. Her eyes had the haunted look of a prisoner being held in a gulag. The idea that this man had kept the picture in his wallet almost like a trophy gave me a sick feeling that I had never experienced before.

'Anything there?' Tracy asked.

I flipped the credit cards back over, concealing the picture, and shook my head.

'Just what you would expect,' I said.

I opened the cash sleeve of the wallet and thumbed through the bills. There were sixty-eight dollars, and a small Post-it note stuck on the back of one of the bills. I pulled it out; there was nothing written on the front side of the note but I could see the indentation of writing on the other side. I peeled the note off and flipped it over.

'What is it?' Tracy asked.

It was a phone number with a Valley area code. The letter T was also written on it. I held it out for Tracy to look at.

'Do you recognize this?' I asked.

She shook her head.

'I've never seen it,' she said.

'A place or a person,' I said.

Tracy looked out the window.

'Tyler?' she said.

'Lots of names start with T.'

'Like mine.'

'But you never saw the number before?'

She shook her head.

'I guess that makes me innocent,' Tracy said sarcastically.

She managed a small smile but it quickly vanished.

'If that is Tyler, then that means there is a connection to Charlotte,' she said and looked at me for confirmation.

'It's possible.'

I took out my phone and started to dial the number.

'Is that a good idea?' Tracy said.

I hit send.

'We'll find out.'

It rang three times then an automated service picked up. *Leave a message at the beep.*

'I'd like to talk about Derek Sexton. Please

call this number back,' I said and hung up.

I saved the number on my phone, looked at the rest of the effects on the table, then reached down and picked up the key rings.

'His apartment?' she said with a shudder.

I nodded. Her eyes filled with dread and she glanced over her shoulder as if expecting him to walk through the door.

20

Darkness was beginning to fall when we stopped outside the apartment her husband had rented. It was an old Spanish-style building painted pale yellow with ornate stonework and a tiled entrance that sat between two dying palm trees. It was the kind of place where old B movie actors from the 1950s were finishing out their days as they waited for one last call from an agent.

People disappear in Los Angeles every day, dozens of them, most with no intention of doing so, they just slip through the cracks of whatever hopes had brought them here and are swallowed up by a city that feeds like a predator on dreams. For every detail we had learned about Charlotte, rather than bringing us closer to her all we really had were new questions that had replaced the old ones. Perhaps April had told us everything. But it was also just as likely that something had still gone unsaid, maybe not because she was intentionally trying to mislead but rather because to open up completely would be an admission that nothing was ever going to be the same between her and Charlotte. Something had happened to her friend beyond her experience; regardless of how hard she tried to understand and as much as she might want things to return to what once they had been, at some level she understood they never would

— even if tomorrow Charlotte walked back in that same door she had disappeared through. That kind of truth is hard enough for anyone to understand, let alone a teenager.

I knew something about that. When finally I had returned home after the coma and was taking my first steps back into the world, the one question that was always there whispering in my ear was why? Not why did this happen to me, but rather, why do I want to return to this? How do I fit in? I don't belong here any more.

★ ★ ★

As we stepped up to the entrance to the building, a window in a ground-floor apartment slid open and a woman with deeply dyed red hair and skin the color of parchment paper, her eyebrows drawn on with brown pencil, leaned out with a long, thin cigarette in a silver holder tucked snugly between her fingers.

'Can I help you?' she asked, doing her best to remember a Brooklyn accent. 'I'm the super.'

There were six mailboxes next to the entrance. Tracy's husband's name was on number six.

'We're going up to number six,' I said.

She shook her head.

'I think Mr Sexton is on a trip,' she said.

'A long one,' I answered.

'Thailand, I think?' she said.

'Further than that. It's all right, we have a key.'

'Are you the police?'

'I'm his wife,' Tracy said.

184

Surprise registered in the woman's eyes and she took a drag on the cigarette.

'I didn't know he was married.'

'Neither did he most of the time,' Tracy said.

'Have the police been here?' I asked.

She nodded.

'I'm good at handling police; I did two episodes of *Adam-Twelve*.'

'When was this?' I asked.

'The second and fourth season. 1969 and 1971.'

'No, when were the police here?' I said.

She thought for a moment. Behind her a Martini glass with a bright green olive in it reflected the light of the television inside the apartment.

'A few weeks back.'

'Detectives or uniforms?' I asked.

'Uniforms, from the Sheriff's Department. They asked if he lived here alone, then left. The detective was here yesterday morning.'

'Detective?'

She took a drag on the cigarette and gave it a little thought.

'I think he was a PI not a cop.'

'Did you show him the apartment?'

'Certainly not. He asked a few questions and left, I respect my tenants' privacy.'

Respect aside, what she really liked was someone paying attention to her.

'You seem like someone who notices things, details,' I said.

She reached up and placed her hand on her chest and smiled.

'De Mille once told me that very thing,' she said.

'What questions did the PI ask you? It would be useful to know,' I said.

She hesitated, then glanced at Tracy and smiled.

'I guess since you're his wife it would be all right to tell you.'

'It would be very helpful,' Tracy said.

'He showed me a picture of a girl, wanted to know if I had seen her.'

I slipped the picture of Charlotte out of my jacket and held it out.

'This girl?'

She nodded.

'Yeah, that's her, real pretty, nice smile, big brown eyes.'

'What did you tell him?'

'I used to see her. Sometimes she would be by herself, sometimes with Mr Sexton, sometimes with a friend.'

Tracy reached out and nervously took hold of my hand.

'When was the last time you saw her?' she asked.

The woman took another drag on the cigarette.

'A week or two, I don't remember.'

'What did the friend look like?' I asked.

'A boy, about her age, he was white.'

'Did you ever hear his name?'

She shook her head.

'I don't think so, but I'm not good with names. I thought she or Mr Sexton might have

186

been here late last night; one of the other tenants thought they heard some voices in the apartment. I knocked on the door this morning, but no one answered. It wasn't you, was it?' she asked.

'No,' Tracy said.

'Maybe Mr Sexton's back.'

'That would be a big surprise,' I said.

We walked up to the apartment at the back of the second floor. The carpet had been cleaned recently and still held the sweet smell of shampoo. A television was on in one of the apartments we passed, music played in another. At the back corner of the building where her husband had lived there wasn't a sound. I stepped past the door to the apartment and over to a rear stairway. Through the window I could see a covered parking structure below where the rear stairs exited the building.

I stepped back to the door and took out the key ring that Tracy didn't recognize and tried the keys until the right one slipped in the lock.

'Do you think Charlotte could have been here last night?' Tracy asked.

I unlocked the door and pushed it open.

'Someone was,' I said.

I reached around inside until I found the light switch and flipped it on. The apartment appeared ransacked. I started to step inside but Tracy held back, staring down at the threshold as if there was a line drawn across it that said 'Do not cross'.

'I'll look around, you wait here,' I said.

Tracy shook her head.

'Last time you said that we found a man dead.'
She reached out and took my hand. 'I think I'll come with you.'

Inside the air was stale with the aroma of dust and cigarettes and a fainter smell of dope. Some of the furniture had been overturned, other pieces just shoved aside. From the marks the legs had left in the carpet I suspected that it was the first time in years that any of it had been moved.

The couch had been flipped over and the fabric covering the underside had been ripped off, some cushions had been slit open, and in one corner of the room the carpet had been pulled back to reveal the aged wood floor underneath. Beyond that there was nothing else in the room that appeared to have been searched, probably because there was nothing that could be called remotely personal.

The small kitchen had the same lack of charm as the living room. The drawers and the contents of the cabinets dumped out onto the floor didn't help much either. The whole apartment felt as if time had stopped inside this place a long time ago, and that whatever lives had passed through here were just making unscheduled stops before moving on to whatever was next.

'This doesn't feel right,' Tracy said and then let go of my hand.

I looked around the floor at the pieces of silver dumped out from the drawers.

'You mean beyond the obvious,' I said.

Tracy looked past me and nodded, then walked over to the dark hallway that led to the other rooms.

'What is it?' I asked.

'This isn't the way he would live. He liked nice things, he couldn't afford them most of the time, but that never stopped him.'

She looked back into the living room.

'This would have been an insult to his sense of style.'

'What are you saying?'

Tracy stared down the dark hallway. 'I'm not quite sure how to put this,' she said, trying to make sense of something she didn't quite understand. She thought for a second then looked over to me. 'The last time that he . . . attacked me. It was different from the others.'

'You don't have to tell me this if — '

She held up her hand and shook her head.

'It's all right. What was it you said? He can't hurt me any more.'

'Yes.'

She turned back to the hallway and stared into the darkness.

'The rage in him was gone. You could see it in his eyes, it was as if hurting me had become as much a part of him as breathing.'

She turned and looked back into the living room.

'Whatever he had once been, the part that allowed him to live a dual life wasn't there any more inside of him. It was gone, that's how he could have lived in this place.'

She shook her head and turned to me.

'I think something bad happened here,' she said nervously.

Tracy looked over to the dark hallway, then rushed over to it and flipped on the light switch — no light came on.

'His bedroom must be down here,' Tracy said.

I started to step past her. Tracy held out her hand to stop me.

'Let me do this,' she said determinedly. 'He's not going to frighten me any more.'

She slowly started down the hallway until she reached the two doors, one on either side. I followed a few steps back, stopping just short of where she stood looking into the open door on the left. It was the bathroom.

She stepped in and looked around at the items spread across a shelf next to the sink.

'I recognize some of this,' she said, reaching out and picking up a bottle of aftershave. 'I remember the scent. He always liked to put some on after he had hurt me.'

Tracy clenched the bottle as if trying to break it, then set it back down and walked over to the door of the bedroom, but didn't open it.

'Charlotte once told me that whenever our bedroom door was closed, she got scared.' Tracy reached down and took hold of the door handle and turned it until the bolt fell open, then pressed her face up against the door but didn't open it. 'She would hide in her room or sneak out of the house for a while. When she would come back in she would stand on the other side of our bedroom door and press her ear against it, listening for the sound of me breathing.'

Tracy's hand tightened around the doorknob.

'All that time I thought I was hiding it all from her.'

Tracy leaned in, pressing her ear against the door to listen as her daughter used to.

'What kind of a mother lets their daughter live like that,' she said disapprovingly, 'standing in a dark hallway on the other side of a door?'

'The same mother who was able to walk away from him,' I said.

She took a deep breath.

'It's no wonder she kept her secrets from me.'

'It was his fault, not yours,' I said.

Tracy shook her head, then pushed the door. Slowly it swung open. The air inside was somehow different from the rest of the apartment. The smell of cigarettes and dust were here, but there was also something else, a heavier, stronger scent, almost metallic, that gave me an uneasy feeling.

Tracy stared into the darkness for a moment, looking for the source of the presence in the room, but it didn't seem to originate from one place, it was everywhere. She reached out to flip on the light, then hesitated, the fingers of her trembling hand gently tapping the plate of the light switch.

'Something's wrong here,' she whispered.

'I know,' I answered.

Her hand shook for a moment then flipped on the light switch. For an instant as the light came on my heart began to pound and I thought my head was moments away from a full-blown event. But it wasn't me at all. A red ceiling light was bathing the room in a dull red hue. Tracy started to take a step and I reached out and took hold of her arm.

'What is that?' she said.

I stepped around her and quickly scanned the room. There was little inside it — a chest of drawers against a wall, a chair and the bed. The drawers had all been opened, the contents dumped on the floor. There was only a bedspread covering the bed, no blanket, and no sheets. A single pillow lay at the head of the bed half covered by the bedspread. The indentation of a head was still faintly visible in the pillow.

'Don't move,' I said.

'What are you seeing?' Tracy asked.

I realized I knew the odor from several fatal wrecks I had investigated. As blood dries it has an odor that some describe as coppery. I reached out and took hold of the bedspread and pulled it down to the foot of the bed.

'Is that blood?' Tracy asked.

'Yes, that's what it is,' I said.

There was a stain around the pillow and a swath of blood swept over to the edge of the bed as if painted by a brush. A small amount stained the carpet right next to the bed. I looked around the rest of the floor but didn't see any other blood anywhere, then I carefully walked along the side of the bed. Up close in the odd red light I could see pieces of thin nylon rope had been tied to the four corners of the bed.

Tracy stepped up next to me, her eyes moving across the bed until they found the frayed pieces of rope. She stared at them for a moment and then at the blood.

'What happened here?' she asked.

Before I could say anything I saw the panic begin to spread in her eyes and she started shaking her head.

'Oh, God no, no, no.'

I took her by the shoulders and turned her towards me.

'That's not what happened here,' I said.

Tracy didn't hear the words.

'No, no.'

'Look at me.'

She looked at me but her eyes weren't focusing.

'Oh, my God.'

'Listen to what I'm going to say.'

She managed to slow the panic and nod.

'That's not Charlotte's blood.'

'How do you know . . . how — '

'I'll tell you, just listen.'

She forced herself to take a deep breath.

'All right.'

'The apartment's cold, there's no heat on in here, it takes a long time for blood to dry. Look at it.'

She reluctantly turned and looked back at the bed. There was no doubt in my mind that whatever had happened here had taken place well before Charlotte had vanished.

'The blood on those sheets is dried and cracked, that would take weeks. Do you understand what that means?'

Tracy stared at the bed for a moment and then looked back at me.

'You're sure?' she asked, her voice still filled with fear.

I nodded.

'I'm sure.'

The fear in her eyes vanished, but not the questions. What had happened here?

'What do you think this is, then?' she asked.

I stepped around to the other side of the bed; a few spots of blood stained the floor.

'You said something had changed in him the last time he attacked you.'

Tracy nodded. 'You think he went even further, did even worse things?' she asked.

'Perhaps.'

I looked at the bed for a moment and then at the ropes.

'There's no blanket, no sheets. Where are they?'

Tracy shook her head and I looked down at the bloodstain on the floor.

'How much did he weigh?' I asked.

It took Tracy a moment to go there. 'Ah . . . he was a little shorter than you, and thin.'

'A hundred and sixty?'

'About that.'

I kneeled down and examined the blood. The edge leading towards the door wasn't as defined and sharp like the back edge. I got up and walked over to the window and pulled open the blinds. Down below was the parking structure out the back of the building. I turned and looked back at the bed and then over to the door.

'I need to go see the crash site.'

Tracy shook her head.

194

'You're moving too fast.'

'Where he died, I need to see it.'

'Why?'

I looked back at the blood on the floor.

'The time frame is about right,' I said.

'What time frame?'

'The dried blood.'

'I don't understand.'

'This is a little difficult to ask, but it would help,' I said.

Tracy nodded.

'I'll try,' she said hesitantly.

'The rope — did he ever tie you up?'

She shook her head.

'No.'

I looked back at the bed.

'What is it you're seeing, Elias?' Tracy asked.

'I think it's possible that the wreck that killed him started right here.'

'You think that's Derek's blood?'

'It will be easy enough to confirm,' I said.

'What makes you think this isn't something he did to someone?'

'My guess is that the blood has been drying here from the night of the accident.'

Tracy stared at the bed, trying to put the pieces together.

'You think the person who killed him tied him to this bed?'

I nodded.

'If I'm seeing what I think I'm seeing, then whoever killed him had bound him to the bed and then struck him with an object heavy enough to duplicate the kind of head trauma

195

suffered in an accident. After he was hit, I imagine he was alive, but unconscious. The ropes were untied and the attacker laid the blanket or sheets out on the floor and rolled his body onto it. Before he could be moved, the wound bled through the blanket and soaked into the carpet. Sheriff's deputies didn't see any of this because they were here on a routine car accident, checking for next of kin, not looking for clues in a murder. They never stepped inside.'

'What about Delgado?'

'She's never been here, it's not her case.'

'But she's right, he was murdered?' Tracy asked.

I nodded.

'When he was picked up they must have dragged him slightly, you can see the movement in the bloodstain where the edge closest to the door was smeared. Since there are no other bloodstains, whoever moved him was strong enough to lift him up and carry him over his shoulder, or there was more than one person in this room who carried him out the door, down the back stairs to the parking area in the back where they placed him in the car and then drove to where they sent him over the cliff.'

Tracy stared at me for a moment and then down at the bed.

'You see all that here?' she asked in wonder.

I looked back at the bed.

'Actually, it makes more sense that there were two people, someone to drive his car, and then the other person followed in theirs.'

'Two people?'

I nodded.

'Should we call Delgado?' Tracy asked.

'I'm not sure that we would be the best people to deliver this news to her just yet,' I said.

Tracy glanced about the room.

'How sure are you of this?'

'If I was standing in an uncontrolled intersection and this was an accident scene, I'd be more sure,' I said.

'But it's not one.'

I looked down at the blood on the mattress, bathed in the strange red light of the room, cracked and dried like mud. 'No, there wasn't a car accident.'

'So it's possible you're wrong, and that's the blood of someone else he tied to that bed?' Tracy asked.

'Anything's possible.'

Tracy looked at the bed as if the things I had just told her were written out in script, then turned away and stepped out into the hallway and looked back into the room.

'How does any of this help us find Charlotte?' she asked, trying to find something to hold on to.

'I don't know yet,' I said.

I walked over to the door, took one last look around to make sure I hadn't missed anything. How did it indeed? Hell, I didn't fully understand why I was standing in a room with a red light bulb and bloody pillow instead of in some parking lot like any normal crash investigator sorting out the insurance claims of a man whose Lexus was rear-ended by a woman texting in a Caprice putting on lipstick instead of looking in the rear-view mirror.

We had taken a step closer to something, but what? I reached over and flipped off the light with the back of my finger. The red glow of the light seemed to linger in the room like a mist.

21

It wasn't far to the accident site, forty minutes at most, about as long as anyone would have wanted to drive with a man wrapped up in blanket that they had beaten nearly to death with a bat or lug wrench.

At a turn on Mulholland west of Coldwater we pulled off onto a wide gravel turnout and came to a stop. Below us, the lights of the Valley coming up in the darkness stretched out in a vast plain until they ended in the dark shapes of the mountains to the east. I turned the engine off.

'This is where it happened?' Tracy asked.

Accident reports are public record; through the database at the office I had it in front of us on my phone. I looked along the edge of the turnout where it met the drop of the canyon. There was no guardrail, nothing to slow down a car pointed at the abyss.

'This is it,' I said.

I put the phone away, stepped out and walked over to the edge of the canyon with a flashlight and pointed down into the chaparral until I saw the faint trail of disturbed soil leading straight down into the darkness where the vehicle had torn through the brush.

Tracy stepped out of the car, but stayed next to it. I turned from the edge of the canyon and walked over to where the road met the gravel of the turnout. The faint scent of roses drifted down from the houses behind the tall fence and grove of trees on the rise across the road. Looking around and across the canyon there were no houses with a direct line of sight to where I stood. I walked along the edge of the pavement until I found the spot, then turned and looked across the turnout to where I had just stood and the deepening darkness of the canyon directly below it.

Tracy looked out at the lights of the Valley for a moment then walked over.

'What are you doing, what are we doing here?'

'What I do best,' I said.

Tracy turned and looked in the direction in which I was staring, across the turnout.

'Which is?'

'This is the spot, right here where we're standing.'

'What spot?'

'Where his car left the pavement.'

She looked down at the ground and the pavement around us and shook her head.

'How do you know that?'

I pointed over to the edge where the BMW would have left the gravel and gone airborne.

'A car going over the edge would have traveled down the slope more or less in a straight line from where it had come, that brings it right back to here.'

'And that means what?'

'Delgado was right to have been suspicious about what happened here, even not knowing what we do about the apartment,' I said. 'If the Sheriff's Department had done their work properly, they would have seen it too.'

'Seen what? I still don't follow.'

'Traveling west as he would have been moving, only a drunk who passed out or someone deciding to kill themselves would miss the turn here; we're already past the apex of the turn.' I turned and looked back up along the pavement towards the east. 'The natural place to have missed the corner would have been another twenty feet in that direction. Where they pulled off the road and pointed him towards the canyon they were already well beyond where an accident would have occurred naturally. A car missing the corner here, nine times out of ten, would be a deliberate act. Turning to miss an animal, or a suicide.'

Tracy shook her head.

'Derek was far too infatuated by his own presence to kill himself.'

'Which brings us to the apartment.'

Tracy looked over to the edge of the turnout where his car would have disappeared.

'So that probably was his blood.'

I nodded and looked back over the turnout trying to understand what I hadn't thought through yet.

'Given what we saw in the apartment it seems logical that they had planned to kill him, they had the rope, a weapon, maybe they hadn't planned on the blood, that was a mistake, perhaps they had intended to clean it up, but panicked or one of the other residents came home, maybe they had even figured that they could put him in his car and point him over a cliff, but I don't think they had planned on this exact spot. Halfway through this turn they pulled off, checked out what the drop was down into the canyon and saw that it would work, no house looked over the turnout, all they had to do was wait for the right moment when the road was empty and then put his foot on the accelerator.'

The headlights of a car illuminated the road then came around the corner, slowed as it passed us, then drove on west along Mulholland. Tracy watched its taillights vanish into the deepening darkness then looked back out at the lights of the valley spread out like the surface of the ocean lit up with phosphorescence. She stared at them for a moment and then shook her head.

'I was happy he died, but I didn't think it would be like this. This is more than I — ' Tracy took a deep breath and then turned to me. 'I don't think I would like being able to see the world the way you do. You look at a small detail and see an entire story in it.'

'Sometimes the stories are good ones.'

Her eyes seemed to fix on a single light somewhere far out in the valley. 'Are they?' she said, her voice empty of belief.

'Yes.'

She turned to me. 'Tell me one.'

There was no moon in the sky, but her eyes seemed to hold the gathering stars like they were her own.

'A long time ago I danced with a girl who had stars in her eyes.'

Tracy shook her head. 'I don't remember,' she whispered.

'I do.'

I reached out, took her wrist and guided it up to my shoulder.

'Your wrist rested right there,' I said, 'then your hand curved around the back of my neck.'

Tracy reached out and gently touched the back of my neck. 'Like that?' she said nervously.

I nodded.

'Just like that.'

Tracy took a deep breath, her eyes struggling to stay in the moment, to not drift back out to that single light she was looking at in the Valley where she could imagine her daughter waiting for her. She tried to say something, then lost it, then tried again.

'Where was your hand?' she whispered.

I drew a blank, resisting the urge to look down at my feet and see if there was lasagna covering my shoes.

'I'm a little fuzzy on that,' I said.

Tracy reached down and took my hand in hers. She held it for a moment then looked down at it and smiled. I remembered that smile; it was full of youth, the kind of smile that can save you in a cafeteria line.

'Your hand's trembling,' she said.

'Is it?'

Tracy nodded.

'I can't feel it,' I said.

The smile didn't go away. 'Try holding me tighter,' Tracy said wistfully.

I pressed my hand against the gentle curve of her back and she shook her head.

'Tighter than that,' she whispered.

'How tight?'

'As tight as you can.'

There was a desperate quality in her voice. I pulled her against me and Tracy wrapped her arms around my neck and held on as if she were trying not to fall. I don't know how long we stood there, clinging to each other, our hands moving only to get a better hold, hoping that the tighter we held on the longer we could keep the reality of the world from slipping back in and taking it all away.

But like any dream, it was fleeting. Too much had happened and was yet to happen. Tracy's hands relaxed and her body slipped away from mine, though I could still feel her pressing against me. Her eyes found mine for a moment, but the stars in them were gone. The years we had tried to snatch back had returned to the gray reality of the past.

I turned and looked over to where the car had gone over the edge into the dark canyon.

'Someone broke into my loft yesterday,' I said.

'Was something stolen?' Tracy asked.

'Not a thing. They went through the files I keep on our accident.'

Tracy looked at me in confusion. 'You keep files on our accident?'

I nodded. 'It's what I had instead of memory.'

'Why would they look at that?' she asked.

'I can't imagine.'

My phone began to ring. I slipped it out of my pocket, it was a text.

'It's April,' I said.

'She talked to Charlotte?' Tracy said.

Her text came up on the screen and I read it quickly.

I shook my head. 'No.'

Disappointment filled Tracy's eyes. I handed her the phone.

Her eyes moved quickly over the short, clipped text and she shook her head.

'I don't understand. Meet her at the Echo?'

'It's Sophie,' I said.

22

Is this what happens when dreams come true? The life that you once comfortably walked through becomes unrecognizable. And in this new life the things you see and feel and experience are not at all what you might have imagined any more than the life you had left behind is still there to return to.

A seventeen-year-old girl had explained it all to me. That alone would be unnerving enough, but that was just the beginning, and not even April's crystal ball could see what was ahead.

We headed back towards downtown, winding our way out of the hills down Outpost and onto Hollywood Boulevard. I couldn't begin to count the number of times I'd driven this street and how many accidents I had investigated along its length to where it merged with Sunset, but it had never appeared exactly the way it did tonight.

For years the city had dressed up Hollywood for the tourists, trying to return it to its former glory when film stars prowled its clubs, and fame lurked behind every door — all you had to do was pick the right one. But the harder the city tried to reclaim the past, the more the boulevard took on the look of a stage set, designed to do nothing more than to open the wallets of visitors believing there might really be a mythical place called Hollywood where dreams come true.

Perhaps it was just the events of the last

twenty-four hours and the fact that nothing outside the windows of the car had changed, it was me that had. Perhaps for the first time since the telephone pole came rushing out of the darkness I was seeing the rest of the world with the kind of clarity that until now I had reserved for crushed and twisted metal and skid marks drawn across an intersection where they came to an abrupt stop. Perhaps it was the touch of her hand on the back of my neck.

Whatever the reason was for this new clarity, I didn't want to lose it — ever. I wasn't willing to accept the fact that there was a timer counting out the rest of my life. For the first time I had a reason and another person to live for, or at least the possibility of it. And I didn't want to give that up. But I didn't know how to stop what was happening in my head any more than I knew how to slow down what was going on in my heart.

As we passed Western and headed into East Hollywood, a bright yellow Mustang with a black prostitute in red-hot pants and matching halter-top sitting on the hood came sliding around the corner, the hooker pounding on the windshield with her fist and screaming at the two teenage boys laughing inside to give her the money. At Edgemont a squad car was stopped next to a Mexican man sitting on the curb wearing a white cowboy hat, and silver-tipped boots, blood covering one side of his face as a young woman in a yellow dress stood a few feet away shaking her fist in the air. Another block on, a long line of customers, of all colors, stood talking and laughing outside a Vietnamese restaurant, the smell of lemon grass and garlic drifting out across the street. In the distance ahead, the night-sun searchlight of a police helicopter cut a thin hole in the darkness as if prowling the landscape of a Philip K. Dick novel for a crime that hadn't even happened yet.

There were no tourists here, no entertainment complexes dressed up like sets, no city elders selling whatever anyone would buy, everything was just as it should be, or at least as it really was; perhaps it was the world Charlotte had slipped out of camera range and vanished into.

In a city defined by the automobile, I was perhaps the logical result of it all. A car wreck had taken my life away. Then I found a new life by immersing myself in the accidents of others where I turned their pain into understandable diagrams and coldly written reports that took no account of what was left when it was all over.

And now I was right back where it had all started, sitting in a car with her just as we once had. And, just as before, I could feel the presence of that telephone pole out there in the darkness, waiting to snatch it all away in the blink of an eye.

Don't stop, whispered the voice in my head as we drove.

Tracy reached out and took hold of my hand. She didn't say anything. Didn't glance in my direction. She just stared straight ahead, her eyes focused on where we were going.

23

A crowd dressed mostly in black was gathered on the pavement outside the Echo. In the cool night air little columns of cigarette smoke rose out of the gathered crowd like steam vents before dissipating into the darkness.

We parked across the street and stepped out of the car. April had sent another text as we were driving telling us to meet her outside. Looking over the crowd I didn't see her. I checked my watch — it was nearing ten.

'She should be here,' I said.

Tracy stared at the crowd then shook her head and started across the street stepping right out in front of some oncoming headlights. I grabbed her arm and pulled her back as the brakes squealed and the car skidded to a stop right where she had been standing.

All heads in the crowd across the street turned towards us. Tracy stared at the car for a moment as if not fully understanding what had just happened, then the driver of the car flipped us the bird and drove away. The crowd returned to their cigarettes and the smoke began to rise again. Tracy watched the taillights of the car move off and then looked back towards the crowd as if nothing had happened.

Tracy started across the street again, not waiting for traffic to completely pass. I rushed ahead and took her by the hand and guided her across Sunset. There were perhaps fifty people outside the club. When we reached them, Tracy again pulled away and began moving around the edges of the people with a kind of frantic energy, her eyes passing over the tattoos and piercings that seemed to cover every bit of exposed skin.

I caught up and she turned.

'I don't see her,' Tracy said, her voice rising with tension. 'Charlotte should be here, where is she?'

'No,' I said.

Tracy turned to me. 'What?'

'It's not Charlotte we're meeting, it's April,' I said.

She started to shake her head, then her eyes filled with a kind of sad understanding.

'April?' she said and I nodded. 'Yes . . . what was I thinking?'

'What you're supposed to be thinking. It's all right.'

Tracy took a deep breath and looked back into the crowd.

'I'll try and keep it together a little better.'

'I think you're allowed a lapse or two,' I said.

She shook her head. 'Falling apart won't find my daughter.'

Tracy glanced at me and then looked back across the street.

'I'm all right now.'

I took her hand and we moved again into the crowd, working our way back towards the entrance of the club. As we approached the doors, the driving beat of a bass line began filtering out onto the pavement. The cigarette smoke seemed to get thicker as the music grew louder.

'Could you be more conspicuous?' said a voice.

I spun around to see a young woman with jet-black hair and a large silver stud in her left nostril. She looked at me for a moment.

'You're late,' she said tersely.

'April?'

She lifted a cigarette to her lips, which had dark purple gloss on them.

'You've changed.'

She rolled her eyes the way a kid would who had just been embarrassed by her parents, then she looked over to Tracy and then back to me.

'I thought you were coming alone.'

'Charlotte is my daughter,' Tracy said.

Standing next to April was a thin, pale young man with a bad complexion. His hair appeared to have had the same dye job as April's. His nose stud was in the opposite nostril.

'Who is this?' I asked.

'This is Rex, he drove.'

'Rex?'

He looked back at me, his dewy eyes looking oddly like a golden retriever's. April glanced again at Tracy and took an exasperated breath.

'If Sophie sees you, Mrs Sexton, I don't think she's going to stick around.'

A crash of a cymbals reverberated from inside the club.

'You don't know that,' Tracy said.

April shrugged. A guitar began to riff, the beat picking up speed.

'Whatever, but I think you should wait outside. It's up to you.' Tracy looked over to me.

'You can't expect me to walk away.'

'If April's right — '

Tracy shook her head.

'No,' she said, not wanting to walk away.

'Do you want to take that risk?'

The crowd outside began to drift back into the club as the music picked up more speed.

'I'll find out what she knows,' I said.

'We're supposed to meet her during the second set, we shouldn't even be standing here talking — she could see us,' April said with annoyance.

Tracy looked anxiously over to Rex and April then back to me.

'You promise me?'

I nodded. 'I promise.'

Tracy resisted for another moment then rushed back through the thinning crowd and headed across the street towards the car.

'We should get inside,' April said.

Tracy got to the car but didn't get in. Just stood watching us.

'Can we go?' April said.

I took a last look at Tracy then turned and started into the club with April, Rex and the rest of the crowd. Walking into a loud, dark space with flashing colored lights and music that seemed to shake the building is not high on the list of things to do for someone with a TBI.

As we stepped through the doors the lead guitarist went into a riff and I thought I could feel the screws in my skull begin to work their

212

way out. The lights behind the stage began flashing on and off and I could feel my grip on the world loosening.

I looked away from the stage towards the crowd. That was little better. They moved like a dark sea swaying back and forth in a violent swell. I turned back to April, trying to stay focused.

'When was the last time you were here with Charlotte?' I shouted over the music.

'January; it was her birthday.'

'Not since then?'

She shook her head.

'How are you supposed to recognize Sophie?'

'She said she would know me.'

I looked at her black hair and nose stud.

'Which you?'

She shot me a look. 'Try not to act your age.'

'No — I like the new look.'

She didn't entirely believe me, but the seventeen-year-old inside was trying to.

'It fits you,' I said.

For a brief instant she almost smiled.

'Did you tell her you're in love with her yet?' she asked.

I wasn't sure if I found April's lack of a filter admirable or frightening. I shook my head and glanced around the crowded club for a moment.

'How is she supposed to find you in this, did she give you any other instructions?' I asked.

'I'm supposed to be dancing with someone towards the back of the crowd in front of the stage.'

I looked over to Rex who was standing a few

feet away. As far as I could tell, he was mute.

'Rex,' I said.

'Rex doesn't dance,' said April.

'What does Rex do?'

'He drives.'

I looked over towards the crowd moving up and down like a set of pistons.

'The message we sent her said I had something to tell her, what am I supposed to say?'

'Just point to me, I'll take it from there. You'd better get out there,' I said.

She glanced at the crowd then stared at me. 'I'm not dancing alone. You do dance, don't you?'

'I have a complicated history with dancing.'

'Do you want to talk to her or not?'

I looked over to the flashing lights above the stage, which seemed to bounce around inside my skull every time a new color blinked. April grabbed my hand and started pulling me into the crowd.

'You'll be fine, just pretend you're not old.'

'I'm not old.'

'Yeah, right.'

April led us through the crowd to where she had been told to go and then let go of my hand and began moving to the beat of the music. I looked at the faces moving around us. None seemed to take any notice of our presence. If Sophie was one of them, she was doing a good job of disguising the fact.

April pressed in next to me and shouted over the music.

'Unless you want to scare her off by just standing there, I suggest you start moving. You know, dance.'

The lights flashed again and an aura like the colors in a prism began to appear on the edge of my vision. A warning that the wiring in my head was about to overload. I turned away from the lights and closed my eyes, trying to slow things down. April reached out and touched my arm.

'Are you all right?' she asked.

I nodded but didn't turn back towards the lights.

'I'll be fine.'

'What is it?' Her hand slipped from my arm.

'I sometimes have trouble with flashing lights, no big deal.'

I took a couple of breaths and then slowly opened my eyes like a kid peeking out from under the covers to see if the nightmare he had been having was now loose in the room. The aura had passed, though I could feel a pinpoint of pain behind my eyes.

'It's all right, it's passed,' I said.

April didn't say anything. The song the band had been playing ended and the room fell almost silent. I turned around.

'Any sign of — ' I started to say.

There was no one standing where April had just been. I looked around but didn't see her in the crowd. The band started another song and the people began moving again, faster and faster to the music as the guitarist began to riff and the drummer picked up speed.

I pressed through several people to my left but

215

there was no sign of her. I started back to the right and saw movement through the gyrating crowd. A woman with jet-black hair was moving several feet away following another woman with blond hair.

I rushed forward and reached out, taking hold of the arm of the girl with the black hair. She quickly spun around and then yanked her arm away. She had piercings in her nose and eyebrows and a big silver stud in her lower lip.

'You got a problem?' she yelled.

I released her arm.

'I thought you were someone else.'

She leaned in laughing. 'In your dreams.'

She took the blond woman's hand and walked off. I turned and looked back into the crowd; moving through the periphery of the dancing a man and a woman stepped into the light of a strobe. In a staccato of flickering light I saw April turn and look back, her eyes desperately searching the crowd, a man holding her by the wrist.

She moved in disjointed flashes of light until they passed the strobe and she vanished back into the darkness. I pressed through the crowd, trying to follow, and then I stepped out into the light of the flickering strobe.

Everything around me moved in bursts of brilliant light. Faces, an arm, hands, twisting bodies, but no April. I stepped out of the strobe and back into the darkness. It took a moment for my eyes to readjust and then I saw the red glow of an exit sign above a door at the back of the building.

I started to move towards it.

'What do you want?' came from behind me.

I turned to see a woman standing several feet away in the darkness, backlit by the strobes. I couldn't see anything other than a faint outline of her face. She wore a hat, which covered her hair.

'What do you want?' she repeated.

'You're Sophie?' I said.

'Do I have to ask you again?'

'I'm looking for Charlotte,' I said.

'Why?' she said bluntly. 'What is she to you?'

The question caught me off guard. I had no answer to that.

'You some kind of a knight who comes to girls' rescue?' she asked.

'She's in trouble,' I said.

'And you can fix everything?'

'No, I can't.'

The drummer smashed the symbols.

'You're him, aren't you, the one from high school who her mother said was dead.'

'I don't know,' I said without thinking.

She started to turn away.

'I'm him,' I said.

She stopped and looked back at me, though beyond the fleeting flash of the lights I still couldn't see her face.

'What do you want?' she said with an edge to her voice.

'I want to talk to her,' I said.

'You don't even know her.'

'I talked to Anna.'

'Why the fuck did you do that?' she said, the

edge getting sharper.

'She told me about the videos.'

'I don't know what you're — '

'Do you know the names Art and Jack?'

'No,' she said way too quickly.

'Was Charlotte's stepfather involved with it, did he supply the drugs?'

'I don't know what you're talking about,' she said, clearly flustered.

'The investigator that her mother hired was murdered,' I said. 'I think whoever did it is looking for her.'

'How do you know that?' she said, tension rising in her voice.

'He could be looking for you, too; so are the police.'

She took several quick breaths and shook her head.

'Someone killed Charlotte's stepfather,' I said.

'He died in an accident.'

'No he didn't.'

'That's not — '

'What is she running from?' I asked. 'Let me help.'

'You can't.'

I started to reach out towards her but she pulled her hand away.

'Just go away,' she yelled, not sounding much at all like the super-chick April described. 'Just walk away before — '

'Before what?'

She turned and started to move away through the crowd. I began to follow when a hand grabbed my arm from behind. As I started to

218

turn I was struck on the right side of the face. There wasn't any pain, no fear, the blow spun me to my left and I looked to see if there was a telephone pole rushing towards me, but there was only the tile of the dance floor.

Everything stopped, all sound, all sensation; I seemed to be drifting in darkness. I saw Tracy's eyes, I thought I felt her take hold of my hand, but in an instant it was gone and I heard the sound of my heart beating and then a sharp pain began to rise on the side of my face.

The flashing colored lights came back into focus and I started to turn my head when a hand took the side of my face and pinned me against the floor.

'This is the only warning you will get. Stop.'

'Stop what?' I mumbled.

His hand pressed my face harder into the floor. 'You don't know what you're doing.' He leaned in and I could feel his breath on the side of my face as he whispered. 'Don't fuck with this any more.'

I tried to move but he pinned my face even harder against the floor.

'You got it?'

I nodded as I heard shouting in the distance.

'That's enough — stop it, stop it!'

He put more pressure on the side of my face and I could feel myself beginning to plunge towards unconsciousness like speeding into a tunnel.

'Stop . . .'

His hand slipped from the side of my face though the sensation of his fingers pressing against me remained like a phantom holding on to me. I lay there for a while without moving, I don't know how long, but I had practice at that. I tried to replay his words but I couldn't hold on to anything.

Focus, breathe, start with that, take a breath.

I slowly drew air into my lungs and held it for as long as I could. The shape of dancers moving around me became visible as I began to emerge from the tunnel. I took another breath and then another. My heart beating against my chest began to slow down. The bitter taste of the dirt and dust on the floor filled my mouth and I started to gag.

A hand took hold of my arm and pulled me up to my knees.

'You fuck!'

Through the flashing of the lights April's face was illuminated.

'I trusted you!'

It took me a moment to catch my breath enough to speak. 'What happened — ?'

'You lied to me! That's what happened.' The moisture of tears in her eyes reflected off the flashing light. 'You bastard!'

'April, what happened — '

She took a step away from me. 'Stay away from me.'

I tried to get up. 'April . . . '

'Leave me alone!' she yelled and then turned and disappeared into the crowd. I tried to get up to follow but fell back to my knees. A hand reached out of the darkness and took my arm.

'Can you get up?'

My head felt like it was spinning on a pinwheel.

'I'm not sure,' I mumbled and looked up at the figure trying to help me. The lights were flashing again, the band driving a beat that was picking up speed with every note. The movement of dancers was all around me like flickering shadows.

'You need to come with me, get up,' she said.

It was a woman's voice, but when I looked into her face the flashing lights made it a blur. She grabbed my hand and arm and pulled me up. 'Now walk.'

I swayed a bit, then we were moving away from the dance floor and into a hallway. Faces passed, some stared at me, others laughing, talking, paying no attention as we moved, the smell of dope hung in the air, beer, sweat. We rounded a corner and then a door swung open and we stepped out into the cool night air.

She leaned me up against the door as the sound of traffic filled in, replacing the music. The blades of a helicopter beat the air somewhere in the darkness. A single light above the door illuminated the alley we were standing in.

'Are you all right?' she asked.

I leaned into the wall for support and took a breath and then another. The pinwheel that was my head began to slow down. My face throbbed from where I had been struck.

'What happened in there?' she asked.

I looked into the face of my rescuer for the first time. It was the woman cop who had interrogated me.

'Delgado?'

'What happened?'

'I asked too many questions,' I said.

'Who was it?' she asked.

I started to ask what she was doing here then I realized the answer.

'You're following us.'

She nodded. 'Who were you talking to?'

I hesitated.

'Last time we talked you accused me of murder,' I said.

'That was Rodriguez; I accused you of being an idiot. Not the same thing. Now who was it?'

'Sophie.'

'Shit . . . who hit you?' she said angrily.

'I didn't see him.'

'Did you get a good look at her?'

I shook my head.

'What did she tell you?'

'It was more of what she didn't tell me.'

'Which was?'

'She's frightened.'

'And the guy with the fist?'

'He warned me to stay away.'

She thought for a moment then shook her head. 'What the hell are you doing, going to a dead man's apartment and dancing with her at the crash site?'

It took me a moment to work back to that.

'What does that have to do with — ?'

'Jesus, I can't figure out if you're the smartest guy I've met or the dumbest.'

'I had to know if it was an accident.'

'Do you?'

222

'You were right, it wasn't.'

'You need to think about what you're doing,' she said.

I started to shake my head.

'A beautiful woman walks back into your life and you just accept it as a natural consequence of your boyish charm and good looks. Wake the hell up.'

'That's not what's happening.'

'Lester was killed about midnight, were you with Tracy?' she asked.

'No.'

'And you weren't with her the night her husband died?'

'No.'

'Anything unusual happen in the last few days, beyond the obvious?'

I started to shake my head, then stopped.

'Someone broke into my loft.'

'And nothing was stolen,' Delgado said, answering her own question.

'No.'

'Was anything left behind?'

'To set me up, is that what you're saying?'

She nodded.

'I don't think so. Why are you doing this?' I asked.

'I told you, I'm not a homicide cop.'

'Vice.'

'But Rodriguez is, and he will burn you.'

In the haze of my head I tried to fill in the blanks of what she was saying. 'Porn?' I said. 'That's why you're here?'

She shook her head.

'It's not porn when they're using young girls like play things and throwing them away when they're finished with them,' she said grimly.

'I talked to a girl named Anna,' I said.

From the reaction in her eyes I could see that she knew Anna.

'She mentioned the names Art and Jack,' I said.

'Art would be Arthur Grunier.'

'Sexton was part of it?' I asked.

'I can't prove it, but I think so.'

It took me a moment to process this to the next logical step and my stomach began to turn.

'Did he do anything to Charlotte?'

'It would be reason to kill him if he did,' she said.

'Tracy didn't murder him,' I said before doubt could creep into my words more solidly than they already had.

'Someone did,' Delgado answered. 'And then they killed a private detective who found out something he shouldn't have.'

'What did he find out?'

'I think his secretary knows something but she's afraid to talk to the police.'

She wrote down a number on a card and gave it to me. 'That's her name and number.'

I glanced at it then stuck it in my pocket.

'You still didn't tell me why you're doing this?' I said.

She took a breath. 'You saw Anna,' she said.

I nodded.

'She's one of the lucky ones.'

The door to the club flung open and a large

group of people tumbled out carrying beers and lighting up cigarettes and making phone calls. A moment later Tracy stepped through the door, saw me through the crowd and rushed over.

'Was that her?' she said, her voiced flushed with adrenalin.

I turned to Delgado but she had disappeared through the crowd.

'No,' I answered. 'Why did you come — ?'

'I saw April run out, so I came looking for you. What happened?'

It still wasn't clear why April had said the things she did. What had I lied to her about?

'I'm not sure.'

'Did you talk to Sophie?' Tracy asked. 'Did you?'

Delgado had been right; I wasn't with her on either of the nights that Sexton and Lester had died. She was also right that if Sexton had done to Charlotte what had happened to Anna, it would be more than enough reason to kill him.

Don't fuck with this any more.

'Sophie didn't come,' I said, lying to her for no other reason than that it seemed a sensible thing to do. That is, if sensible even applied to my life any longer.

Tracy reached out and touched the side of my face.

'What happened to you?' she asked.

'Someone warned me to stay out of it.'

Tracy shook her head.

'I don't understand. Who? Why?'

I studied her eyes, looking for the truth, but if

225

it was there in her words, her eyes kept their own counsel.

'I don't know,' I said.

'You're not telling me something,' she said. 'What did you find out?'

I tried to imagine the words we heard Anna say coming out of Charlotte's mouth as she stood on stage in the school play video. If what Delgado believed Sexton was involved with was true and Tracy didn't know any of this, how would you tell her? And if she did know, then all of this had been theater.

My knees started to buckle and Tracy reached out and held me up.

'I'm taking you home,' she said.

24

The beginning of the day and the events I had witnessed now seemed so long ago that they had taken on the unreal quality of memories from years before as opposed to just hours.

Don't fuck with this any more.

No kidding. There were just two problems, and when she looked at me with those eyes, the life I had apparently left behind didn't matter any more. I was all in, whether Tracy was part of two murders or not. I didn't know how to 'just walk away', as Sophie had told me, any more than I knew what was coming.

It was near midnight when we left the club. We were closer to my place so we drove downtown to my loft just beyond Little Tokyo. We didn't talk on the drive, though the silence that filled the glances we took at each other felt as if they were words, and the closer we got to the loft, the faster Tracy seemed to drive and the greater the urgency the silence took on.

We parked out front on the street, not bothering to go into the secured parking lot. As we stepped up to the entrance of the building and I reached for my keys, I felt her hand gently touch my back and then she leaned into me, pressing her face against the back of my neck. Her hand slipped around and pressed against my chest over my pounding heart.

'Tell me what you know,' she whispered.

Why? Was I here to find a daughter, or to take a fall into the abyss? I didn't want to believe Delgado, but her words were there as I looked up the stairs wondering if whoever had broken in to my loft had done more than just go through my files.

Her hand tightened around my chest, and I thought my heart was going to explode. No other woman had this effect on me, not like this. Why was her hand like a match to my heart?

'You,' Tracy whispered.

'Yeah,' I said, having lost none of the conversational skill I once possessed on the night of a long-ago dance.

Her fingers tightened around the fabric of my shirt. I felt her breath on the back of my neck as she pressed herself against me. I closed my eyes, wanting to give in to it.

'The police have been following us,' I said.

Her hand stiffened then she pulled away and turned around scanning the street.

'How do you know?'

I looked up and down the street but didn't see anyone that appeared to be watching us, but that didn't mean they weren't there.

'Delgado was at the club,' I said.

Tracy reacted as if she had been slapped. 'That was who you were talking to.'

I shook my head. 'She just picked me up after I was knocked down, that's all.'

Tracy looked at me and shook her head. 'Do you think I killed my husband — do you?'

I hesitated a fraction of a second, but it was long enough to hurt. 'No.'

Her eyes moistened with tears. 'Why are you lying to me?'

I started to answer but she shook her head and began to walk away.

'The men Anna talked about, your husband might have been one of them,' I said.

The words stopped her.

'Is that possible?' I asked.

She stood still for a moment then shook her head. 'I don't know,' she said softly.

I took a step towards her but she held up a hand to stop me.

'Delgado thinks Lester found something, and that was why he was killed,' I said.

'What does this have to do with Charlotte?' Tracy said.

'I don't know, maybe nothing.'

It took a moment, but then the terrible meaning behind my words became clear to her. She spun around, stared at me for a moment.

'Maybe?' she whispered, then reached up and covered her mouth as if to stop herself from screaming, then she shook her head and gritted her teeth. 'That's not what happened to my daughter.' Her eyes found me. I had seen fear in them before, but this was different. The horror they held seemed to have no end. 'Oh, God, don't tell me this,' she cried.

'We don't know that yet.'

'It isn't — ' she whispered.

There was nothing I could say, so I just nodded and Tracy turned and rushed back to her car and drove off into the night towards the lights of China Town.

25

I should have gone after her, but I didn't. As much as I wanted that match that was the touch of her hand to burn a hole right through me, Delgado's words were there, pulling me back. *Wake the hell up.*

And for every argument I could muster to deny her words, nothing I could come up with was able to push away the feeling that Tracy still held secrets I had yet to learn.

I turned to go upstairs and the words and images of the last day began to bombard me. You don't know what you're doing . . . this is the only warning you will get . . . the vacuum . . . the bloody water in the sink.

With each step I took they came faster.

The shoe in the middle of the floor, a sock half pulled off, the bruises on the neck . . . don't fuck with this any more . . . did you kill Lester . . . strands of cord on the bed . . . the tire tracks leading towards the cliff . . . the flashing lights of the club . . . it can be dangerous to play detective . . . her hand on the back of my neck . . . you're in love with Charlotte's mother.

I stepped into the loft. It was just as I had left it, as it always had been. But it wasn't mine any more. It belonged to a past life that was as distant as the darkness of the coma.

I stepped over to the filing cabinet that had been gone through. Why that? Was Delgado right, had something been left behind? I turned and slowly looked across the rooms.

Rodriguez will burn you.

What was it? What did they leave behind? Where would you put it? I stepped over to my desk and pulled open the drawer.

Run, said Tracy.

I dumped the contents of the drawer onto the floor. There was nothing there. I did the same with the next drawer and the next.

Faster, hurry.

The kitchen followed, furniture was overturned, cushions ripped open. Where would you hide it? The boxes in the closet, open, check everything, one after another. Go through the books, every page, throw them in a pile, now do the same with the files, empty them out, now the clothes, under the rugs, the refrigerator, the shelves of food.

Don't stop.

The front ends of the cars came down, pull apart any opening, pound it with a hammer. Flip the bed, strip the sheets, the pillows, the night table, the bathroom, the tank of the toilet. The walls they could have put it . . .

'Elias.'

I stopped. Sweat dripped down my forehead.

'What the fuck are you doing?'

Buzz was standing in the doorway. I looked at him for a moment, then around at the wreckage scattered across the floor. I tried to take a breath but there didn't seem to be any air left in the room.

'I was looking for something,' I said.

Buzz's eyes moved over the debris in disbelief. 'You find it?'

I shook my head. 'Anything else?' I asked.

He hesitated. 'Maybe this isn't the right time.'

'For what?'

'The friend I told you about, he found some things out about your dream girl.'

A piece of metal fell from one of the front ends onto the floor.

'Fourteen years ago she was arrested for drug possession and shoplifting. She's had a dozen jobs in as many years, mostly clerical, one after another. A year ago she was arrested for DUI and drug possession, went through rehab at a clinic.'

'That's all?'

'All?' he said as if disappointed. 'You need more than that, she's got problems.'

'There's a lot of that going around.'

He glanced at the mess surrounding us. 'No shit.' He started to turn to the door, then stopped. 'Elias, tell me you're not getting involved with her.'

Was that what this was? There were no skid marks, no bits of glass or twisted steel. The evidence was concealed in the beats of the human heart, and the answers hidden there, or at least the understanding of them, was just as elusive as that beating muscle had always been to me.

'What's it look like?' I said.

He was silent for a moment, then shook his head.

'In my experience, this looks like love.'

26

What little rest I did get was in a chair surrounded by the wreckage that had been my life. I'd drift off for a while and enter a dream where I was running through a forest of eucalyptus trees, their pale trunks lit up in the moonlight like enormous bones, the ground covered in a thick layer of leaves that filled the air with their pungent aroma smelling like dried blood as I ran. I was chasing someone, weaving in and out of the trees and every time I was about to catch them I would bolt awake, seeing their face.

Between the nightmares I would try to find the connection I may have missed that would open that door concealing Tracy's secrets, but the harder I pushed the more elusive the answers became and I would drop back into exhaustion and drift off to the sound of Buzz's voice.

Are you getting involved with her?

★   ★   ★

In the morning I tried the number Delgado had given me for Lester's secretary. I left a message on her service. A few minutes later she called back, hung up, then called again and agreed to meet me at a diner in Silver Lake, but only if Tracy were there, and only if she was satisfied that we were alone.

I rang Tracy to arrange to pick her up. She said nothing about the events or words of the night before as we drove back from the Valley.

We arrived at the Astro Coffee Shop in Silver Lake a few minutes before ten. Several police cars were parked in the lot, but there was nothing unusual about cops stopping in a coffee shop at the end or beginning of a shift.

There was no one obviously watching us as we walked to the entrance of the restaurant and stepped inside, but I knew, just the same, that the secretary was there watching, making sure it was safe to step back into the light where her employer had been killed.

We took a seat in the front of the restaurant where we were easily visible and ordered coffee. She walked through the front doors wearing what appeared to be a bright red wig under a baseball cap, dark glasses and jeans.

She looked in our direction then walked down the aisle passing us without saying a word, then turned around and came back.

'I'll be in a booth in the back,' she said without stopping and then walked down to the end and around the corner.

We took our coffee and followed her to the rear of the restaurant. She was sitting in the far corner booth away from the windows out front. Of the six booths, two were occupied by uniformed cops, the others were empty.

One of the cops looked up from his pancakes and watched us pass, then returned to his food. We stopped at her booth without sitting.

'Joan?' I asked.

She glanced past us towards the restaurant's entrance.

'Too many windows out front.'

Her eyes moved from the entrance to the booths full of police then to Tracy.

'I remember you,' she said. 'Sit down before every cop in LA decides to join us.'

We slid in on the other side of the booth.

'Were you followed?' she asked.

'I don't think so.'

She shook her head. 'You don't think? Not exactly a ringing endorsement of your detective skills.'

'I'm not dead,' I said.

She lowered her sunglasses, revealing bright green eyes that were bloodshot, then leaned across the table and looked at my bruised cheek.

'Not yet anyway.'

She slid her glasses back up and sat back. Joan looked to be in her early thirties, though the hat and wig gave her the ageless appearance of a mannequin in a store window. She took a pack of cigarettes out of her pocket, removed one and put it in and out of her mouth without lighting it as she began to talk.

'In case it's not obvious to you, I'm fucking scared. I signed up to answer phones and run appointments, not to be some Girl Friday hiding from bad guys.'

From the brief glimpse of her eyes it was clear that she had been doing a lot of crying.

'The police said you were the ones who found Earl's — Lester's body,' she said.

'Yes.'

235

She drifted with the thought for second.

'They wouldn't let me see him, wouldn't even let me look in the office.'

'You were in love with him, weren't you?' I asked.

She looked at me in surprise then took a nervous drag on the unlit cigarette and shook her head. 'I don't know, when you figure out what love is, you give me a call.'

She stared at the cigarette for a moment in silence, sighed, then stuck it back in the pack.

'Yeah, I loved him. I've always been really good at picking just the right guy to break my heart, though this is the first one to ever do it by getting killed.'

A waitress stepped up and Joan ordered coffee and a large tomato juice.

'Have you found your daughter yet?' she asked Tracy.

'No,' Tracy answered.

Joan shook her head, and then wiped another tear away as it slid out from under the dark glasses.

'I'm sorry. Everything's fucked up.'

'Do you know what Earl had found out about Charlotte?' Tracy asked.

Joan sank a little deeper into the booth, took a breath and shook her head. 'I don't know details. He called me the night before he died. He said he had found a girl who he believed knew where Charlotte was.'

'Did he say a name?' I asked.

'Sophie.'

'Did he meet her?' I asked.

'Not yet. As we were talking, he said he was outside a building where he thought he might get some answers.'

'Where?'

'He didn't say. It must have been near an airport, though, because I heard a plane landing or taking off.'

'What kind of plane?' I asked.

'What do you mean?' she said.

'Was it a jet or a little plane?'

'No, it wasn't a jet.'

'Did you tell the police this?'

She hedged.

'Not all the details.'

'What did you leave out?' I asked.

'Not everything Earl did was exactly legal.'

That didn't seem to be the entire truth, but I let it slide.

'That was the last time you talked to him?' Tracy asked.

Joan nodded. 'Before he hung up he told me to take yesterday off.'

'Did he say why?'

'No, but other times when he'd done that it was because he was meeting someone at the office who wouldn't like anyone else to know they were there,' she said.

'And he didn't say who?'

She shook her head.

'Was he working on any other cases?'

'Nothing with any drama, just screwed-up kids.'

'Did he ever mention the name Derek Sexton?' I asked.

She looked at Tracy.

'Your husband.'

Tracy nodded.

'Yeah, he said something.'

'What did he say?' Tracy asked.

'He told me not to tell anyone this.' She hesitated, conflicted about telling us. 'Earl said he thought your husband had been murdered, and that he was close to knowing who did it,' she said.

'He never told you who?' Tracy said.

'No.'

'Do you know why he didn't want you to tell anyone this?' I asked.

'He said the wrong people would get hurt and he didn't want that to happen.'

'The wrong people?' I said. 'That's what you didn't tell the police, isn't it?'

She nodded and glanced over to the cops at the other tables. 'I should be going.' Her voice was on edge.

'Do you know anything else about Charlotte?' Tracy asked.

She looked at Tracy and hesitated.

'If you know something, I need to know — it doesn't matter what, you can tell me,' Tracy said.

'All I know is that Earl had said she wasn't the girl her mother thought she was.'

'Thank you,' Tracy said.

Joan looked at Tracy for a moment, then shook her head. 'Earl spent a lot of time looking for runaways, he didn't exactly see the same world as most people do, especially parents. It doesn't mean anything. It's just different.'

Tracy shook her head. 'No, it means something.'

The waitress walked up with the glass of tomato juice and coffee. Joan picked up the juice and drank half the glass then set it down and started to slide out of the booth.

'I should be going,' she said then stopped. 'There's more.'

'What?' Tracy asked.

'Drugs?' I asked.

Joan nodded.

'That was part of it.'

'I had my suspicions,' Tracy said.

'He used the gallery to sell them. I don't have any proof, but I think that's how Earl may have made the connection to Sophie.'

'What's the other part of it?' I asked.

'He didn't say anything specific.'

She looked towards the door as if wanting to leave but something was keeping her.

'What is it you want to say?' I asked.

She hesitated.

'I don't know if this is connected, but Earl mentioned it.'

She glanced again at Tracy.

'There were some things he found out about your husband that were pretty ugly.'

'There're not many things about Derek that would surprise me,' Tracy said.

Joan looked over to me as if she were searching for a way not to tell us what she knew.

'It surprised Earl, not many things surprised Earl.'

'What things?' Tracy asked.

'There were sexual things. Earl didn't say it was connected to the rest, but I don't think he had figured it all out yet.'

'What did he say?' Tracy asked.

'Earl said he preyed on young girls, thought it was possible that he might have been photographing them and filming them . . . selling the pictures.'

'This isn't porn, is it?' I asked.

She shook her head.

'No, I think it was violent.'

'You said young, how young?' Tracy asked, her voice filling with dread.

'Underage — sixteen, seventeen, maybe a little younger too.'

What I saw in Tracy's eyes was more than just shock, but what it was I didn't understand yet.

'My daughter's age,' Tracy whispered.

Joan nodded.

'Like I said, Earl didn't know if any of it was connected to — '

'Was Charlotte one of them?' Tracy managed to say.

'I don't know.'

'Tell me,' Tracy demanded.

Joan shook her head.

'I really don't know, I'm sorry.'

She slid over to the edge of the booth.

'If I need to talk to you again — ' I started.

She shook her head. 'You can't. I'm leaving, going back to Minnesota. If I think of anything else, I'll call you,' she said.

She stood, looked towards the door, then back to Tracy.

'I really hope you find your daughter.'

She turned and walked out past the cops, vanishing into the bright sunlight. We sat in silence for a moment trying to add Joan's words to an already desperate palette of hearsay and rumor.

'We don't know — ' I started to say.

Tracy grabbed my hand and shook her head. 'I need a moment.'

She released my hand, slipped out of the booth and rushed out of the restaurant.

I nursed my cup of coffee for a few minutes, not quite sure if any amount of time would be enough to process the kind of news we had just had, then I left enough for the bill and followed her out.

Tracy was bent over behind a bus stop bench, sick to her stomach, convulsing. I started to walk towards her but she looked in my direction and shook her head. When the convulsions passed she stepped around and sat on the bench staring at the traffic moving by in a steady stream.

I gave her another few moments then walked over and sat next to her. I didn't say anything; I just watched the cars pass, as Tracy did. If she was seeing anything beyond the hell she had found herself in, I didn't notice it reflected in her eyes. They were as far away from this world as I had ever seen in a person. The lights changed from green to yellow and then red, then did it all over again and again. I'm not sure how many minutes had passed when Tracy reached up and touched the fingers of my left hand and shook her head.

'I wonder if this is what it's like for a blind person to regain their sight,' she said. 'You see the world for the first time, but it's not the world you expected.'

'I need to know some things,' I said. 'And you need to tell them to me, no matter how difficult it is. All of it.'

Tracy closed her eyes and nodded.

'Back inside, when she told us about the girls, it wasn't surprise I saw on your face, was it?'

Tracy opened her eyes, but if they took in any of her surroundings, it would have been a surprise.

'No, not all of it,' she said flatly.

'Tell me,' I said.

Tracy looked up at the bright sun, as if searching for memories hiding in the glare.

'When I first met Derek, he leased a warehouse space. He called it his studio. He wanted to be a photographer, but it never went anywhere.'

'Did you ever see it?'

She hesitated. 'Yes.'

'He photographed you?' I asked.

She nodded, then began to slowly replay the past.

'But it wasn't like this. It was supposed to be artistic when we started. Nudes, like in a museum . . .'

'But something happened?' I asked.

'The last time he photographed me it got violent — sexual. I never went back there and he never talked about it.'

'Could that be the place Lester went to?'

242

Tracy shook her head. 'He stopped renting it years ago.'

'Are you sure?'

Tracy took a heavy breath that seemed burdened with history. 'You mean more secrets?' she asked.

I nodded.

'It would be foolish for me to say no, wouldn't it?' she said.

'Was the warehouse near an airport?'

She again sifted through the past. 'It was under the flight path of a small airport out in the North Valley.'

'You were arrested for drug possession and DUI?' I asked.

I could see the words stung.

'I told you I had been in rehab.'

'I'm sorry, but I need to know everything,' I said.

Tracy looked down at her hands clenched in her lap.

'I tried all kinds of ways to escape from him, some of them weren't very healthy. I became addicted to pain killers . . . other things.'

'Are you clean now?' I asked.

Tracy nodded. 'Thirteen months. I couldn't have done it without Charlotte, she saved my life.' She reached up and covered her mouth with her hands and shook her head as tears welled up. 'When we met Anna, as horrible as it was, there was no connection to Charlotte . . . but now . . . If Charlotte was one of those girls that he . . . ' She couldn't finish.

'We don't know that she was,' I said.

'What do we do?'

'Do you remember the address?'

'No.'

'Could you find it?'

She thought for a moment, fear creeping into her eyes.

'I don't know.'

Tracy stood up. For the first time she seemed to notice the traffic streaming by.

'What did she mean?' Tracy asked.

'Joan?'

She nodded.

'About what?'

'Lester told her he didn't want the wrong person to get hurt,' Tracy said.

She turned to me. 'Who's the wrong person?'

27

We left the Astro coffee shop and headed north on the 5 freeway into the endless sprawl of housing subdivisions and strip malls of the Valley.

Hurt the wrong person? I had missed that, and I shouldn't have. What had Lester meant? Hurt them how? There's no end of those possibilities. Was he trying to protect someone, an innocent, or was it something else? Something darker? And who was it and why?

Lester had been paid to find a missing girl, that's all, not to risk his life by doing the right thing, but that's exactly what he had done, and it seemed he had been killed for it. What had he found that was worth that kind of risk to someone like him? He wasn't an amateur on leave from another life or hopelessly in love with the client. He was paid to do a job, and when it was done, the only part of that job that really mattered to a professional was that at the end of each day you went home, stuck dinner in the microwave, opened a beer and watched a game on TV. And now, instead of a Bud and the sofa, he had a toe tag and a body bag.

Just past the interchange of the 5 and the 170, the red and white smoke stack of the DWP generating plant rose in the distance. Tracy had said nothing most of the drive, but when the stacks came into view, it was as if a light had gone off in her head.

'Those,' she said.

'You remember them?' I asked.

She nodded.

'I remember the stripes, and at night, there're lights on them.'

Her eyes fell on the road sign ahead. 'We would get off at the next exit.'

I maneuvered through the traffic to the exit and dropped down the off ramp to the traffic light.

'Left or right?' I asked.

She looked both directions, seemingly unsure. 'I thought I would remember. But it doesn't look familiar. It was a long time ago.'

'Would you still see the smoke stacks after you got off the freeway?' I asked.

She looked off towards the stacks and stared at them for a moment.

'I think so . . . yes.'

I took a right and we headed north on Branford. Like most of the Valley the area had once been citrus groves that after the Second World War had been sold off to house the new middle class that worked at the defense plants and automakers.

Most of the plants were long gone, as were the white workers who had left the area. It was mostly Mexican and Central Americans who lived here now. The aroma of hamburgers and french fries cooking in strip-mall restaurants had been replaced by the scent of grilled pork, chilies and grilled corn from taco stands.

At San Fernando we stopped and Tracy again

looked up and down the street for something familiar, but she shook her head. 'I don't remember,' she said as if hesitant to go back in time.

'You need to try,' I said, pushing her.

Her eyes looked up from the street as the sound of a small plane coming in from the east caught her attention. She found it in the glare of the sun, a small white and green plane descending for a landing to the north.

'I remember that,' she said.

She watched the plane until it disappeared from view over a series of industrial buildings and warehouses that lined the streets to the north across the railroad tracks.

'Follow it,' she said. 'Go across the railroad tracks and follow it.'

When the light changed I crossed San Fernando and then a set of railroad tracks and began to follow the line of the plane's descent. I had a strange sense of familiarity about the place that didn't make sense until we had driven a block and a large salvage yard of thousands of wrecked cars, stacked like broken and discarded toys, came into view.

'I know this place,' I said. 'I examined a destroyed Ford Galaxy in that salvage yard.'

Tracy looked over towards the stacks of cars in the yard. 'He had some pictures on the wall of his studio from there. Twisted steel and chrome, he called them figure studies.' She looked ahead as the tower of the airport came into view in the distance. 'I remember the planes used to come right over the studio when they landed and took off. When we pass the salvage yard we take a right.'

The salvage yard extended for another two blocks where it came to an end.

'Here?' I asked.

Tracy looked off down the street — a mix of warehouses and steel and concrete-sided industrial buildings — searching for something familiar.

'This must be it,' she said, 'but I still don't see anything.'

The sound of another small plane approaching from the east became audible and Tracy turned. 'Drive until it's right over us,' she said.

I stepped on the gas keeping an eye on the descending plane until it appeared to be coming directly at us. It passed over so low I could see the pilot's face tense as the wings wobbled in an updraft.

'Is this the place?' I said, turning to Tracy.

Her eyes were fixed on a small stucco building to my left. The windows were covered with paper on the inside. The faded letters on the building's façade above the door were barely visible.

'Electrical — '

'Supply,' Tracy said.

She stared at the building and its faded red door.

'You remember?' I asked.

Tracy nodded, her eyes focused on it like it was a living, breathing thing.

'Yes, this is it,' she said with dread.

There was an empty fenced yard overgrown with weeds and trash to the right of the building.

The structure to the left was a shell of a storefront gutted by fire.

'Why would Sophie meet Lester here?' Tracy said. 'Why would she know about something out of the past like this? How could it possibly mean anything?'

'If Lester was right, perhaps it's not just a part of the past,' I said.

I reached into my pocket and removed Sexton's key ring with the unidentified keys on it. Tracy looked down at it as if her dead husband had just walked back into her life.

'You can wait here if you want,' I said.

Tracy looked over to the building for a moment, then opened the door and stepped out. 'I'm finished being frightened by him.'

I followed her across the street to where she stopped a few feet from the door. The pavement was cracked and full of weeds; bits of trash, scraps of plastic and paper and various menus from takeout restaurants littered the doorway.

I walked over to the front window and tried to look through a hole in the paper covering the inside.

It was too dark to see anything so I stepped over to the door.

'Which were the keys you didn't recognize?' I held them up for her to examine.

'The ones on the right,' she said. 'The others are for the gallery.'

I took the first key and tried it but it didn't fit. The second key slipped easily into place. I turned it and the lock's deadbolt fell open with a soft click.

'More secrets,' Tracy whispered to herself.

I pushed on the door but it stuck and then I leaned into it with my shoulder and it swung open. The light streaming in revealed a small empty room and another door leading further into the building. The plasterboard wall had been painted white. A large photograph of the sun setting over the Santa Monica Pier and its Ferris wheel hung on the wall to the left of the door.

'Do you remember this?' I asked.

Tracy shook her head. 'No, this room wasn't here,' she said.

I stepped up to the next door and tested the handle, it turned and I pushed the door open. A faint chemical odor drifted out from the darkness of the next room.

'What is that smell?' Tracy asked.

'I don't know.'

We looked through the open door into the darkness for a moment.

'He used to have a dark room here,' she said.

'People don't use dark rooms any more,' I said.

I stepped through the door, ran my hand over the wall until I found a light switch, and turned it on. Several bare fluorescent lights began flickering to life, lighting the room like a passing thunderstorm. One of the bulbs engaged and began to illuminate the room with a soft glow as the other lights continued to flicker.

'What is that?' Tracy asked.

'It's not a darkroom,' I said.

Two large folding tables were pushed against

two of the walls; on the other wall was a sink. The tables were covered with various sizes of glass beakers and bottles, a scale and some stainless-steel cooking pots. Everything was a mess, as if it had been shaken up by a small temblor. A propane tank sat on the floor with its hose connected to a burner sitting on one of the tables.

I stepped over to one of them; on the floor underneath it were several large brown bottles. I recognized the label on one of them.

'Acetone,' I said.

'Why is that familiar?' Tracy said.

'It's a meth lab,' I said.

Tracy looked around and at the mess. 'It's true, then.'

I nodded.

'You had no idea?' I asked.

'No — ' She stopped herself. 'That's not true.'

'Drugs?' I asked.

Tracy nodded.

'I saw him sometimes with people I didn't know. There would be telephone calls and meetings at strange hours. He always seemed to have a lot of cash. I didn't dare confront him about it, I was afraid. I thought it was something he did to keep the gallery open, but this is more than that.'

She took another look and shook her head.

'This isn't what Joan had said Lester was looking for,' Tracy said and then her eyes fell on another door at the back of the room as another plane passed low overhead. 'If I remember, the studio was towards the back of the building.'

251

I crossed the room to the last door and tested the handle — it was locked. I took the key ring out and tried the second key that Tracy didn't recognize. The lock clicked open and I gave the door a push. I stepped inside and turned on a light. Tracy hesitated a few feet from the door. The room was double the size of the others. The sharp residue of fire hung in the air.

'Something's been burned in here, and recently,' I said.

'What is that?' she said, pointing across the room.

At the far end of the space were three false walls of what looked like a cheap movie set. Several lights were set on stands in front of the open end of the room. A tripod stood at the front of the room without a camera.

I walked over to the open end of the room where I had a clear view inside the false walls.

'A bedroom set.'

There was a mattress on a box spring with dark brown stains of dried blood across it in various places. Leather restraints were secured to the floor through metal loops driven into the concrete. The walls had been painted black and were marked with glow-in-the-dark graffiti in what looked like the obscene writing from inside a truck stop restroom. I fought off a physical urge to be sick.

'I was wrong,' I said. 'This isn't a bedroom. It's a nightmare.'

'Oh, my God,' Tracy said, her voice cracking.

Tracy cautiously walked over and stood a few inches behind me staring at the scene in front of us, imagining, I suppose, things that no parent should ever contemplate. She stared for a moment more then turned away and looked off into the empty portions of the rest of the building.

She began to hyperventilate, her breaths becoming shorter and shorter as she tried to get air into her lungs. I walked over and put my hands on her shoulders.

'This is . . . oh my God,' she said, barely able to form words.

'Take a breath and hold it in, then do it again,' I said gently.

Gradually she regained control of her breathing, but the horror I saw in her eyes didn't go away with a deep breath.

'When he first took pictures of me it was nothing like this. He called them figure studies. There wasn't anything ugly about them. I was nineteen with a baby. He made me feel beautiful again, that I mattered.' Tracy shook her head. 'Oh, God . . . is that how he got the girls he used to come here? Made them feel special, to be perfect for a moment in a world that has never been anything but imperfect for them. And when they trusted him because for the first time they think they have worth, and would do anything for him, he would bring them here, and destroy it all.'

Her hands were trembling.

'Tell me Charlotte wasn't one of them,' she whispered.

'There's no evidence that she was,' I said.

'Was this what she was running from?'

'If Charlotte was running from this, she would have done it when he was alive, not dead.'

'Maybe she ran because she couldn't face me finding out about this.'

Tracy turned and walked to the other side of the studio where several filing cabinets that had been lined up against the wall had been tipped over onto the floor. I walked over. The cabinets were charred and smelled of burned paper and plastic.

'These were burned,' Tracy said.

On the floor a few feet away was a can of charcoal lighter.

'Recently,' I said.

'How do you know that?'

'I've been around enough burned cars, the strong odor you're smelling only lasts for few days, it gets duller with time. Whoever did it used the lighter fluid because they wanted to contain the fire just to the files. If they had done it with gasoline the whole building would have gone up.'

'What are they?' Tracy said.

I kneeled down, wiped the soot off the front of one of the drawers. On the front was written 'Stills'.

'Photographs. He kept pictures in this.'

As if in reflex Tracy took a step back away from it. I reached over and wiped off some soot from a drawer on the other cabinet. The writing was just visible.

'This one had videos in it.'

I pulled open the drawer, inside were dozens of DVD cases, burned and melted into unusable globs of plastic. I pulled open another drawer and it was just the same, the DVDs had all been destroyed or least appeared to have all been ruined. I reached inside and removed one that had been heavily burned on one half, the other remaining intact. Some writing was still partially visible.

'What's it say?' asked Tracy.

'It says 'Amber', I can't read the rest.'

A visible chill ran through Tracy and she tightly crossed her arms across her chest and held onto herself.

'Someone's daughter,' she said.

I moved over to the cabinet marked stills and pulled open the drawer. The remnants of brown envelopes were scattered inside along with bits and pieces of photographs that hadn't burned completely. I reached in and removed a corner of a picture that had remained intact. All that remained of the photograph was a bare ankle and foot. There was red nail polish on the toes. The fingers of a hand grasping the leg were just visible where the photograph had been burned away. It wasn't a girl's hand.

'What is it?' Tracy asked.

Until that moment the reality of a young girl living and dreaming in this world had remained abstract at best. Not even Anna's battered psyche painted as complete a picture. But in one fragment of one ugly little photograph it all came flooding in. In that instant I knew the fear and panic that had been strangling Tracy's heart.

I crushed the fragment of the picture in my fist and put it back in the drawer.

'Nothing, it's been destroyed,' I said.

I pushed the drawer shut and looked around the rest of the room. There was another door at the back of the building. I walked over to it. It was locked; nothing about it suggested that there had been a break-in.

'You think Sophie did this?' Tracy asked.

I walked back from the door and looked around again. I felt like I was standing inside an open wound.

'If Charlotte — ' she started to say.

'Don't do that to yourself,' I said.

Tracy looked around for another moment; she seemed on the verge of coming apart.

'This whole thing should be burned, nothing left,' she said. She walked over to the can of lighter fluid and picked it up. 'We have to destroy this, all of it!'

I rushed over and grabbed the can out of her hand and put it down, then took hold of her shoulders.

'If there are other girls who are missing, there could be something here that might help,' I said.

Tracy shook her head. 'There's nothing here that can help anyone,' she said angrily.

'I'll light the match myself when this is over,' I said. 'We need to be smart.'

'For Charlotte,' Tracy said, the rage slipping from her voice.

'Yes.'

Tracy shook her head, as this nightmare appeared to be on the verge of sweeping her away. 'I have to get out of here.'

'I'll look around a little more,' I said.

Tracy turned and rushed out. I surveyed the room, trying to do exactly what I had done countless times at accident scenes, understand what wasn't visually obvious. But there was no sudden turn of a wheel or uncontrolled acceleration hidden within the walls of this place. There was only the twisted residue of a cruel man left behind in bits of melted plastic and charred paper.

Tracy could be right about who had struck the match. If what we knew about Sophie from April was accurate, perhaps what had taken place here was an attempt at justice for Sexton's victims. Perhaps she had been here with Charlotte and together they had set fire to a past that deserved to be turned to ashes.

Or maybe this is what Lester had meant by not wanting the wrong person to get hurt. By burning the files he had protected every one of the girls who had stepped into this room, not knowing that the monster who had made them feel special was about to turn on them.

I looked around one last time at the set where Sexton had played out his twisted world but there was nothing else to see. Everything one needed to understand about him was right there, only the pain he caused would remain in the shadows of damaged spirits and violated bodies.

As I turned to leave the sound of another plane making its approach rose outside. I closed the door on the studio and started to step into the meth lab when I heard the other sound, just hidden in the roar of the plane's engine — a cry of pain was coming from the next room.

I started rushing for the other room as the plane began its pass directly overhead.

'I don't know,' Tracy said.

The plane's throttle revved and the sound rose.

'I don't know!' Tracy repeated.

She must have been nearly yelling for me to hear it. What didn't she know, what had happened to her daughter or why, why any of it? There was no shortage of questions. Or had it all just finally become too much?

'I don't know anything,' she pleaded.

Her voice was higher than normal, like someone pleading for help as they clung to a ledge. I reached for the door leading out of the meth lab as the plane's sound began to fade.

'Where's my money?' said another voice from the other room.

I froze where I stood.

'I told you, I don't know anything about money,' Tracy yelled again.

'Liar.'

'I'm not lying.'

I slowly turned the handle on the door and opened it just enough to look through as the sound of the plane fell away completely.

'Where's my fucking money?'

'Please — '

A figure was holding Tracy against the wall by her throat. He had long black hair that seemed to lie on his head like pieces of string. I could see a tattoo of a snake on the arm that held Tracy's throat. The handle of a knife was visible sticking out of his back pocket. He wore a black leather

258

vest over a white T-shirt and heavy black biker boots.

'You're his bitch. He told me about you. Showed me some old picture of you — you're pretty sweet.'

Tracy shook her head.

'I'm nobody's bitch,' she said, gritting her teeth as his hand tightened around her throat.

A sound like a laugh came out of him.

'We'll see.'

He reached up with his other hand and placed it on her chest.

'Where's my fucking money?'

I stepped back from the door and looked around the meth lab for something to use as a weapon. What do you use? I've never even been in a fight, not even in junior high school. And once you have a weapon in your hand, what do you do with it? And how? My mind started flying with the possibilities, the sounds; how it could all go wrong. What do you do?

Tracy cried out, 'Don't!'

I looked at the bottles of chemicals. I could throw one in his face, but it could hit Tracy, and even if I missed her, what would any of them do to him?

'I want my fucking money,' he repeated.

I looked across the room trying to imagine what, out of all the things I was seeing, could be used as a weapon.

'Where's the girl and her boyfriend!' he yelled.

'I don't know — '

'Sophie! Where is she?'

She gasped for breath. I quickly crossed the

259

room and picked up a large metal cooking pot by the handle and started back towards the door.

'I don't — ' Tracy yelled.

'Don't you fucking lie, where is she?'

I reached the door and looked through the opening. The front of Tracy's shirt had been torn open. His hand was moving inside over her chest. I pushed the door slowly open and Tracy's eyes found me as I stepped into the room, then they looked down at the pot in my hand.

'I'll give you everything you want,' Tracy said.

'Fucking right you will.'

He reached down and began pulling at Tracy's pants. My hand tightened around the handle of the pot and I halved the distance across the room, my eyes focused on Tracy.

I took another step and then another. I glanced down at the pot in my hand. *What do I do with it? Swing it; swing it as hard as you can. Where?* I looked at the back of his head, took two more steps. *Right there, behind the ear, above his neck.* I raised my hand, but I couldn't feel the pot any more, was I still holding it? *Don't look away; focus on the back of his head. Swing it, as hard as you can, but what if I dropped it and I didn't know it?*

I hesitated, looked at Tracy's eyes. I felt the pot in my hand again, but it was too heavy now, how did it get this heavy, how could I swing it? I could barely hold on to it.

Tracy nodded.

Look back at his head, don't look at anything else, focus on one spot, and take one more step and then swing it.

I took the step.

'Yes,' Tracy said.

'What?' the man said.

'Do it.'

The man started laughing.

'Do it,' said Tracy.

I lifted the pot.

'Now!' Tracy yelled.

The man hesitated for a second, then in a blur of motion, his left hand reached back and slid the knife out of his back pocket.

'Do it!' Tracy yelled.

The silver knife blade caught the light like a grill of a car reflecting a headlight. He started to turn and raise the knife as I swung the pot as hard as I could.

'Son of a bitch — ' he started to say as the pot hit the side of his head with a dull hollow thud.

He reeled back with a look of surprise on his face, staggered for a moment then dropped to one knee.

'Fuck!' he said.

A bright crimson red rose in his ear like a flower opening and he reached up to it with his free hand and touched the blood.

'Fuck,' he said again.

He raised the knife jabbing it wildly through the air, then his eyes seemed to focus on me and he smiled.

'You're dead,' he said.

In an instant he sprang forward, coming at me with the knife, swinging it wildly. I stepped to my right as the blade sliced through the air and I swung the pot again, striking him in the face with a sharp crack like a piece of china breaking. He seemed to freeze in mid-stride for a moment as if suspended in time, neither standing nor falling, then he stumbled forward onto his knees and shook his head.

'No!' he yelled as I stepped around behind him.

He pushed himself back to his feet and began to raise the knife.

'What the fuck happened?' he said, then started to turn.

I swung again. The pot hit the back of his head and reverberated in my hand. He stiffened up like a jolt of electricity had coursed through his body, then the knife slipped from his hand and fell to the floor, then he collapsed liked a puppet whose strings had been cut.

The only sound I heard in the room was the drum-like beating of my heart. I don't know how much time passed — a few seconds, perhaps more. I looked at my hand holding the pot, the knuckles were as white as chalk. I couldn't feel my fingers or the handle I was gripping. My stomach began to turn and I fought off the urge to be sick.

I looked down at the man spread out face down on the floor. His ear was now swollen and bright red with blood. His chest rose with a shallow breath. I lifted the pot and stared at it for a moment, then I let it slip from my fingers and fall to the floor, hitting it with the same empty, dull thud as when I had used it on his head.

I stood over the man for a moment, watching the shallow rise of his chest, then I stepped around him and kicked the knife across the room and turned to Tracy.

She was standing against the wall where he had pinned her, her eyes staring at his motionless body on the floor. Her shirt was torn open; her pants had been partly pulled down. I stepped over to her.

'Are you all right?' I asked.

If she heard me she gave no indication.

'Tracy?' I said.

She still didn't react. I reached out and took hold of her hand. 'Are you all right?' I asked again.

She turned and looked at me, staring past me for a moment.

'I'm fine.'

'Let me help you here.'

She shook her head. 'Help?'

I reached down and carefully pulled her jeans back up to her waist as she looked at the man on the floor.

'Let me get this too,' I said, and buttoned a couple of buttons on her shirt that hadn't been torn off.

'I'm all right,' she repeated, seeming to take no notice of what I had done.

She stepped around me and walked over to the man spread out on the floor.

'Is he dead?' she asked.

'No.'

She stared at him for a moment longer, then looked over to the pot on the floor, reached down and picked it up.

'I'm nobody's bitch, do you hear me!'

Tracy lifted up the pan and started to swing it down towards his head. I rushed over and pulled her back as she began to bring it down. Tracy wrestled away and glared at me.

'What are you doing?' she demanded.

Her hand tightened around the handle as if it was the only thing keeping her on her feet.

'You don't want to do that,' I said.

'You don't know what I want.'

'I know you don't want to know what it feels like to do what I just did. And it won't bring us closer to Charlotte.'

At the sound of her daughter's name, Tracy immediately appeared to return from the abyss the man on the floor had taken her to. She stood there for a moment then looked down at the pot in her hand as if seeing it for the first time.

'I don't know what I . . . ' Her words slipped away.

'I know,' I said.

She flung the pot aside, then looked down at her torn shirt and tried to piece it back together.

'I think I lost some buttons,' she said, then looked at me.

'You saved me again.'

'And I didn't even have to wreck a car to do it.'

She tried to smile, though couldn't really manage it, then she looked over to the man on the floor. 'Who is he?' she asked.

'I think he's the business partner of your husband Delgado told me about.'

The sound of another plane began to make its approach.

'I want to get out of here,' Tracy said.

I looked down at the snake tattoo that wound around his arm and then over to the knife across the room. The man began to groan as he began to ease back towards consciousness.

'Now!' Tracy said.

We ran to the car and started to drive away. With each passing block the sound of the pan hitting the man's head became louder — a dull metallic thud as it hit flesh and bone.

When it became too loud I pulled over and stopped next to a 7-Eleven. We didn't say anything for a moment, just sat in the same kind of silence that exists the instant after an accident where your mind tries to catch up with reality. I had never been in a fight in my life, not even a wrestling match during recess.

I took out the card Delgado had given me and then started to text her the location of the warehouse.

'What are you doing?'

'She's trying to help,' I said.

'How do you know that, because she told you?'

'We have to trust someone.'

'She's a cop, and my daughter's a black teenager; you're being naive.' She reached out and took hold of my hand holding the phone. 'I trust you,' she said and looked into my eyes. 'That's enough.'

Was it? It didn't feel like it. I put the phone back in my pocket.

'I don't know the person who did what I did back there,' I said.

Tracy looked over to me. 'I do, it's the second time he saved me.'

'My one natural skill.'

The sound of the pot hitting his head finally began to slip away. My heart rate slowed. We sat for a moment, trying to understand what we had seen and what had happened.

'He said Sophie,' Tracy said.

'And her boyfriend. That must be Tyler.'

'The one who hit you at the club.'

'Do you have any idea what money he was talking about?' I asked.

She shook her head. 'Why would Sophie have Derek's money?' The answer was on her lips even before she had finished asking the question. Tracy looked over to me and I could see the worry in her eyes. 'Sophie and Tyler . . . they killed Derek. They went to his apartment — ' She hesitated as if by not speaking it wouldn't be true. 'Charlotte is somehow involved, isn't she? It's why she ran.'

It was the only answer that made sense. I nodded.

'It's why they warned you to stay away at the Echo,' Tracy said.

I was rapidly running out of ways to avoid saying she was right.

'The wrong person,' Tracy whispered. 'Was Lester talking about Charlotte?'

'It's possible.'

Tracy looked over to the 7-Eleven where a teenage boy and girl walked out holding hands, moving together as if in a slow dance. She watched them for a moment in silence.

266

'We missed all that,' she said.

'What?'

'Being normal kids. In one night we grew up and everything slipped through our fingers.'

She shook her head and took a deep breath. 'I thought I could protect my daughter from the things that go wrong. I should have known better.' She fell into silence and watched the two kids walk away holding hands. 'You know why I said yes to you at the line in the cafeteria?' Tracy asked, her voice filled with melancholy.

'My natural grace with lasagna.'

She turned and looked at me.

'I said yes because when you looked at me, you were the first boy whose eyes weren't hiding anything. It was all there to see, your panic, fear — everything your heart was trying to contain without bursting,' Tracy said. 'And it's all still there.'

I put the car back in gear and began to drive on.

'That was a long time ago.'

28

I thought I had known something about the dark corners of this world that most people spend their lives trying to avoid. But the glimpses I have had of it in the aftermath of road rage and booze-fueled smash-ups did little to illuminate how dark those corners of the world really could be. I had seen what a ton of colliding steel could do to the human body, how the results could be so unrecognizable that they no longer seemed to belong to this world, so not even Lester's battered body had fully shined a light into this black hole.

What I had not witnessed was the kind of ugliness contained within three walls of plywood and a fragment of a burned picture of a young girl's ankle. There was no forensic engineering to explain this. No measure of physics to understand how and why it had happened.

It was like holding a mirror up to the world, but instead of reflecting only that which is visible, it had also shown what was not, but always there just the same, hidden in a twisted mind that masquerades as a neighbor, or husband, or the person you pass on the street whose face seems designed for slipping through every day in anonymity.

And now that mirror even held my reflection in it. With the first swing of the pan that hit the side of his head I had stepped into that world and with each blow to follow I stepped even further. I knew the face of violence now. It was no longer only to be found in the folds of bloodstained sheets. I knew how it sounded. How it felt in your hand and how it sank to the pit of your stomach where there was no getting rid of it and its memory.

For the first time I had fully stepped into the world that before had only existed in the grainy image of a surveillance video where Charlotte looks back over her shoulder towards the life she was leaving behind.

Tracy already knew this world, had known it from the first day her husband had put his hands around her neck. But I was there with her now, and knew what I hadn't before, that even when it was over, I would never leave it behind; it would always be there over my shoulder, whispering to me a warning not to stray from the light again.

29

When we pulled up to the outside of Tracy's small bungalow to retrieve some fresh clothes and whatever else she needed, she didn't immediately rush inside in the hope that Charlotte had miraculously returned while we had been away. I suppose she had done that when Charlotte first vanished, but she was beyond that now.

Hope had been replaced by a determination to see the small details which, if seen before Charlotte had run, perhaps would have told of what was about to happen.

'You can't stay here,' I said. 'We'll get your things, you can stay with me.'

Her eyes moved slowly over the walk up to the front door, then over each window; every corner of the house and yard was subject to examination.

As I opened the door Tracy shook her head. 'Wait,' she said and I stopped.

Her gaze was focused on a window along the side of the house.

'Something's different,' she said.

I looked over the house, but didn't see anything.

'What is it?' I asked.

'Someone's been here.'

I didn't notice anything to suggest that she was right.

'Look at the window on the side,' she said.

It was barely noticeable, but it was there just the same, a faint reflection on the glass of the window.

'There's a light on inside,' I said.

'Yes,' she answered, her eyes not leaving the window.

'Could you have left it on?' I asked.

Tracy shook her head.

'No, you don't leave lights on when you have a teenager obsessed with global warming.'

I stared at the faint glow on the glass of the window. 'Maybe he came here before the warehouse.'

'Charlotte,' Tracy whispered.

'Charlotte is only one possibility.'

Tracy shook her head. 'No, it's Charlotte,' she repeated.

Her hand grabbed the door handle and before I could stop her she was out of the car and running towards the front door. I jumped out and followed, reaching her just as she pushed open the front door.

'Charlotte!' Tracy called out.

There was only silence inside the house.

'Charlotte?'

I reached out and gently took hold of Tracy's arm as she stared at the glow spilling out into the living room from the light that was on back in the kitchen.

'Wait,' I said.

I crossed the room to the entrance of the small dining area that led to the kitchen. There was nothing out of place. No sound coming from the source of the light, no movement, so I stepped over to the open door to the kitchen.

Tracy eased up behind me the way you might step up to the edge of a cliff that made you nervous.

'Do you notice anything?' I asked.

Tracy looked around for a moment.

'No, but something's not right.'

I started to nod, then stopped. Across the room on the counter by the back door was a can of Coke.

'Do you drink Coke?' I asked. I motioned towards the can of Coke. 'Did you drink that?'

Tracy stared at it for a moment.

'I don't remember.'

I stepped across the room to the counter, reached out and started to pick up the can, then released it.

'We need to check the rest of the house,' I said and turned to Tracy.

'What?' asked Tracy.

'It's still cool.'

Tracy turned and looked towards the hallway that led to the bedrooms.

'She was here?' Tracy said.

I stepped over to her.

'We don't know that.'

'Then who?' Tracy said.

I shook my head and put a finger to my lips. 'Someone could still be here.'

I stared down the dark hallway towards the bedrooms then glanced over to the stove where a heavy cast-iron pan sat.

'No, it's Charlotte,' Tracy said.

I turned as she rushed down the hallway.

'Charlotte, is it you?' she yelled.

I ran into the hallway after her leaving the pan sitting on the stove. Before I could reach her, Tracy pushed open the door to the bedroom and stepped inside. She was standing there frozen as I reached the door and stepped around her. The room was empty.

'I was sure she was here,' Tracy said dejectedly.

I glanced quickly over the room. The only things out of order were several drawers of a chest that were partially opened.

'Were these open?' I said and walked over to the chest against the wall.

Tracy stared at it for a moment.

'No.'

'Why would anyone look in these?'

'There's nothing in those except her clothes,' Tracy said.

'You're sure nothing was hidden here?'

'Yes.'

'How would you know that?'

'After she vanished I needed to keep myself occupied. I did all of her laundry, folded it and put it away myself; there was nothing in these but . . . '

Tracy came over to the chest and as she looked into the drawers she clenched her fists into tight balls.

'Oh, my God. It was her, clothes are gone.'

'You're sure?'

Tracy's eyes welled up with tears.

She reached into the drawer and began to go over the clothes inside, then went through another drawer and another.

'She's taken things,' Tracy said.

'How many?'

'I'm not sure — three, maybe four, changes.'

Tracy stopped going through the drawer, staring at its contents, then turned and rushed over to the closet, opened it and began to go through the shirts on the hangers.

'This is all wrong,' she said.

I stepped over to the closet.

'What's wrong?'

'It wasn't her,' she said.

I shook my head. 'How do you know?' I asked.

'The clothes are gone, but they're the wrong ones.'

I still didn't follow. Tracy rushed back to the chest of drawers and began pulling out the shirts inside.

'They're not here, it wasn't her,' she said and wiped a tear away.

'What aren't here?'

Tracy took a deep breath to slow herself down.

'You've never lived with a teenager, so you wouldn't understand this.'

'Explain it.'

'I gave her two shirts for Christmas. They're gone.'

'And that means what?'

'She was so embarrassed by them, she's only ever worn them inside the house to make me feel better about getting them. She would even take them off to talk on the phone.'

'And they're both gone,' I said.

Tracy nodded. 'Charlotte wouldn't have taken

274

them. Someone else did. Sophie?'

'Perhaps.'

Tracy took another look around the room.

'Why didn't she come herself?' She shook her head and answered her own question. 'Oh, God — she didn't want to see me.' She looked over to Charlotte's computer. 'Maybe she — '

Tracy rushed to Charlotte's computer and logged on to her Facebook page. There were more than a dozen new posts, friends asking for her to come home or call them, but there was nothing from Charlotte.

Tracy read them all over again to be certain that she hadn't missed anything, but nothing changed.

'Nothing,' she whispered, 'I thought perhaps with the clothes . . . '

My phone rang and I slipped it out. It was a text with a picture attached to it from Delgado. 'Is this the one who hit you at the club?'

I opened the picture. It had been taken outside the Echo as April and I were about to go inside. Several feet away in the crowd a face was focused on us. It wouldn't have been noticeable if the picture hadn't been enlarged. The image had softened from zooming, but his features were just clear enough to see. His hair was short, light brown or sandy blond. He had the thick shoulders and neck of an athlete.

What was striking was the mask of intensity that was his face. It was strangely young and old at the same time. His eyes appeared to be seeing through us like a weapon. Was this the voice that had whispered in my ear?

Don't fuck with this any more.

'What is it?' Tracy asked.

'Delgado.'

She immediately began to react. 'Don't — '

'Have you ever seen him?' I said, holding out the phone for Tracy to see.

She started to shake her head.

'Just look,' I said.

Tracy reluctantly stared at it for a moment.

'Is it him?' she asked.

'I don't know.'

Tracy looked at the picture, then started to turn away out of the expectation of disappointment, but then she stopped.

'You've seen him?' I asked.

Tracy continued to stare at the face. She rushed back to Charlotte's computer and her Facebook page.

'When Charlotte disappeared I went through everything, again and again, thinking I was missing something, all the posts, the pictures. I might have seen him in one of her photo albums.'

Tracy began going through her daughter's picture albums. School . . . Fun . . . Friends . . . It was a travelogue of a teenager's life. As interchangeable with any other teen except for the small detail that Charlotte had vanished and people were dead. With each passing picture the normalness of it all seemed to focus Tracy's pain even more. One after another, album after album, the photographs passed by like bits of memory. The hope in Tracy that perhaps she had recognized the face began to slip away until she stopped on a photograph.

She took a breath. 'I don't know,' she said.

It was a picture from a party taken with a flash at night. Charlotte was standing with a group of four other kids mugging for the camera. To her left I recognized Hunter, the boy I had met at the Thai restaurant.

I looked again at the picture Delgado had sent, then back at the face next to Charlotte. Were they the same? I couldn't tell.

'Is that him?' I asked.

Tracy just stared at the boy on Charlotte's right with the Cheshire cat grin.

30

There were almost a thousand students in Charlotte's grade at school; if the face in the picture was one of them we couldn't find it in her yearbook. Perhaps it was nothing more than the kind of smile you couldn't turn away from. It was infectious and unnerving at the same time. It was as if he knew that at any moment he could slip away down the rabbit hole just out of frame of the picture the way Charlotte had. Or was that what we saw lurking just out of sight in every teenager? Was the real mystery they held, the youth that we had lost and now belonged to them? But was it him?

Tracy texted Hunter and he agreed to meet us when school let out.

We took Charlotte's laptop and enough clothes for Tracy until it would be safe for her to return home, then I drove us to the school. The campus was a sprawling complex of buildings and temporary structures that had grown like weeds in an attempt to keep up with the exploding population.

Hunter was standing by a gate near one of the entrances to the athletic fields when we pulled up. Given the choice of location he had picked he clearly didn't want any of his or Charlotte's friends to know that he was meeting us. He glanced quickly around then slipped into the back seat.

'Have you found her?' he asked.

'No,' Tracy said.

His eyes found the bruise on my cheek from the club. He wanted to ask about it, but didn't.

'We need you to look at a picture,' I said, opening up the laptop.

He started to shake his head.

'I don't want to get anyone in trouble.'

'They already are,' I said and held out the computer with the picture.

'Who's the kid on the left?' I asked.

His eyes again found my face.

'What happened to you?' he asked.

'Please,' Tracy said. 'Do you know him?'

He looked at the picture and quickly shook his head.

'No.'

Tracy's shoulders slumped.

'That is you with Charlotte,' I said.

He nodded.

'Take another look,' I said.

He did and still shook his head.

'It was just a party, I didn't know most of the people there. Everybody is always taking pics.'

'Charlotte put it on her Facebook page. Did she know him?'

'I don't know, everyone posts everything, you don't even think about it.'

If he was lying, he was better at it than any of the other kids we had talked to. He took one more look and again shook his head.

'Why didn't you know most of the kids at the party?' I asked.

'It was at a party house, most of the kids were

from a few different schools.'

'A party house?'

'Big place that rents out.'

'Which schools?'

'I don't know, maybe April knows, she took the pic.'

I started to take out my phone.

'She isn't in school. I texted her but she didn't answer. She always answers texts.'

He looked at my face again, more with concern than curiosity.

'April said she was meeting you last night. Did something happen?'

'Yeah, something.'

He thought for a moment, then started to reach for the door, but stopped.

'He was a baseball player, I remember that.'

'Anything else?'

'No, just that.'

Hunter then got out of the car and quickly walked away into the steady stream of kids now leaving the school.

'In the club last night, April was angry about something, she said I had lied to her,' I said.

'Lied?' Tracy asked, as if the meaning of the word was confusing to her. 'About what?'

'I don't know.'

31

April lived a few miles south of the school just off Laurel Canyon. Most of the houses on the block had long ago been torn down and replaced by apartment buildings. The few homes that remained had the appearance of besieged holdouts clinging to a life that was already gone.

April's Honda was parked on the street outside a Tudor-style apartment building, which was next to a Mediterranean-style complex which was adjacent to a building with no style at all.

According to Tracy, April lived with her mother who was a secretary at Warner Brothers in Burbank. We parked and I started to get out but Tracy hesitated, still staring at the photo on her daughter's computer.

'At the club, why would she say you lied to her unless you know something or she thinks you do?' Tracy asked.

I shook my head.

'You know everything I do,' I said, which was at best half true.

Tracy's eyes were beginning to fill with tension.

'What is she talking about?' she said then looked at me nervously. 'What does she think you know?'

'You can ask her,' I said.

Tracy stared at the computer screen for a

281

moment then shut it.

'Maybe it was nothing. She was probably just scared,' Tracy said.

Maybe, but I doubted it.

'Probably,' I answered.

Next to the entrance was a large coat of arms, 'The Radford Arms', no doubt put there in the hope of enticing wayward Saxons to this home away from home. That seventy-five per cent of the residents were brown, yellow or some color in between would have come as a great surprise to the builders. You had to be buzzed through to get through the front door and into the lobby. April and her mother lived in apartment 209.

'She told me to leave her alone. Don't tell her I'm with you,' I said as Tracy pressed the intercom button.

April answered almost immediately, as if she were waiting for someone to walk through the door.

'It's Mrs Sexton,' Tracy said. 'I need to talk to you.'

April hesitated.

'About what?'

'Please,' Tracy responded.

'Are you alone?' she asked.

Tracy looked over to me.

'Yes,' she said with such certainty that I almost believed her.

The intercom fell silent for a moment then the door buzzed and we walked through. The building consisted of four wings built around a central courtyard with what appeared to be an English rose garden planted in the center.

We took the stairs up to the apartment and rang the bell, Tracy standing in front of the peephole as I remained out of sight. A moment later the door opened. April took a half-step out and her eyes fell on me before the door was fully open.

'Fucking great,' she said.

'Please, I need to show you something,' Tracy said.

April stood blocking the door for a moment then shook her head and walked back into the apartment. We followed her in to the living room where she took a seat on an overstuffed chair and we sat on the couch. For all of April's hipness and piercings the inside of the apartment could have been a set for a middle-class sitcom.

'What do you want?' she asked.

Tracy set the computer on the coffee table.

'That's Charlotte's laptop,' April said.

Tracy nodded and opened it up.

'Who is this?' Tracy said, motioning towards the picture on the screen.

April's eyes fell on it and then looked too quickly back to us.

'I don't know.'

'You took the picture,' I said.

'Did I? I don't remember.'

'You're lying,' I said.

Her face flushed.

'You would be the expert,' she said angrily.

'Is that Tyler?' Tracy asked.

April said nothing. I took my phone out and pulled up the photograph from the Echo and handed it to April.

'That was him at the club last night, wasn't it?'
I said.

She barely looked at it.

'If you say so.'

'What did he say to you last night?' I asked.

'Like you don't know,' April said.

'No, I don't. Why are you protecting him?'

'This isn't about him,' she responded.

'What is it about?'

She glanced at Tracy and shook her head.

'Why did you do this?' she said.

The reaction in Tracy's eyes gave me the impression she knew what April was talking about.

'I think we should go,' Tracy said and started to get up.

'You're protecting Charlotte?' I asked.

April got up from the chair.

'From what?'

'You should leave,' she said.

'From what?' I repeated.

'Lies!' April said.

'Let's go,' Tracy said.

April started to walk towards another room and I got up and blocked her way.

'What are you protecting Charlotte from?'

'Get out!' April yelled.

'Come on,' said Tracy.

'What are you protecting her from!' I said back.

'Her father!' April shouted.

'I'm leaving now,' Tracy said.

'Her father's dead,' I said.

April's eyes focused on me like two daggers.

'You!' she yelled. 'I'm protecting her from you!'

All the air in the room seemed to vanish. There wasn't a sound beyond her words, which had the presence of another person standing silently in the corner in shadow.

I looked over to Tracy and she looked away. She was trembling.

I'm protecting her from you?

My head began to spin.

'What are you . . . ?'

The scent of eucalyptus filled the air.

'No snappy comeback,' April said.

Run . . . faster . . .

I took a breath.

'Last night, you said you were at the club for Charlotte's birthday, when was that?' I asked.

'You would know,' April said.

'When?' I demanded.

April shook her head in confusion. 'Don't fuck with me,' she said.

I looked over to Tracy. 'When is her birthday?'

Tracy struggled to take a breath and looked away and I turned back to April.

'When?'

'January twenty-second,' April said.

I turned and looked over to Tracy as the edges of my vision began to fill with a bright white light, like advancing headlights.

'Nine months,' I said.

Don't stop . . .

Tracy shook her head.

'Oh, Jesus,' April said in astonishment and looked over to Tracy. 'He didn't know?'

285

My heart began to race out of control. Flashes of images flooded my head — her hand, her neck, her eyes. I was running, barely able to breathe.

Faster . . .

'Why?' I asked.

Tears fell down Tracy's face and she shook her head.

'Why!' I repeated.

She shook with the words. 'You were dead,' she whispered.

The room began to vanish into the white light.

'*Don't sto* — '

I felt myself begin to fall, then the sound of glass shattering filled my head and the light turned to darkness.

32

The room came back into focus slowly like a camera struggling for a point of reference. The faint sound of music was present.

'She said this happens to you.'

I turned my head. April was kneeling on the floor next to me. The faint music I was hearing was coming from her iPod earpieces round her neck.

'She said if you didn't wake up in an hour I should call the paramedics.'

I sat up too quickly and my head felt like it was going to spin right off onto the floor. I looked around the room. Charlotte's computer was no longer on the coffee table.

'Would you like a drink of water or something?' April asked.

I nodded. April got up quickly and walked into the kitchen and returned with a glass of water. I took the cool glass in my hands and held it up to the side of my head, took several deep breaths then looked around the room again.

'She left a while ago,' April said.

'How long?'

'Half an hour maybe, she called a cab, ran out.'

Her eyes drifted over me with the curiosity of a treasure hunter, settling eventually on my head.

'Are you all right?' April asked.

I nodded, carefully.

'She say anything else?' I asked.

'A little.'

'How little?'

'She said you saved her life once . . . and you were in a coma.'

'I don't remember.'

The spinning inside my head began to slow. I reached out my hand and April helped me up and I took a seat on the table. She sat in a chair and stared at me in silence until she couldn't contain her curiosity any longer.

'You really didn't know?' she asked.

The words seemed to snatch the breath right out of me. Was it true? Was that the emptiness I had carried with me since waking from my long sleep? Was I a father?

'No,' I said, barely managing even that.

April tried to get her head around it.

'I don't . . . that's fucked up. How is that possible?'

You were dead.

I thought I knew what it was like to be alone. To peer out from a dark room unable to find the door through which to step back into the light. I was wrong. This room was far darker.

'We went to a dance,' I said. 'Until a few days ago I didn't even remember that . . . I was dead.'

April reached out and gently touched my knee with her fingers then withdrew them. I looked up at her and she smiled in a way that only comes with youth before time and life steals it away.

'You got better,' she said.

'I need your help, April,' I said.

'If I can.'

My phone with the picture from the club was still on the coffee table; I picked it up and looked at the intense eyes in the photograph staring out from the crowd at the club.

'Was he the one sitting next to Charlotte at the party?'

April hesitated for just a moment as she tried to understand if she was violating a trust before deciding it was OK.

'I'm not sure, but I think so.'

'Tyler.'

'That was what he called himself in the club.'

'Was he the one who told you I was Charlotte's father or did you talk to Sophie too?'

She shook her head.

'I didn't see Sophie, it was him.'

'What else did he say?'

She struggled with the answer for a moment. 'Do you really want to know this?' she asked almost protectively.

'Yes.'

She took a breath to steady herself.

'He said you abandoned Charlotte and her mother, and that's why everything happened that did.'

Everything . . .

April shook her head. 'But that's not true,' she said.

'Truth isn't always just one thing,' I said.

'That's not what they teach in school.'

For all of her worldly street knowledge that had taken me on a drive through teenage hell in Hollywood, she now looked every bit a kid.

'There's a connection between what happened to Anna and Charlotte.'

April played it out in her head and I could see the fear rise in her eyes.

'Porn,' she said softly.

'It's far worse than that, there was drugs and violence, and it's connected to her fath — ' I stopped myself. 'Sexton, he was one of them.'

She looked at me in silence, the pace of her breathing picking up.

'Was Charlotte . . . did what happened to Anna . . . ' She didn't want to say the words.

'I don't know,' I answered.

I held up the picture on my phone.

'He and Sophie are involved.'

'Involved in what?' she said nervously.

'If I'm right, Sexton's murder. I need to find him.'

'What about Charlotte? Are you saying — '

'I don't know.'

She started to shake her head in disbelief.

'The party at the house, was that the first time you met him?' I asked.

'Yes.'

'What do you know about him?'

'Nothing, we barely talked, he was interested in Charlotte.'

'Do you know what school he went to?'

'A lot of the kids at the party were from the Woodward School, but I don't know if he was one of them.'

'Did you tell Tracy any of this?'

April shook her head, then glanced nervously at her watch.

'You should go before my mom gets home,' she said apologetically.

'Is there anything else you remember about him, or did Charlotte say anything?'

She started to shake her head. 'She said he was cute.' She shook her head in frustration. 'That's all I know.' She took several shaky breaths. 'It was at that party where we started drifting apart,' she said, her voice filled with sadness.

A tear slipped down her face and she wiped it away. I hadn't seen until that moment, but it was there in April's eyes, a broken heart; she was hopelessly in love with Charlotte.

'Can you find her?' she asked softly.

Find her? Could I? How could I not? I needed to find her as badly as she needed finding. I slowly stood. My knees felt a little weak, my head hurt a bit, but there were no flashing lights and the room wasn't moving. It was the world that had been turned on its head, or, at least, my world.

'I'm sorry about . . . ' April started to say. 'I'm sorry about what happened to you . . . about everything.'

We stood in silence for a time — a shared moment of loss, perhaps, I thought, but when I looked at April's eyes, I knew that even with the innocence of youth, what she carried in those eyes wasn't reconcilable, and I knew just as well that she understood that — mine at least remained a mystery. I stepped over and she looked up at me as more tears formed. I gently kissed April on the top of her forehead.

'I'll find her,' I said.

33

I had hoped to drive away from The Radford Arms with a name to match a picture, perhaps a school, that was all, not this.

You really didn't know.

No.

If she had walked back into my life to tell me, why hadn't she? If she had . . . if . . . if.

How could I not know? I had remembered the dance, the touch of her hand on my neck, the feel of her hair on the side of my face. Isn't there some sort of genetic spark that gets lit up that tells you these things? We're not supposed to be alone.

Or was this how it's meant to work when you're damaged goods? A sort of Darwinian plan that keeps incomplete people in the dark so they don't drive into another intersection and make an even bigger mess of things.

It wasn't that far from April's apartment, so I drove back to where it had begun once again and pulled over and stopped just before the intersection. Were the dreams I had carried all these years about her in fact bits of memory? But from where? What had happened between leaving the dance and the crash?

I didn't stop the engine or get out. There was nothing here, no more secrets, just a few old gouges in some concrete that had nearly disappeared with time.

Whatever had happened between Tracy and me, whatever fantasy had been lived out for a few moments, remained locked away, at least from me. Perhaps Tracy carried it with her — the one true moment in a life filled with secrets? Perhaps not; you live a lie long enough, the fiction can take on the weight of truth.

My phone rang and I took it out. There was a text from Delgado.

Have you found him?

Was Tracy right, should I not trust her? There was that word. Trust. Who might I be betraying if I did?

I started to type in no, but stopped and then typed in the address of Sexton's warehouse instead and then quickly hung up.

It was getting dark as I arrived back at the loft. I looked for Tracy's car where it had appeared that first day, but it wasn't there so I went straight up to the loft.

I stepped inside and flipped on a light. I had forgotten that I had torn the place apart looking for . . . looking for what? Trouble. I shouldn't have bothered; it had found me all on its own. The wreckage of the past had nothing on the present.

Buzz must have been out because no music drifted down from upstairs. I needed a drink and food, but I was too exhausted for either so I lay down and watched night fall over the lights of Little Tokyo and waited for sleep to take hold, but each time it drew close I took out my phone and dialed her number, and each time I hit quit instead of send.

Dance with me . . . the light in the gym reflected off her eyes . . .

I bolted up out of a half-sleep to the sound of a police helicopter flying low overhead. An hour had passed since I had given in to exhaustion, though even in sleep she was there, not quite a memory, but not a dream — a whispering presence on the other side of a dark room.

As the helicopter moved off I heard the other sound at the door — a knock, and then another, and another, the pause getting longer between each one.

I got up and stepped over to the door but instead of opening it, I reached out and placed my hand against it, waiting to feel the knock on the other side. It came like her voice in my head, on the verge of disappearing altogether. Was it Tracy outside the door? I started to call out her name, then stopped. Another knock pressed lightly against my hand.

I leaned into the door waiting for another but it didn't come. There wasn't a sound on the other side. I quickly unlatched the door and pulled it open. She was halfway down the hallway walking away.

'Don't,' I said.

Tracy stopped and turned. We stared at each other in silence for a moment.

'I was afraid to go home,' she said finally. 'I didn't know where to go.'

'Is that why you came here?'

She looked down at the floor and shook her head.

'No.'

For just an instant she appeared as if she might shatter into a thousand pieces.

'I've been trying to tell you . . . every day,' she whispered.

'You should have tried harder.' I paused. 'You had better come in.'

I pushed my door open the rest of the way and stood aside. Tracy hesitated, then walked slowly down the hallway and into my loft. I stepped inside behind her and closed the door. She was looking in wonder and perhaps fear at the wreckage across the floor.

'I re-did the place to look like the inside of my head,' I said. I walked over and put some cushions back on the couch and made a place for her to sit. She walked right past it and over to the window and stared out at the cityscape glowing in the night sky.

'I think we left off where I was dead,' I said.

Tracy's shoulders tensed and she clenched her fists.

'Am I Charlotte's father?' I asked.

Her shoulders sank and she nodded. 'Yes,' she whispered.

We fell into a silence that felt like hands pushing us apart.

'It was an accident,' Tracy finally said softly.

'I have extensive experience with accidents.'

Tracy turned around, looked at me for a moment then slowly sunk to her knees and buried her face in her hands. I walked over and sat down against the wall next to her. Her eyes began to moisten with tears.

'You kissed me as we were finishing the last

dance,' she said and shook her head. 'It was just supposed to be a dance.'

She took a few breaths to steady herself.

'I never planned on liking you so much,' she said.

My heart was beating against my chest. A mixture of confusion and anger was flying around in my head.

'You might have tried telling me.'

'We were kids, you were practically a stranger. When I found out I was pregnant you were still in a coma and months away from leaving the hospital, if you left it at all. Everyone said you were never going to be . . . '

'What?'

She glanced at me, struggling with the words.

'Normal,' I said.

Tracy nodded.

'I was scared,' she whispered.

'I know what scared is,' I said. 'It's lying in a bed, trapped in darkness with a machine doing your breathing.'

A tear slipped down her cheek like a slowly spoken word.

'I kept hoping there would be a way to turn the clock back and make everything right,' Tracy said. 'But it doesn't work that way. It was as if my life had been taken away and I was given another one. It didn't matter what I wanted. So I went away to school, and thought I would never see you again.'

'You never thought to see if I had recovered?' I asked.

'Charlotte was two when I heard you had

come out of the hospital. I put everything into raising her on my own. It was all about her. We had spent a part of one night together that ended terribly; I didn't know how to look back.'

Her dark eyes found mine; they were full of a kind of sadness I had never seen.

'I told Charlotte that her father had dumped me when I told him I was pregnant.'

'She thinks I abandoned her,' I said.

Tracy tried and failed to look at me, then nodded.

My heart sank. I could feel the possibilities slipping away again just as they had once before. If for a brief moment I thought I might step out of the life I had known and into another, I knew now that it wasn't that simple. And as much as I wanted to blame Tracy for keeping the truth from me for all these years, I knew now that that also wasn't so simple.

'Charlotte found your picture in the year book once, asked if I knew you.' She looked away. 'I said no.' Her voice cracked with emotion. 'Why did I do that?'

'You did what you thought you had to do.'

She shook her head. 'No, I did what was easiest.'

Tracy looked at me for a moment.

'She has your eyes, I think she sensed that.'

'The rest of her is you, she's beautiful.'

Her body began to tremble. If she had been made of glass, I think she would have shattered.

'How did she find out?' I said.

Tracy shook her head. I looked over at the files that had been gone through in the break-in. Had

297

she been in this room? Putting the pieces of her past together, filling in the blanks?

'If I lose her, I'm lost,' Tracy said.

I wanted to reach out and take Tracy's hand in mine, but I held back. More tears fell down her cheek. I had been ready to judge her, but she was right, we had been little more than kids, who were strangers. What right did I have to judge? But that didn't change the sense of loss I felt; perhaps it was even stronger because of it.

'I wish I had seen her grow up,' I said softly.

'Oh, God,' she said, her voice cracking again. 'I wish you had too. So much might have been different.'

Her words had an effect that I had never experienced. They seemed to land on my shoulders with a physical weight that I felt in every muscle, every nerve in my body. Whatever I had believed about my life, the things I thought I knew, all the things I didn't, it had all changed in a heartbeat. It was like waking from another coma. It would be so easy to imagine the life that might have been, but it was folly, like trying to touch a shadow.

'You're right, we were just kids who barely knew each other, and you were alone,' I said.

'We both were.'

She leaned her head on my shoulder, took a deep breath. Had the last of Tracy's secrets been revealed? Could I finally trust her completely? I didn't have an answer for that, any more than I understood the feelings let loose inside me. I had long ago accepted the reality that you can't get back the things you lose. That those moments that had slipped away into that gray world, where not even memory travels, were better left unsought because, even if found, you could never touch them or embrace them.

When Tracy had walked back into my life I had let myself begin to believe that I was wrong, that the things you lose were retrievable. I should have known better. But Charlotte wasn't a misplaced moment in time that had drifted away in the wind. She was a living, breathing piece of my own reflection in the mirror. And if I didn't find her, and she, too, slipped into that gray untouchable world, any chance I ever had of finally escaping that intersection would be lost for ever.

★ ★ ★

What little rest I did get was in a chair next to the bed where I watched Tracy try to sleep as she fought off the demons that had invaded her life.

Several times she woke from dreams after calling out Charlotte's name into the darkness, and each time I held her hand until she gave in to exhaustion and drifted off.

Between the nightmares I would try to find the connection I might have missed that would open that door concealing Charlotte, but the harder I pushed the more elusive the answers became and I returned to watching Tracy, listing to the sound of her breathing, waiting for the next dream and the feel of her fingers holding mine as she whispered in the darkness, 'Are you there, Elias?'

34

In the morning we said almost nothing to each other about what had happened the night before. It was as if a door had been opened to another world, but neither of us was ready to walk through it, at least not yet.

The morning after — only without the sex.

It took most of the day and finally a phone call from the principal of Charlotte's school for the officials at the Woodward school to finally agree to meet with us.

The school, tucked in a canyon at the base of the Santa Monica Mountains, had the look of an elite ivy-league campus that had been misplaced in Los Angeles. The grass along the walkways seemed to have been trimmed with scissors. The trees all appeared to have been transplanted from a New England forest. The buildings were made of large blocks of dark stone with vines of ivy winding up its sides and around the windows.

School had just let out when we arrived. The students lingering on the grounds before heading home in their blue blazers with the crest on the pocket or the lacrosse players walking towards the field seemed as out of place in Los Angeles as their surroundings were, or at least the Los Angeles I grew up in. The kids were mostly white or Asian, none were overweight, and they had a look in their eyes that suggested they already were preparing to take over the universe, or at least expected it to be handed to them.

On the insistence of the school officials Charlotte's principal had agreed to sit in on the meeting. Even the suggestion that a student from their school was somehow connected to Charlotte's disappearance had clearly sent shudders through the hallowed halls built to keep the rabble at arm's length. The principals of the two schools were waiting in the office for us. The walls were paneled with dark oak like an Oxford don's might be. Pictures of what I assumed were former students who had gone on to win Nobels, run movie studios or at least make a ton of money, lined one of the walls.

The principal from Charlotte's school was a woman in her mid-forties named Fuentes. She had an exhausted look in her eyes that seemed more suited to a soldier than an educator. A distinct difference from the shark-like gaze the principal from Woodward named Keller projected.

We took our seats as a secretary brought in a tray with a pot of tea and cups. As we sat down his eyes found the swelling on the side of my face. From the look he gave me I suspected he thought a homeless drunk must have wandered into the room by accident.

'I'm sorry, I was only expecting Mrs Sexton. And you are?' he asked.

I never much like the idea of privilege, perhaps because I had never had any, but still, the air of superiority that clung to the crest on his jacket pocket made me want to look around for another soup pan.

'I'm an investigator,' I said, hoping to perhaps make him feel even more uncomfortable with my presence.

'I'm sorry, but we have strict privacy guidelines surrounding any information regarding our students,' he said.

I think he had just told me to get the hell out.

'I'm also Charlotte's father,' I said as a paternal tsunami rose up inside me.

He coughed.

'Really?' he said and glanced at Tracy.

'He dotes on her,' Tracy said.

Keller looked back at the swelling on my face.

'Have you had an accident?'

'No, I think this is exactly what he had in mind when he threw the punch.'

He tried without much luck to smile.

'How colorful,' he said.

The door to the office opened and another official from the school stepped in and took a seat.

'This is Vice Principal Burns,' Keller said. 'He conducts all inquiries regarding any student or staff.'

Burns had all the charm of an FBI agent rather than an educator.

'Now what is it you would like to show us?' Keller said.

Tracy opened Charlotte's laptop with the picture from the party and set it on the desk for them to look at.

'That's my daughter. We believe the one on the left is a student here and that he is involved with Charlotte's disappearance.'

'His name's Tyler,' I said.

'What do you mean by involved?' Keller asked.

'They may be involved together with another girl named Sophie.'

Burns and Keller both looked at the picture then quickly traded glances that seemed anything but casual.

'Our students' privacy is of the greatest concern to us,' Keller said.

'That would be a yes, he is a student here,' I said.

'We of course would require proof of this connection before we could violate that privacy.'

And their enormous tuition fees.

'You're looking at it,' I said. 'He's the one who hit me.'

'You must be mistaken; he's one of our best students, a star athlete with a bright future. His name's also not Tyler. You must have the wrong person.'

I took out my phone with the picture from the club and handed it to them.

'This is him shortly before he hit me. He may also be involved in the deaths of two men,' I said.

'Deaths?' Keller asked.

'They were killed.'

'What are you suggesting?' he asked.

'I'm suggesting it would be better for all concerned for you to help me rather than the police.'

Keller looked over to Burns who nodded.

'As I said, he's an outstanding student in every way,' Keller said.

'And?' I said.

He paused to carefully craft what he was going to say next.

'A week ago he failed to come to school. After several days of missing class we called the family, as is our protocol regarding missing class time. The family told us it was a personal matter and that they were handling it. When a week passed without the return of the student, we contacted the family again, and again we were told it was a personal matter and that they were taking care of it and would prefer it to remain private.'

'When a student misses a specific amount of class time it is our protocol to conduct an internal investigation to make sure that nothing has happened here in Woodward that might have contributed to the student's absence,' said Burns.

'You were covering your ass,' I said.

From the look on Keller's face I don't think he found my comment particularly helpful.

'We hold our students to a very high standard, and when they don't meet that, we do everything to make sure that we are helping them as much as possible to achieve their goals,' Keller said.

'What did you find out?' I asked.

'Nothing specific that pointed to anything within the school was responsible,' Burns said.

'But you found something,' Tracy said.

Again Keller glanced over to Burns.

'What did you find?' Tracy repeated.

'I think, for clarity, it would be better for me to show you,' Burns said.

* * *

They walked us out of the office and to another wing of the school filled with students' lockers. A Hispanic maintenance worker in a gray uniform with a name patch saying 'Luis' on his shirt was waiting for us.

'Again, it must be made clear that nothing in what we found was actionable. Your information perhaps puts that in a different light,' Keller said.

'Nothing has been touched, there have always been two people present when the locker has been opened,' Burns added.

'I gather the student's parents are lawyers,' I said.

'This protocol would be followed with all of our students,' Keller said and nodded to the maintenance man. 'You can open it, Luis.'

He took a key off a ring he was holding, opened the lock, and stepped back as Burns swung the door open. As Tracy looked inside she gasped.

'Oh my God,' she whispered in a mix of confusion and fear.

'When we saw this, we of course didn't know the connection to your daughter,' Keller said.

The inside of the locker looked exactly as I remembered high school lockers looked. The back of the door, however, was another story. It was covered with photographs, laid out with an obsessive quality and attention to detail, and they were all of Charlotte or Charlotte and him.

'How long ago did you find this?' I asked.

'Two days ago.'

'I guess you missed the pictures of Charlotte on the six o'clock news,' I said.

'All this may be nothing more than a case of adolescent infatuation,' Keller said, ignoring my comment.

There were pictures from in and outside school, at her house, inside and out of restaurants, clubs, holding each other, laughing, kissing, sleeping. Only one photograph wasn't of Charlotte and I had seen it before. It was the shadowy profile photograph from Sophie's Facebook page.

'We've made no ID on that picture,' Burns said.

Tracy stared at it all for a moment, then looked over to me, struggling to find the words to what was raging inside her.

'Their whole lives are in here, it's like a secret diary,' she said.

'I must repeat that this all may be entirely innocent,' Keller said.

'I have experience with infatuation, Mr Keller. I know it when I see it.'

I looked over to Fuentes.

'As a professional educator, would you call this innocent?' I asked her.

She shook her head.

'No, I wouldn't.'

'We have no proof of anything,' Keller said to Tracy. 'I don't believe it serves anyone to jump to conclusions.'

'My daughter is missing, Mr Keller, what conclusion should I jump to?'

'We'll need his name,' I said.

'Again, the parents have requested that this remain a private matter. Even showing you this is

306

probably more than we should be doing.'

'This isn't private, those are pictures of my daughter.'

Keller hesitated.

'If he's missing with Charlotte, then his parents need to talk to us as much as we need to talk to them,' I said.

'Our hands are tied on this, I'm afraid. I'm sorry,' Keller said.

Tracy's frustration was about to blow.

'What about his friends — any rules against talking with them?' I asked.

Keller looked over to Burns for a moment.

'I think we can do that.'

Burns took out a phone and began making calls as he walked away.

★ ★ ★

Burns was waiting for us at the door as we left the building and began walking us towards the parking lot. Dozens of students still lingered on the grounds and by their cars.

'I apologize,' Burns said, 'but with privacy laws what they are now, there's little we can do.'

'Are there any other pieces of information you would like to not pass on to us?' I asked.

'Such as?' he said in such a way as to suggest wriggle room.

'If I had asked before if this student had any history of violence or drugs, what would have been the answer?'

We reached the car and stopped.

'If you had asked that before, I would have

307

said he has no history of drugs as far as I know. He was disciplined once for a fight during a baseball game, but that's sports, those things happen.'

'What things?'

'A pitcher threw a ball at his head, he went after him with a bat. It was stopped before anything happened. No harm done. As we said before, he's a fine young student.'

'What would you say to that question now, knowing what we've told you?'

He gave the answer some thought.

'I would say things can go wrong very easily when you're seventeen, no matter what we do.'

Burns turned and looked through the gates to the school at a small group of students waiting to be picked up out on the street.

'I think the tall girl with the long black hair would be the one you shouldn't talk to,' he said. 'She may even be expecting a ride home. Her name's Amy.'

'Thank you,' Tracy said.

Burns looked over to her.

'You don't need to. I have a fourteen-year-old daughter myself.'

He then walked away and we jumped in the car and drove through the gate of the school, stopping next to the group of students out on the street. The tall girl with thin athletic features and long black hair wearing a soccer team jacket turned and looked at us for a moment. She hesitated before stepping over to Tracy's window carrying her backpack full of schoolwork.

'Are you Amy?' Tracy asked.

308

She hesitated, then nodded.

'Mrs Sexton?'

'Yes.'

The girl turned and said something to the other kids then stepped over and opened the back door of the car and got in.

'Principal Burns said it would be best if we drove away as quickly as possible.'

I stepped on the gas and pulled away from the Woodward school.

'Your daughter is the missing girl?' she asked.

'Her name's Charlotte,' Tracy said.

'I know, I'm sorry,' she said.

'How do you know?'

'I've seen her Facebook page, everyone has. I think I even friended people who had friended her before this happened. But everyone has so many friends, you never know, I get poked and posted forty, fifty times a day.'

The girl made me feel ancient.

'Do you know anything yet about what happened to Charlotte?' she asked.

Tracy shook her head and started to introduce me.

'This is Charlotte's . . . ' The words seemed to stump her.

'Elias,' I said.

'Hi,' the girl answered.

'You know the boy whose locker we just looked at?' Tracy asked.

'Yes, Darren Coles, I live only a few blocks from him. I can show you his house on Sunshine Terrace, it's off Laurel Canyon.'

I knew the general area; I turned back to the

east and headed for it.

Tracy showed her the picture on the computer.

'Is this him?'

Amy looked at the picture, surprise in her eyes.

'He was going out with your daughter?' she asked.

Tracy nodded.

'You didn't know?'

'No. I don't think anyone knew.'

'How well do you know him?' Tracy asked.

'We went out for a few times.'

'Why just a few times?' I asked.

'We just didn't click, no drama.'

'What's he like? I need you to be specific,' Tracy asked and Amy nodded.

'He's like really smart in some ways, and in others totally normal, almost too normal.'

'You mean he was boring?'

She shook her head.

'It was like he was always keeping something from me. I don't think he liked opening up. Not exactly a news flash when it comes to guys.'

'You think he had secrets?'

She thought about it for a moment.

'Everybody has secrets, it's just that most everyone can't wait to post them on Facebook.'

'He was different?' I asked.

Amy nodded.

'He kept his.'

'He have any history with drugs or violence?' I asked.

'No drugs, I don't think he's even smoked pot.'

'He was in a fight at a baseball game, do you know what happened?'

'He tried to hit the other player in the head with his bat, but somebody grabbed it,' she said, shrugging her shoulders. 'I don't really get sports, I guess that happens.'

We started up Laurel Canyon into the neighborhood where he lived.

'Is he on Facebook?' I asked.

She looked at me as if I had flown in from another planet.

'Everyone's on Facebook,' she said. 'Even my mother — it's embarrassing.'

'Have you ever seen his page?'

'Sure.'

'There was nothing on his page about the two of them.'

She shook her head.

'Nothing.'

'Does the name Sophie mean anything to you?' I asked.

'The Facebook Sophie, yeah, she's cool.'

'How is she cool?'

'She talks about how to be real, how to get out of bad relationships, how to deal with fucked-up parents, things like that.'

Tracy's eyes found mine for a moment, then looked away so I wouldn't see the embarrassment in them.

'You ever meet her?' I asked.

'She was at a party once, someone pointed her out, but I didn't meet her.'

'Could you recognize her?' Tracy asked.

She shook her head.

'It was a big party and she was in a crowd.'

'Darren ever talk about her?'

'Not with me, but that doesn't mean he hasn't with someone else.'

'Does the name Tyler mean anything? Or did Darren ever use it?'

'No, I don't think so.'

I handed her my phone with the photograph from outside the club.

'Is that Darren?' I asked.

She stared at it for several seconds.

'The hair's different, everything looks a little different, but I think it's him.'

'What do you mean different?' Tracy asked.

She looked at it again.

'Intense . . . a little like he was at the baseball game after the fight.'

I turned off of Laurel Canyon onto Sunshine Terrace.

'You can drop me here, I'll walk home. I live that way,' Amy said and wrote down the address on a piece of paper. 'His house is a few blocks ahead on the left.'

I pulled over to the pavement and stopped. Amy opened the door and stepped out.

'Has there been any talk in school about why he's missing? Or have any of his friends talked to him?' Tracy asked.

Amy shook her head.

'No, it's kind of weird; no one's talked to him. A few people have started making up jokes about why he's gone.'

'What kind of jokes?' I asked.

'Ridiculous.'

'How ridiculous?'

'There was a rumor going around that he had murdered his parents and is on the run. Like I said, it was ridiculous.'

35

The neighborhood was one of those post-baby boom developments that seemed designed specifically to house family dysfunction or at least confusion. On one side of the street there would be a row of houses with faux Greek columns with gold trim, while on the other were miniature versions of southern plantations and New England cottages.

A few blocks on, we stopped across the street from the address Amy had given us. The house, which appeared to have been inspired by an episode of *Hawaii Five-O*, sat on the top of a short slope covered with ivy. If there were windows facing the street, they were covered by a thick stand of bamboo on either side of the oversize double front doors. A series of Tiki-shaped lights lined the walk from the driveway to the house where a black 700 series BMW sat in the driveway.

I started to get out, but Tracy hesitated a moment.

'What is it?' I asked.

'The story Amy heard,' she said.

'I doubt his parents are lying dead inside.'

Tracy stared at the house and shook her head. 'Not them. What if he killed Derek?'

'It's not impossible that Grunier did it,' I said.

'How would he get his money with Derek dead?'

'That is a problem,' I said.

She again stared at the house for a moment.

'Things can so easily go wrong,' Tracy said, quoting Burns. She turned to me. 'Why would he kill Derek? This isn't about money.'

I shook my head.

'You saw the pictures of the two of them. He's in love with my daught — our daughter. Why would the model student do something like that? Why?'

Short of it being an accident, there was only one answer that made sense, and I could see in Tracy's eyes that she knew it just as I did.

'He was rescuing her,' I said. 'Or thought he was.'

'You have some experience with that.'

Tracy sat in silence for a moment as the meaning behind those words crystallized.

'If this is true, then what we found in the studio, the set, the pictures . . . Charlotte was one of those girls.'

'We don't know that,' I said though the words sounded hollow.

Tracy shook her head.

'But you think it's true.'

I nodded.

'Oh, God,' she whispered.

★ ★ ★

A Hispanic housekeeper answered the door. When we said we were here to talk to Darren's parents, she looked at us and then asked, 'Police?'

315

I didn't answer the question. Letting someone think you were the police rarely failed to get you in a door that otherwise might close in your face — it was an old technique for insurance investigators.

'We would like to talk to his parents,' I repeated.

She asked us to wait by the door then stepped away. From another room the sounds of a hurried conversation took place and then a moment later a woman in her mid-forties, wearing a sleek dark business suit that looked like it cost more than every piece of clothing I had ever owned in my life, rushed in.

She had the thin-drawn features of a harried show biz professional who, after working twelve hours a day, put in hours on the Stairmaster or running up and down the Hollywood Hills in a manic quest to put off aging for one more day.

'Mrs Coles?' I said.

She nodded. 'You have some news about Darren?' she asked, then looked us both over more closely. 'You're not the same officers we had talked to before,' she said.

'I believe your housekeeper was confused, we're not policemen,' I said.

'I don't — ' she said, confused. 'What is it you wanted?'

'We understand your son is missing,' I said.

She looked at us both for a moment and again shook her head.

'I'm afraid you're mistaken. Who are you?'

I introduced us.

'What is it you want?' Coles asked.

'My daughter is missing,' Tracy said.

'What does that have to do with me?'

'We believe she is with your son,' I said.

She looked at me as if I had spoken Aztec.

'I don't know where you get your information but our son isn't missing.'

'My daughter is the girl in the pictures in his school locker,' Tracy said.

A faint look of panic began to be visible in Mrs Coles's eyes.

'I'm sorry about your daughter, but I'm afraid you will have to leave.'

'Two men have been killed,' I said.

Coles's steely resolve just took a broadside.

'I don't know what you're talking about.'

I took out my phone and showed her the photograph from outside the Echo.

'This is your son, isn't it?'

She took the picture in both hands, which began to tremble as she looked at it.

'When was this taken?' she asked.

'Two nights ago outside a club on Sunset.'

'It's my son, but he's . . . '

'Changed?' I said.

She looked at it for another moment and then nodded.

'The police are eventually going to connect all the dots,' I said. 'And when they do, they are going to find your son right in the middle of it all. Now you can wait for them to knock on your door when it will be too late to do anything about this, or you can talk to us now, and we will help each other before it gets worse.'

The rest of her professional veneer crumbled

and what was left standing in front of us was a panicked parent. She took a look outside the door then glanced at her watch, then seemed to have a confused internal dialogue as she figured out what to do.

'You said people have been killed?'

'Yes,' I answered.

She didn't begin to know where to go with this.

'This is not possible, you must be mistaken.'

'It's not a mistake,' I said.

Until this moment, perhaps, she still believed this was about a boy running off to be with a girl.

'This can't be true.'

I told her just enough of the details of the events to give her some understanding. As she listened silently, the denial left her face, replaced by the blank look of a lost traveler who, though holding a map in her hand, still has no idea where she is. When I finished, she took several short breaths to steady herself, then softly said, 'Come in.'

We stepped inside and she closed the door behind us. She took a step, then stopped and turned to ask a question, but was so lost she couldn't form one.

'We need to know anything you can tell us about the things he did or said before he disappeared,' I said.

'I'd better show you his room,' she said.

She walked us through the fashionable house that played out like the turning pages of an *Architectural Digest* photo spread. Her son's room was at the back of one of the wings, as isolated as possible from any other room in the house.

As we stepped up to the door she stopped a few feet short and stared at it as if it were an open wound, then averted her eyes.

'My husband and I were out at a function the night Darren . . . ' The words slipped away from her. She was so practiced in not saying that he had vanished that the fiction that he was just away still held a grip on her. 'We came home just before midnight and found his room like this — and he was gone.'

She reached out and took hold of the door handle with her shaky hand and pushed it open. She stepped inside, though stayed next to the door as if not willing to travel any further than was necessary into her son's world. The room had been torn to pieces, nothing seemed untouched; the furniture had been shattered, the other pieces that littered the floor had been so thoroughly destroyed that I couldn't even guess what they had once been. If it were possible to erase all physical evidence of a life, I couldn't imagine it being any more complete than this.

Tracy looked about the room for a moment then turned to Mrs Coles.

'I'm sorry,' she said gently.

Mrs Coles nodded.

'We thought there had been a burglary, that's why we called the police. It was one of the officers who suggested that perhaps Darren was responsible.'

'Was that a surprise to you?' I asked.

She nodded.

'The police told us that if we had been home that night — well, there's no telling where this would have ended.'

'Has he ever been violent to either of you before?' I asked.

'No,' she said in wonder.

'There was an incident at a baseball game,' I asked.

She turned to me in surprise.

'Our son is a talented — a good student — that was a game.'

She looked around the room in resigned wonder. 'We don't understand this, any of it.'

It would be easy to describe this as crazy, a kid out of control, but the feeling in my own hands of having torn my loft apart was too fresh in my memory. Perhaps the real surprise is that more people don't do this.

'Did he have any secrets?' I asked.

She nodded without hesitation. 'Your daughter.'

'My daughter didn't tell me about him, either,' Tracy said.

'What have the police said to you so far?' I asked.

'He's considered a runaway, they don't have the resources to do anything about it unless he breaks the law. We hired an investigator, but so far he's found nothing.'

'One of the people who have been killed was the investigator I hired,' Tracy said.

Coles made no attempt to hide the shock in her face.

'Why?' she asked.

'We believe he found something that was a threat to someone,' I said.

'Someone?'

Until this moment denial had kept the reality of what had happened in their lives at bay, but from the look on her face, that was over. Any hope that he would just walk back through the front door and everything would return to the way it had been was gone.

'How did this happen?' she whispered.

She played something through her mind, then looked uneasily around the room, her eyes full of pain.

'I wanted to clean this up, but my husband insisted that Darren would do it when he came home.'

She turned and looked away from the mess towards the door.

'I think I would like to talk in another room.'

She turned and walked out and we followed her into the living room. It was a large, open space with floor-to-ceiling windows looking out on to a black-bottom pool in the back yard.

Mrs Coles took a seat on the couch and we sat across from her in sleek leather chairs. The housekeeper stepped into the room.

'Is everything all right, Mrs Coles?'

'Yes, it's all right, Maria, go on with what you were doing.'

The maid glanced suspiciously at me and then walked out. Mrs Coles took a breath as if to steady her nerves.

'Did he take anything with him?' I asked.

'Some clothes.'

'Did he ever mention the name Sophie?' I asked.

She looked at me and nodded.

'Yes, she was a friend of a girl he dated for a while named Anna.'

'He dated Anna?'

She nodded.

'Not for very long, I think meeting Sophie may have had something to do with it.'

'Before my daughter vanished,' Tracy said, 'she met someone on Facebook named Sophie.'

'Charlotte and your son are somehow connected to her, but we don't know how.'

'Did he tell you anything about her?'

She shook her head.

'Does the name Tyler mean anything?'

Her face flushed with color and she stared at me for a moment.

'How do you know that name?' she asked.

'We think it's the name your son is using.'

She whispered something under her breath and shook her head.

'That name means something to you, doesn't it?' I asked.

She closed her eyes for a second and took a breath, her anguish more visceral.

'What does it mean?' asked Tracy.

'We had another son, he died when he was fifteen; Darren was twelve.'

'His name was Tyler,' I said.

She nodded and looked past us into the backyard.

'I'm sorry,' said Tracy.

'It was a type of aggressive bone cancer. He only lived six months after the diagnosis.'

'How did it affect Darren?' I asked.

She shook her head.

'During the illness and immediately after, it was a difficult time for me, I coped badly, so did my husband. Darren was the strongest one of us all. He saved us.'

'How about since then?'

She thought for a moment; the memories were clearly difficult for her.

'He became more serious, focused. I think he wanted to be both him and his brother for us.'

'You've tried to contact him?'

'Of course: calls, emails, messages on Face-book, nothing has worked.'

'Is the phone being monitored?' I asked.

'The detective was doing that, but it hasn't produced anything yet that has helped, just the GPS coordinates of the calls or where he connected to the web, the locations have all been different. Darren's too smart to be found that way.'

'Would you have those addresses?' I asked.

She nodded. 'I'll get them.'

She left the room and came back with a sheet of paper.

'The addresses are approximate,' she said. 'You can keep that if it will help.'

I started to look over them but when I recognized an address my heart seemed to try to jump out of my chest and I slipped the paper into my jacket pocket.

Tracy looked at me, knowing that I had seen

something, but I let it pass for the moment.

'What about money?' I asked.

'He has a checking account and a credit card, but he hasn't touched either.'

She wrote down something on a piece of paper from a note pad.

'Why did this happen?' she asked, desperate for some understanding.

Until this moment I hadn't fully understood why the wheels had so completely come off Charlotte's life. But it was clear now. A teenage life is black and white, there's no gray area; that comes with age. Their world is both more chaotic and clearer at the same time. Darren had done the one thing that had made his world understandable. He was being a hero.

'I think he was trying to protect Charlotte,' I said.

'From what?' she asked.

I looked over to Tracy.

'Her stepfather,' she said. 'He was abusing young girls; she may have been one of them.'

They looked at each other for a moment, sharing a world perhaps only mothers understood.

'He's one of the men who is dead?' she asked.

Tracy nodded. Coles's face flushed as her reality took on an entirely new weight and detail.

'Oh, my God,' she whispered, then removed the piece of paper she had written on from the note pad and handed it to me.

'That's the name and number of the detective. My husband will be home shortly, he wouldn't want us to be having this conversation, it will take some time for him to accept this.'

I glanced at Tracy and she nodded and we both stood up.

'Thank you,' Tracy said and she started to leave.

'The picture of Darren outside the club,' Mrs Coles said.

We stopped.

'What was it?' I asked.

'The face, his hair, even the eyes, were different, but I've seen it before.'

'This isn't the first time he changed his appearance?'

'I'm not talking about Darren.'

The uneasiness that had lodged itself in my gut since we had walked in this house just kicked me in the side when I realized what she was saying.

'Tyler?' I said.

Mrs Coles nodded.

'It's like looking at a ghost. He's become his brother, or what his brother might have looked like if he had lived,' she said.

36

We sat for a while in the car trying to fit what we had learned with our own understanding. How could so much go wrong inside of a house? How do you explain that? It wasn't just secrets that had been hidden beyond the faux Hawaiian lights and bamboo plants. It was the perfect suburban family turned into a nightmare.

'A ghost,' Tracy said.

'He's not a ghost.'

'No.'

We sat in silence for a moment trying to find a place in the puzzle for what we had learned.

'Anna, Sophie, Charlotte, he was involved with all of them,' Tracy said.

'They haven't spent any money,' I said.

The understanding of what I was saying appeared in Tracy's eyes almost immediately.

'Oh, God, that's what he was talking about — 'Where's my money?',' she said, referring to her husband's partner with the knife. 'They took it. It must have been in Derek's apartment. He'll be looking for them.'

I nodded as a white Mercedes came down the block and pulled into the Coles's driveway. Mr Coles stepped out wearing a suit and carrying a briefcase. His hair was prematurely gray; his skin tanned, his frame lean. As he walked to the front door he carried himself like a man whose every movement was designed to never allow a moment of doubt to creep into his world. The Maginot Line of the family.

He paused at the door and glanced towards the street in our direction. I couldn't tell if he was looking at us. Perhaps it was just something he did every day when he returned home, looking for a son, or maybe he was looking for a past that had slipped out of his control. Then he went inside.

'You recognized an address on that sheet she gave you, didn't you?' Tracy asked.

I slipped the paper out of my pocket.

'A few,' I said and handed it to her.

Tracy looked at it for a moment.

'This is my house,' she said. 'When he took the clothes.' She went on down the list. 'And your loft,' she said.

'Do any of the others mean anything to you?' I asked.

She finished going over the list and then nodded.

'This is the gallery. I don't recognize any of the others,' she said.

'There's one more,' I said. 'The second from the bottom.'

Tracy looked at it and began to shake her head, then stopped and stared at it in silence.

'That can't be right,' she said, turning to me.

'It is,' I said. My head seemed to wind up like a top that was going to begin spinning.

'Our accident site?' Tracy said.

I nodded.

'I drove there the night after you had left my place,' I said.

'Why?'

'A salmon returning home, I suppose.'

A hand reached out the window of a Ford and tossed away a cigarette.

'I don't think I was alone,' I said.

The red taillights disappeared into the night.

'They must have followed me — a Ford Taurus. I didn't think anything of it at the time.'

'Did you see . . . could she have been there?' Tracy asked.

'Have you ever seen Charlotte smoking?' I asked.

'No, never, she wouldn't — '

Tracy stopped herself, nearly laughed, but didn't. Certainty wasn't something she could count on any more.

'That would be my old life. Why?' she said.

'There were at least two people in the car, the passenger on the driver's side tossed a cigarette out the window.'

'Sophie?' she asked.

'Could be.'

'How did they find you?'

'They didn't, you did,' I said.

It took her moment, then she realized what I was saying.

'They were following me. I led them to you.'

'That would be my guess.'

'You think they're the ones who broke in?' Tracy asked.

'Could be how she put the last pieces together that I was her father,' I said, the word father sounding as if someone else had spoken it. Tracy looked at me for moment, then turned away, perhaps not used to me saying it any more than I was.

I took a last look at the house trying to imagine the conversation that was taking place inside.

'What did the principal at the school say? The parents preferred it to remain a private matter. If anyone needs help, it's that family, why didn't they want it? Why wouldn't the husband want us talking to his wife?'

'Knowing you need help isn't the same as asking for it,' Tracy said with a certainty that only comes with experience.

'What if there's another reason?'

'You think they know something?'

I nodded.

'I don't think Mrs Coles was lying to us,' Tracy said.

'I'm not talking about her.'

Tracy looked over at the house.

'A husband keeping secrets from a wife,' Tracy said. 'I have some experience of that.'

I reached out to start the car and the front door of the house opened. Mr Coles walked out, his jacket and tie left inside. Mrs Coles was reaching out towards him.

'Bill, don't — '

'What are you thinking!' he yelled. 'He's our son!'

He stormed over to his Mercedes, jumped in and backed down into the street and started to speed off.

37

We caught up with Coles as he headed south over the top of Mulholland and began winding his way down the narrow canyon towards Hollywood. I've never actually followed anyone before, except for going to a party or a restaurant at an address I didn't know. I suppose because we've seen so many people do it on TV we just assume we know what we're doing, like it's a natural occurrence that springs up in everyday life in LA.

That's not entirely accurate.

We were one car behind him when he reached the bottom of the canyon and was approaching the light on Sunset. Coles put on his right turn signal as the light turned yellow.

'He could be going to Beverly Hills,' I said.

I started to slow when Coles stepped on the gas and shot straight through the intersection as the light turned red.

I hesitated for a moment. I know everything about accidents. I know that 71.5 per cent of all collisions that occur in LA happen in those three seconds when yellow changes to red. In the business we call it the blank space — an extra space between two words in a sentence, the moment when no one remembers what or if they were thinking when they made the worst decision of their lives.

I pulled around the Buick in front of us and

stepped on the gas as cars began to enter the intersection. Tracy reached out and touched the dash with her right hand.

'What are you — ' she said.

A brown pickup driven by a Mexican slammed on the brakes and others hit their horns. A man in a red Porsche with a cigar in his mouth gave me the finger. A woman in a mini-van full of kids in soccer uniforms began shouting asshole out her window.

The rear of the car began to slide right, I corrected, we straightened for a moment then began to drift the other way. A catering truck painted with flames on the front and the words Burning Dogs spelled out in sausage-shaped letters on the front closed towards Tracy's door.

She turned and leaned away from it, her hand gripping the dash.

'Don't . . . ' she whispered.

I pressed the gas, turned the wheel. For a moment there didn't seem to be a sound in the entire world, as if we had slipped into an alternative reality where the line between the past and present had been lost. Tracy's eyes found mine. The sound of traffic returned and the red flames of the catering truck moved across the plane of the rear-view mirror. We were through. Tracy took a breath and looked back, then at me, appearing as if she was going to say something then turned and looked down the street.

'Your driving has improved,' she said softly.

Coles was almost a block ahead moving in and out of traffic. I did my best to follow, but he was still pulling away. The Mercedes started to take a right, and then the roof lights of a squad car lit up in our rear-view mirror and a siren began to sound. Tracy turned and looked back at the police car behind us, and then looked at me, her eyes pleading with me not to stop.

'We'll find — ' I started to say, not because I believed it but because I gave in to the male instinct of saying exactly what a woman wants to hear in a moment of stress even though all evidence points in exactly the opposite direction.

As I pulled over to the curb the Mercedes disappeared from view. The cop was speaking on the handset of his radio inside the squad, his eyes moving back and forth between the computer screen and us, then he put the radio down and stepped out. As he began to walk towards my side of the car, I saw his hand casually reach down and take hold of the handle of his pistol.

'Why is he grabbing his gun?' Tracy asked.

'They always do that on traffic — '

He slipped it out of the holster and held it at his side.

'Do they always do that?' Tracy added.

I shook my head. 'No.'

The cop stepped up to my window.

'Would you turn the engine off,' he said.

I did as instructed.

'I guess I missed the light change,' I said.

I started to reach for my wallet.

'Keep your hands where I can see them and step out of the vehicle, Mr Hawks.'

He hadn't seen my license. How the hell did he know who I was?

'Step out of the car,' the cop said.

I glanced at Tracy then eased out.

'Put your hands on the roof,' he instructed.

I did exactly as I was told.

'Do you have any weapons on you or anything sharp that could poke me?'

I shook my head.

'No.'

He holstered his pistol and quickly frisked me, took out my wallet, then walked me back to the squad.

'Have a seat,' he said.

'Just out of curiosity, I'm wondering how you knew my name before looking at my ID?' I asked.

We stepped up to the squad and he opened the back door.

'Did I?' the cop said and placed me in the back of the squad.

He walked back to our car and repeated the process with Tracy and brought her back to the squad and sat her inside next to me.

'Is this normal procedure for a red-light violation?' I asked him.

He closed the door without responding.

'What's going on?' Tracy asked.

'I'm not sure.'

We sat there for twenty minutes confined in the tight back seat that seemed designed to stifle words the same as movement. The real reason we had been stopped finally drove up behind us. Delgado stepped out of her squad, exchanged a few words with the officer, then walked over to the patrolman's car and slipped into the front seat.

'Why are we sitting here?' I asked.

'You don't answer your phone,' Delgado said. 'I found the warehouse,' she said, looking at us like a displeased teacher.

Tracy shot me a look knowing I had betrayed her wishes and informed Delgado.

'You didn't — ' she started to say then looked angrily away.

'If you keep trying to do this by yourselves it will be a disaster,' Delgado said. 'Do you understand? You need help.'

Tracy shook her head. 'Why should I believe you?'

'Because I've seen the inside of that warehouse and others just like it. And I know more about what your husband and his partner did in there than you should ever think about.'

Tracy looked away.

'Listen,' Delgado said, 'I've looked into those girls' eyes. I've held their hands as they told about their nightmares. You need to understand something. Homicide doesn't care about the horrors that happened in that warehouse. They don't care because someone still beat Lester to death and probably killed your husband.'

She looked at us for a moment.

'I'm not the enemy,' she said.

Tracy thought for a moment, looked at me and then turned to Delgado. 'I didn't kill my husband,' she said.

'I believe you,' Delgado answered.

'What do you want, then?' she said.

Delgado leaned back against the dash of the squad.

'Did your husband ever bring your daughter to the back of that warehouse?' she asked.

'I don't know,' Tracy said.

'Do you understand where this is going?' Delgado said.

Tracy started to answer, then stopped.

'What are you saying?' she asked.

'Listen to me. If Charlotte and her friend Sophie think they can be Thelma and Louise,' said Delgado, 'you need to remember how that movie ended.'

Perhaps Tracy had thought about it before, but this was the first time someone had said it out loud, and it was a cop saying Charlotte might have killed her stepfather.

'My daughter wouldn't . . . that's not possible,' said Tracy.

'You've seen the warehouse; you saw what it did to Anna — '

'My daughter was not in there!' Tracy said angrily, fighting off reality as long as she could.

'Who is the boy with them, the one who hit you, Tyler?' Delgado asked.

Tracy was trembling, didn't respond. Delgado looked at me. Tracy's eyes found mine, pleading with me not to tell her. Perhaps a day ago, or even a few hours, I might have told Delgado what she wanted to know. But now . . . Charlotte . . . If there was ever going to be any evidence beyond a few accident reports and hospital charts that I had lived, it was going to be found in the lines of her face, her eyes, the sound of her voice. If there was any chance that I would not be alone in this world, there could be only one answer to Delgado.

'I don't know,' I said.

'You think my daughter has killed someone and you want my help to catch her? No, you're wrong,' Tracy said.

Delgado shook her head.

'That's not what I'm doing.'

'What do you call it?' Tracy answered.

'I'm trying to save her,' she said and again looked at me. 'Give me something, a name, anything.'

Again Tracy looked at me, her eyes demanding the right answer. I started to say something and Tracy glared at me to stop.

'Before he was killed, Lester told his secretary that he didn't want the wrong person to get hurt, I think he was trying to protect Charlotte,' I said.

'What are you doing?' Tracy asked angrily.

'Trust me,' I said.

'Is there a point to this?' Delgado said.

'Why would Charlotte hurt someone who is trying to protect her?' I said.

Tracy's eyes stayed on me, trying to figure out what I was doing. Delgado thought about it, then nodded.

'So who's the right person?' she asked.

'Sexton owed his partner money,' I said.

'Grunier?'

I nodded.

'And you know this how?'

'He told us.'

'You talked to him?'

336

'It was a short conversation.'

Delgado sat back and thought it through for a moment.

'Charlotte and her friends have the money, that's why they ran,' she said.

I didn't know if that was the truth or not, but it was at least part of the truth, and one that didn't have the word murder attached to it.

'I think so,' I said.

Delgado looked over to Tracy.

'Is this what you think happened?'

'Yes,' she said.

'All right,' Delgado said then turned back to me. 'Anything else you want to tell me?' she asked me.

From the moment this had begun it had felt like trying to hold mercury in my hands. No matter how hard one tried to put an order to the events that had transpired, there was always something out of our control, something that wasn't right.

'There's something we're not seeing or understanding,' I said.

'You want to be specific?'

'I don't know.'

Delgado sat there for a moment digesting it all.

'All right. Maybe I would do the same thing if she were my daughter, but it would still be the wrong choice. When you're ready to tell me more, I hope it won't be too late.'

She stepped out and looked at the uniformed officer who had pulled us over.

'Let 'em go.'

38

We sat in silence and watched Delgado and the other officer drive away. Where we were going next seemed as unclear as where we had been. The silence that now sat uncomfortably between us seemed a greater gulf than the eighteen years we had been apart.

I was a father in name only without memories to fall back on. If for a moment after learning about Charlotte I had allowed myself to believe in a different future, that had fallen apart as easily as the past had slipped away. 'You think what she said is possible, that Charlotte was part of what happened — Thelma and Louise?'

I looked at her for a moment trying to understand if Tracy really wanted to know. When finally I nodded, I could see in her eyes that she knew it was a possibility also.

'I'm not sure,' I said.

'Is that what you meant when you said there was something we aren't seeing or understanding?'

'Maybe, I'm not sure.'

'You were trying to protect her,' Tracy said.

'Trying.'

'But you didn't tell Delgado Tyler's name, why?'

'At the club, Tyler — Darren — told April that Charlotte thinks everything that has happened started the day I abandoned you and her when she was born.'

Tracy shook her head.

'She doesn't understand. You know that's not true.'

I nodded. 'But it feels true,' I said.

We slipped back into silence and I began driving. We had traveled about a mile when Tracy started to speak.

'It was during the last dance,' she said, her eyes focused on a distant point in time that appeared as clear to her as the road ahead.

'The lights had been turned down, the disco ball was swirling around us. I don't remember the song.' She paused and took a nervous breath. 'I had kissed a lot of guys, I was thinking it would be fun to kiss you.'

I turned and headed east on Sunset driving back towards downtown. As I drove Tracy's eyes remained fixed on that point in time oblivious to where we were or going.

'Then you kissed me.'

She shook her head, seeming to slip even further into the memory.

'I was wrong,' she said, her voice quaking. 'It wasn't fun — it scared me. It was perfect.'

The muscles of her jaw tensed as she grappled with the intensity of the memory.

'I pulled away from you and ran out of the gym, hoping you wouldn't follow and yet wanting you to. I was running across the lawn outside the gym when you grabbed my hand. I pulled away. I yelled at you to leave me alone. I told you it was nothing, the whole night was a joke, that I went out with you because I thought my girlfriends would think it was funny — the kid in the cafeteria.' She struggled to take a breath. 'You just stood there listening to me saying these terrible things and when finally I was done, you just shook your head and said 'That's not why you're here'. Then you turned and started walking away.'

Tracy closed her eyes for a moment as if my words of all those years ago still unsettled her.

'Then I ran after you. It was crazy, I don't remember where we went or how we ended up there. I remember running again, I remember how my heart was beating, I remember the taste of your lips, your hands taking off my clothes . . . the way you touched me . . . felt inside me . . . nothing had ever felt like that before . . . or since . . . '

I continued winding our way across Sunset, passing through East Hollywood and the abandoned buildings and mean streets where April had shown me a shadow world, and then into Silver Lake and Echo Park, listening to Tracy tell the story, our story, but I had no memory of it. It was like listening to someone read a book out loud; the story wasn't about me, and no matter how desperately I wanted to be the person in that story, her words opened no window to that lost world of my past. Seeing the intensity in Tracy's eyes and hearing it in her voice made the sense of loss even stronger.

In the time it had taken for Tracy to lift the lid on our past and look inside, perhaps in a way she had done in isolation for far too long, I had driven home and stopped the car outside the loft and turned off the engine.

'And then in that instant everything changed again and you were gone,' Tracy said, then looked around for the first time at where we were. 'I want it back,' she whispered, looking at me. 'I want to know it was real . . . that what I felt that night was real.'

Her eyes found mine for a moment and then looked away towards the towers of the city.

'And I know I can't ask for that now, not while Charlotte's gone.'

Neither of us made a move to get out or said anything for several moments, the silence offering more comfort than any words might have provided. Tracy shook her head as she stared out at the lights just beginning to come up with the approach of dusk. She fought with a thought or words for a moment, then finally spoke.

'The things that happen to you, the blackouts — are you going to be there when this is over, or are you going to disappear again?'

Was I? Perhaps over time I had become comfortable with the idea. But everything had changed.

'The truth,' Tracy said.

I started to answer her, then saw my mother reaching out, her fingers just touching the skin of the grapefruit as she began to feel the sensation that something wasn't right.

'I'm not going to disappear,' I said.

39

We didn't talk as we walked upstairs. We didn't talk about us, not Charlotte, not the future or the past, but it was right there, like a person in shadow walking right behind us — a fear that regardless of where we had been, whatever was ahead might be far worse.

The smell of fresh oil paint drifted out from one of my neighbor's lofts. Polka music was again filtering down from Buzz upstairs. For a brief moment everything appeared just as it should be. I even managed to steal a glance at the curves of Tracy's ear. As I stepped up to my door and started to slip the key in, I remembered that the lock had been broken.

The polka morphed into Pearl Jam.

'Does he always do that?' Tracy asked.

As I pushed the door open Tracy's hand fell gently on my shoulder and it nearly took my breath away.

'I'll cook something,' she said.

I closed my eyes. There it was, the future I never let myself dream about; all it took was the touch of her hand and the kind of words that were so commonplace in a normal life that they are forgotten almost as soon as they are said.

I stepped inside and Tracy followed. The mess in the loft was hardly visible in the fading light.

'I'm a good cook,' she said and her hand slipped from my shoulder and as quickly as that

I could feel the dream begin to fade away.

A good cook?

The normalness of the words was startling. Right at that moment it became clear that we were still strangers, just as we had been eighteen years before. We knew none of the little things about each other that fill most of the moments in a shared life. I was still standing in the cafeteria line, staring at a girl who was as much dream as flesh and blood. We had never had a chance to get past those first awkward words the morning after that open a door to whatever will follow.

Say something.

I could think of nothing. I closed the door and reached for the light switch as Tracy walked past me towards the kitchen.

'What do you like — ' she started to ask.

The movement came quickly towards her from the kitchen. She started to raise her hands.

'Wait!' Tracy yelled.

The figure knocked her down and started moving towards the door. I ran towards him and we collided and went backwards over the top of the couch, flipping heavily onto the hardwood floor with a thud.

He gasped. I could feel his breath on the side of my face. He started to pull away, trying to get to his feet. I reached and grabbed the hair on the back of his head and wrapped my other arm around his neck as he got to his feet, spinning around, trying to pull me off. We hit a chair and tumbled over onto the floor and he landed on top of me, knocking the wind out of my lungs and I lost my grip on his neck and head.

'It's not — ' he started to say and Tracy jumped onto his back, covering his face with her hands.

They fell back over the top of the couch and he yelled, 'No, no!' as they landed with another thud.

'It's not!' he yelled again.

As I got to my feet he pulled himself free from Tracy and bolted for the door.

I took a step to follow but with one breath I fell back to my knees, desperate for air. The door opened and he ran out, slamming it behind him as I crawled gasping for breath around the other side of the couch where Tracy was just sitting back up.

I got to her side and reached out, touching the side of her face. I took a clipped breath and then another.

'Are you all right?' I managed to say.

Tracy nodded.

'I don't understand.'

'I know.'

I pushed myself up and reached the door, pulling it open.

'What the fuck is going on?'

Buzz was standing there.

'And who the fuck is this?' he asked.

The intruder was lying on the floor of the hallway a few feet away, moaning softly in pain.

'You OK?' Buzz asked.

I nodded and looked down at the guy on the floor. He was white, perhaps in his thirties, dark hair, dressed in jeans and the khaki kind of jacket you see foreign correspondents on TV wear when they want to look rugged.

I glanced up and down the hallway; none of the other neighbors had stepped out.

'What the fuck is going on?' Buzz repeated.

'I don't know. Bring him inside,' I said.

I went back in and turned on the light. Tracy was sitting up on the couch, her arms across her chest. Buzz came through the door with his right arm wrapped firmly around the guy's neck as he half walked, half dragged him over to a chair. Tracy got up and stepped around behind the couch.

'Who is he?' she asked.

His eyes were a little dazed, the side of his face red where Buzz must have smacked him. Buzz tossed me the guy's wallet as he kept his other hand on the collar of the man's shirt.

'It's a mistake,' the guy said softly.

I opened the wallet and looked inside. I recognized the name.

'He's a private detective,' I said, showing Tracy the ID.

'The name's Osgood,' he said, getting his breath and equilibrium back.

'You're working for the Coleses,' I said.

He had almost black hair and eyebrows with a thin nose that gave him the appearance of an angry crow. He looked at me in surprise.

'You're looking for their son,' I added.

'How did you know that?' he asked.

'Mrs Coles told us,' I said. 'How did you find me?' I asked.

'I didn't.'

'You were following Darren?'

He nodded.

'I was tracking him through his phone but he stopped using it.'

'What are you doing here?'

I handed him back his wallet. He took a deep breath.

'I wanted to find out why he came here. I knocked — the door was open, you need new locks.'

'Darren and Charlotte were the ones who broke in before?' I asked.

'Charlotte?' He shook his head. 'Her name's Sophie.'

'Do you know where they are?' Tracy asked.

'I wouldn't be here if I did.'

'But you did know?' I asked.

'I'm really not at liberty to disclose — '

'People are dead, maybe you would like to talk to the police.'

Osgood shook his head.

'When was the last time you saw them?' I said.

'When they met you at the Echo,' he said. 'I followed him inside, saw him walking away from you on the floor. When I got outside they were gone, haven't seen them since.'

'When did the Coleses hire you?'

'About three weeks ago.'

It took me a moment to fill in the blanks.

'Before he disappeared?' I asked.

Osgood nodded.

'Why?'

'It's what I do.'

He reached into his wallet and removed a

business card and gave it to me.

'Teen Watch.'

'Parents hire me to find out the things their kids won't tell them . . . We monitor their on-line activity, their phone . . . and sometimes find them when they've gone missing.'

'You spy on people's children,' I said.

He nodded. 'It's a booming business.'

'Were you following them the night they went to Sexton's apartment?'

He hesitated, then nodded.

'Was he alone?'

'He was with the girl.'

'Charlotte.'

He shook his head.

'I've only seen him with Sophie. If there's someone else with them they must have hooked up with her later.'

'You're certain?' Tracy asked.

He nodded.

'What did you see at the apartment?'

'The girl went in first, Darren went in about twenty minutes later. I waited almost an hour, and started to get a bad feeling about things so I went inside. When I got upstairs to the apartment I didn't hear anything so I went in. When I stepped into the bedroom I heard a car and looked out the window and saw it driving away, the girl was running down the driveway after it. By the time I got back outside the building they were gone.'

'And so was Sexton.'

'Well, I never actually saw him in the car or the apartment.'

'You said she was running after the car?' I asked.

'Yeah.'

'How?'

'What do you mean?' Osgood asked.

'Was she running to catch up, was she angry, scared, surprised?'

He thought for a moment. 'Surprised, maybe — no, she was scared,' he said.

'You're sure?'

He thought for another moment.

'Yeah, I'm sure. She yelled something as she was running,' Osgood said.

'Yelled what?'

' "What are you doing?" '

'You're sure that's what she said?' I asked.

'Yeah, that's what she yelled.'

'Did you look around the apartment?'

'Just for a second.'

'What did you see?'

'I saw the ropes . . . there was some blood.'

'Blood?' asked Buzz, trying to catch up.

'I got out of there after that. I didn't know what it all meant.'

'Were you able to follow them?'

'No.'

'And you didn't call the police.'

He shook his head.

'I only made the connection to the accident about a week later. And, like I said, I never actually saw anything.'

'Did you tell Coles?' I asked.

He nodded.

'He didn't believe it. Then Darren vanished.'

'Does his wife know about this?' I asked.

'I don't think so. Coles's instructions were that I only talk with him.'

'So my daughter wasn't there?' Tracy asked.

'I didn't see her.'

She closed her eyes and took a deep breath in relief and whispered, 'Thank God.'

'Did you see the pictures in his locker in school?'

He shook his head.

'His father told me about it, but I haven't seen it. He said they were pictures of Sophie.'

'The pictures are of my daughter,' Tracy said.

Osgood looked over to her in confusion.

'Coles said they were of Sophie,' he said.

'No,' Tracy said.

'So Charlotte is Sexton's and your daughter, not Sophie?' Osgood asked.

'She's his step-daughter,' Tracy said.

'I'm her father,' I said.

Buzz's jaw nearly fell right off his face.

'You're what?' he said.

The unease that was buried deep in my gut since this had started began to feel like a rising storm. I looked over to Tracy.

'Something's not right with this,' I said.

'I'm telling you what I know,' Osgood said.

The shadowy picture of Sophie on her Facebook page flashed in my mind.

'They're not Thelma and Louise,' I said.

Osgood started to shake his head. 'You lost me,' he said.

'Would you be able to identify Sophie if you saw a photograph of her?' I asked.

'Yeah.'

'What are you doing?' Tracy asked.

I reached into my pocket and slipped out the photograph of Charlotte and handed it to him, a sick feeling spreading like a fever through me.

'Take a close look,' I said.

Tracy got up and started to shake her head.

'No, don't,' she whispered.

'And you're sure you've never seen her?' I asked.

Osgood studied it for a moment. 'What do you mean?' he asked in confusion.

'Stop it!' Tracy yelled.

'You have seen her?' I asked.

'What are we talking about here?'

'Stop!' Tracy pleaded.

'Have you?' I repeated.

Osgood looked at Tracy. 'No.' He looked back to me.

'Please,' said Tracy.

Osgood shook his head.

'The hair's different . . . but that's her.'

Tracy fell silent and backed away.

'Sophie,' I said.

40

'You're certain?' I asked. 'You want to take another look at it?' Osgood shook his head.

'I'm sure, that's her.'

'You're lying!' Tracy said angrily.

'I got nothing to lie about,' Osgood said.

'Liar!'

She started to take a step towards him as she clenched her fists. I stepped between them and stopped her. Tracy looked over to me and her entire body shuddered. She tried to say something but lost the words, then turned and walked over to the window and stared out into the deepening darkness. I put the photograph away.

'I'm sorry,' he said.

'When was the last time you talked to Coles?' I asked.

'This morning.'

'What did he tell you?'

Osgood hesitated, then shook his head.

'He told me about the locker at school,' he said.

'Is he in contact with his son?' I asked.

He thought about it for a moment.

'There have been a few times where I thought he already knew something I was going to tell him,' Osgood said.

'Is it possible he's protecting him?'

Osgood considered it for a moment.

'They have a Malibu place for the weekends.

Coles told me he had a neighbor keeping an eye on it and that his son hadn't been there. I had no reason not to believe him.'

'Did you ever track them to a warehouse in the North Valley?' I asked.

'The one by the airport?'

I nodded.

'Once,' Osgood said.

'Did you go inside?'

'I didn't have a chance,' he said.

'Does the name Anna mean anything to you?' I asked.

'Former girlfriend who was in rehab.'

I started to nod but stopped.

'Was?' I asked.

'She walked out of the clinic this morning, left with a guy on a motorcycle.'

'Arthur Grunier?' I asked.

'That would be my guess.'

'How do you know this?' I asked.

'Many of the kids I follow have addiction issues, I have contacts in most of the clinics.'

'I think Grunier is looking for Darren and Charlotte,' I said.

He looked over to Tracy then back to me.

'If that's true, that's bad.'

'The detective Tracy hired was murdered,' I said.

He looked over to Tracy in surprise, then back to me.

'Lester was working for you?'

'I think you should be careful,' I said.

He shook his head. 'Shit,' he said softly to himself.

352

We talked for a few more minutes but there was nothing new or that we didn't know. He gave us the address of Coles's place in Malibu then made a beeline for the door and was gone. Tracy just stared out the window in silence after he left. Buzz looked over to me.

'Daughter?'

I nodded.

'And murder?' he added.

'Yeah.'

'I think I'll go play some music,' he said, then glanced at Tracy and started to walk away, then stopped.

'Maybe you should — '

'What?'

Buzz looked at me for a moment, glanced at Tracy.

'Do you know what you're doing?'

I shook my head. 'No.'

Buzz left us and I stepped over to the window next to Tracy. Her eyes held the stunned gaze of someone who had just walked away from a terrible accident, the only one who had not been injured.

'He's got to be wrong,' she said softly.

He didn't sound wrong. It all made a terrible kind of sense. If she was already living a secret life, was it such a stretch to create an entirely new person to escape it? How many other kids living their lives on-line do it every day in lesser ways? In a world where the only rules are those of speed of connection, why wouldn't the real world be something relegated to the same closet where your old laptops and modems, hardwires, phones and CD players collect dust.

New is better. New is faster, bigger. New is everything, every need, every want, every dream. In a world where every desire can find its equivalent in pixels and four or six or eight Gs, held in the palm of your hand, does the line between fantasy and reality even exist any more?

'You don't think he's wrong, do you?' Tracy said.

'No,' I said.

Tracy turned and looked back out the window.

'But it doesn't make her guilty of anything,' I said.

Tracy shook her head. 'She was in his apartment, she was there when he was tied to the bed and . . . ' She let the rest slip away. 'This is a nightmare.' There was an edge of desperation to her voice.

The sound of Buzz's guitar began to drift down from upstairs.

'I keep wanting to ask myself how this happened,' Tracy said. 'But I don't know where to begin, where did I make the first mistake, what sign did I miss, what didn't I do? How could I be so clueless? Was my husband abusing my daughter and I didn't see it? What kind of a person lets that happen?'

Perhaps twenty-four hours ago I might have judged her, maybe I even wanted to, but now it seemed petty, or at least useless, no matter how much I would like to think that it would have all been different if I had been in their lives.

'What matters is now, not the past.'

Tracy shook her head.

'Every day you've gone to work to try to understand an accident that happened eighteen years ago, the past is everything to you, what do you know about now?'

She was right, or at least she wasn't wrong. A police siren began wailing out in the distance towards Chinatown. A single coyote, alone on the streets of the warehouse district, began to answer with a singsong of cries.

'I shouldn't have said that,' Tracy said.

The siren faded but the coyote kept calling as if expecting an answer.

41

Since Tracy had walked back into my life I had passed out a couple of times, seen more flashing lights than I had in years, been hit in the head, survived two fights, learned that I was a father, and was falling in love. If my own history meant anything, I couldn't help but think that the next time I slip back into darkness would be the one that plants me for good in the vegetable patch.

There wasn't time to waste, not a second, not mine, not Charlotte's.

What did Charlotte's words as she ran after the car mean?

What are you doing?

What words do you use as you chase a car carrying a man who had been nearly beaten to death? Like looking at a set of skid marks on a pavement you could read into them whatever you wanted. I knew what Tracy thought they meant, what they had to mean, what they must. Charlotte was trying to stop what was happening, she didn't help kill her stepfather. She was innocent, and if Osgood's interpretation of her words was accurate, perhaps she was right to believe it. In four short words it was all there if your belief was strong enough. She could see it as if she had witnessed it all.

Darren had wrapped Sexton in a sheet and dragged him off the bed onto his shoulder and began carrying him out of the apartment the way you would help a drunk. Charlotte said it the first time there: 'What are you doing?'

Darren didn't even hear her; his plan was already in progress.

'Get the door and check the hallway,' he said.

'What?'

'Do it.'

She hesitated.

'Do it now!' he yelled.

She ran to the door, opened it and looked out into the hallway. It was empty; she turned and looked back at Darren.

'What are you going to do?'

'Help me get him down the stairs.'

Charlotte started to shake her head.

'Help me.'

They carried him, dragged him down the back stairs to the door to the parking area.

'Now look outside.'

Charlotte stepped out and looked around; there was no one there.

'Go open the back door of his car.'

Charlotte wasn't thinking any more, her heart was racing, she could barely breathe. She ran to the car and opened the back door. Darren carried him over and rolled him into the back seat.

As he closed the door Charlotte reached out and grabbed his arm and tried to pull him away from the car.

'Stop it.'

He pulled his arm free and then rushed around and got in the car and started it.

'What are you doing?'

He began to drive away and she ran after him.

'What are you doing?'

But words are elastic things whose meanings can bend and twist. You change an inflection on a single word, and all of history changes.

They stopped at the bottom of the stairs; Charlotte let go of Sexton's arm and looked out into the parking area.

'It's clear,' she said.

She helped drag him across the pavement to the car and they put him in the back seat. As Darren ran around the car and climbed in behind the wheel Charlotte looked back up towards the windows of the apartment . . . had they left anything, did they close the door?

'I'm going to go check — '

Darren started the engine and she turned to see him begin to drive away. She stared for a moment in disbelief as he left her behind.

'What are you doing?'

She started to run after him.

'What are you doing?'

Which truth was it, or was it neither, or both? What did truth even mean any longer? Did I care? How do you measure it? Or do you just give it a value and measure it like time? There was the world before Charlotte. And there was the world after Charlotte. Nothing else applied any longer. Not truth, not right or wrong. All that remained unanswered was how far was I willing to leave behind the life before Charlotte.

If the second version of the words Osgood had heard her say was closer to the truth, what would I do to protect her — a girl whom I had never seen, whose eyes I had never looked into, whose voice and the sound of whose laugh I had never heard, whom I had never held in my arms as any father would? How far would I go for her? What price would I pay, and what would I be giving up if I cross that line for good, what's on the other side? A fantasy life in the suburbs with a yard and picket fence where we all live happily ever after and quietly bury the memory of a murder every day as we sit around the breakfast table?

I had been a father for a little over seventy-two hours, but it was all the time I needed. The home video of her standing on that stage and the sound of her voice had not stopped playing in my head since the moment I had seen it. Every gesture she made with her hands, every syllable she spoke, felt like a match to my heart. I would do exactly what any father would do, what Tracy had been doing from the very beginning. I would believe the first version of Charlotte's words, not because the facts said they were more likely to be right. I would believe them because to not to, meant I was alone in this world and I couldn't go back to that.

42

On the way to the Coleses' place in Malibu we stopped at Anna's home and sat with her mother and father in their post-modern dream house and told them all the details that they had either avoided trying to see about their daughter or that had remained secret to them.

They had heard nothing from her since she had left the clinic. As they listened to the story of what had happened to their little girl, the stylish surroundings took on the quality of a set designed for an entirely different film than the one they found themselves in.

Perhaps they had suspected or had even known some of the details, but when we were finished, they sat in silence staring straight ahead, caught in their private hells, as separate from each other as they were from their daughter.

Her father finally broke the silence.

'This man, Grunier . . . he was one of them who made the — '

'Yes,' his wife said, cutting him off before he could put into words the images they now held in their heads.

'We tried to do what we thought was right for her — always, from the very beginning,' he said.

'Shut up, Jim,' his wife said, her voice shaking with emotion. 'We were wrong.'

We left them with Delgado's phone number

and instructions to tell her everything we had told them. They promised to contact us if they learned anything, though I doubted the promise would be remembered for any longer than the time it took for us to walk out to the car.

The address for Coles's Malibu home was at the end of a winding drive in the hills above Las Flores Beach. From the street a walkway descended to the house through a thicket of century plants and bougainvillea. No lights were visible. All we could see of the house was the peak of the roof in the moonlight rising just above the vegetation. Coles's Mercedes was parked out front.

We stopped across the street, shut off the engine and turned out the lights. The landscape that surrounded us was empty except for the circular trunks of dead palm trees; the blackened shapes of chimneys that rose up out of concrete slabs. A fire had roared down out of the hills on the hot Santa Ana winds the previous fall and had taken every house on this end of the block except for the one Coles was in.

'If you were right and he was trying help his son, it would have been here,' Tracy said, staring at the house. 'This is where secrets come.'

I glanced around at the surroundings; a charred mailbox was all that remained of the house across the street.

'Coles told Osgood that the neighbors were keeping an eye out for his son — there are no neighbors.'

'Is she here?' Tracy said softly.

I shook my head.

361

'His car isn't here,' I said.

Tracy's eyes were fixed on the stairs leading down through the vegetation to the house.

'Something's here,' she said and got out.

Twenty steps led down to a small patio in front of the house. We stopped at the bottom. The house was dark. The front door was open a few inches. I reached out and took Tracy's hand.

'Wait,' I said softly.

There was something on the patio a few feet in front of us just visible enough to see in the darkness. I stepped forward and picked it up as Tracy came up behind me.

It was a patient's ID bracelet. The thin plastic had been torn as it was ripped from the wrist.

'Anna's,' Tracy said.

My eyes moved to the opening in the front door and the darkness inside. The wood had cracked and splintered from being forced open. A radio or a TV was playing somewhere inside. I pushed it open a few inches more, half expecting some kind of reaction, but none came. I turned to look at Tracy.

'I'm not waiting out here,' she said, trying to keep it together.

'If something happens —— '

'What?'

I hadn't worked the rest of that out. 'Stay behind me.'

I gave the door a gentle push and it slowly swung open; the hinges, rusted from the salt air, softly squeaked. The windows must have been shuttered because there was no moonlight, no lights from the houses on the slopes below filtered inside. The only light that was visible was that coming through the door we had just opened, and that illuminated only a few feet inside until that was swallowed by the intense darkness.

'Should we turn on a light?' Tracy whispered.

I imagined the light coming on and seeing Grunier standing there with a knife.

'No,' I said.

The sound was coming from somewhere in the house to the right. I took a step and stopped, a wooden dining-room chair lay broken on the floor as if it had been propped up against the door handle to help secure it and then was shattered as the door was forced open.

As Tracy looked at the broken pieces her fingers tightened around mine.

'Is Charlotte here?' she whispered.

I started to shake my head.

'She's here,' she said.

'I think the sound is coming — '

Her hand pulled from mine before I could stop her and she ran off into the house, disappearing into the darkness somewhere to the left. I started to go after her then stopped as her footsteps fell silent.

'Tracy,' I called softly.

She didn't respond. I eased up to where she had vanished from sight. What appeared to be a hallway led off in the direction she had gone, but I couldn't be sure, and there wasn't a sound except the TV or radio and that was coming from the other end of the house.

'Tracy,' I said softly again into the darkness of the hallway.

I started to take a step, then the sound of the TV fell silent and I stopped. Was I wrong about the direction of where the sound had come from? Now that it was gone, I couldn't be sure. The silence and the darkness were so complete, they seemed to take on a presence, as if someone was standing just beyond arm's length, waiting for me.

I took another look in the direction Tracy had gone, then turned again and looked back towards the other end of the house where I thought the sound had come from. I heard a thump, and then another. It was my heart pounding against my chest.

I turned back and took a step towards the direction Tracy had gone, then took another and another, my hand reaching out in front of me into the blackness until I found the corner of a wall. Something appeared to move ahead, the darkness seemed to swirl like smoke.

'Tracy,' I said softly.

My heart beat harder, but there was no other sound. I eased my hand forward, moving along the wall until I found a doorway. I moved my hand across the opening, half expecting another hand to reach out and grab me, then I stepped around the corner and looked into the room. The darkness had layers of density — heavier near the floor, lighter as I looked up, but nothing moved, no knife came swinging out of the emptiness.

'Tracy,' I whispered.

Nothing.

I started to turn when a flash of light moved across my field of vision as if the darkness were a fabric that had just been torn open, and then just as quickly the darkness returned. Was that a light or was it something else? I reached up and touched the scar on my head. Was it starting? Was I about to unravel?

No, not now, don't do this now, I said to myself as if I could negotiate with my own frailty.

I closed my eyes and counted out a few heartbeats, waiting for the sound of a hemorrhage inside my head, bursting like a broken dam. There was nothing, no pain, no sound.

Maybe it's not happening.

I opened my eyes. At the end of the hallway a faint line of light was visible and it wasn't coming from inside my titanium-encased brain. A shadow moved across it.

Had I imagined that?

I moved forward, guiding myself down the hallway with my hand. I hadn't imagined it. It wasn't a short circuit in my head. There was a light — a thin, pale line that seemed to float just above the floor.

'Tracy,' I said again.

A few steps more and the thin line of light became clearer. It wasn't floating, and it was real, spilling out from under a closed door. The round knob of the handle reflected just enough light to be visible in the darkness. I stepped up to the door as a shadow moved across the light again inside the room from left to right. I leaned in and listened for movement, for a voice, for anything.

I started to whisper Tracy's name again, then stopped and looked down at the doorknob and took hold of it. I started to turn it. The shadow moved again and then appeared to stop directly on the other side of the door.

'Tracy,' I whispered.

No response, the shadow didn't move. I continued to turn the handle again until I heard the faint click of the bolt clearing the lock. There was still no response from the other side of the door. I looked down at the light. The shadow was still right there. I took a deep breath then started to push the door open.

As I began to move, the door was pulled violently out of my hand from the other side. I tried to stop my momentum but I was falling forward. I looked up to see something move towards me. There was a flash of silver coming at my face. I reached up to protect myself from the attack when a hand grabbed my wrist.

I tried to pull away then started to swing.

'No — '

'Elias.'

Her silver bracelets jangled as I pulled my hand free and then saw her face. We stared at each other for a moment in silence.

'Tracy.'

'Jesus, I thought you were — '

'She was here, Elias, Charlotte was here!' she said, her voice full of heartbreak.

'How do you know that?'

She turned and walked back into the room and I followed. A small lamp sat in the corner of

366

the room providing the dull light. It was a bedroom done up like a Cape Cod beach house. The bed had been slept in. The contents of a chest and a closet were strewn about the floor. Tracy stepped over to a cardboard box that sat on the floor next to the bed. I went over and looked down at the box.

'Look,' she said.

She held out a shirt and I took it from her.

'Her clothes,' she said.

It was one of the shirts that Charlotte would never have been caught wearing. Tracy clutched the shirt in her hands and held it to her chest as she looked around the room.

'We missed her,' she said softly.

I looked around at the mess — it wasn't the aftermath of violence, the room had been searched. I kneeled down and looked through the box of Charlotte's things. Along with the clothes were some shampoo and toothpaste and a brush.

'They must have left before Grunier got here,' I said. 'He wouldn't have searched the room like this if Charlotte and Darren were here.'

The sound that I had heard at the other end of the house began again and we both turned and looked into the dark hallway.

'Charlotte?' she said.

Whatever was waiting at the other end of the house, I doubted it was Charlotte.

'I don't — '

Tracy began to move towards the door and I grabbed her. She started to call her daughter's name and I covered her mouth with my hand

and shook my head.

'I don't think it's Charlotte,' I whispered.

Tracy shook her head. I reached up with my free hand and put a finger to my mouth.

'Sssh.'

Her eyes looked away from the hallway and into mine, still trying to believe that her daughter was waiting at the other end of the house.

'Don't make a sound,' I said.

The panic in her eyes passed and she nodded. I slipped my hand from her mouth.

'OK?' I asked.

Her eyes were drawn back to the hallway for a moment, then she looked at me and nodded.

'It's got to be her,' she said.

I reached out and took her hand in mine. If the last few days had been a lesson in anything it was that nothing 'had to be'.

'No it hasn't,' I said.

She looked away from the hallway.

'Maybe,' she whispered.

'Stay with me,' I said and we started back into the hallway.

The light from the room provided enough illumination for us to be able to find our way down the hallway and into the large central living room. I started to walk through it then stopped. A coffee table had been turned over in the center of the room. On the light-colored couch were a few dark stains on one of the cushions. Blood.

The sound stopped again, then started and then continued to go on and off, on and off. I kept moving before Tracy saw the couch. We stepped into a small kitchen and stopped. On the other side was another hallway. At the far end a dull glow illuminated an open door, but it was a different light to that in the other room, it was blue and rose and fell in intensity as the channel was changed from one to another.

The TV volume was just loud enough to distinguish the changing sounds, the bang of a gunshot, a car horn, a woman screaming, a storm front was moving, a regime was collapsing, beer was cold as a mountain stream.

I started to step forward and Tracy stopped and shook her head, staring at the light.

'It's not Charlotte,' she whispered.

The television fell silent again, but the glow continued, its intensity rising and falling as the channels now silently changed. Tracy's hand closed more tightly around mine.

'We shouldn't go in there,' she whispered.

'I'll check it out,' I said quietly and started to loosen my grip on her hand, but Tracy wouldn't let go.

'I'm all right,' she said.

We moved across the kitchen and into the hallway and slowly started towards the room at the end. Halfway to the room Tracy stopped, her hand pulling at mine.

'Look at the wall,' she whispered.

I turned as Tracy backed away. There was a dark handprint on the wall that in a few feet more became a smear.

'What is — ?' Tracy said. 'Oh, God, blood.'

'Wait here,' I said and slipped my hand from hers.

She didn't protest this time. I stepped forward

keeping against the opposite wall from the bloodstains. The sound of the television came back on, louder this time.

. . . This offer is good for the next twenty minutes and if you act right now . . . secure your family's future as generations before us have with gold . . . storms are extending across the entire mid-Atlantic . . .

I took another step and the sound fell silent again. I waited a moment, looked back at Tracy.

. . . The miracle cooker will change your . . .

Tracy shook her head.

'Let's go.'

. . . The accident occurred when an eastbound semi —

Tracy mouthed the word 'please'.

I took another step. The sound fell silent again.

'Don't,' Tracy whispered.

I stared at the flickering light coming out of the open door for a moment, then started forward, slowly taking one step.

'I have a gun,' came a voice from the room.

I stopped, looking into the blue light of the doorway. Was it from the television? I wasn't certain. I waited for another half-minute, but there was only silence. I glanced back at Tracy.

'No,' she whispered.

I turned to take another step.

'I have a gun,' the voice repeated.

It wasn't the TV.

'I don't,' I answered.

He fell silent.

'Mr Coles,' I said.

Tracy stepped back up behind me, took hold of my hand and tried to pull me away. The light began to flicker faster.

'If you're hurt, we can help,' I said, stepping up to the edge of the doorway.

There was a metallic click.

'I have a gun,' he yelled, his voice cracking with tension or pain.

'The gun isn't for me, Mr Coles, is it?'

'Don't come any closer.'

He turned the TV off and the hallway fell into darkness.

'Get out of my house,' he said softly.

'You're injured?' I asked.

Silence.

'Charlotte — Sophie — is our daughter,' I said. 'She was here, wasn't she?'

He didn't respond.

'It's too late to hide what's happened, but we can help each other,' I said.

Again nothing. I glanced back at Tracy, motioned for her to not move. She shook her head. I looked back at the open door, the TV cooling made a soft tinkling sound.

'No,' Tracy whispered.

I took a breath then stepped into the open door. On the other side of the room a window was open, letting in just enough starlight and moonlight to make out the shape of Coles standing in the corner, holding a small brass lamp with sailboats on the shade in his hands as though it were a club.

'I have a . . . ' He didn't finish the sentence.

'It's not me you're afraid of,' I said.

As my eyes adjusted to the light I could see blood on the sleeve of his shirt and on his face. He appeared to have been badly beaten. His nose was bloodied, the side of his face bruised and swollen. His free hand was wrapped around his chest. Each breath he took was a struggle for air as if he were breathing through heavy cloth. I started to reach for the light switch.

'Leave it off,' Coles yelled.

I pulled my hand back.

'Do you know where they are?' I said.

I took a step into the room.

'Stop,' he said.

I did.

'I know what happened,' I said.

'What do you know?' he said.

'I know you were trying to protect him, just like he was protecting Charlotte.'

'Get out.'

I heard movement behind me and Coles raised the lamp as if he was going to throw it. Tracy was standing there. His hands tightened around the lamp and he began to shake his head.

'You don't know anything.'

'I know I love my daughter, just as you love your son,' Tracy said.

His hands holding the lamp began to shake.

'Please put that down,' I said.

'Love?' Coles said.

'Yes,' Tracy answered.

Coles began to laugh, then he lowered the lamp.

'If I loved him, how did this happen?' he said softly. 'What kind of a father am I?'

I took a step forward and he motioned me away with the lamp again.

'You need help,' I said.

'No.'

Tracy started to move towards him. He swung the lamp through the air. 'You don't need that,' I said.

'Please, let me help you,' Tracy said.

'How?' he answered. 'You can fix all that's gone wrong?'

Tracy shook her head.

'No, but we can get you to a doctor.'

'I don't need anything.'

'Please,' Tracy said.

He shook his head.

'I have everything in the world,' he said, his eyes filling with tears.

In the faint moonlight filtering into the room I saw the glistening of tears fill Tracy's eyes.

'I don't,' said Tracy. 'I need my daughter.'

Coles shook his head and tossed the lamp aside as whatever veneer from his former life of master and commander crumbled completely and he sank slowly to the floor.

'What have I done?'

I stepped over and kneeled in front of him. He had the look of an animal caught in a trap with no understanding of how to escape. Finally his nervous eyes fell on me; for just an instant they seemed to take hold of the moment.

'You're the ones who talked to my wife?' he asked.

I nodded. He looked over to Tracy and then he drifted back towards the hell he was in.

'Your wife didn't know, did she?' I asked.

'No. They had been staying here . . . I thought I could control the situation . . . fix it . . . I'm a lawyer . . . ' He laughed at the word.

'You drove here after we left her?' I said.

He nodded.

'I was going to convince Darren it was over.' He shook his head at the thought. 'Their fiction . . . they thought they could end whenever they wanted to.' He shook his head. 'It doesn't work that way. There's no such thing as fictional consequences. They're scared, and don't know how to stop. I told them I could do it for them. That was my fantasy. I was a fool. We had an argument this afternoon. My son thought I was betraying him. They left.'

'What happened here?' I asked.

He reached up and wiped some blood from his face.

'I heard something at the door, I thought they had come back. When I opened it the girl was standing there.'

'Anna?' I asked and he nodded.

'She said she was looking for Darren. I told her she had to leave and he came up from behind me, I never saw him. He had a pipe in his hands. He was already swinging it.'

'His name's Grunier,' I said.

'Where's my daughter? Please tell me,' Tracy said.

He shook his head. 'I don't know,' Coles said.

'You must know something,' she asked.

He shook his head again. 'Do I look like I know anything?'

'Do they have the money with them?' I asked.

He took a heavy breath. 'I didn't know anything about that until the guy with Anna started asking me about it. He said he was going to fuck me just like he did the detective if I didn't tell him where it was.'

'Lester?'

'He never said a name. It only stopped when Anna told him she could find them. She was screaming at him.'

'Do you know what she meant?'

He shook his head. 'No. Can you find them?' he asked.

Tracy looked at me, her eyes hoping I could answer.

'Yes,' I said, though I didn't believe it, but I was getting good at hiding lies, not even Tracy saw it. 'We'll get you an ambulance,' I said.

He shook his head.

'Just go find them.'

He winced in pain, then leaned his head back and closed his eyes.

'I think you should go now.'

Tracy looked at Coles for a moment wanting there to be more, but there was nothing else to come from him. Whatever fiction he had tried so desperately to cling to was gone.

Tracy dialed 911 for an ambulance as we walked away. Before we reached the end of the hallway the television came back on and Coles began silently flipping through the channels one after another after another.

43

We drove to the end of the block and waited until the paramedic unit and its flashing lights passed us heading for Coles, then sat for a moment in silence looking out at the landscape that had been reduced to ashes. I hadn't noticed a scent in the air before — the salt of the ocean blending with the charred soil and the remains of homes and all that had once been inside them. The plastic, furniture, food, metal, clothes; what part of it were the dreams the homes once held?

'He killed Lester,' Tracy said.

I nodded. She sat for a moment trying to understand it, all of it.

'Why?' Tracy whispered. 'How did it get this far?'

'They're seventeen,' I said. 'Who doesn't want to be someone else when they're that age, someone smarter, sexier, cooler — someone different from who you are? A whole new life is right there in their phone or laptop.'

Tracy looked out towards the lights of a boat moving offshore.

'You don't have to be seventeen to want that,' she said.

'No.'

'Were you telling the truth in there — do you know where they are?' Tracy asked.

Did I? There wasn't time for anything but the truth now, not a second. I reached down and picked up my phone. I had missed two messages. One from April, one from Delgado. I looked at Delgado's first.

Rodriguez saw Sexton's apartment . . . it's out of my hands.

The words hit Tracy like a blow.

'Oh, God,' she whispered.

I brought up April's text.

Look at Sophie's Facebook page . . . something's happening.

I quickly brought up Sophie's page. Everything that had been there was gone, replaced by a single sentence. *We're giving it all away tonight at the mansion. Come and party.*

'They're talking about money?' Tracy said.

'They must be.'

'The mansion, what does that mean?'

I shook my head as I dialed April's number. She picked up on the second ring.

'Did you get my text?' she asked.

'Yes. Where's the mansion, is that where the party picture was from?' I asked.

'No, I took you there.'

'The empty building?'

'Yes. What's happening? Is Charlotte all right? I'm on my way there right now.'

'April, turn around and go home.'

She didn't answer.

'April, stay away from there — '

She hung up.

'Where is she going?' Tracy asked.

'April took me there, it's in Hollywood, an empty building where kids go party and live.'

'Live? Charlotte went there?' Tracy asked.

I nodded. In the distance the sound of a siren began to grow in intensity as it came in our direction.

'The paramedics would have called the police, this will be them, we should move,' I said.

'Does Anna know about this place?'

'She knows.'

I stepped on the gas and drove out onto Los Flores Canyon and started down to the coast highway just as the flashing lights of a squad car came racing towards us. I started to look away from the lights but in that second the flash seemed to penetrate my eyes and travel to the back of my skull like the point of a hot wire. I closed my eyes, but the red of the lights still filled my field of vision as if my eyes were open.

'If he tells them what happened, the police will start looking for them,' Tracy said, but I didn't hear her, or rather I was listening to a doctor's words.

'*The warning signs of a hemorrhage can be subtle or dramatic; there're no rules here. It could be a sharp and sudden pain, it may travel, or it may be localized, or in some instances there may be no pain at all. Your vision may be affected, blurred, auras, flashes of light, color, you may be dizzy, you might black out, you may lose sense of smell, there could be numbness in a limb or hand. Depending on the severity, this may last anywhere from a few seconds to —*'

'For ever.'

'What if he tells them?' Tracy asked.

I pulled over to the side of the road and stopped. The pain in my head began to dissipate

378

and then vanished. The red in my field of vision faded to a soft pink and then slipped away like sparkling fairy dust.

'*Consider yourself warned, and get checked out,*' *said the doctor.*

'Elias?'

I opened my eyes, looked over at Tracy and took a breath. The sea was there, the scent of her hair.

'Are you all right?' she asked and reached out and took hold of my hand.

I felt every inch of her fingers on mine, no numbness. I nodded — carefully. Nothing went wrong.

'Coles isn't going to tell the police anything, he's going to keep on doing exactly what he's always done, he's going to lie, and protect his son.'

I reached into the door pocket and pulled out the *Thomas* guide to find where I had gone to with April. As I scanned the streets of Hollywood the lines and names began to soften and the dull ache began to rise again in my head.

Shit, it was happening. No, not now, not yet.

I looked away from the map and out at the dark landscape, the lights of houses, the car headlights, they all seemed suspended in a sea of ink. I closed my eyes for a moment, then opened them. The world seemed a bit more solid, but when I looked back at the map the lines and words still refused to focus completely.

'I don't have my reading glasses, I need you to find the right street,' I said handing her the map.

She looked at me for a moment but took it

without asking any questions.

'What am I looking for?' Tracy asked.

'It was a few blocks after Sunset crossed the freeway,' I said. 'Read me the names.'

As Tracy began to go through the names block by block a siren began approaching from back up the canyon.

'That will be Coles,' I said.

The flashing lights of the ambulance began to light up the mirrors and reflect off the glass of the windshield. I turned away as it passed in a rush heading for a trauma center, but the lights still danced across the darkness in flashes of color like small explosions. I closed my eyes and kept them closed until the sound faded into the distance.

That was normal, lights do that to everyone, the darkness plays tricks, that's all it was.

A pulse of pain went through the left side of my head like an electrical current had been switched on and then off.

'Within boundaries you can expect to live a normal life,' the doctor said.

'Normal, until it stops being normal?'

I had had just about every kind of imaginable headache before, but that was different.

'Stress is not your friend,' he said.

'What is?'

'Vascular integrity.'

'As opposed to personal integrity.'

He shook his head.

'They're inseparable, they each require a hundred and twenty over eighty.'

'Normal.'

'Exactly.'

'How will I know?'

'Know what?'

'Will it be different from what I've felt before?'

'Oh.'

'Will it?' I asked.

He sat back in the chair and shook his head.

'When that time comes, there's no one form it will take, there're no rules for what could happen; for all we know about the brain, there's even more we don't.'

'Is that a yes?'

He took a breath. 'My sense is it will be different enough from what you've experienced before that you will know.'

'And then?'

'That I can't tell you.'

I wanted to tell him that he had to be wrong, that things had changed. That there was a tomorrow in my life, and she had straight black hair, brown eyes and was more frightened than he could imagine.

'Hobart,' Tracy said.

I opened my eyes just a bit and looked out at the lights in the darkness. None were doing anything unusual. I took a breath and shook the doctor's words off.

'Serrano.'

I turned to Tracy.

'That was it.'

Tracy looked at me, panic beginning to fill her eyes.

'Hurry,' she whispered.

44

The lights and the road began to soften again. I looked away and closed my eyes for a moment. Maybe it was just lack of sleep, maybe it was just the usual sensory anomaly that had been my companion on and off for years. And maybe that clock I heard ticking in my head when I closed my eyes was nothing. And maybe the doctor was wrong, maybe it would be the surprise of a lifetime and I wouldn't know anything.

Sure.

I looked back down at the map. I could see the grid of streets, the names began to come into better focus, but there was still that other sound, counting out the time left, tick, tick, tick.

'I need you to drive,' I said.

Tracy looked at me in concern.

'Something's wrong. I can see it in your face.'

I shook my head.

'My night vision isn't good, that's all,' I said, trying not to let on that it was much more than that.

I walked around and got back in and Tracy started driving down the rest of the canyon to head back towards town.

'Sunset will be fastest this time of night,' I said.

We headed east through Pacific Palisades and Brentwood and the gated mansions of Bel Air before entering Hollywood. It had been a long time since I had sat as a passenger and just watched the city pass by, not that the city that I know is like anyone else's. My landmarks weren't the Chinese Theater, the walk of fame, the studios, Venice beach, the Hollywood Bowl or any of the other snapshots of the city traveling the world on the net with the caption having a wonderful time wish you were here.

My landmarks were a two-vehicle collision at the corner of Ivar and Santa Monica. A single-car rollover on Barham. A hit and run at Ventura and Woodman. Had I really believed I would find meaning in life by looking backwards? Why hadn't I understood that if answers existed they weren't in the twisted steel and broken lives of strangers, but in this very instant and my own wounded heart? How much time had I wasted? Was there a figure? And now that I was here with all or at least some of the riddles from the past answered was it too late, was the clock nearly finished counting?

'Something is wrong, isn't it?' Tracy said.

A group of Japanese tourists were taking snapshots of a policeman arresting a hooker in red leotards as her john sat in the squad car, hiding from the cameras by covering his head with a jacket.

'Wrong?' I asked.

The cameras all flashed at the same time. One seemed to go through my head like a needle.

'I saw it in your eyes when you passed out at your loft, I see it again in your eyes now,' she said.

'No, that was something else in the loft; that

was seeing you for the first time.'

'And what is it now?' Tracy said. 'Something happened driving down the canyon, didn't it?'

I started to shake my head.

'Don't,' she said. 'Don't you dare lie to me!'

The traffic on Sunset began to back up with the evening's cruisers.

'We need to get off the strip,' I said.

'What happened, Elias?' she demanded.

We stopped behind a car full of teenagers on the prowl for just enough danger to send them back happily home to the parents.

'I don't have that answer,' I said. 'It might be nothing.'

'Don't confuse me. What does that mean?'

'It means I'm still sliding across that intersection in my parents' Volvo. That telephone pole is still waiting.'

Tracy shook her head.

'Don't do this to me.'

'If I remember, it was a Pontiac that did it, not me,' I said.

She reached out and grabbed my hand in hers. The tips of my fingers had no sensation in them.

'What's wrong!' she pleaded.

'It means our accident isn't over for me yet.'

She looked at me in alarm. Tears began to form in her eyes.

'This happens from time to time, it's nothing to worry about, it will pass,' I said.

'Your hand is cold,' Tracy said.

'That's because I'm looking at you.'

'Don't make jokes, not now.'

'I'm not joking.'

Her eyes looked up at my head.

'I'm taking you to a hospital,' Tracy said.

'We don't have time for that.'

She shook her head.

'If I really needed to be in a hospital, then there's probably nothing they can do for me, so we'd just be wasting time. Charlotte's time.'

Tracy released my hand and stared at the traffic ahead.

'What's happening? Tell me now, or I'll . . . ' She looked away. 'Tell me!' she demanded.

My mother took the grapefruit in her hand, raised it to her face and breathed in its sweet, sharp scent. Did she know this day was coming, was that her secret that she had kept to herself in a terrible silence?

'They fixed the injuries from the accident . . . they couldn't fix me, though,' I said.

A tear fell out of the corner of her right eye and down her cheek.

'This wasn't supposed to happen.'

She turned the wheel hard and stepped on the gas going against traffic and onto the nearest side street to get off Sunset and head towards Franklin, shaking her head.

'Damn you,' she whispered. 'Damn you for doing this to me.'

I looked at the line of her long neck and the soft curve of her perfect ear.

'It was an accident,' I said.

45

How do you measure trauma? What yardstick do you use to understand the effect on a heart and mind the first time Sexton put his hands on Tracy's throat or touched Charlotte? Tomorrow the sun will come up, but the world is not the same one they had greeted the day before. And from that moment on, no matter how many times they might try, they will never get a chance to have a single day back and make that one decision that would have put them in a different place or moment to change the past. The headlights never veer off to the right or left; they never stop, they just keep coming straight at you.

Halfway through Hollywood a picture was posted on Sophie's Facebook page. I stared at it for a moment before I recognized it. There were some lights inside the empty windows now.

'They're there,' I said.

Messages posted by kids going to the party were quickly filling the page. Tracy glanced over and noticed me staring at the screen.

'What is it?'

'There's a message from Anna,' I said. '*I'll C U there.*'

Tracy gasped. 'Oh God.'

Another picture appeared on the page.

'They've posted another pic,' I said.

'Is it Charlotte?'

'No, it's a picture of a bag of money.'

There was a caption above it.

Everyone is going to share, this is the end.

'Oh, Jesus,' Tracy said, her hands tightened around the steering wheel.

Another message appeared from Anna.

I have something for U. Meet me in the Penthouse.

'It's Grunier,' I said.

'Post something, warn her!' Tracy yelled.

'If I do that, Grunier will see it,' I said.

Tracy handed me the phone and stepped on the gas.

'She might be using her phone, tell her to get out,' Tracy said.

I dialed her number but it was busy. I tried again and it was the same result.

'Post on her page!' Tracy said.

I looked back at my phone, there were now dozens of messages and they were still streaming in.

'There're too many.'

'Do something!'

I started to type, but with my fuzzy head my fingers moved painfully slowly and inaccurately.

'Hurry!' Tracy said.

Grunier there . . . don't meet Anna . . . get out.

I posted the text but it quickly seemed to be lost in the other posts streaming in.

'She'll never see it,' I said.

'What do we do?' Tracy said desperately.

I stared helplessly at the screen of the phone as more postings appeared. Entire governments have fallen with the touch of the finger, but it couldn't get us any closer to Charlotte.

'I don't know — ' I started to say, when I looked up from the screen to see the light turn red in the intersection.

Tracy was shaking her head and stepped on the gas.

No said the voice in my head. I looked past her at the headlights coming from the left towards us out of the darkness.

The shot never changes, there's nothin' here but an old wood floor.

The lights began to reflect off the glass on the inside of the windshield.

Don't . . .

Brakes began to squeal. Tracy started to look to her left.

'Don't stop,' I said.

The headlights caught her eyes.

'Faster,' I said.

Her hands tightened around the wheel.

'Faster.'

I was pressed back against the seat as a car horn blared and the headlights began to fill the inside of the car with light. I reached out to brace myself against the door and closed my eyes.

'Oh God,' Tracy said.

There was silence. Not a sound. Not even the ticking of the clock in my head. I opened my eyes as the lights of the other car slid past behind us, the horn still blaring.

We both stared straight ahead down the road, neither looking back. Tracy took a breath and glanced at me. She was shaking, but it wasn't from fear. For just an instant her eyes seemed to hold all the time that we should have had but never did. My heart began to race. That's what we'd lost that night so long ago. We couldn't see any of it, we couldn't touch it, but for the first time perhaps we both felt it. A tear fell out of the corner of her eye and she looked back down the road and just like that all those moments slipped away again.

I glanced down at the screen of the phone; another picture had been posted from inside the building. Blurred faces half frozen by a flash as they danced in the darkness.

'Call the police,' Tracy said.

'If they think Charlotte is a killer?'

Tracy looked at me, playing out the possibilities.

'What do we do?' she asked.

I dialed Delgado's number. She answered on the third ring.

'Where are you?' she said.

'I need you to meet us at a building in Hollywood,' I said.

'Why? What's happening?' she asked.

I looked over to Tracy and she nodded.

'Charlotte is Sophie,' I said.

'I'm listening,' Delgado said.

'She's with a boy named Darren Coles. They took some money from Sexton. Grunier's money, he's after them and knows where they are.'

'How do you know this?'

'I'm watching it on-line.'

She was silent for a moment.

'What is it?' I asked.

'Rodriguez saw Sexton's apartment. He thinks Charlotte and her friend may have killed Lester.'

'You know that's not true.'

'I'm not in homicide.'

'Grunier killed Lester,' I said. 'He just nearly killed Darren's father, he beat him with a pipe just like he did Lester, you can check with Malibu Sheriff.'

There was silence on the other end for a moment. I looked back down at Sophie's page again. Another picture appeared. It was a picture out the window of the building of dozens of people arriving.

'Will you help!' I said.

'I need the address,' Delgado said.

'Just you, no other cops to make a mistake.'

'I'll check with Malibu Sheriff,' Delgado said. 'If it's true, I'll keep the other cops away. That's the best I can do.'

I looked over to Tracy and she nodded. I gave Delgado the address.

'Hurry,' I said.

46

Tracy slowed just enough to veer around a truck, then sped through the next intersection as the light turned red.

'We won't get there in time,' she said, her voice cracking with tension. 'Call her again.'

I started to dial when a new flash of pain went through my head and the touchpad of the phone went out of focus. I pressed myself back against the seat and closed my eyes.

Just a little longer, not yet, please.

The spasm weakened and I opened my eyes.

'Elias,' Tracy said with alarm.

I took a breath to steady myself, then looked down at the phone, the numbers came in and out of focus. I tried to dial the number.

'Thank you for using AT&T, the number cannot be reached as dialed, please try again or check —'

'Elias!' Tracy said, her voice cracking with tension. 'Do it again.'

I stared at the phone for a moment and my focus began to sharpen. One at a time I punched in the numbers, double-checking each one.

'It's ringing,' I said.

'Put it on speaker.'

Tracy gripped the wheel like she was holding on to a lifeline as we listened to the rings. One, two, three . . .

'Pick up, pick up, pick up,' Tracy began to chant.

Five, six —

'Yes,' said a male voice.

A pounding electric bass was audible in the background.

'Darren?' I said.

The music got louder, but no reply came. Tracy looked at me and shook her head.

'Tyler?' I said.

Nothing came back.

'Do you recognize my voice?' I asked.

Still no answer.

'You have to listen to me,' I said.

Tracy began to shake her head.

'He's not — '

'What?' he finally said.

'Tell him!' Tracy yelled. 'Get out of there!'

'Don't call again,' Darren said.

'Listen — '

The line went dead and Tracy pounded the steering wheel.

'No,' Tracy screamed. 'Get him back.'

I started to redial and looked at the screen on the other phone. There was another message posted from Anna. *I'm here, meet me.*

'Grunier's there,' I said.

'Call them back!' Tracy said.

I finished dialing. The line was busy. Tracy pounded the steering wheel.

'Try again!'

Still busy.

'Again!'

I looked down at my phone and there was another picture. In the dim light of the camera's flash, Charlotte and Darren stared solemnly into the camera. The caption said *Goodbye*. Tracy looked at it in disbelief and started to shake her head as I dialed the number again.

'Make them understand!'

It started to ring. Two . . . three . . . four . . .

'Answer it!' Tracy yelled.

It rang again and again.

'Please,' Tracy whispered.

More rings, again and again.

'Please — '

They picked it up.

'Listen to me,' I said. 'Get out of there right now. Grunier is there.'

There was just silence on the other end.

'You have to believe me,' I said.

'Charlotte!' Tracy yelled.

'Leave the money and get out!'

Silence.

'Go now!' Tracy said.

Nothing.

'Listen to us!' Tracy yelled.

The line was silent.

'Charlotte, please!' Tracy pleaded. 'Trust me!'

'Mom?'

'Yes, it's me, now get out, run!'

Nothing came back.

'Charlotte!'

The silence on the other end almost sounded like a breath.

'Honey, listen to me,' I said. 'You've got to listen — '

The line went dead.

47

The line of red taillights on the 101 as we passed over the freeway looked like an open wound in the dark night. Tracy glanced at her watch and said the only words she had spoken since Charlotte's phone went silent.

'Ten minutes.'

She looked at me and started to say something more, then just shook her head and continued driving. What could happen in ten minutes? How many lives could begin and end within that brief window? How much fantasy could spin into a real nightmare? No new picture had appeared on Sophie's page in the time it had taken us to drive. Was that a sign that the transition from fantasy to reality was complete? And what did this new world of theirs look like?

The lights, the clubs and the Hollywood dream were behind us now. These streets were darker and emptier, as if the energy needed to fuel the glitz just a few blocks west had drained the life from here. A man sat on the curb outside a pool hall holding his head. A young white street hustler stood in the doorway of a closed Thai restaurant waiting for a trick. A lone food truck selling late-night goat tacos was parked in front of a free medical clinic that was scrawled with gang graffiti.

There was a secret world just around the next turn or a step away from the light.

'*A girl named Kelly died here, I think she was from Ohio . . .*'

'This is it,' I said.

Tracy turned and headed down the dark side street. Two blocks down past shuttered houses and low-rent apartment buildings parked cars began to fill the street. Teens driving their parents' BMWs and Volvos had come over from the Valley to a party. Another block on we came to a sliding stop at the end of the cul-de-sac.

The empty building behind the chain-link fence where I had seen ghostlike figures moving in the empty windows with April was now lit up with beams of flashlights that cut the darkness like shooting stars.

We parked. The heavy beat of rave music drifted from the building. More kids were arriving and climbing through the hole in the fence to join the party.

Tracy didn't rush out of the car as before, but instead sat staring at the building, her hands still holding on to the steering wheel, trembling ever so slightly.

'My daughter is in there?' she asked as if hoping I had made a mistake.

I nodded and motioned towards a Crown Victoria parked across the street.

'That's a cop car, Delgado's here,' I said.

Tracy loosened her grip on the wheel and then looked back over to the building.

'I thought I would know what to do,' Tracy whispered.

As I got out of the car my head felt light and I closed my eyes for a moment. Tracy came around from the driver's side, took hold of my hand, then stole a glance at my head, inspecting for any cracks in the metal siding.

'Are you all right?' she asked.

I looked down at her fingers wrapped around mine. I couldn't feel any of it.

'Sure,' I said.

We started through the maze of parked cars that filled the street. The music rose and fell. Kids were shouting in excitement, beams of flashlights moved to the beat of the music. We came around the back of a van and I stopped, staring at a shape in the darkness.

'A motorcycle,' Tracy said. 'It's his.'

She let go of my hand and rushed towards it, then stopped a few feet behind it. I stepped up next to her.

'What if — ' She didn't finish.

The bike was parked right behind a Ford Taurus. The driver's window had been smashed. The seat was covered with glass and some fast food wrappers and empty Starbucks cups, but nothing that gave a clue about what was to come.

I looked over to the building. The third and top floor were mostly black, the dozen or more windows looked out on the street like lifeless eyes. I saw no movement, but the darkness wasn't empty. There was something there I wasn't seeing, or was just missing.

Tracy stepped up behind me.

'What is it?' she asked.

'The penthouse. Anna must have been talking about the third floor.' The glow of a light appeared in one of the third-floor windows then vanished. A flashlight beam cut across a window, then was extinguished.

We stepped past the car over to the hole in the fence. The music rose. A flash lit a window on the third floor for an instant. There was a scream or was it just the party?

I took out the phone connected to Sophie's page. It had gone dark.

'No!' Tracy cried.

I dialed Delgado with the other phone and she answered on the second ring.

'Where are you?' I said.

'What?'

We started through the fence. The intensity of the music began to rise.

'I think they're on the third floor.'

'I can't hear you,' Delgado said.

'The third floor,' I repeated.

'Find her!' Tracy yelled.

The faint glow of light in the center of the third floor began moving towards the right.

'I'm on the third floor,' Delgado said.

'There was a flash,' I said.

'Where?'

The light crossed from one window to the next.

'It's moving.'

'I don't see anything,' Delgado said.

The light was still moving towards the right.

'It's still moving!' I said.

'I don't see . . . '

The light appeared and disappeared as it moved from room to room.

'Do you see it still?' she asked.

The movement of the light stopped, then it went out.

'Wait . . .' Delgado said.

The music picked up speed, two kids ran past us laughing and smelling of grass.

'There's something,' Delgado said.

The music was turned up.

'What?' I yelled.

'I thought . . .'

'Find her!' Tracy screamed.

A Roman candle started shooting into the air in front of the building and people started screaming with excitement. There was another flash of light in the building.

'Did you see that?' I said.

'What?' she said.

'He's there,' I said.

She didn't answer.

'He's there!' I yelled.

The phone crackled with static. Another candle started shooting into the sky in front of the window, lighting up the darkness.

'Delgado?'

'Wait,' she said.

'Oh, Christ — '

'Did you see Charlotte?' Tracy took the phone from my hand and yelled. 'Do you see Charlotte?'

Silence.

We stared at the building, waiting for another word from her.

'Delgado?'

She didn't respond.

'Delgado?' I repeated.

Still nothing.

48

We were running towards the building before either of us consciously thought to do it. Whatever thread of reality that we had been clinging to was gone. We were a part of Charlotte's and Darren's fiction as if they had created us, playing a role whose fate was already decided.

I knew I was running because I could see Tracy ahead sprinting towards the glow of lights and the sound of music, but I couldn't feel the sensation of movement. I wasn't conscious of breathing harder than normal; no air seemed to move across my face.

I focused on Tracy, the movement of her legs, her arms reaching out and trying to grab the air, her feet seeming to barely touch the ground. I tried counting the steps as a way of measuring the distance but the voice in my head wasn't counting steps. It was the past.

Come on, faster.

Where?

It's a surprise, come on. Run.

I'm running.

Faster.

I stumbled and fell to my knees, the air smelled of eucalyptus. Tracy reached down and took my hand. The bracelets jangled as they slid down her thin wrist.

'I had a dream about you once,' she said. 'It was just like this.'

She leaned over and kissed me.

Hurry, we're almost there. Faster.

The scent of eucalyptus vanished as my legs gave out and I fell. Tracy had reached the building, and was standing at the open door staring into the flashing lights and darkness inside. She turned and looked back at me.

'Don't,' I said. The pain was getting worse.

She shook her head and looked back inside.

'Wait,' I yelled.

Tracy turned and disappeared through the doorway. I tried to get to my feet and failed, then tried again. More people were running past me waving light sticks and laughing.

'What's happening?' said a voice and I looked up.

Another Roman candle lit up the darkness blinding me for a moment.

'What happened?' was said again.

The sound of my heart beating seemed to echo in my head. I took a deep breath. I heard the voice again but couldn't make out the words. I forced another breath and another. My focus came back and I saw April kneeling next to me. She was crying, and trying to say something; her eye make-up had streaked down her cheeks.

'Wherc's Charlotte?' she said, her voice full of desperation.

I shook my head.

'Get up!'

April grabbed my arm and pulled me to my feet.

'Where is she?' she yelled.

There was a dull pain in my head as if the

point of a finger was being pushed against it.

'Tell me about the third floor?' I said.

She shook her head. 'I don't understand, is that where she is?'

'What's up there?'

'Just rooms, they used to be apartments.'

'How many hallways?'

'One.'

'How many stairs?'

April shook her head. 'Where is she — '

'How many?' I repeated.

'One on each end,' she said. 'Is that where Charlotte is? Is she with Sophie?'

'There is no Sophie.'

She didn't understand.

'Charlotte is Sophie,' I said.

The beam of a flashlight cut across the darkness and seemed to tear a hole through my vision.

'What's happening?' April cried, her eyes glistening with tears.

'I need you to call the police.'

'No,' April cried and started to turn to run inside.

I grabbed her wrist and pulled her to me and wrapped my arms around her to keep her from breaking free. Her chest was heaving with sobs.

'What's happening?'

'Listen to me!' I said.

She tried to pull away but I held her in place.

'Are you listening?' I said.

She nodded.

'I'll find Charlotte. You need to call the police and tell them Detective Delgado needs help. And then you need to wait here and I'll bring Charlotte to you. Will you do that?'

'Oh, God!'

'Will you?'

April's hands tightened around me and she nodded. I slowly released her and looked into her eyes.

'Now call them right now. Tell them to hurry.'

Her fist clung to my shirt for a moment then slipped away and I ran towards the building. As I stepped inside the music went through me like a blade. Bodies were moving everywhere, voices, yelling, laughing. I couldn't see Tracy anywhere.

I moved away from the crowd until I saw the vague shape of the stairs and thought I heard something above.

'Tracy,' I yelled, but it was useless to try to yell over the music.

I started up as fast as I could when another flash of light tore a hole in the darkness. There was no sound this time, no candle being lit up, there was no flashlight pointed in my eyes.

'If that time ever comes there's no one form it will take, there're no rules for what could happen.'

A pain hit the side of my head where the plate lined my skull, my knees buckled.

'My sense is that it will be different enough from what you've experienced before for you to know.'

Blood moving through the blood vessels inside my head sounded like rushing water flowing through pipes.

He was right.

The flash of light faded, though a faint aura remained circling my field of vision. I got back to my feet and looked up the stairs. There were no footsteps, not a sound anywhere, or maybe it was there and I just couldn't hear it.

'Tracy!' I yelled.

If she could hear me over the sound of the music and the crowd she didn't answer.

'Tra — '

I took a step, and the pain hit again.

Eucalyptus filled the air . . .

I closed my eyes, but the aura was still there. I tried to say no, to fight it off, just a few more minutes, but I couldn't hear the sound of my own voice.

'We've run far enough,' she said. 'This is the place.'

We were standing in a small circular clearing, the moon sending shadows of the trees across the thick bed of leaves like the pattern of a quilt. Tracy's fingers moved down the row of buttons on her shirt and it fell open.

Is this what the doctor meant? What's different is you begin to trade the present for the past. Just a moment at first, then more and more until the present becomes what memory used to be. This is how we die.

Her shirt fell away and she reached out and began to unbutton mine, her fingers slipping inside, pressing against my chest as if listening to the beating of my heart.

Not yet, please not yet.

'It's all right.'

There was a scream and I opened my eyes. I

403

was at the top of the stairs, though I didn't remember taking any of them. The hallway extended into the darkness to the left.

I started left, then stopped and listened, then started again until I reached a door. I placed my hand against it but felt nothing, then hesitated and pushed it open as more pain moved through my head like flowing water.

'*This was my dream,*' Tracy whispered in my ear.

The shadows of the trees began to wrap around our bodies like ribbons pulling us tighter and tighter together. Her fingers pulled against mine and her body began to tremble.

'*Don't stop . . . don't . . .* '

The spasm began to fade and the darkness of the hallway came back into focus. I checked another door then another and all the rooms were empty. At the end of the hall was a faint light. I started towards it, using the wall as a guide when my foot hit something on the floor. I stepped back and looked down at the shape, trying to understand what it was. I reached down to touch it, and then stopped a few inches short. The shape of legs stretched out through the open doorway came into focus.

She was face down, one arm underneath her, the other at her side, her fingers still clutching her phone. I tried to take a breath, but couldn't as I kneeled down next to her. In the darkness I couldn't make out any features on her face. I ran my hand up her arm and shoulder until I felt her short hair on the back of her head.

'Detective?' I said.

She didn't move.

'Delgado?'

I reached out and placed my fingers across the side of her neck. I felt a faint pulse. I leaned in next to her face; blood was dripping from a wound just above the hairline. The fabric of her shirt was damp with more blood from another wound.

'I'll get you help,' I whispered.

She faintly exhaled — a word hidden in her breath.

'Gun.'

I reached down and ran my hand over her waist until I found the holster. It was empty.

'It's not here,' I said.

She started to say something else, but could only manage a breath.

'Tell me again,' I said and leaned in even closer. 'What did you say?'

She tried, then tried again. 'The room,' she whispered.

'Which room?'

She managed to barely shake her head. A short, clipped breath came out and she slipped into unconsciousness. I checked her pulse and it was still faintly beating. I reached over and took the phone out of her hand, then looked down towards the end of the hallway and the door with the faint light under it.

The room, was that what she meant? I got to my feet when the phone in my pocket began to ring. I quickly reached for it before the ringing gave my location away.

'Do you see her?' said Tracy.

'Where are you?'

'Oh, God, find her, Elias.'

The line went silent.

'Tracy, where are you?'

She didn't answer. I heard movement coming up from the stairs. I turned and started towards the room at the end of the hall, staring at the thin line of light under the door as a guide. The pain came again on the third or fourth step and I felt myself begin to fall.

The headlights illuminated the inside of the car. The air was filled with gasoline.

'*My leg, oh God. Fire.*'

The smashed engine ticked like a clock as it cooled.

'*Don't leave me.*'

'*I won't.*'

I pulled on the door as she pounded on the glass.

'*Oh God, do something.*'

I felt the blood running down the side of my face as the door gave way and opened. Tracy tried to move and screamed in pain and then the light of flames erupting filled the interior with an orange glow.

'*Don't . . .*'

I pulled on the dash trying to move it and free her leg.

'*Don't leave me. Please don't leave me.*'

The dash moved an inch or two and her leg pulled free. She wrapped her arms around my neck and I lifted her out of the car as fingers of flames began to reach under the dash. I took a step and then another and I heard the sound of liquid flowing inside my head and felt the moisture slipping out of my ear and I started to fall.

My eyes began to focus; as the wave of pain subsided I heard the footsteps stop just behind me. I didn't move, didn't breathe. I had fallen through a door and was lying just off the hallway. In the darkness I could barely make out the shape of his foot as he took a step past me, then stopped. A few inches from his foot the faint glow of Delgado's phone became visible on the floor; the sound of an automated operator's voice came on.

'Please hang up and dial again . . . '

His fingers began tapping the wall of the hallway, he took a breath, stepped back then stopped. I closed my hand into a fist to deflect the blow. The floorboard creaked under his foot then I heard movement and I started to raise my hand towards my face. He reached down and picked up the phone.

He closed the phone and stood absolutely still, then began to rock back and forth on his feet and his fingers started tapping the wall again, then he turned and ran back down the hallway.

I took a breath and another, waited for the sound of his footsteps to disappear, then pushed myself up, leaned against the wall and ran my fingers over the side of my head. There was no blood, no fluid coming out of an ear.

I took out my phone, but the screen was no longer lit up, there was a depression in the center of it from where I had landed on it. I got to my feet and leaned out into the hallway listening for a moment, but the only sound was the thump of the music downstairs. I turned and moved along the wall towards the door with the line of light under it.

There were no prisms shimmering in my vision, no pain in my head, no ticking clock. I seemed fine, and that wasn't possible. I thought it would end with the sound of a crash or a flash of light, not in silence, not peacefully, not without a struggle. I didn't want to just slip away.

'Hurry,' Tracy said.

I rushed to the door, pushed it open, stepped inside and closed it behind me. A muffled cry came from behind and I turned. A glow stick on the floor lit the room in a faint yellow light.

Duct tape covered her mouth and her wrists were taped to a pipe in the wall. It was Anna. Her eyes fixed on me like a traumatized animal. I started towards her and she tried to crawl away to protect herself, but her bound hands held her in place.

'I'm not him,' I said. 'It's all right.'

She still pulled against her restraints and tried in vain to kick at me with her legs to protect herself. I stopped a few feet short and kneeled down.

'Look at me, I'm not him.'

Her eyes stopped looking for an escape and focused on me.

'All right?' I said.

She nodded. I eased forward and pulled the tape off her mouth then reached up and began to untie her hands.

'Are you injured?' I asked.

She shook her head and I began to pull the tape off her wrists.

'Where's Charlotte?' I asked.

She shook her head. 'I thought he wanted me,' she said.

'Where's Charlotte?' I repeated.

She looked at me in confusion. 'Who's Charlotte?'

'Sophie, where's Sophie? Where?' I yelled.

She shook her head again. 'He didn't want me, he wanted her.'

'Where is she!'

For just an instant her eyes appeared to slip back into reality and tears appeared. 'Oh, God.' Then reality slipped away just as quickly as it had appeared. 'Why didn't he want me?'

The music downstairs doubled in volume and cheers rose up from the crowd.

'I'll take you out of here,' I said.

She shook her head. I started to stand and Anna began to panic.

'Don't leave me!'

I reached down, took her hand, and walked her out of the room and started down the hallway. As we passed Delgado lying on the floor Anna tripped over her legs and let out a squeal and clutched my hand.

'Keep walking,' I said. 'Hold on to my hand.'

We made it to the stairs and I stopped. Light was coming up from below, I could hear people running up to the second floor and shouting in excitement as we started down.

'What's happening?' Anna said.

As we hit the landing a steady stream of kids were running up into the second floor shouting and yelling as the music continued to pound out its intense rhythm.

'Is he here?' Anna said, slipping back from reality and trying to pull away from me to join the others.

I clutched her hand even tighter and pulled her along.

'He's not there,' I said.

We pushed through the kids running up and reached the ground floor. I ran her outside where another crowd had gathered and was shouting in excitement over the sound of the music.

'April is over there,' I said motioning towards where I had left her. 'You need to find her.'

She shook her head in confusion.

'April?'

She looked around at the crowd and slipped back into self-awareness.

'What am I doing here? Oh, God.'

She looked at me in confusion then her eyes focused even more.

'There's blood coming out of your ear,' she said.

I reached up and touched it as the sound of police sirens became audible in the distance.

'April is waiting for you,' I said. 'Run.'

Anna looked at me for a moment then turned and ran as the crowd erupted in cheers and shouts. I turned to see a figure standing in a second-floor window, the beams of flashlights illuminating him as he threw a handful of money into the sky and it began to fall towards the crowd like leaves drifting down from a tree.

The crowd made a dash for the money as I looked up to see Charlotte step into the window next to Darren and throw another handful out and then they both vanished back inside. I started back through the crowd to the building. The faces scrambling for the money became a blur and my head began to spin. I reached up and touched my neck, more blood was slipping down onto the collar of my shirt.

'No, Elias, hurry . . . don't leave me.'

I didn't feel any pain. Didn't feel anything. I was moving but felt no sensation. Perhaps this is how you leave — like a ghost, eavesdropping on the living, hearing, seeing, but you can't touch, can't feel. It would be so easy to just let go and give in to it, one last chance to do it all again. To stop at the intersection and watch the other car pass harmlessly by.

'Hurry,' Tracy whispered.

I stepped back into the building and started towards the stairs when screams came from behind me. I turned and looked at the crowd waving flashlights and glow sticks as they yelled for more money, and I saw the abrupt movement of bodies. There was another scream, but this time it wasn't for money, it was fear.

More frantic movement in the crowd, a girl ran past, her mouth open in a silent cry. I tried to stop her but she ran on and I turned to see his face for just an instant in the flash of lights — a mask of gritted teeth and violence, then the light moved and he vanished back into the crowd as

411

the music again picked up speed and another cheer rose outside as more money came floating down through the flashing lights towards outstretched hands.

I started to follow in the direction in which he had gone. Another spasm of pain went through my head and took my breath away.

Tracy reached down and picked up my hand and placed it on the back of her neck . . . 'I want to be with you,' she whispered.

'Somebody do something!' someone yelled to my left.

I turned and saw a figure lying on the floor in the flickering light. A girl was on her knees next to her, her hand under the figure's head as she screamed for help, but no one was paying any attention.

Another cheer rose outside as more money floated through the beams of flashlights. People rushed past, jumping, climbing out the window to reach the money.

'Do something!' the girl yelled as I reached her side.

I reached down and took hold of Tracy's hand. My fingers felt nothing.

'I thought they were dancing,' the girl said frantically. 'He had his hands around her neck.'

In the flashing lights I could see the imprints of Grunier's fingers on Tracy's skin.

'Do something!' the girl yelled again.

I put my hand on Tracy's chest. There was no movement.

'She's not breathing!' the girl yelled.

Gently I lifted Tracy's neck and placed my lips

412

on hers and breathed into her mouth. Her chest rose, then fell and remained still.

'Again, do it again!'

I cradled Tracy in my hands and breathed into her again and again.

'Is she breathing yet?' she asked.

I placed my face against her mouth but felt no breath on my cheek.

'It's not working!' the girl screamed.

I did it again and again as the crowd outside erupted in cheers one more time as the music rose another octave. A tear slipped from my eye onto Tracy's cheek.

'*Don't stop . . .* '

I breathed into her mouth again.

'*Don't . . .* '

'No!' the girl cried.

Another breath. Her fingers tightened around mine.

' *. . . stop.*'

Her chest rose and her breath touched the side of my face, then she gasped for a breath again, and then slowly took in another and began to breathe steadily.

'Stay with her, help is coming,' I told the girl. 'Tell them there is a policewoman injured on the third floor.' She started to shake her head. 'Tell them!' I repeated.

I released Tracy's hand and stood up as screams erupted from the second floor. I ran through the crowd oblivious to anything other than the music and the money falling from the sky.

As I reached the steps more screams came

413

from above but they weren't yelling for money and I heard the rush of panicked movement on the stairway. I took a step and my knees buckled. Frightened faces streamed past trying to get out of the building. The room began to spin. The edges of my sight began to darken. I closed my eyes and reached out and steadied myself against the wall, then opened them. The room had stopped moving but the tunnel of my vision was getting smaller and smaller.

'*Hurry.*'

49

One step then another and another. A girl slipped and fell on the stairs and began to cry as others tried to jump over her. I grabbed her hand and tried to pull her up then the next wave of people running down swept her out of my grip.

I stayed against the wall and rounded the turn of the stairs. I reached the second-floor landing as the last few people ran to get out. There was a scream, the sound of a body hitting the floor. I ran through a doorway, then another and stopped. The walls had been demolished, creating a large open space.

'Oh, God,' Charlotte cried out.

The crowd outside let out a jeer of excitement. Darren stood next to a window holding the bag of money out into the darkness. Charlotte was on her knees in front of Grunier; one of his hands held her by her hair; the other pointed a gun at the side of her head.

'Let her go!' Darren cried.

The crowd outside erupted in more cheers. The music began to pound out an even faster beat.

'Throw it!' the crowd yelled.

'Give it to me!' Grunier demanded.

'Let her go!'

I stepped into the room.

'Now!' Grunier yelled.

'Darren!' Charlotte cried.

I took a step and the pain returned, slicing through my head, taking my breath. The tunnel of my sight was closing.

'*Don't stop, hurry.*'

More blood slipped down my neck from my ear. Charlotte cried out again as he pulled her head back and pressed the gun against her.

'Do it, do it,' the crowd began to chant, unaware of what was happening.

I took another step. Charlotte was shaking with fear and crying.

'Give me my money!' yelled Grunier.

'Oh, God,' Charlotte cried. 'Oh God, oh Go — '

'Let her go!' Darren yelled.

'Now!' Grunier screamed.

The light of a flashlight hit the few panes of glass still in the window where Grunier stood holding Charlotte, blinding him for a moment.

'Now!' the crowd yelled.

I started to run towards Grunier as he held up his hand to shield himself from the light, then Darren heard my steps and turned to see me.

'God!' Charlotte cried out.

I halved the distance.

'Throw it!' the crowd yelled.

Grunier turned and saw me, then started to raise the gun in my direction.

'*Don't stop . . .*'

A flash of light lit up the room as we collided and Charlotte fell to the floor screaming. I heard the glass of the window shattering and I was falling weightless through darkness. The air was cool rushing past. The flashing lights of squad cars reflected off the building, glow sticks and flashlights lit the ground like fireworks. Grunier's hand holding on to my arm began to tremble and his breath raced out of control.

I stepped up behind her in the line at the cafeteria and she turned and looked at me.

'I wouldn't eat that,' Tracy said.

My plate began to slide off the edge of the tray towards the floor. Tracy reached out to catch it but it slipped just out of reach past her fingers and she smiled.

'Do you want to go to the dance?'

The ground raced towards us. Money floated in the air. I could see faces staring at us as we fell. I looked away towards the night sky, took a last breath, caught a faint hint of eucalyptus in the air and closed my eyes.

'Sure — ' Tracy started to say.

50

For days I seemed to keep falling, twisting and tumbling in the darkness. At times there would be a hint of light slipping in, the descent would slow then it would begin again all over. Occasionally, there were sounds, an electric tone, a beep, half a voice saying half a word, but then I would return back to my fall and darkness.

I don't know how much time passed. That's the thing about unconsciousness; a second and an eternity are interchangeable. So I waited for the ground to hit and for it all to end, but instead of that stillness the light began to filter back in, and the beeps and the tones, and the rhythm of the sound of my heart beating began to return. And once I thought I heard music, a polka.

'Open your eyes, and try to follow the light.'

I tried and failed. Perhaps more time passed, days, weeks . . . or maybe no time at all.

'Try again, open your eyes.'

To see what? What was I to find? What was I going to wake to?

'Squeeze my hand. Do you feel that?'

Did I? I wasn't sure.

'Now open your eyes.'

The walls were pale yellow like flowers.

'The feeling in your throat is the ventilator. We're going to remove that in another day.'

A day. How long is that? How many breaths, heartbeats?

I dreamed that night for the first time. I wasn't falling any longer. There were no electric tones, no distant voices. She was there standing next to me, her small hand holding mine, and I could feel it. *Once upon a time you saved me from pirates.* But the dream ended.

The breathing tube was removed. The first breath came like a sweet drink of water, washing away the taste of plastic and medicine, and then slowly, in small steps, the world began to pour over me in waves. Slowly I began to return to the light. The sounds of intensive care, the movement of nurses and doctors swirling around like a windstorm. It was too much, too fast. I wanted to slip back to my darkness. I would try, but they pulled me back, prodded and poked.

One day at time. One hour. A minute was a start. Sure, whatever. And then gradually the long twisting fall and finally the darkness stopped for good. It was morning, I think. The light coming through the window was soft and warm.

'This . . . is . . . intensive . . . care?' I asked, the words slipping reluctantly through my lips.

The doctor standing next to my bed nodded. He had short gray hair under a chili pepper surgical cap and was wearing dark blue scrubs.

'I'm Dr Stone,' he said. 'I did your surgery. Actually, there have been several surgeries.'

I reached up and felt the heavy bandage that covered my head.

'Successfully?' I asked.

He smiled and nodded. His bright slate-colored eyes had an intensity that must only come with sawing open a skull.

'Yes. We've replaced the plate in your skull, there's no more bleeding. We think many of the problems you experienced before should not happen again.'

'The problems?'

'The fit of the old plate was causing pressure on the brain and hemorrhaging, that's all been corrected.'

He didn't understand. The problems were who I was, the way I saw the world. What did that mean? Who would I be now?

'The old plate did save your life, though,' the doctor said. 'The bullet glanced off it instead of penetrating your skull.'

The bullet, what . . . ? The blast of light just before the window.

'Do you remember anything of what happened?' he asked.

The clock ticking in my head was gone.

'I remember everything,' I said.

He nodded and smiled.

'Good. It'll take time, but I expect a full recovery,' he said.

'And what should I expect?' I asked.

He patted me on the arm.

'Another day, another chance.'

'How long have I been here?' I asked.

'We kept you in a coma for three weeks until the swelling in your brain went down and we were able to replace the plate. The last surgery was four days ago. We'll be moving you to a regular room later in the day.'

'Has anyone visited?' I asked.

He smiled at something and shook his head.

'Someone named Buzz. He says you like polka.'

'No one else?'

'A few policemen.'

'That's it?' I asked.

As he nodded, I felt my heart sink. Why hadn't she come? What had happened? Was she all right?

I rested and slept, and slowly healed. Buzz visited and played music and made me laugh. But there were no voices in my head any longer. The silence was lonely.

On the third day of my return a nurse woke me from a sleep and told me I had a visitor.

'A woman,' she said with a smile.

My heart began to race as the door opened. Delgado stepped in.

'I'll leave you two alone,' the nurse said, not understanding the nature of the relationship, and left.

Delgado walked slowly over to the side of the bed. She had lost weight, her skin was pale and her cheekbones seemed more defined. Her dyed blond hair was returning to its natural color. What was in her eyes was something I had not seen before in her — a hesitation, doubt.

She stepped up to the side of the bed and looked me up and down and then smiled.

'You're looking better,' she said.

'They say I'm a new man,' I answered.

She reached out and took hold of my hand.

Her fingers felt almost as thin as sticks.

'Are you all right?' I asked.

She nodded and tried to smile.

'All things considered. You saved my life,' Delgado said, emotion welling up in her throat.

'I don't think that's exactly accurate.'

'You saved quite a few that night.' Tears began to form in her eyes. 'I don't know how to thank you,' she said softly, only able to hold eye contact with me for a moment before looking away.

She slipped her hand from mine and wiped away a tear.

'I get to see my daughter grow up,' she said, her voice cracking. 'Because of you.'

She walked over to the window and looked out over the city for a moment.

'Has she been here?' Delgado asked and turned around.

I shook my head.

'They've been through a lot,' she said.

'Are they all right?' I asked anxiously.

She nodded hesitantly.

'What's happened?' I asked.

'You went through the window,' Delgado said. 'After that.'

'We arrested Grunier for Lester's murder. Apparently he thought Lester was digging into their drug business or was hiding the money. It was a senseless killing. He'll go away for a long time.'

'That wasn't what I was asking about,' I said.

She nodded. 'I know.' She took a breath. 'The Sheriff's Department is revisiting the investigation. The belief is that Darren acted while trying to protect Charlotte life; if he's charged, it would be with involuntary manslaughter or even less.'

She still hadn't answered what I really wanted to know.

'And?' I asked.

She stepped over to the bed.

'From the beginning,' I said.

'Darren helped her create Sophie as a way to escape what was happening in her life.'

My heart began to pound against my chest.

'It's true, then,' I said. 'Sexton.'

Delgado nodded. 'We found fragments of photographs and videos in the burned cabinets. What Sexton did to her no child should ever endure.'

Her words struck like a blow, the pain that filled my chest was unlike any I had ever felt, worse than any loneliness I had ever known.

'Together they set about to live a second life, the one that would fix all the wrongs that had happened in the real one.'

'Lester had figured it out. He didn't want an innocent person to get hurt, he was trying to protect Charlotte too,' I said.

'Seems so.'

'Why did Charlotte run? The police thought it was an accident.'

Delgado shook her head in frustration.

'That was my fault. If I had been as smart as you, this might not have happened.'

'I don't understand?' I asked.

'When I started asking questions about Sexton's death, Charlotte thought her mother was going to be blamed for it. They're kids, they did what kids do when scared, they ran.'

'She thought she was protecting her mother,' I said.

'Something like that.'

'This didn't have to be like this, did it?' I said, grasping for an understanding of things that perhaps one never would understand.

Delgado shook her head with a sad resolve.

'It never has to happen, but it does,' she said resignedly.

Neither of us said a word for a moment, letting the silence fill in the spaces that violence had torn apart in each of our hearts.

'What now?' I finally asked. 'What's going to happen to her?'

'The DA has no stomach to charge her with anything given what had happened to her.'

Delgado took a deep breath.

'It's over,' she said, though her voice lacked the kind of conviction that had been present before any of this.

'Is it?' I asked.

'My part,' Delgado said.

'What are they going to do?' I asked.

'Last time I talked to Tracy she said they were going to work very hard at putting the past behind them.'

I tried to say something, but the words slipped away. This is what a broken heart feels like. Delgado's sunken eyes found mine for a moment, she started to say something else, then stopped and looked across the room as if it were an entire ocean full of mystery she was gazing out at.

'I'm just a cop,' she said softly, 'what do I know?'

'You're more than that,' I said. 'You're a mother.'

Delgado stepped over, took hold of my hand.

'And you're a father.'

'For a brief moment maybe.'

Delgado clenched her jaw as if trying to contain the anger she felt at my being left alone in this room.

'I'm sorry,' she said. 'Perhaps when some time has passed, and they've healed, she'll come back through that door.'

Would she?

'Time is the one thing I have again,' I said.

'You're a good man, Elias,' she said, her voice cracking with emotion.

If there was more that Delgado knew she didn't or couldn't share it with me, and I didn't press her.

'Thank you,' was all I could manage.

Delgado bent over and kissed my cheek, looked into my eyes for a moment, then turned and walked out of the room.

So I waited for them to walk through the door. And when I couldn't wait any longer I tried to remember all the details of every moment we had had together in the brief time we had shared. I had lost the memories once, but they were there now and I wasn't going to let them slip away again. Her smile, the sound of her voice, her touch, the way she had guided me through our first dance, the shadows of trees making a quilt on a bed of leaves in a forest.

I took my first steps and sat at the hospital window looking for them, hoping I would glimpse them somewhere out in the city that stretched to the slate-blue line of the ocean on the horizon. The hours turned to days and they didn't come.

Perhaps it was enough to have a dream come true once. Perhaps.

On the day of my discharge a nurse woke me early, gave me some papers to sign and then left. After I had filled them out, I went to the window to search one last time, were they there? I tried to imagine what they would be doing at that very moment, what they were talking about, what plans for the day they were making, where they were going, and all the small moments that pass unnoticed in shared lives, but I couldn't, or maybe I didn't want to because I knew I wasn't there; it had all slipped away again.

The nurse opened the door to retrieve the paperwork.

'Your ride is here,' she said.

I turned to see Buzz standing at the door smiling.

'Time to go home, dude,' he said, his smile getting even bigger.

Home, is that where I was going? Yeah, why not.

I glanced one more time out the window in the chance that I would find them, though I knew the view didn't hold them any longer, and when I turned to leave, they walked into the room. Tracy wore a neck brace. Her arms were placed firmly around Charlotte's shoulders. She started to say something, then stopped, her eyes looked over the bandages covering my head and a tear fell down her cheek.

'I'd like you to meet . . . ' she said and stopped, the words not escaping the secret so long held in her heart. 'I'd like you to meet . . . your daughter,' she just managed to say.

Charlotte's eyes looked me over cautiously. She started to take a step towards me but Tracy's arm's remained protectively around her shoulders. Like a nervous deer stepping cautiously out of cover, Charlotte slipped from her mom's grasp and walked across the ten paces of the room towards me, testing each step before taking the next. Her eyes held all the wonder of a child who had just discovered a secret, and all the hesitation experience had burdened her with.

She stopped a foot away, looking me over like an unopened piece of long-lost mail and took a deep breath to steady herself, then tentatively put her arms around me, and I put mine around her and we each held on and didn't let go. The voices that had been my companions in my head for so long were gone, but my new world wasn't silent. A new one had replaced them.

'You,' Charlotte whispered.

We do hope that you have enjoyed reading this large print book.

Did you know that all of our titles are available for purchase?

We publish a wide range of high quality large print books including:
Romances, Mysteries, Classics
General Fiction
Non Fiction and Westerns

Special interest titles available in large print are:
The Little Oxford Dictionary
Music Book
Song Book
Hymn Book
Service Book

Also available from us courtesy of Oxford University Press:
Young Readers' Dictionary
(large print edition)
Young Readers' Thesaurus
(large print edition)

For further information or a free brochure, please contact us at:
Ulverscroft Large Print Books Ltd.,
The Green, Bradgate Road, Anstey,
Leicester, LE7 7FU, England.
Tel: (00 44) 0116 236 4325
Fax: (00 44) 0116 234 0205

Other titles published by Ulverscroft:

ONE KICK

Chelsea Cain

Kick Lannigan was kidnapped when she was six and rescued when she was eleven. In the early months following her freedom, Kick's parents put her through therapy and support groups, but nothing helped. Then the detective who rescued her suggested Kick learn to fight; before she was thirteen she had mastered marksmanship, martial arts, boxing, archery and knife-throwing. She excelled at every one, vowing never again to be a victim. But when two children in the Portland area go missing in the same month, Kick is approached with a proposition: use her past experiences and expertise to help investigators find these abductees. She has never forgotten what happened to her. And never forgiven those who did it . . .

A WANTED MAN

Lee Child

When you're as big and rough as Jack Reacher — and you have a badly set, freshly busted nose — it isn't easy to hitch a ride. At last he's picked up by three strangers, two men and a woman. Within minutes it becomes clear they're all lying about everything — and there's a police roadblock ahead. There has been an incident, and the cops are looking for the bad guys . . . Will they get through because the three are innocent? Or because they are now four? Is Reacher just a decoy?